SURVIVAL BENEATH
YUCCA MOUNTAIN

MONTY NEREIM

ARCHWAY
PUBLISHING

Archway Publishing books may be ordered through booksellers or by contacting:

Archway Publishing
1663 Liberty Drive
Bloomington, IN 47403
www.archwaypublishing.com
1 (888) 242-5904

ISBN: 978-1-4808-8942-2 (sc)
ISBN: 978-1-4808-8940-8 (hc)
ISBN: 978-1-4808-8941-5 (e)

Library of Congress Control Number: 2020906892

Print information available on the last page.

Archway Publishing rev. date: 04/20/2020

To: Natasha, Isabella, Sterling, Monty, Kate and Ty.
May you live in a world shielded from peril and extinction.

"A retrofitted, former nuclear waste repository is a costly but safe alternative to human extinction. Fifty families buy in to the underground bunker and consider themselves lucky. But are they really?"

FOREWORD

THE BASIS FOR THIS NOVEL IS A DREADFUL TOPIC—UNDERGROUND survival in a bunker complex. The bunker Monty Nereim envisions is the abandoned nuclear waste repository called Yucca Mountain, located ninety miles from where I live. In his novel, it is converted into an ultra-safe "sanctuary" for privileged families escaping apocalyptic disaster—a fascinating scenario of survival.

As the former mayor of Las Vegas, I was woefully familiar with Yucca Mountain. Over $12 billion was spent drilling and testing the 1,000-foot-deep tunnel for the potential storage of the nation's nuclear waste. Mr. Nereim's story develops from the real-life blunder of Yucca Mountain.

I warned them of the Achilles heel of the project. It wasn't in the five-mile tunnel they drilled under Yucca Mountain. It was the transportation routes leading to the nuclear waste storage site. They all passed through major populated cities, including my city. Transporting nuclear waste is a real safety risk. Adding to the problem was the nation's neglected infrastructure: its deteriorating highways, bridges, tunnels and rail networks. You can understand the conundrum. Nobody had any expertise of a potential hazmat calamity.

The good news is that the author envisioned salvaging the $12 billion investment in the nuclear waste repository by making it into a valuable asset—an ultra-secure underground bunker. In his novel, that is. This captivating story features the consummate sanctuary for the super-rich. The fictional scenario is entertaining to read and also intriguing in what may be technologically feasible.

Equally absorbing is Mr. Nereim's spotlight on developments in space launch systems, survival foods and machinery, air and water filtration and even underground farming techniques that are all woven into the creative plot.

I asked my wife, the current mayor of Las Vegas, if it were possible that a creative novel could possibly influence governmental action. Could the $12 billion squandered in Yucca Mountain be recouped and made good, into a worthwhile asset? You never know.

Oscar Goodman
Las Vegas Mayor (1999-2011)

FOREWORD

SIXTY-FIVE MILLION YEARS AGO, THE DINOSAURS WERE WIPED OUT BY A catastrophic asteroid impact. What would happen *today* if an asteroid struck? Civilization would cease to be. Maybe, or maybe not.

Innovation and technology may offer some "lucky" humans the means to survive. Preppers are the people who we think of as being most equipped to persevere. Their underground bunkers and converted silos are a novel approach to surviving for a short-term disaster. But a world calamity may require a deeper look, literally.

"Underground slums" is the term used for the amateur prepper's bunker compared to the Sanctuary under Yucca Mountain. Built one thousand feet underground in an abandoned, 5-mile long tunnel, a small village complex, accommodates fifty families in a plausible scenario.

Monty Nereim's novel exposes the unimaginable. A monumental asteroid slams into earth near the apex of the "Ring of Fire," setting off a chain reaction of earthquakes, volcanos, tidal waves and fires that envelop the earth. Only a few well prepared could possibly survive. The residents under Yucca Mountain do, but that's only part of the story.

George Noory
Host, *Coast to Coast AM*

George Noory has co-authored seven books. *Coast to Coast AM* airs on more than 641 stations in the U.S., as well as Canada, Mexico and Guam, and is heard by nearly three million weekly listeners. It is the most listened to overnight radio program in North America.

AUTHOR'S NOTE

SPACE EXPLORATION TECHNOLOGY CORPORATION (SPACEX) AND THE National Aeronautics Space Administration (NASA) represented in this novel are organizations of dedicated, professional, and hardworking men and women, though I have taken some literary license in their endeavors to advance the plot of this story.

PROLOGUE

THE IMPRESSIVE LIST OF APPLICANTS HAD ALL BEEN PROCESSED. IT WAS not the usual, well-heeled society types vying for head-table privileges. All were in their thirties and early forties, had families, and were extremely healthy—physically, mentally, and emotionally. They were accustomed to privilege because of their substantial fortunes and yet they nervously awaited their acceptance letters like high school seniors applying for prestigious universities.

Only fifty slots were available, yet hundreds applied. Screening was thorough, uncompromising, and heartless. The lucky ones were not from The Hamptons or Beverly Park. They sprinkled the map, the professions, and sources of wealth. Here were the demographics:

PROFESSION	INDUSTRY	NUMBER
High Tech, Software, Developers	Silicon Valley	12
Brokers, Bankers,	Wall Street	8
Investors, Developers	Real Estate	7
Investors, Entrepreneurs	High Tech, Energy	7
Heirs	Family Estates	4
Bio Med	Pharmaceuticals	4
Entertainer, Musicians	Hollywood	3
Professional Athletes	Sports	2
Royalty	Foreign Monarch	1
Drug Baron (Acquitted/Retired)	Illicit Drug Industry	1
Power Ball Winner	Lottery	1
	Total	**50**

When the letters arrived, they celebrated quietly so as not to attract attention or create panic. Later, when the ultra-secret alarm came, they would gather their families and slip away without notice. They would supposedly survive. The rest, well, that's another story.

CHAPTER I
DISASTER STRIKES

THE REGULARS AT THE BOARD OF TRADE WERE THREE ROUNDS INTO happy hour, toasting one another's jokes, good fortune, and any other excuse on this Friday night. Still grumbling over last month's influx of Iditarod visitors, they were now reclaiming their favorite bar. But in a matter of minutes, the patrons and their blissful community of Nome, Alaska. would become the first American casualties of *Onesimus*, vaporized by an explosive energy six billion times more powerful than the atomic bomb of Hiroshima. They would not be warned or prepared, nor did they have any chance for escape.

On the other side of the Bearing Straight, just 157 nautical miles away, Lavrentyia, Russia, population 1,459, would become a hole in the ground 7 miles deep and 90 miles wide; ground zero for the impact. Officially known as *1989DP Onesimus*, the asteroid's effect would be instant, painless, and without warning. A similar fate would be dealt to a number of small communities located in this area of the Arctic Circle.

The intense heat at impact could melt ice layers and boil much of the Arctic Ocean. The shock wave created a tsunami more than 900 feet high would reach California and Hawaii in less than a day. The tsunami would cough up big ships and underwater submarines like wiped-out surfboards in a Banzai Pipeline. Coastlines would be consumed by the rise in ocean levels. Global earthquakes and volcanic eruptions triggered by the colossal shock waves would redefine land and ocean boundaries. California may only be identifiable by its mountain tops. The impact would generate an environmental calamity that extinguishes most life forms and would take decades if not centuries to allow any recovery.

A cloud of vaporized rock, dust, ash, and steam sulfates spread from the crater as the asteroid burrowed into the Earth in a fraction of a second. Rock and pieces of the asteroid were ejected out into space by the blast, then were heated to glowing hot fragments while re-entering the atmosphere, broiling the Earth's surface and igniting massive wildfires. The resulting cloud of dispersed particulates covered the globe and caused temperatures to drop, conditions that would persist for years.

An impact of any sizeable magnitude, on or near the critical point of what seismologists call the "Ring of Fire," would be cataclysmic for land masses on both the eastern and western shores of the Pacific Ocean. Like falling dominos, a chain reaction of earthquakes, and volcanic eruptions would initiate from the arctic and trigger similar eruptions along the fault lines of the Pacific basin.

The Aleutian Island chain had several dormant volcanoes that would become sympathetically active with *Onesimus'* impact. Mount Spurr, Mount Redoubt and Mount Augustine would erupt along with other nearby North American and Asian volcanos. The Cascade Range would become sensitized resulting in eruptions at Mount Rainier,

Mount Shasta, Mount Hood, and Mount St. Helens. Working its way down the coast, seismic activity would become catastrophic if the swarms of Long Valley caldera volcanoes became active, especially the super volcano east of the Sierra Nevada Range near Mammoth Mountain.

The domino effect would include seismic activity and earthquake eruptions along prominent fault lines including San Andreas and Rose Canyon. The combination of earthquakes, volcanoes and the resultant tsunamis would result in portions of California, Oregon, and Washington disappearing into the Pacific Ocean, and perhaps the entire Central Valley becoming a vast inland sea.

CHAPTER II

THEY'RE CALLED "PREPPERS"

MONTHS EARLIER

RANDALL MEREDITH DID NOT CONSIDER HIMSELF A "PREPPER."

But there he was in Las Vegas satisfying his curiosity. His staff, even his wife, had no idea this business trip was a fact-finding mission of survival.

Prompted by fears of terrorism, pandemic, natural disaster, nuclear holocaust, EMP, economic collapse, or even anti-government paranoia, millions of survivalists around the world meticulously prepare for Armageddon. They eschew being called "tinfoil hatters." They purchase weapons, survival gear, generators, gas masks, medical emergency supplies, and even plant seeds. They stockpile food and water in underground bunkers. They read dozens of books, watch videos, attend conventions, and join like-minded groups and review their websites. They're not comfortable relying on the government for their personal safety *when the shit hits the fan-* -WTSHTF in Prepper parlance.

Unlike survival *purists*, however, some Preppers are not interested in living in the woods, catching small animals in snares, or fishing with hooks and strings. Recognizing and consuming edible plants or learning the skills necessary to live with virtually no assistance is not in their wheelhouse. They acknowledge that such skills are admirable, but learning, training, and becoming proficient at them can be daunting.

Even with the best technology, preparing for WTSHTF can be a problem. Home-oriented food dehydration machines are burdensome. Freeze-dried and pre-packaged survival food is pricey and handling and storage a hassle. Actually, all the items on the astute prepper's checklist—there must be hundreds—can be overwhelming. Dedicated preppers must somehow persevere.

An enviable subset of preppers, who are concerned with survival but are too busy or too rich for the prepping mundanities, falls into the *EP* category. They are a small, wealthy minority who can afford the very best, without the inconvenient learning curve or personal slog necessary to prepare. They're considered privileged and can simply pay others to make things ready.

Technological convenience is more suited for "Elite Preppers" (*EP's*).

During his desert recon trip, Meredith navigated the Executive Air Terminal and easily spotted the limousine driver holding the placard with his last name. The Yucca Mountain Sanctuary logo on the placard's lower-left corner confirmed it. He travelled light— khaki pants, sport shirt, blue blazer, and Top Sider mocs—no socks and no luggage. The over-and-back trip required little provisions; he carried only a laptop.

Meredith and driver quickly navigated through the gated areas of McCarren International Airport. The desert air beyond the automatic glass doors of the terminal hit Meredith like a 49'ers linebacker. Pressing on, the young executive followed his driver to the idling limousine. He sank into the cool, black leather seat as the driver secured the door, hustled to the other side of the vehicle, and assumed his position behind the wheel.

"Weather nice in Santa Barbara?" the driver politely asked.

"A lot cooler than here. How do people survive in this oven?"

"A marvelous invention—air conditioning," he said with a laugh.

"How long have you lived here?"

"I'm Mr. Globitz' driver. I travel wherever he goes. We've been coming here twice a month for the last four years. New York is where I call home."

"Nice."

Meredith paused from the pleasantries and pulled up the file on his laptop. He scanned the information pertaining to his appointment, occasionally glancing out of the backseat window. He marveled at the Las Vegas skyline, the billboards, and the hectic traffic. His thoughts drifted to the harebrained venture he was on, investigating a doomsday safe haven for his family. *If Eve knew what this trip was about, she'd declare me insane,* he mused.

Word of an underground super-bunker had spread at the speed of light amongst the financial elites. Meredith was one of them. "Insiders" secretly scrambled to make an appointment to reserve one of the prized suites. Ownership was suddenly becoming a sought-after position for the powerful and wealthy. Meredith had to investigate.

After a fifteen-minute ride, he found himself in the elegant Encore Hotel and Casino where he was greeted in the lobby by a very well-spoken representative for the Yucca Mountain Sanctuary project. The nametag with logo helped, but her gray pinstriped business suit, silk blouse, and high heels separated her from the hotel staff and its patrons.

"Welcome to Las Vegas, Mr. Meredith. Did you have a nice flight?"

"Ah, yes. Thank you."

"I'm Gretchen Kensington," she said with a smile as she extended her hand.

He responded, shaking her hand. Pleasantries aside, his misgivings about this Yucca Mountain trip were broadcast on his furrowed brow.

Ms. Kensington recognized the look and immediately took charge.

"The elevator is over here. Our Yucca Mountain display suites are on the penthouse level."

Conversation with Gretchen during the brief ear-popping elevator ride was cordial but limited. When the doors opened, he was greeted by a tall gentleman in his forties with a German accent.

"Mr. Meredith, I'm Hulbert, your advisor to YMS, the Yucca Mountain Sanctuary."

The entire sixty-third floor of the five-star luxury, Encore Hotel and Casino was devoted to a survival sanctuary exhibition—the sales room. Globitz' designers had laid out a mockup of the new Yucca Mountain facility, some ninety miles away from Las Vegas. No expense was spared installing his exhibition suites. The scale model of the shelter he built within the catacombs of the former nuclear waste repository was only part of the presentation.

During the next two hours, Randall learned of the impenetrable doomsday bunker complex they called YMS. Heinz Globitz envisioned an ultra-secure fallout shelter for affluent inhabitants like Meredith. Different from the thousands of luxury bunkers being built around the world for wealthy preppers, this one would be unparalleled.

Globitz considered farcical the personal family shelters built ten to twenty feet underground, no matter how luxurious. Even the avant-garde, underground "Luxury Silo Condos" didn't meet his standards, Hulbert explained.

Absolute protection from the risks of nuclear fire, fallout, or an electro-magnetic pulse attack required extreme measures. Biological contamination, pandemic, government revolution, and economic and monetary collapse necessitated more than blast-proof underground bunkers.

"Yucca Mountain was an ideal solution," Hulbert explained.

Meredith's intellect was unmatched in computer technology, but suddenly he found himself a total neophyte in the complexities of world catastrophes. Masking his naiveté, he engaged Hulbert in theoretical questions of survival. With reassuring confidence and tutorial detail, the Yucca Mountain authority put every question to rest.

Hulbert explained that fifty select families would be allowed to survive a cataclysmic disaster "if the balloon goes up," as he put it. *They* would be the lucky ones; their children would become the next generation of Earth's inhabitants. Yucca Mountain was a prepper's ultimate survival solution.

With his authoritative European inflection, Hulbert tactfully pushed all of Meredith's insecurity buttons: family safety, progeny, investments, security, health, and well-being. He stressed the exclusivity of those lucky enough to be accepted into the YMS family of patrons. Hulbert recognized the familiar gaze Meredith revealed from his experience with other well-heeled prospects. They didn't want to deal with the ugliness of having to survive, but knew it was prudent. They weren't typical preppers, but they were ripe for the picking.

And Heinz Globitz, the insightful opportunist, was poised and ready.

It was his brainchild to capitalize on survival hysteria. Globitz, an East European-born American and one of the wealthiest men in the world, made his fortune through questionable hedge fund and currency trading as well as shrewd investments. Educated in England and later convicted of insider trading, he was accused of meddling in several foreign government affairs. Rumored to have been released from a Russian prison on financial terms, he had an uncanny ability to recognize moneymaking opportunities while escaping liability. Converting Yucca Mountain from a nuclear waste repository to a survival facility required visionary genius. Globitz' genius.

In the 1980s, the U.S. government determined that Yucca Mountain was the preferred site for safe storage of the nation's growing amount of unspent nuclear waste. The military's portion accounted for about one-third of the total requirement, while nuclear power plants and other civilian sources, the rest. A consolidated nuclear waste repository was needed. This obscure mountain in a rather remote part of the nation became the focal point of attention.

The Yucca Mountain Nuclear Waste Repository[1] project was a windfall to the Nevada economy. Billions of dollars were spent to study and build (bore) into the Nye County mountain range. Nevada politicians and businesses were all smiles with the influx of capital expenditures and employment.

Then came the environmentalists and the few NIMBY (not in my back yard) alarmists. Concern about potential water contamination from nuclear waste seepage and fallout caused by future earthquakes brought the project to a temporary halt. For good measure, the antagonists also stirred up concerns about overland transportation vulnerabilities of the nuclear waste.

The *coup de grâce* came when a controversial senator from Nevada and the president of the United States bowed to the dictates of the environmental lobby and killed the project. The good senator and his president amazed their adoring "save-the-earth" fans with dazzling contortions, patting themselves on the back.

When the taxpayers' $12 billion investment in a nuclear waste

---

[1] The 1987 Nuclear Waste Repository Act authorized an underground storage facility for spent nuclear fuel and radioactive waste at Yucca Mountain. It became a "political hot potato" and scuttled after over $12 Billion expended and 5-miles of underground tunnels were bored under the Nevada mountain.

storage facility went south, the multi-billionaire was eagerly waiting in the wings.

The financial bailout by the shrewd businessman for a dysfunctional U.S. Government project became a bonanza. For nickels on the dollar, Globitz purchased the ready-made fallout shelter that was constructed 1,000 feet below the Earth's surface and directly above an untapped aquifer.

The five-mile long, "U-shaped" tunnel complex was bored into a compressed volcanic tuff rock formation in the mountain range that formed some ten million years earlier. The abandoned tunnels and off-shoot alcoves were still equipped with an electrical distribution set up, air filtration, and an internal road network among other amenities; all salvageable by Globitz' design engineers. The purchase cost, plus the calculated $1.5 billion buildout and expected profits, would be recovered handsomely by the YMS visionary."

The government's saving grace to the sad state of affairs was its recoupment of a portion of the taxpayers' layout from the parsimonious offer by Globitz. The billions of dollars the local economy would have benefitted from later, during its operation, was quietly dismissed. Like many government waste projects, Yucca Mountain sat boarded up and vacant for years. It eventually evaporated from public scorn—along with the politicians responsible.

Meredith was dazzled by the meticulous details of the presentation. Hulbert, his convincing and knowledgeable guide, was more teacher than salesman. More consultant than agent. More compassionate friend than stranger.

As they walked through the replica 1,500-square-foot living quarters of the project, Meredith found himself getting lured into the survival mindset. His insecurities about family and their safety weighed heavily. He was no "prepper" and yet, maybe he should be. Hulbert subtly reinforced his concerns.

Globitz' spectacular exhibition showroom was convincing. Prospective residents like Meredith could walk through, inspect, and "kick the tires" of the model of the safe-haven dwelling. Three bedrooms, two baths, a kitchenette, and a great room consisting of a dining area and a living/family/media area were staged with the very best furniture and appliances. A reinforced security chamber was thrown in for good measure. The diminutive but luxurious suites were suitable for a family of four.

A warm, crackling virtual fireplace, simulated windows with programmable high-definition sceneries of pastureland, meadows, or ocean coast lines, and surround sound background music provided an ambiance patently different from the reality of its one-thousand-foot-deep bunker superstructure. Each of the fifty resident suites available could also be personalized as necessary.

Big, bold letters of the catchy phrase appeared throughout the presentation rooms: *Leave the Prepping to us!*

Bright, colorful foldout sales brochures and ubiquitous video monitors throughout the sales and marketing showroom avoided any unpleasant reference to Armageddon. The topic was assumed but not mentioned. Rather, they boasted the sanctuary's modern living conveniences and pleasant environment.

Meredith's emotions were convinced, but the pragmatic engineer required details.

Technical issues like infrastructure were all covered in fine print. The volcanic ash scrubbers, with HEPA filters for nuclear, biological, and chemical filtration supported the air duct system. Electrical power, converted from geothermal heat energy, and backup lithium-ion batteries charged by stand-by diesel generators ensured an infinite supply of uninterrupted electricity for the facility. One of the alcoves was dedicated to a water reservoir and a reverse osmosis water filtration system. With a viable source of food, residents could conceivably survive indefinitely.

A food storage locker contained enough dehydrated, freeze-dried, and canned food to last the occupants twenty years. Dried and preserved meats, fish, and fowl augmented by instant milk, white rice, and black beans, et cetera, promised a less-than-gourmet, but palatable sustenance. Fresh food cravings could be appeased by tilapia raised in an aquaponics alcove along with vegetables and fruits.

An aeroponic garden would also accommodate seed potato and tomato production, leaf crops, and micro-greens. Nutrient-rich mushrooms would be grown without much space or light. Nuts, like white walnuts, would be stockpiled because of their incredible twenty-five-year long shelf life and nutritional value if uncracked and kept dry.

To combat boredom and muscle atrophy, a workout facility, lap pool, and a virtual golf course would occupy one wing of the complex, replete with men's and women's locker rooms, sauna and steam rooms. Vitamin D sun lamps would be located throughout.

A smaller-sized soccer field with Astroturf would accommodate youth activities. Three classrooms with the latest desktop computers, white boards, equipment, and supplies would serve their educational needs. A virtual library would be stocked with millions of digitized books, DVDs, CDs, games, and the equipment for library use or in the comfort of a resident's suite.

Meredith learned that a probable two-to-three-months stay in the complex, by the fifty or so families, would be a cakewalk. In fact, ten, even twenty years would be possible if required.

A resident support staff would occupy the back wing of the underground complex. A medical wing would contain a hospital bed, a procedure table, and a dental chair. Maintenance, security, medical doctor, dentist, psychologist, teachers, agricultural and nutrition specialists, activities coordinator, and entertainers would all be included in the total occupancy of the shelter.

Meredith, like the selected, potential patrons, was mesmerized.

Globitz knew his investment would pay off. His hand-selected staff, including Hulbert, was warm and friendly, and very convincing. Similarly, but unadvertised, his criteria for qualifying resident prospects included a religious and political profile. Religiously observant candidates were preferred. It was assumed that they would accept stress and hardship more readily and would better deal with the prospect of fear. Radical religious zealots, however, were politely denied. Anyone with a history of political activism was tactfully disallowed. An underground utopia required friendly and obedient neighbors. What lay behind the façade, however, was something no one anticipated.

Buy-in terms? When Meredith and the other prospective residents finally learned what was required for their buy in, they were shocked. To even "qualify for acceptance," an extensive screening was part of the agreement: medical, intellectual, financial, and genetic. Families with children under ten years of age were preferred. A hefty, non-refundable deposit was also required to hold a reservation (and eliminate the play-actors). The remainder, delivered in advance, before occupancy: two hundred, "Good Delivery" gold bars (400 troy ounces each), roughly $120 million.

"What currency will survive Armageddon?" Hulbert calmly posited.

Meredith gulped when faced with the price tag.

A beautiful, welcoming wife and two adorable kids would not assuage a miserable flight home and two sleepless nights.

CHAPTER III

THE SITUATION ROOM

WHITE HOUSE, WASHINGTON, DC

"Good morning, Madame President."

"Good morning, General. Staff. Please be seated. Now, what's this all about?"

A concerned President Lucille Cranston seated herself in the designated leather desk chair opposite the General's end of the heavy, mahogany conference table. With her trusty tablet device in hand, the wary executive artfully measured eye contact of everyone in the most portentous, decision-making room in the world.

The popular president was not a politician. Cranston worked her way up through the ranks of business, eventually becoming chairman and CEO of Cargill, one of the top ten corporations in America. She was later summoned to overhaul the U.S. Postal Service, where she successfully restructured and privatized it, employing robot and drone technology, small package and document delivery pods, and a high-speed data delivery network for all of the United States. Mrs. Cranston was affectionately called "Linebacker Lucy" for her aggressive nature in tackling tough problems, if not her endomorphic silhouette. But she was not prepared for today's nightmare.

Despite his Brooks Brothers pinstriped suit, crisp white oxford shirt, and navy silk tie, the square-jawed, no-nonsense former Army Ranger still commanded the respect and salutation "general." He and the nervous, unrecognized attendee were an exception to an uncharacteristic sparsity of advisors and cabinet members for a subject so serious that it demanded the security of the Situation Room.

White House Chief of Staff General Sterling H. Addington, still standing, called the gathering to order. Michael F. Maganti, the Secretary of Defense, Ida Drabek, National Security Advisor, and the unfamiliar face, Robert Wilcox, director of the White House Office of Science and Technology, were present.

President Cranston was the dubious beneficiary of an election process where the government's change of command, jokingly called "sausage making," left her in the dark on many of the long list of names of her advisors. The most uneasy member of this morning's meeting was one of them.

Either because of his generous campaign contributions, his connections and affiliations, or unfortunately, expertise in his field, Wilcox was one of many political appointees the administration blindly "knighted" following her election. The retired Rensselaer Polytechnic Institute Dean of Engineering often admitted that it was the impressive title and occasional invitations to White House soirées that were his motivations for moving to Washington and joining the White House team. Little would be required of him. Now this!

Looking directly at the bespectacled visitor wearing a green bow tie, the president asked, "Who are you, sir?"

Before he could respond, she asked General Addington, "Where's the rest of my cabinet?"

Florence Woods, the ever-faithful Secret Service agent assigned to Cranston, sensed the restricted and serious nature of the gathering and exited, closing the heavy door behind her. The ultra-secure Situation Room on the first floor of the West wing of the White House was now sealed.

General Addington responded, "Madame President, Dr. Wilcox is here to help explain some very disturbing news from the NASA's Jet Propulsion Laboratory in Pasadena. We thought it best to limit the exposure and avoid any possibility of leaks to the public, so we invited only pertinent staff."

"NASA is live on the SVTC monitor number one," he declared.

The Secure Voice TV monitor flickered, and all focused their attention on an image that appeared of Stuart G. Sutton, the Administrator of NASA, who had flown out to California to hear firsthand his JPL scientists' report. The three-hour time zone difference was not the reason Sutton's eyes bagged nor his tie loosened. His face was ashen, brow furrowed, and with a trembling look of fear, he cleared his throat and waited for the prompt.

"Madame President, I am sorry to report that a PHA my staff has been tracking has deviated from its orbital path and is on a catastrophic collision course with Earth," blurted the NASA executive from the video conference monitor.

Composed but obviously displeased, the president queried, "Remind me, Mr. Sutton, what's a PHA?"

Sensing an opportunity to be relevant and leaning forward in his seat at the conference table, Wilcox attempted to explain, when the video again erupted with Sutton's voice.

"Potentially Hazardous Asteroids (PHAs) are the asteroids with a potential to make threateningly close approaches to the Earth," Sutton said.

The two-way conversation suddenly shifted to one-way, rapid-fire questioning from the astute president, now sitting upright in her leather chair.

"How close; how catastrophic?"

"When will it hit?"

"Where?"

"What plan of action do we have, sir?"

Wilcox was now stammering as he interrupted the president's focus from the monitor. "We are working on a plan, madame, but there are problems."

Turning toward her pesky advisor, she asked, "What kind of problems? When did we first learn of this PHA anyway?"

The monitor with Sutton's voice broke in again with a long explanation, much to Wilcox's relief. The murmur among those in the Situation Room went quiet while the NASA head spoke.

"An analysis of the new data conducted by our Near-Earth Object Program Office here at JPL, and the Planetary Defense Coordination Office, shows that in twenty-seven months and four days, the risk of collision by a four-mile wide PHA, known as *1989DP* is almost certain—ninety-six percent."

Onesimus (pronounced: **oh-nis'-a-mus**), the given name of the Russet potato-shaped asteroid, had been observed for years on its merry orbital path around the sun. It was considered a no risk, Near Earth Object (NEO) on the *Sentry Risk Table*[2] and also on the *Palermo Technical Impact Hazard Scale*. Regardless, it was routinely monitored, along with 10,912 other NEO's.

Astronomers, physicists, and mathematicians have followed asteroids for centuries, calculating and tracking their orbital paths around the sun, similar to the orbital paths of all the planets. Asteroid detection, tracking, and defense is one of the missions of NASA, its interagency partners, and the global community. Their concern over

---

[2] *Sentry Risk Table. and Palermo Technical Impact Hazard Scale*. Astronomer's data forecasting tools for measuring potential impacts with Earth by NEOs.

Onesimus was elevated four years earlier when the predicted position on its orbital path exactly coincided with the position of Earth.

Earth's latest threat from space had occurred in 2013. A meteoroid, which broke off from an unknown, larger asteroid, initially exploded entering the atmosphere over Russia at 40,000 miles per hour. Its high velocity and shallow angle of atmospheric entry luckily caused an air burst at an altitude of around 97,000 feet (18 miles). The meteoroid was only 50 feet in diameter and weighed approximately 30,000 pounds when it entered the atmosphere. Yet, the total kinetic energy was equivalent to a 500-kiloton bomb; 20–30 times greater than that of the atomic bomb at Hiroshima.

It wreaked widespread destruction and injury in and around the city of Chelyabinsk. Over 1,500 people were hospitalized. Because most of the mass burned up entering the atmosphere, the largest fragment found was merely 2 feet in diameter and weighed 660 pounds.

The Chelyabinsk incident would be microscopic compared to the destruction posed by Asteroid *1989DP Onesimus*.

A Japanese Hayabusa spacecraft had actually rendezvoused with *Onesimus* on an unsuccessful, platinum metal-mining expedition. Platinum metals are some of the most rare and useful elements on Earth. Platinum exists in such high concentrations on some asteroids that even a small platinum-rich asteroid can contain more than has ever been mined on Earth in its entire history. Despite the disappointment in platinum mining, the Japanese mission resulted in a great deal learned about the composition and mass of *Onesimus*.

More recently, and after the Japanese mining mission, a near collision with a rogue asteroid disturbed *Onesimus*, pulling it into a new and slightly different orbit. The observations made by the Gemini 8-meter telescope in Mauna Kea, Hawaii, and confirmed by the orbiting Sentinel Infrared Space Telescope amended its risk potential with Earth. After several other observatories noted it had deviated from its orbital path, a new risk assessment upgraded its probability to ninety-six percent. It meant that in less than three years, Earth's orbital position was on a direct collision course with the asteroid on its new orbital path. The collision with Earth would be catastrophic.

"It will not be a direct hit, like a head-on collision, but more like an accident-causing lane change of two cars on a freeway—with considerably more devastation," explained Sutton.

"Unless we divert it, it will initiate a disastrous and potential end-of-civilization situation, starting at impact near Lavrentyia, Russia. Evacuation and civil defense measures would be all that's needed with an impact by a smaller asteroid. However, at over four miles in diameter and a consistent solid mass of rock and metal, *Onesimus,* presents significantly greater danger."

"There are numerous ways to divert asteroids, depending upon their mass, consistency, and the available reaction time. The simplest measure for an asteroid of this nature would be to build a large spacecraft and basically ram it into the asteroid a few years before it would hit Earth. But it could take years to build a large enough launching mechanism for the size of a 'kinetic impactor' spacecraft needed for *Onesimus*. The rendezvous alone could take another year or more."

"I thought we took care of this a few years ago," the president said.

"We tried, Ma'am. When we first suspected the asteroid's altered orbit, we scrambled the experimental NEOShield Impactor Spacecraft using a Russian Soyuz rocket system. It probably would have worked on a smaller-massed asteroid. Unfortunately, it failed.

"This asteroid is larger and more dangerous than our current kinetic-impactor capabilities," Sutton continued. "The size, mass, and the reaction time we have for *Onesimus* would require a blast-deflection solution using a nuclear warhead—which we're not prepared for, either."

The president swallowed. Attempting to muster her "never say die" persona, she looked at each staff member. No one looked up. Slumping into their seats, they quaked as she barked out another question. "What about that Japanese rocket you mentioned? Couldn't that be relaunched?"

Sutton exhaled deeply, then lamented, "The Hayabusa is too small for a kinetic-impact application."

The two minutes of silence in the Situation Room felt like two hours to the nervous staff. Reluctant to accept the naked truth of the situation, the president again scanned her staff for suggestions. Even a small glimmer of hope from her team of advisors would have been welcomed. Without looking up, Ida Drabek quietly cleared her throat. NASA remained mute on the SVTC monitor. Wilcox sat speechless. Except for the faint whir of the air conditioning, the silence was palpable.

"What about the Asteroid Mitigation projects we've spent billions on? What about the Europeans? What are the Chinese saying? There must be some solution!" the president desperately pleaded.

"We've considered every possible resource working through the Planetary Defense Coordination Office (PDCO), which works directly with foreign nations as well as our own," Sutton said. "Nothing."

"So, you're saying we're screwed! There's nothing we can do?"

The oxygen was unceremoniously sucked from the room.

Moments passed, painfully. Then, Wilcox blurted through the dark silence, "SLS! NASA has the Space Launch System being developed for Mars. It could reach an asteroid in deep space. With an appropriate nuclear payload, we would have a chance—albeit a very slim chance."

"Can you confirm any of this, NASA?" the president directed toward the monitor.

"Ma'am, we considered that," he sighed. "The Space Launch System is two years away from being launchable. Accelerating the development of SLS within the window of opportunity we have for *Onesimus* is not possible."

More silence.

Every member of her staff sat mortified in gloom; palms sweating, stomachs churning, and hearts pounding. "Linebacker Lucy" looked stunned. It didn't take NASA's rocket scientist to explain the consequences of Earth's collision with *Onesimus*.

This wouldn't be the first major history-making asteroid to collide with Earth, either. There's evidence of four previous encounters billions of years ago. More recently, some 65 million years ago, an asteroid six miles in diameter hit Earth near Chicxulub, Mexico, blasting a crater more than 110 miles wide. The impact set off fires, earthquakes, and volcanoes and threw so much sulfur, dust, and moisture into the atmosphere that it cut off sunlight for years. Earth's temperatures lowered and may have caused the eventual extinction of dinosaurs and three-quarters of all species. The Chicxulub asteroid was only slightly larger than *Onesius,* but then dinosaurs, not human civilization, were the casualties of extinction.

The reality of the end of civilization was soaking in with the transfixed staff. Then a thunderous interruption:

"Elon Musk!" exclaimed Wilcox. "SpaceX and Elon Musk have the *Falcon Heavy* space launch vehicle. They just launched his TESLA roadster into deep space with it."

"We thought of that," said Sutton. "We would still need a very large space vehicle with a huge payload to fit in *Falcon's* nosecone."

The rivalry between NASA's darling and the privately funded outsider played politics even for space flight. Boeing's costly and protracted development of the behemoth Space Launch System was jealously guarded as the intended heavy space launch vehicle for NASA. SpaceX, on the other hand, was a pesky, private-sector stepchild.

Both NASA and Boeing downplayed the successful launching of the *Falcon Heavy* launch vehicle in 2018 where Elon Musk's TESLA roadster was the advertised payload. They said it was "too small" for NASA's deep-space needs. NASA fancied big. SpaceX's more nimble approach to space exploration preferred smaller, re-useable space launch rockets and more practical development schedules. The payload differences were 154,000 pounds (SLS) to 141,000 pounds (FH) at lift-off. This meant the SLS could accommodate a 38,000-40,000 pound space craft for a Mars mission, while the FH only a 26,400 pound space craft.

The faceoff between tomorrow's "perfect" launch system funded by government contracts and the privately funded "smaller, but good" launch system available today was playing out with the highest of all possible stakes—world civilization.

"If we loaded up a *Dragon Space Craft* designed by SpaceX with a monster nuclear device, we could probably nudge the *Onesius* off-course. Just one degree would likely cause it to miss Earth!" Wilcox shrieked.

"NASA?" the president asked, looking skeptically at the SVTC monitor.

"It's possible, Ma'am. But a very-very long shot," Sutton opined. "Like betting on the Old Gray Mare."

Total silence. And more contemplative pause. After a few minutes, a welcomed break in the silence was voiced by a revived Linebacker Lucy.

"Gentlemen, and lady," she commanded. "If we do nothing or if we try and fail, no one will be here to even criticize our decision anyway."

Then, one eyebrow arched as she flashed the old "Linebacker" smirk and asked a question of her advisors, "Is anybody here a hockey fan?"

The befuddled staff looked at each other; then at the president. No takers.

She continued, "One of the greatest hockey players to ever lace up a pair of skates once said: 'You miss one hundred percent of the shots you don't take.'"

"Dr. Wilcox, I'm appointing you in charge of this situation. Get

Mr. Musk and assemble all the necessary parts you need to this puzzle. NASA, you guys back him up. Notify me directly if you get ANY resistance. Get that *Falcon Heavy* rocket going and fix this problem!"

"General, see that they have the full cooperation of all agencies, including DOD, STATE, NSA, and the CIA."

"Mr. Sutton, my iPad indicates that part of your mission is to inform the public of NASA's space activities."

"Yes Ma'am," Sutton responded.

"This mission will be an exception to that. No public announcements."

"And, I want this held in complete secrecy. A warning to all of you, including NASA—this is the highest security situation we have on our plate. Do not notify FEMA or any press. We don't want ANY unnecessary and premature panic to consume the public. NO LEAKS!!"

"Mr. Sutton, I assume your organization is on board and will cooperate."

"Absolutely, Madame President," he stated.

Now, let's get going," she commanded.

The Situation Room attendees responded, "Yes, Ma'am."

The president rose and exited before anyone could respectfully muster to their feet.

CHAPTER IV
WILCOX'S MISSION

"MY GOD, I CAN'T TAKE A PEE WITHOUT THESE GUYS WATCHING,"

Nobody but Bob Wilcox would feel a transformation in lifestyles like he would. The Saturday before his dreadful White House meeting, he was raucously cheering at his grandson's soccer game over in Annandale, oblivious to any scientific advisory requirement of the president. One week later, he was across the Potomac, stone sober in a hurricane's eye of civilization's worst nightmare.

The Secret Service agents looming outside his Georgetown rowhouse made the neighborhood aware and uneasy that someone important resided within. Wilcox was forbidden to discuss the reason for their presence even with his wife, and admitted he felt safer in obscurity than with their protection. No one, especially the press, could enter or leave the Wilcox residence without the agents' scrutiny.

Dr. Wilcox's new office was deep within the bowels of the

Pentagon. An armed guard outside his suite of offices prevented any unauthorized visitors. The walls, floor, and ceiling were lined with impenetrable metal mesh so that no intrusions could intercept the secure voice environment inside. All communications and coordination were considered Top Secret, SCI (Special Compartmented Information) for Wilcox and his team. Daily briefings with the White House Chief of Staff would be conducted by SVTV conferencing. Weekly briefings with the president would be scheduled in the Situation Room.

The once-retired, happy-go-lucky Wilcox pined for the halcyon days at Duke University, where he was considered the "party animal" at Pi Kappa Alpha. "Why did I ever move to Washington and accept this White House appointment?" he grumbled.

Dr. Wilcox was assigned a host of NASA engineers and administrative support staff for his team. They were given an unlimited budget and a license to steal. Their super-secret office complex was in the E Ring basement of the Pentagon. A "Wilcox Commission" cover story was fabricated with a goal of developing a satellite defense system for the military. Anything from the Pentagon was considered more plausible to deny, veiling its real, doomsday-prevention mission. Also, the Federal Emergency Management Administration, FEMA, could be kept in the dark and thus avoid public scrutiny and panic.

The government and JPL's official statement was that the previous routine mission redirecting *Onesimus* was successful. Meanwhile, the National Security Agency (NSA) was directed to intercept and alter "any and all" communication dealing with *Onesimus* and imbed the official storyline. No agency, government, NGO, or private citizens were exempt. NSA had to ensure complete opacity on the subject so that world panic would not occur. Foreign governments, even allies, were kept in the dark by the State Department.

The Central Intelligence Agency (CIA) had a supporting role, as well. An aggressive disinformation campaign was called for, "to redirect attention from *Onesimus*" to some other international concern. There were plenty of small wars occurring to choose from; plenty of tin-pot dictators and human tragedies to divert the world's attention. This would be a perfect opportunity for a "Wag the Dog" narrative.

A symphony of government agencies commenced the allegro from the same score, and Wilcox, it seemed, benefitted from its music. Despite his moaning, the reluctant warrior performed masterfully. His team's tireless effort became a virtuoso performance into what might be the only option available to thwart the extinction of life on Earth.

Wilcox's warriors embraced the "millennial geniuses" from SpaceX and brought them up to speed on the secret *Onesimus* mission. Office space was provided for key members of Elon Musk's team within the sensitive area of the Wilcox Commission suite in the Pentagon. All were sworn to secrecy and placed on the Secret Service watch list.

A *Falcon Heavy* (FH) launch vehicle was requisitioned by the government from the fledgling SpaceX's private inventory. Since the SLS was not yet in service, the *FH* offered the highest payload capacity of any currently operational launch vehicle in America necessary to reach GEO (geostationary orbit). Only NASA's big daddy, Saturn V, retired in 1976, had a larger capacity. From a GEO, a space craft could be launched and hopefully, rendezvous with *Onesimus*.

SpaceX's *Dragon* space craft was too small to be a kinetic impactor for the massive *Onesimus* asteroid, but it had three best-hope considerations: it was designed to fit into the nose cone of *FH*, it could carry a nuclear bomb (to compensate for its small, kinetic impact mass), and most importantly—it was available.

The *FH* was reprioritized from any other future mission in deference to *Onesimus*. With full cooperation by the SpaceX ground crew and builders, *FH* was readied for an immediate mission and moved to the modified Launch Pad 39A at Kennedy Space Center in

Florida. A matching SpaceX *Dragon* spaceship was designated as the *Falcon Heavy* payload.

The CRS-13, SpaceX's thirteenth Commercial Resupply Service spaceship, was a previously flown *Dragon* capsule made available for the *Onesimus* mission with some major modifications. It would need a new first- and second-stage booster and interior cargo mounting brackets, but its hull, structural elements, thrusters, harnesses, propellant tanks, plumbing, and many of the avionics could be reused. Since this was a one-way mission and acceleration weight was an issue, the heat shield, batteries, and components exposed to sea water upon splashdown were no longer necessary and removed.

Next the US Air Force had to prepare and deliver one of its heaviest nuclear bombs. The B83, a 1,200 KT bomb was selected. It was still maintained in the Air Force's inventory despite being built in 1983. It was designed for relatively hard impacts on irregular reinforced concrete surfaces; comparable to the solid rock surface of *Onesimus.*

The heavy steel weapon body had a nose cone and three hollow, shock-absorbing frangible rings to prevent ricochets or sliding. The warhead was mounted forward in the bomb body in the first compartment to make the bomb nose heavy. The mid-case contained the firing set and fusing controls, surrounded by a fiberglass-reinforced resin honeycomb for protection. The aft case contained the arming system and thermal batteries. The B83's parachute system in the afterbody were obviously unnecessary and removed.

The B83 would snuggly fit inside the *Dragon's* cargo capsule and be held in place with newly configured cargo brackets. Its weight of 2,400 pounds, 12-foot length, and 18-inch diameter allowed for extra rocket fuel for the *Dragon's* acceleration and navigational thrusters.

It was all coming together quite nicely. Time, however, was elbowing out any wiggle room for errors. NASA's scientists calculated the last best hope for a successful rendezvous with *Onesimus* was November 11, and would require eleven months, ten days of travel time for the spaceship.

The concept was entirely feasible. The elliptical orbit of the 35,421 miles per hour asteroid was precisely mapped by NASA. At a critical juncture, the asteroid would be intercepted by the fast-approaching *Dragon,* crashing into a preselected area of the asteroid's rocky surface. Bomb detonation would occur upon impact.

The forces generated by the payload and nuclear explosion would compensate for its lack of mass, and thus, disrupt the inertia of the asteroid. With zero atmospheric conditions and little gravitational forces in outer space, the blast from the attached nuclear device would hopefully, nudge the asteroid from its orbital path. Even a slight alteration of *Onesimus'* orbit would render it mitigated.

Dr. Wilcox reflected on his eighth-grade science class covering Newton's three laws of motion. Fifty years later they would be dramatically on display with earth-shaking consequences.

"Madame President, NASA and SpaceX have been exceptionally cooperative," Wilcox expressed by secure phone. "We are progressing on our mission and planning for a launch within the window of opportunity, on or before December first."

"Excellent, Dr. Wilcox. Have you had any reporters snooping around?" she asked.

"Negative. However, officers from FEMA have inquired about our work. Not sure how they got wind of our project, but they were rather insistent; they wanted to be given the heads-up."

"Damn it," she responded. "Another leak. It's imperative that FEMA and any other "outsider" not learn of this project, lest it fails. Do I make myself clear?"

"Yes, Ma'am."

Wilcox understood the implied message, without her spelling it out. If the mission failed and *Onesimus* couldn't be diverted, FEMA would not really be needed. In fact, mobilizing the entire National Guard to control things in the United States would be a waste of effort. Same for the rest of the world.

CHAPTER V
NASA TO THE RESCUE

IF ONLY...

Ideological differences were dissolved. World leaders opened up their treasuries, their veiled labs, their secret technologies, and their coveted brainpower for the cause. This one time in recorded history offered global unity.

JPL, PASADENA CALIFORNIA

The world's preeminent asteroid-mitigation scientists considered all conceivable mitigation techniques for the Potentially Hazardous Asteroid (*1989DP Onesimus*). The realistic marshalling of technology and assets however, eliminated two of the three most viable approaches:

- Gravity Tractor Device. A large spacecraft would orbit alongside the asteroid for a long period (several years, even decades) and slowly pull it out of the Earth's orbital path. Time would be the disqualifying factor for this approach.

- Kinetic Impactor. Launched years in advance, a large massed spacecraft could ram an asteroid, pushing it from Earth's path. The mass of the impactor would have to be proportionate to the asteroid. However, due to the size and proximity of *Onesimus*, there was no chance for success and thus, the kinetic impactor was eliminated as an option.

- Blast Deflector. A nuclear standoff explosion, using propulsion rather than mass, could divert an asteroid's impact with Earth. Technically banned for use in space, radioactive fragments could still impact the Earth's surface. Using the energy from a surface-mounted nuclear blast to nudge, rather than shatter the asteroid mass, would *conceptually* divert it from its perilous rendezvous with Earth. Time and the deployment of an ideal nuclear device are the critical elements for a fast-approaching asteroid. Space treaties be damned, this was the only remotely possible approach for dealing with *Onesimus*.

Each hand-selected JPL team member, with his or her unique training and specialty, was responsible for a segment of a series of tasks that would detonate a nuclear device on one side of the 4½ mile wide, potato-shaped asteroid. Knocking it from its orbital path, even one degree, would prevent a catastrophic encounter with Earth. The nuclear option was unanimously preferred over two other options by the assembled space scientists. Other options considered technologically unfeasible involved laser beam blasting and companion asteroid-bumping options.

Despite the abundant flow of air conditioning, beads of sweat rolled off the brow of thirty-six-year-old Richard Campbell (MIT '93), seated before three of the many brightly lit computer monitors of JPL's Command Center. His keen focus on the mission at hand supplanted all thoughts of his pending divorce.

A small, black-and-white placard above his desk bore the words "Docking and Platform Assembly." The high-definition video image of a four-foot square area of the rocky surface of *Onesimus* and two ominous mechanical arms projected on one of Campbell's computer monitors exactly matched the image on the massive video wall at the front of JPL's control room. The same images appeared on the SVTV monitor in the White House Situation Room until it went dark.

The cool blue lighting within the command center accentuated the curved banks of computer monitors and control stations but did nothing to prevent the accumulation of perspiration in the armpits and the back of Campbell's white shirt. His concerns also transcended the presence of the armed Department of Homeland Security Police guards, wearing their black fatigues and bullet-proof vests, positioned in every corner and at the entrance and exit of the room.

His hands moved swiftly between the keyboard and the two adjacent joy sticks, controlling every move of the robotic arms appearing on the monitors. A small diode light near the corner of one screen indicated the activity of the directional jet nozzles of the parent space craft. Bursts from the nozzles were carefully doled out to complement the asteroid's gravitational pull, keeping the module engaged with the 35,000 miles per hour orbiting object.

The three men hovering over the sweaty engineer were focused on the precise movements of the mechanical arms, responding to Campbell's brain surgeon-like skill. Providing moral encouragement rather than technical oversight, all three remained respectfully silent.

This was not one of the one thousand simulated practice runs Campbell had performed over the last few months. This was game day: the real deal, and life on Earth depended upon its success.

What appeared to be a pneumatic drill popped onto the scene in the computer display. Maneuvered into position by Campbell's encouragement, the drill proceeded to bore through the guide holes of a metal template into the hard, rock surface of the critical area in focus. A snake-like hose followed in trace of the pneumatic drill and vacuumed the debris fragments and dust emitted from the drilled rock. In a perfect circular pattern, the snaking hose moved in concert with the drill leaving behind a clean, one-inch hole, then another and another, until all five holes under the metal template had been bored.

The cast of performing space paraphernalia, drill, template, robotic arms, and snaking vacuum were all illuminated by klieg lights from the mother spaceship. Captured and transmitted back to Earth in high definition under the masterful direction of aerospace engineers, they appeared like puppets performing in a home video. Without taking a bow, the robotic performers disappeared as if the curtain were dropped, ending Act I.

Deep breath.

Campbell, his three bosses, and JPL space scientists all exhaled, and prepared for the next phase of the docking platform assembly. Moments later, a refreshed computer screen signaled Act II.

The mechanical arms floated back onto the screen, each bearing a two-feet long by one-inch diameter bolt. The bolts were inserted through two of the template holes and into the drilled holes of the rocky surface. Magically, the robot arms twisted and rotated the bolts clockwise into a firm, temporary position. Responding to commands of JPL's sweaty maestro, the arms exited and returned with two more bolts and repeated the process. The last bolt was secured by one of the arms when the other returned with the pneumatic socket wrench to permanently seat the bolts into the rock.

With five bolts solidly mounted into the asteroid's surface and docking plate, the engineer sighed relief. His small, but important part of the Earth-saving mission was an indisputable success. *If only my estranged wife appreciated my critical work*, he mused. One of the overseers did, however, and offered a pat on Campbell's back as the three shuffled behind another specialist's workstation.

The image on the massive video screen at the front of the command center zoomed out from the small stage of the subject area to reveal a

SURVIVAL BENEATH YUCCA MOUNTAIN

large smooth object, the size of a Volkswagen. The man at the controls for the "Device Placement" event was but another of the fifty-member team of the world's finest aerospace engineers ever assembled.

Everyone in the room knew about the asteroid encounter sixty-five million years ago near Chicxulub, Mexico. *Onesimus*, slightly smaller at 4½ miles in diameter, could cause similar devastation to a more inhabited Earth. Power grids would disintegrate, nuclear reactors explode, dams crumble, buildings topple, and nature's fury unleashed. Because of the Earth's development and human population, man could witness his own extinction from an encounter with an asteroid this size.

The catastrophic event of Chicxulub was about to be replicated. The end of mankind would almost be certain. Almost.

Campbell and his colleagues at JPL knew the consequences all too well. Today, they were on the world stage and they did their level best. When it was over, the SVTV monitors and computers shut down, the lab lights turned off, and they all went home to be with their loved ones, sworn to secrecy. Campbell would embrace his gin and tonics, preferring his neighborhood bar to the empty home he used to share with his estranged wife.

THE WHITE HOUSE

"Madam President, Dr. Wilcox is here with news from the JPL," announced General Addington, the Chief of Staff.

"Yes, can we squeeze him in before President Jeong?" she asked regarding her scheduled meeting with the newly elected Democratic Capitalist Korean leader.

"Five minutes?" Addington asked.

"Yes, that's all we need."

An anxious Wilcox was led into the Oval Office by the Chief of Staff and positioned in front of her desk. If he were a puppy, his tail would be wagging and the folder he was holding would be gleefully dropped in front of its rewarding owner.

"What's this, Dr. Wilcox."

"It's a press release, Madam President. We propose you schedule an Oval Office broadcast to the Nation, a-a-and to the world!" stuttering with excitement.

President Cranston frowned and half smiled from the side of her mouth as she looked at Addington standing to the right of her desk.

"I have a staff of speech writers and a Press Secretary, Dr. Wilcox. You don't need to advise me on communications with the American public. Now, what would you propose we say to the Nation?"

Unnerved and panicky, Wilcox fidgeted his sweaty fingers and said, "It's all detailed in our proposed announcement: the magnificent accomplishment of our scientists. We can all breathe easy. We diverted the asteroid that would have destroyed the Earth!" Then pausing to compose himself, he continued, "Madame President, this single event will define your presidency. You saved the world."

Not amused, General Addington cut in, "And the coming election will be a shoe-in, right?"

A more considerate and genial response was offered by the president, "Mr. Wilcox, I would rather the JPL be allowed to herald their success. Let's let them make the announcement."

A puzzled Wilcox smiled, accepting her dictate. "Of course." He turned with a contemptuous look at Addington and exited. It was obvious he was the *useful idiot* for the situation and not in the loop between JPL and the White House.

JPL's press release and announcements of its extraordinary success had already been written and waiting for public disclosure—before the outcome was even confirmed. As history reveals, governments and leaders are not always truthful.

The alternative would be to ask the nations of the world to prepare for a catastrophe that they could never surmount. Massive panic would be uncontainable and agonizing.

Quoting her favorite philosopher, M.B. Matthews, President Cranston confessed to her trusted chief of staff, "Blissful ignorance in certain death is preferred over futile hysteria."

CHAPTER VI
GOODBYE, SANTA BARBARA

AT THE MANSION.

Prompted by an ominous alarm that was secretly transmitted from Nevada, a series of events was set in motion that would forever alter the Meredith household.

Drew Cummings sat patiently on the right front fender of his limousine. His ill-fitting chauffer's outfit contrasted significantly from his weekday campus attire at University of California, Santa Barbara. Two tours in Iraq and one in Afghanistan fostered in him an appreciation for his current weekend assignments. Today: the Randall T. Meredith residence, overlooking East Beach and the Pacific Ocean. Witnessing the tranquility of the ocean breezes spilling over the cliffs, the gliding red-tailed hawk overhead, and the manicured hedge bordering the circular driveway to the Merediths' 18th-century French-style chateau, he conceded that today's assignment was indeed better than college studies and far better than combat.

Inside the 10,000-square-foot mansion, just steps away from Drew's perch, a conspicuous pall engulfed a pair of occupants. Low voices emerged from the library where the thirty-six-year-old Meredith and his trusted butler, Alejandro, were talking.

Randall Meredith, a self-made millionaire at age nineteen, had been considered a computer nerd from age ten. A software algorithm he developed in his teens had become an integral part of an Oracle system for which he was paid handsomely. His computer genius was recognized early on and a budding career was launching, but his dad insisted that he first attend college.

Stanford. Social development, academic exposure, and long-lasting associations were dad's idea of "polishing" his diamond in the rough. He was right. Randall graduated with honors and with numerous lifelong friends. Somehow, his popularity among the Sigma Nu fraternity brothers didn't lower his standing on the Dean's list, nor did it hinder the progress of his courtship of Eve Donovan, the blue-eyed beauty and debate team member. Eve had grown up in Omaha and was the daughter of a large insurance company executive. She was a slender, petite, and refined intellectual who rarely called attention to herself, displaying a consistent allegiance to God, family, and country. She was the perfect complement to Randall T. Meredith.

His neatly trimmed dark hair was speckled with gray, revealing the price paid for success in a very competitive line of work. The self-discipline of morning laps in his pool and regular weightlifting bolstered Meredith's confidence. But, the thirty-six-year-old software entrepreneur had more pressing concerns.

"Alejandro, you know what this is about," warned Mr. Meredith.

"Yes, I have an idea, sir."

"It's only immediate family. I can't take you with us."

"I understand, sir."

Pulling a bound file from the desk drawer, Mr. Meredith opened and spread its contents on the inlaid, leather surface of the walnut desktop.

"Alejandro, hopefully, we'll be back in a month or two and this won't be an issue. But these are the necessary documents you'll need to run the estate in our absence and to authenticate its transfer, should it become necessary. The adjacent property is now yours. Please accept it with our family's sincerest gratitude."

"Yes, sir. Thank you."

Turning from his desk and leaning forward in his chair, the sad billionaire looked directly into the glistening eyes of his loyal servant. From his own finger he removed a well-worn ring bearing a black onyx stone encircled in gold and the words "United States Marines." Barely discernable imprints of "Tunn Tavern" appeared on one side of the ring and the image of the Iwo Jima memorial on the other. He placed it into Alejandro's palm and gently folded the reluctant recipient's fingers into a tight fist, sealing their bond of respect and loyalty.

As he patted the top of his trusted butler's hand, he affirmed, "This is a little more personal. It was given to me by my father. I pray that it may someday be handed down to your own son."

"Thank you, sir."

"Now, please assemble the staff for our goodbyes."

Lining the marble-tiled entry hallway, the dutiful staff of maids, cook, gardener, janitor, and nanny awaited the exodus of the family they loved and served. One by one, the Merediths shook hands and hugged their employees. Leading the way was their gracious but stoic wife and mother, Mrs. Meredith. The wagging tail of Winston, the family's golden retriever, was accompanied by liberal hugs from the twin six-year-olds, Rex and Samantha.

The dog had been their best friend since birth, and both kids expressed a teary-eyed farewell. Winston was instinctively aware of the gravity of the situation and returned an unusually affectionate concern with sloppy licks to their faces before being heeled by Alejandro.

Approaching the doorway, young Rex turned, broke from the family procession, and ran back to Maria with his outstretched arms. Hugging and sobbing, young Rex pleaded with his father to take Maria with them. Always composed and comforting, the devoted nanny knelt to eye level with her charge.

"Be strong, Mi'jito. Now go."

With an assuring push, she directed the boy back to the front door and his waiting parents.

At the limo, Drew abruptly came to attention as the four Merediths emerged from the resident's main entryway. With authority, he swung open the right-rear door and cheerfully greeted his distinguished clients. A forced smile was returned by Mrs. Meredith as Rex and Samantha bounded into the limousine. The subdued adults followed as the attentive driver closed the doors, assumed his position behind the wheel, and slowly drove his passengers through the iron gates. Their day of return—unknown.

CHAPTER VII

THE ALARM SOUNDED

LAS VEGAS, NEVADA

SHORTLY AFTER DAYBREAK ON A HAZY TUESDAY IN MAY, MARSHALL Retzlaff had just completed a routine clearance of United flight 723 arriving from Boston. The foam from his second sip of a favorite espresso-latte had not yet been licked away from his upper lip when the radar screen flashed trouble. Then the call from the pilot. "Low Fuel Situation. Request priority landing!"

Then, more trouble. And more, again. A series of "emergencies" from several unscheduled, approaching aircraft resulted in Retzlaff's arms to flail and his voice to rise. Then screams shattered the otherwise controlled monotone inside the control tower at McCarran International Airport. "Clearance NOT granted! Abort! Abort! You are not cleared to land, on runways 19 or 26."

Defying the warning, the avalanche of rogue aircraft broke

through the patchy clouds and dangerously touched down just minutes apart. Shrieking commands by the air traffic controller went unheeded. Retzlaff spontaneously waved off the scheduled airliners and placed them in holding patterns until the main runway was cleared of inexplicable and unapproved emergency landings.

"Bingo Fuel Emergency" was the magical phrase Randall Meredith's pilot used. The request radioed from his Gulfstream G650 was a recognized military term and falsely represented an empty fuel tank to a "hopefully" friendly former military air traffic controller. It was one of the few granted priority landings at the Las Vegas airfield. Magical phrases be damned, most of the pilots were not so reverent, as the flood of unauthorized planes poured from the sky.

Whining engines propelled the taxiing aircraft to the once vacant, south-west apron of the airfield. The pilots coaxed their planes into uncontested parking spaces amongst an accumulation of a wingtip-to-wingtip, cluttered mass of corporate jets. One by one, the aircraft terminated their deafening shriek, as they came to rest. Ignoring the protestations from the control tower, the pilots turned off their communication systems as well, and began deplaning their passengers.

Hardly by coincidence, a fleet of idling black limousines snaked through the NO ACCESS gate and pompously formed an improvised queue inside the airfield boundaries.

The kicked-up dust and hot Las Vegas air momentarily stunned the exiting passengers. Like the other wild-eyed moguls with their immediate families in tow, the Merediths scrambled from their plane, each carrying but a single suitcase. Eve's slacks caught on the exit ramp and ripped the left leg of her Lisa Perry wool pant leg up to her knee. Husband Randall's grip on her right arm prevented a fall as the two steered the twins toward the idling limousines.

Meredith acknowledged one of the arm-waving chauffeurs next to his vehicle and directed his wife and kids through the maze of parked aircraft, swirling dust, and other frantic families. It was the seventh vehicle in a long line of limousines that the Merediths finally reached, throwing their luggage into the trunk before plunging into the vehicle's back seats. The deafening whine of still-arriving corporate jets was hardly silenced by the limo's doors closing. The panting passengers sunk into the deep leather seats while their hearts waited for calm.

One by one, the idling long black sedans were loaded with their VIP patrons before barreling out through the airfield's unauthorized access gate. The haste of loading luggage suffered a casualty of one family's belongings, which became a speed bump for the lumbering limos. Cynical drivers seemed to enjoy the opportunity of flattening the forsaken luggage, whose contents spewed out onto the dusty pathway of the airfield's exit.

Left stranded in a cloud of exhaust smoke, tire tracks, flying rocks, and debris, were the bewildered pilots and air crews. Abandoned by their owners, the planes were parked like cords of wood against the perimeter fence of the airport's boundary with crew members embarrassingly watching from the cabin doors, wondering who would explain their actions, pay their fines, and be responsible for removing their aircraft from McCarran International's property.

CHAPTER VIII

JOURNEY TO SAFETY

AFTER THE FLIGHT

IT WAS QUIET BUT ANXIOUS IN THE PASSENGER SEATS OF THE MEREDITHS' Las Vegas limousine. Eve's death grip on her husband's hand during the drive was noticed by the fidgeting twins, who seemed to sense the gravity of their trek. Earbuds dangled, and their electronic games were yielded to the scenes of Las Vegas casinos and billboards flying by the limo's windows.

It was only four months earlier, they remembered, when their dad returned from his Las Vegas business trip bearing an extraordinary gift: a Mini Quadcopter Drone. He had told them that the International Consumer Electronics Show provided this delightful souvenir, which he gave them as a reward for good behavior while he was away on business.

Beyond the Las Vegas valley, the scenery north along Veteran's

Memorial Highway (U.S. 95) intrigued Rex and Samantha. An Air Force base on the right, a prison complex on the distant left, mountains on the horizon, and desert everywhere.

"Moonscape," kidded their dad.

The two unusually quiet kids were captivated by the contrast of scenery from their familiar California home base. An unprecedented interlude of silence transpired, especially from Samantha. With foreheads pressed against the windows, they found themselves hypnotized by a land indescribably foreign. Giant meandering tumbleweeds, an occasional trailer park, and road signs warning drivers against picking up hitchhikers, it all seemed like a video game.

Their desert-gazing tranquility was suddenly interrupted by the appearance of two black limousines racing past them.

"Weren't they speeding, Dad?" asked Samantha.

"In a hurry, for sure, Sam. Probably going where we're going," he responded.

Several minutes passed.

"Did we just see the *Road Runner?*" exclaimed Mr. Meredith.

The silence was broken. It was a feeble attempt to inject some levity into the situation. The twins turned toward their jokester father to see where to look, then quickly realized the hoax. A dig from Eve's elbow indicated that his humor was not appreciated.

Despite the ensuing small talk, the hour and a half of highway miles drudged on, uneventful. The limo finally began to decelerate as they approached the intersection with State Route 373, where there was an unlikely minimart/truck stop called Amargosa.

The twins sprang to life at the prospect of a time-out and a cold soda. Their observant father noted the raised eyebrow of his wife, who was focused on the bright pink building adjacent the truck stop. He quickly told the driver to press on. His reluctance to explain one of Nevada's "ahem" (brothel) businesses to his innocent kids was understandable and appreciated by Eve.

Then, driving a few hundred feet further, the limo made a right turn onto an unmarked, paved road. Roughly a mile later was a rusty Department of Energy sign forbidding firearms, cameras, and recording devices. The limo continued as the road meandered through mountain and desert terrain for a few more miles, when they came upon a small sign with the words "Yucca Mountain."

Passing a man-made mountain of rock and earth, the limousine came to a rolling stop. A security guard directed them toward a gate that opened to a large parking lot and a series of temporary buildings. All eyes were fixated on what appeared to be a small town on the desert floor snuggled between the crevasses of two mountainous ridgelines.

One corrugated steel building about 200 feet long was surrounded by several single-story buildings and a street network. A parking lot, water tower, railroad tracks, and a fuel tank mounted ten feet in the air added to the bizarre appearance of a boom town of days gone by.

Swirling gusts of wind and dust frustrated the orange-vested parking attendants who were waiting for the incoming limousines. The parking area was marked by bright orange, windblown banners.

Resting on railroad tracks fifty yards from two massive trapezoidal prisms of rock and dirt sat a colossal piece of machinery—the tunnel boring machine. It was a long cylinder with an ugly frontend that lay along a pair of railroad tracks and was at least two stories high. Connected to the cylinder and stretching beyond the length of a football field was a mysterious-looking train that could have been built by aliens from another world. The behemoth machine had obviously burrowed out of the side of Yucca Mountain and expired from its last mission.

White paint on the gnarly looking cylindrical auger head yielded to patches of rust and corrosion. A metal ladder ran up to the operator's compartment which featured a cloudy window. Hydraulic pistons, hoses, and cables resembled a contemporary piece of art gone bad. Conveyor belts, a debris cart, and mechanical bucket loaders comprised the back portion. It was an impressive display of power all on one railroad track, linked together with steel, nuts, and bolts; a monument to mining technology, albeit grave worthy.

The parking attendants were positioned throughout the area to direct the incoming limousines into a barb-wired compound. The once clean and shiny black vehicles were maneuvered into a recently configured parking lot. White chalk lines designated parking spaces on the gravel and spotty asphalt, while chalked arrows pointed to the reception area of the compound.

A disoriented Meredith family clambered from the dusty vehicle and anxiously waited for the trunk lid to be opened. Randell quickly grabbed his and the twins' suitcases while Eve wrestled her own valise from the limo and followed her family along the chalk-lined path toward the Spartan-like facilities.

The attendants guided the well-healed patrons to the first of a series of temporary shelters. Guards, conspicuously positioned outside of each of the five temporary shelters, maintained order in the fast-forming queue. Large red signs identified each shelter: Station 1 (Credentials), Station 2 (Interview and Application Checklist), Station 3 (Medical Examination), and Station 4 (Final Interview). Noisy generators powered the skid-mounted A/C units beside each facility and added to the carnival-like atmosphere.

Three or four families like the Merediths were lined up in front of one of the structures. Mr. Meredith smiled and inquired if this was the back of the line for Station 1. A nod in the affirmative was given by a gentleman holding the hands of two tow-headed toddlers. Randall's follow-up comment about the desert heat prompted another nod followed by a conspicuously cold silence. Rex and Samantha picked up on the situation's tension, especially noting the obedience of the other youngsters in the line in front of them.

Like edgy soldiers in a boot camp chow line, the Merediths patiently waited their turn to enter the first station. Finally, a gruff voice was heard as the guard motioned them toward the entrance.

Schlepping their luggage through the aluminum access door was an acceptable inconvenience under the circumstances. The blowing air conditioning within the shelter was a welcome relief from the 90-degree, morning desert heat.

"Passports or photo ID's, please," barked the weasel-looking clerk behind the computer monitor at the folding table.

The bug-eyed twins watched as Meredith placed all four passports on the table next to the clerk's coffee cup and stated, "We're the Merediths. We should already be registered in your system."

"Gimme a few minutes to find you. Okay, here it is. Yes, Meredith." He paused, then with a condescending smile, said, "Your financials and references are in order. Welcome, Mr. Meredith."

Handing him a clipboard, the clerk stated, "Here are some forms for you to complete at the table to my left. When you have filled them out, proceed to the gentleman at the table behind me."

The Merediths successfully navigated the various credential-related wickets of Station 1 and exited to join the line outside Station 2. Again, there was an eerie silence among the families waiting their turn to enter.

Suddenly, they were all startled by a verbal disturbance that erupted behind them in Station 1. "No! You can't do this to us. Take your hands off me!" A distraught family was ushered out of the structure at gunpoint, then back to the parking area, where they were forced into a waiting limousine. The anxiety barometer surged upward.

At Station 2, the luggage of other patrons was conspicuously parked outside of each of the six cubicles, three on the left and three on the right, leaving a cluttered hallway down the middle leading to the rear exit. The fabric-covered partitions provided some modicum of privacy, yet hushed voices broadcasted throughout. Folding chairs in the Merediths' cubical accommodated knee-to-knee conversations with their assigned counselor. "Dr. Elizabeth Sanchez, PhD," was prominently displayed on the nametag of her white lab coat, providing an aura of authority that might otherwise be questioned. The Merediths yielded the completed forms from Station 1, their updated vaccination records, medical and dental records, and DNA certificates.

Politely responding to all questions, Meredith wondered if Ms. Sanchez really knew what Yucca Mountain was all about. Her enquiries about current medications, drug or alcohol abuse, phobias, special needs, and handicaps were predictable. The ones pertaining to their marital relationship and family harmony seemed intrusive and beyond the margins of reasonableness.

Reminding himself of the goal, Meredith forced a smile and answered affirmatively. Eve nodded in corroboration. Once Dr. Sanchez entered her notes on a laptop, she smiled and directed the Merediths to proceed down the hallway, and out the exit to Station 3.

The pause between stations prompted Randall to recall his grandfather telling of his experience entering the land of opportunity years ago, through Ellis Island. A scared nineteen-year-old dealt with long lines, multiple interviews, vaccinations, delousing showers, and the uncertainties that lay ahead. He smiled from those memories related by his grandpa.

The health exams conducted in Station 3 amounted to brief discussions about the Meredith family medical history with a foreign-born doctor named Dubashi. This friendly chap, with an Indian accent and deep dark eyes, eventually deployed his stethoscope and checked all four of the family members' lungs, heart, blood flow, and intestinal sounds. "All good," he happily declared.

He then focused on Rex and Samantha whose immunization records were flagged in the computer records on his laptop. Apologizing, he explained a need for an MMR (Mumps, Measles, and Rubella) vaccination. Eve respectfully challenged the doctor stating that the twins had an MMR shot at fifteen months of age. The good doctor reminded them that a second shot was required at age six, and that admission into the Yucca Mountain facility would require the vaccinations. With calming assurance, he said, "A minor issue. The nurse in the back will administer the vaccination."

The twins immediately looked at each other and knew this was not good. The scrunched face of Rex and teary-eyed expression of Samantha declared an unspoken objection to an encounter with the nurse's needle. However, they soon realized that protest was futile.

A concerned Mrs. Meredith was pleased to find the nurse very efficient and gentle with the twins. A swab of alcohol and a colorful Band-Aid quickly eradicated each child's setback, and the Merediths advanced to Station 4.

Unfortunately, any smiles they may have had quickly disappeared. Armed guards positioned at the entrance to Station 4 and at the side and rear doors raised concern in Randall. The line to enter was two families deep and small talk among them was nonexistent.

Yelling and screaming erupted from inside, triggering quick entry by the guards. The troublemakers? A terrified family of four emerged with the guards shadowing at port arms. The mother, with a baby in her arms, was wailing uncontrollably. The father, towing his toddler son by the hand, turned to curse the officials. It was an ugly scene, witnessed by the Merediths along with two other families waiting in line. Rex and Samantha hugged their mother's leg.

Then with obvious trepidation, the next family in line entered the facility while the Merediths and the others watched the guards escort the unhappy family of four to the parking area and a waiting limousine. Their haunting cries reverberated throughout the compound, while the families awaiting entry in Station 4 were seized with an unspoken tension.

Unlike the family that was refused entrance, the Merediths' final interview went well. They were assigned quarters #9, which prompted a sigh of relief by Eve.. A packet of instructions, four identification badges, and a conspicuous "Welcome Aboard" certificate signed by Heinz Globitz were handed to Randall.

"Wait outside for the shuttle to drive you to your quarters," the attendant directed.

The weary family stumbled out the back door and walked to the benches, just twenty steps away. Rex and Samantha sat down and inserted their earbuds. However, they both turned abruptly toward the loud wop-wop sound hovering over the parking lot. With mouths agape, they watched a helicopter land and a bright yellow golf cart magically appear next to its port side. An elderly gentleman wearing a blue blazer and khaki pants exited and turned to assist a younger, long-haired woman wearing white cargo pants and a gold halter top. The two VIP's climbed aboard the golf cart and were whisked away behind the dirt mound in the direction of Yucca Mountain's entrance.

"Did you see that, Daddy?" asked Samantha.

"Must have been Mr. Globitz and his wife, Sam. They're going where we're going."

Lacking immediate shuttle service, Randall sat down with his family and nervously scanned the mounds of earth obscuring a view of the tunnel entrance. "I wonder how long we'll have to wait?" With a sigh and a deep breath, he finally had a moment to enjoy the deli sandwich prepared by his staff in Santa Barbara. It had been a long day.

CHAPTER IX
ENTERING YUCCA MOUNTAIN

ANGELA MURPHY WAS WEARING HER SANCTUARY UNIFORM, A SNUG-fitting yellow jumpsuit resembling a Formula One racing team outfit with a bright red "YMS" logo on the left breast pocket. Her assignment today: hostess and greeter for incoming Sanctuary residents.

Piloting a three-passenger, yellow golf cart, with its tag-a-long trailer, the energetic hostess sped from the red-carpeted tunnel entrance toward the bus stop area and the waiting patrons. She executed a perfect U-turn in front of the Meredith family. Quickly dismounting, she hustled around the carriage and greeted her guests.

"Good afternoon, Merediths! Welcome to Yucca Mountain."

"Uh-a-a…, good afternoon," was Randall's delayed response.

The twins sprang to life. Earbuds were now dangled as they pondered a Disneyland-type ride on the golf cart trailer.

Angela cheerfully offered to help load the Merediths' minimal luggage on the rack behind the seat of the trailer. Randall was already loading the bags and politely declined help. When she asked, the twins provided their backpacks to Angela, and watched her secure the baggage to the trailer with a heavy nylon strap.

"All aboard," she broadcast with broad grin and a wink.

Rex was the first to immediately clamber onto the seat of the trailer and dutifully fastened his and his sister's seatbelt. Eve and Randall stepped up to the rear-facing back seat of the cart facing the kids. Mom's forced smile was an attempt at cheerfulness for the kid's sake, not her husband's. With its precious cargo onboard, the cart lurched in the direction of the mountain. The forward motion prompted all the Merediths to grab their armrests.

Through her headset microphone, Angela offered a tour guide's narrative as they approached the first of the three berms.

"I'm Angela Murphy, one of the three schoolteachers honored to serve here at Yucca Mountain. Today is Welcome Aboard day, so I get to do that too," she said. "We'll start by driving around each of these dirt mounds, and then will actually see the entrance to the Sanctuary."

Listening while looking beyond the twins, their nervous parents watched the next set of patrons settle into the distancing bench seats they had just vacated. Sam and Rex excitedly panned forward toward the approaching mountain, oblivious to the adults in front of them. "Where's the tunnel?" asked Rex.

"After these berms, we'll be on the final approach to the tunnel entrance. We'll pass through a four-foot thick, air-tight door system that weighs thirty tons," she continued.

"Look up and to your right. Notice the dome-like, framed glass structure above the tunnel entrance? That's the outside of the Sanctuary's observation chamber. The mechanical arm, cameras, and antennas you see are all part of the environment-measuring instruments. A similar cupola is mounted on the International Space Station for astronauts to look out into space or back toward Earth. It's a super-strong bubble window that will enable us to safely monitor conditions on the outside of the Sanctuary after we've been sealed up."

"Cool, just like the astronauts!" exclaimed Rex.

Randall turned to look over his shoulder to see where they were headed and to look at the observation cupola just described. He was impressed with these capabilities, but when he turned back to look at the view of where they had come from, the words "sealed up," sent shivers down his spine.

Shadows had now swept the entire reception area and parking lot. As the cart progressed, the relatively smooth asphalt created a pleasant humming sound for the apprehensive passengers. Steadily advancing, Murphy slalomed around each of the massive berms. Then she eased on to the red-carpeted straightaway; the final approach into Yucca Mountain. Without realizing, the Merediths were experiencing their last natural light and fresh air for the foreseeable future.

A noticeable bump upon leaving the red carpet announced that the caravan was now entering the tunnel's opening, and a slight descent on the smooth concrete surface was detected. A cool draft of musty air wafted across their faces. Meredith looked upward at the archway forty feet overhead. He gazed in awe at the engineering marvel of the bunker's substantial security door system.

Their tour guide beamed as she described the hydraulic secondary door with tempered steel rods that locked into the apertures in the surrounding encasement when closed. "The massive, hardened steel doors" she added, "have brass seats and a heavy rubber grommet to provide an airtight seal, protecting against any chemical, biological, and gas intrusions."

Randall's nervous swallow went unnoticed during a brief pause in her narrative. Inside the tunnel, she pointed out the stairs on the wall that led up to a small, circular metal hatch and locking wheel that provided the entrance to the Observation Chamber.

"That's the same kind of hatch used in Navy submarines," she mentioned.

"'Hope you enjoy our twenty-minute ride as we proceed down into the bunker complex. It's a thousand feet below the surface we just left," she happily conveyed.

The gravity of the situation was beginning to distress Eve and Randall. They were having second thoughts. Was it possible this was all some big mistake? Couldn't they just return to the comfort of yesterday and their home in Santa Barbara?

The cart rolled on.

Eve's tears blurred her rearward view of the fading entrance as they proceeded. Each second of the cart's descent seemed to shrink the size of the tunnel's opening behind them. Her husband's arm around her shoulders was comforting but could not conceal the fact: there was no turning back.

The twins were fascinated by the long row of lights hanging along the walls of the tunnel that seemed to converge in the distance ahead. The periodic darkness between the lights provided a spooky, funhouse atmosphere, and belied the terror their mother was feeling. Clenching the armrests, each parent tried to maintain calm. Eve closed her eyes and said a silent prayer. Down, down, down they rolled into the depths of Yucca Mountain.

The golf cart's speakers now caused an eerie echo effect in the tunnel as Angela happily rattled off facts about the complex.

"On my right is Alcove Number 1, used as a garage for some of the rescue equipment, tunnel drilling machines, trucks and spare golf carts," she said.

Deeper and deeper they went. Cheerfully oblivious to her passengers' discomfort, Angela continued to expound on the design genius of the shelter.

"Our hardened sanctuary is capable of withstanding a nuclear blast, a fire storm, biological and chemical agents, shock waves, earthquakes, tsunami, electro-magnetic pulses, and virtually any armed attack," she blithely shared.

"We're all safe here, no matter what happens outside."

Her merriment somehow did not transfer to the passengers. From the rearward-looking view, the tunnel's entrance had now disappeared. Reality had snuffed out all enthusiasm.

"Hold up, Ms. Murphy. Stop!" yelled Randall.

The cart and tag-along trailer came to an abrupt halt, as everyone turned and looked at him.

"Come here, Sam. Sit with me."

He had noticed his daughter quaking in fright, on the verge of crying. The compassion he had for his children was obvious. His daughter was the first to openly show her fear and Randall hastened to intervene. Samantha unfastened her seat belt and immediately leapt into her father's comforting arms. Eve added warm assurance, reaching over to stroke her hair.

Turning toward their driver, he calmingly said, "Okay, Ms. Murphy."

After a modest jerk, the procession was again underway. Sitting alone in the back seat, Rex was trying to "cowboy up" under the watchful eye of his mother. His legs were curled under his seat, one hand on the seat belt and the other gripping the armrest. His head was tilted, lower lip protruding, eyes staring through the passengers in front of him, focusing on nothing.

A few minutes later and deeper into the mountain, Rex blurted, "My ears, my ears!"

"Hold your nose like this Rex, and blow," his mother said as she demonstrated. "Your ears should clear. If not, do it again."

Success was confirmed with a cautious smile from her little man. The cart rolled on.

"How much farther?" Rex whined.

Angela spoke up, "Hang in there, guys. We'll be at your new residence in less than ten minutes."

The procession continued. Each passing tunnel light served as a reminder of the distance between Yucca Mountain and the comforts of the home they had left behind.

Gradually the dimness of the tunnel began to lighten. There was a hint of music in the air—elevator music, and kids' happy voices. The twins raised up to view the tunnel expanding into a brightly lit cavern. A parkland village. Their parents craned their necks too, as Angela announced, "Welcome to Sanctuary Square!"

Two rows of perfectly shaped maple trees lined a village green, where kids were throwing a frisbee. Reflective lighting on the overhead trompe l'oeil artistry of blue sky and fluffy white clouds produced a beautiful, pseudo-daylight atmosphere of City Park, Anytown, USA.

Angela's microphone went silent as she drove the Merediths on to the curbed pathway encircling the trees and village square setting. Slowing her cart and enabling her passengers to absorb the surreal landscape prompted the desired response. Mom and Dad quietly voiced their amazement; the twins were more vociferous.

"Wow! Look at that, Dad! A miniature soccer field, surrounded by trees," exclaimed Rex.

"And other kids we can play with!" squealed Samantha.

Eve chimed in, "Look, there's an amphitheater at the far end of the plaza."

"And a pizza shop and ice cream store!" shouted Rex.

"And a beauty salon," declared Eve. "This is unbelievable, like a small village just for us."

The speakers sputtered back on as Angela spoke, "This is Yucca Mountain's Sanctuary Square, your hometown for the time you are staying here. You'll find all the conveniences of any small community, right at your doorstep."

Noting an open-air Grotto and several families seated at white linen-covered tables near the far end of the square, Angela cheerfully suggested, "If you can unpack in time, dinner is available until 8 pm. Otherwise, you can order out: Chinese, burgers or pizza."

Eyebrows raised in pleasant disbelief as the Merediths turned, looked at each other, and mouthed, "Wow."

"Now let's take you to your new home," said Angela as she steered the cart right and accelerated down a residential corridor.

The cart stopped at the sixteen-foot wide façade of Residence #9. It was identical to numbers 1 through 8 which they had just passed. (It was actually identical to all the other fifty-plus residences.) Two steps and a landing led up to a beautiful teakwood front door with beveled-glass side panels.

Angela quickly dismounted and strode up to the entryway. "Come on, let's go inside."

CHAPTER X
SETTLING IN AND THE ROUTINE

WITHOUT WAITING FOR HIS FAMILY, REX NEARLY TRIPPED OVER ANGELA'S foot as he leaped through the doorway. Having little interest in a tour of "grown-up rooms" (front room, kitchen, dining, etc.), he raced down the long lighted hallway toward the back to lay claim to one of the bedrooms.

Samantha remained with her parents politely following Angela into the front living room. Expectations of their Yucca Mountain living quarters were nominal, particularly as compared to their Santa Barbara estate. Mrs. Meredith once referred to Yucca Mountain as a "trailer home," albeit underground.

Delightful surprise! Immediately impressed by the ten-foot ceiling and the crystal chandelier over the dining table, the Merediths ruled out all further reference to a trailer home. It was surprisingly pleasant.

Trading apartment width for height was a subtle strategy the designers used to reduce the cloistered effect for the rather confined living quarters. Wall coverings of bright, airy pastels, accent lighting, warm carpeting and tastefully appointed furnishings provided the right touch for what otherwise would have been a cave dwelling.

"It doesn't seem like a bunker residence to me," quipped Eve as she stood on the plush wool carpet near the sofa.

"No," assured Angela. "Mr. Globitz's team of designers did an excellent job to make it bright and cheerful, and as close as possible to your normal, above-ground residence."

"Milano Italian furnishings?" joked Randall.

"In fact, many are," affirmed Angela. "Designer-direct."

"Wow, Mom, Dad!" Breathless and panting, Rex came running back to interrupt the front room gathering. "There's a window in the bedroom, and I can see the *ocean*."

Blushing, Angela revealed, "All of the windows you see are LED crystal panels with programable scenery of infinite variety."

"What does that mean?" quired Eve.

"The views from the windows are virtual reality...they appear like the views from any of the windows you are used to—including the views from your windows in Santa Barbara."

"Yeah, I noticed the trees moving in that picture window," Randall acknowledged, pointing.

"There are sounds of nature available, too. Tiny speakers integrated into each window. Birds chirping, day and night sounds, wind, rain—infinitely variable in high definition," she responded. "They change with night and day, as well."

Eve and Randall's eyes met as they silently mouthed, "Nice," to each other.

"Your kitchen is smaller than you are used to, but quite well equipped. The appliances, furnishings, even the linens are all top-notch. And, the refrigerator should be stocked to your liking—replenishable from our company store, of course."

The hallway past the kitchen and dining area led to the master bedroom and bath. Next was the office den and finally the kids' sleeping quarters with a shared bath. Windows (LED crystal panels), high ceilings, and light-bright color schemes all contributed to a feeling of spaciousness; compensating for the reality of the home's 1,600-square foot floor space.

"The three bedrooms are ready made for your arrival. Linens can be exchanged weekly. Our inhouse TV channels and music are available twenty-four hours, and there's an infinite listing of movies available. Behind this door is an emergency bunker, if needed for extra safety."

"The binder on the desk in the den will answer any questions you may have about your residence. Or, you may dial zero from any one of the phones for assistance.

"Now, I'll leave you to explore and unpack. Remember, dinner is available until 8 pm at the Grotto. Take-out pizza, burgers or Chinese 'til 10."

"Get a good night's sleep. Tomorrow's a full schedule and an itinerary of more get-acquainted events."

Exiting, she paused and cheerfully said, "And, welcome to Yucca Mountain Sanctuary!"

The Merediths watched the front door close. They were now alone. There was total silence—except for the easy listening music Rex must have initiated with a remote in one of the back rooms. Despite the residence's elegant trappings, the warm reception by Angela and the friendly village square outside their door, their hearts couldn't hide from what their eyes revealed.

Trying to deal with his wife's tears, and visibly shaking himself, Randall quickly gave Eve a comforting embrace lest their distress carry over to the kids. Without a word exchanged, Samantha immediately knew anyway and leaped forward to wrap her arms around the waists of her parents. Rex watched his family's emotions play out. His enthusiasm expressed just moments earlier was now eclipsed by concern. But the boy held strong and did not engage in their group hug.

"Let's all unpack and get something to eat," Eve suggested, preventing a lapse into a family dirge. "Kids: hang your clothes in your closets; shorts and socks in the drawers. Dad and I will be ready in five minutes. Let's check out town square for dinner."

"I wanted pizza!" Rex protested.

"Too bad, your mother and I want dinner at the grotto."

The contents of the twin's luggage took exactly ninety seconds to unpack and stow away. They were waiting in the front room when their smiling and composed parents emerged from their bedroom.

"Ready for a short walk to dinner?" quipped their mom.

Out the door, down the residence avenue, and turning on to village square's tree-lined promenade, the four walked. Rex led the way, running and then stopping and waiting. It was a friendly family venture. The ten-minute walk found the Merediths in front of the YM Grotto, an open-air restaurant like one might find on any big city's restaurant row.

Rebecca, the gushing hostess, greeted the Merediths and asked for a few minutes to clear a table. "It's opening night at the Grotto," she explained. "It seems all the residents had the same idea for dinner."

Moments later found them taking inventory of the several families already dining. Eve noticed the gigantic "rock" on the ring finger of the lady sitting near the entrance. The kids assessed their future playmates and Rex looked for any recognizable public figures. Each of the families in the restaurant had its own set of circumstances, worries, and histories. They would soon unfold in their mutual experience in Yucca Mountain.

"Thanks for waiting. Your table is ready, Mr. Meredith and it is next to the Willinghams," Rebecca said. "Here are your menus. Gerome will be your server."

Dinner was unremarkable by the Merediths' standards but excellently served. Normally fussy eaters, the twins devoured their baked chicken and mashed potatoes with gusto. It helped that everyone was hungry, with their having not realized the day's activities didn't include lunch. Full tummies including apple pie and ice cream would hasten dreamland for the twins in their new and unfamiliar bedroom arrangements.

"Good evening, we're the Willinghams," a smiling gentleman offered. A handsome couple in their early forties with two girls, five and nine years old (plus or minus), were all standing having completed their diner and about to exit. It was a polite, neighborly introduction and a welcome occasion for both families to realize they were not alone in this underground venture.

"We're the Merediths. My wife, Eve, Rex, and Samantha. And I'm Randall." The Merediths all smiled and remained seated in front of their desserts.

"Parker, Eloise, Julie, and Gretchen. I'm sure we'll get to know you more, but now we'll leave you to finish dinner." The children's eyes all converged in positive but inhibited reaction as the Willinghams made their way out of the Grotto.

The walk back to their new home was more pleasant than anticipated. Randal and Eve were holding hands and the twins were scurrying about, leading the way. The overhead ceiling of blue sky and fluffy clouds gave way to a nighttime effect of sparkling stars and a glowing moon, thanks to the special reflective lighting strategically hidden in the tunnel's facade. The streetlamps interspersed between the trees lining the walkway provided a romantic charm. *Maybe things will be okay*, Eve thought.

Randall opened the door to Residence #9 and called to the twins, who were still exploring. Eve indicated that it was past their bedtime and told them that tomorrow would be a big day. Samantha and Rex were happily responsive and raced each other to the front door.

Just then, the warning siren sounded. A pulsating screech shattered the tranquil environment. Reverberating off the walls of the tunnel complex and amplifying to headache levels, the siren signaled the closing of the massive steel doors at the entrance of the tunnel a mile away and some one thousand feet above. It blasted for two solid minutes, then paused for ten seconds before blasting off and on for four more minutes.

The rumble of the monstrous, hardened steel gate closing and locking into place caused a body-shuddering chill to even the most hardened of Yucca Mountain staff. They knew: This was it. The growling, thirty-ton shield was rolling into place. The siren screeching suddenly stopped. A deep-voiced announcement rattled the bones of every inhabitant, "ENTRANCE SEALED; ALL SUPPORT MECHANISMS ACTIVATED." This confirmed the total isolation of Yucca Mountain from the rest of the world.

The twins shrieked and ran to their parents, grabbing and holding with all their might. Randall gathered his composure and ushered his family into their quarters and slammed the door. Eve grabbed both kids' hands and pulled them to the sofa, where they huddled and cried.

Pajamas on, teeth brushed, and covers nervously pulled up to their noses, both twins awaited a final tuck-in by Mom and Dad. Eve with Rex, and Randall with Samantha, they tried to provide a reassuring appraisal of the day before prayers. Then alternating bedrooms to offer goodnight and forehead kisses, the parents retreated to the family room for their own, end-of-day, nerve-calming embrace.

The twins' excitement meter had shattered all records for the day and luckily, exhausted them in the process. They had fallen fast asleep. For their worried parents, however, the first night in Yucca Mountain was going to be a long one.

CHAPTER XI
DAY ONE ORIENTATION

"What's that?" whispered Eve. "Randy, wake up! Someone's in our front room. I hear them talking."

Her groggy husband raised up on one elbow to listen. Still drowsy he reflexively reached for the loaded .45 caliber Sig Sauer P220 in the hidden compartment of the nightstand—in his bedroom in Santa Barbara. But this was Yucca Mountain. Thinking more clearly, he rose from the bed, trying not to wake the twins, who were now snugly positioned between their parents.

"Damn that *no weapons* clause in our contract," he cussed under his breath.

Barefoot, pajama-clad, and unarmed, the provisional warrior cautiously crept down the hallway suffused in early-morning sunshine, albeit virtual reality sunlight. His pulse was pounding with every deliberate step. He had no plan. Confronting danger was always more natural for his dad, the Marine, he lamented.

Safely investigate, he thought. *Engage, only if necessary to protect the family.*

Past the den, then the kitchen, Randall quietly tiptoed. Peering around the partition separating the dining area from the living room, he witnessed the source of the talking—the wall panel television. He sighed in relief.

The intrusive video broadcast was the Yucca Mountain closed circuit TV announcing the Residents' Orientation meeting in the Village Square at 10 am.

"All clear, Eve!" he confidently yelled in the direction of the back rooms.

Thirty-minutes later, the man of the house called out, "Breakfast! Come and get it."

"Breakfast. Come and get it."

"Why Randall Meredith, where did you learn to cook breakfast?"

"Don't kid yourself, Eve, men are quite capable of a lot of stuff. How would you like your eggs, scrambled or scrambled?"

"Come on, kids. Dad made breakfast."

The twins, hearing the news while still nestled under Mom and Dad's comforter, climbed down from the bed and headed for the door. Still in pajamas, they came running to score some breakfast: scrambled eggs, bacon, toast, and juice. The smell of freshly brewed coffee also made it feel just like home. Yesterday's trauma faded and was replaced by excitement for the day's new adventures.

Row after row of white folding chairs were in place near the enclosed end of the massive cavern called Village Square. A large white projection screen hung from what appeared to be a loft carved into the stone wall twenty feet from the floor. The concrete stairwell going up to the loft suggested someone important might occupy the residence behind the loft. A raised platform and a standing microphone in front of the screen would be the focal point for the day's briefing.

Smartly dressed ushers in burgundy blazers were strategically positioned to guide the uncertain residents into their alphabetized seating. Each folding chair had a label bearing the name of a resident family and all fifty families were accommodated.

They all came at once. The four ushers were overwhelmed. Two hundred total, kids and adults, were assigned the ten rows of chairs. The incoming gaggle annihilated any thoughts of meticulous organization demanded by Mr. Globitz. The hunt for assigned seats added to the confusion. Eventually, the rows filled, and confusion was reduced to a general murmur.

A thick packet marked "Meredith" was waiting on one of the four seats in the fourth row, near the middle. The family to the right was already seated but were distracted by a discipline problem with their boy. Four chairs on the left were still empty. Randall surveyed the arrangement and noted that several more rows of chairs in the back were filled with uniformed personnel, obviously Yucca Mountain staff.

Like their first exposure on the previous day, the cavern appeared bright and sunlit with pleasant music broadcast throughout. Under the virtual reality of fluffy white clouds and blue sky, the assembly could have been a middle school graduation ceremony on a campus lawn.

Randall panned the audience as if to analyze each family's qualifications for being there. Could he identify with these people? Where were they all from? What were their backgrounds? It was going to be an interesting venture.

Similarly, Rex and Samantha scanned the occupants of the chairs around them. The prospect for playmates was excellent. Predictably, the other kids were also assessing the new people. Their eyes often met each other's but modesty or shyness prohibited any familiarity.

"Good morning, I'm Jim Ogilvy," said the man sitting to Randall's right. "What did you think of the entry gate closing last night?"

"It frightened the crap out of my family," Randall said. "I'm Randall Meredith, and this is Sam, Rex, and Eve." Eve leaned forward to acknowledge the introduction, while Rex and Samantha were ambivalent; engaged in people watching. The pleasantries were interrupted, and the audience hushed when a staff member tested the microphone up front.

The background music stopped, and the audience anxiously focused its attention forward, as if to see an orchestra conductor take the podium. The huge, white screen behind the stage came to life with the YMS logo focused in the center and a music-laced message in a pleasant masculine voice:

Good morning and welcome to Yucca Mountain Sanctuary.

And, congratulations! You qualified for entry into this facility, having undergone a very thorough screening process. If anyone deserves to survive a catastrophic disaster, it is you. Your ethical, moral, and professional standards have been scrutinized to the minutest degree. Your prospect for health, vitality, and longevity have been verified by your DNA. You and your family are disease-free, inoculated, and mentally stable.

We hope your stay with us will be pleasant and brief, while the world outside resolves its issues and environmental disturbances. Rest assured that you are safe here in Yucca Mountain and that your family can enjoy the time you are away from your home in the security of the most technically sophisticated shelter in the world.

Before introducing the founder and the inspiration of the Sanctuary, we'd like to point out some of the features that you will learn to appreciate during the course of your stay.

*Yucca Mountain Sanctuary is like a giant, multi-corridor submarine. It is completely air-tight, self-contained, and provisioned to support all residents and staff for up to twenty years. It is powered from the Earth's core by a binary geothermal power plant for our turbines which generate enough electricity for every electrical outlet and every electrical demand, **forever***!

There is a freshwater aquifer directly under the south wing. There is also a back-up recycling water purification system and a hundred-thousand-gallon reservoir providing enough water for all of our needs.

Oxygen-recycling technology employing high energy, vacuum ultraviolet lasers has enabled us to convert used air or carbon dioxide to fresh air and oxygen. Then we use a system developed by NASA, a state-of-the art HEPA air filter, ultraviolet light and charcoal system to provide purified air down to point three microns. Ozone generators provide a reliable back up during brief maintenance intervals. NASA would be proud of our air quality.

Yucca Mountain is indeed the safest, most technically advanced sanctuary on Earth.

Now, for you kids we have some special programs. Here to explain is our Activity Director, Coach Frank Lowe.

Coach Lowe appeared on the stage wearing an athletic jumpsuit with the familiar *YMS* logo. The tall, trim, and energetic educator took the microphone and enthusiastically greeted the audience with his booming voice, "Good morning, kids!"

The kids perked up and responded, "Good morning."

Placing his hand to his ear, he hollered, "That was pretty weak. Now let's try it again, GOOD MORNING, KIDS!"

Delighted to be recognized, the special segment of the audience approvingly responded, "Good morning!"

"That was much better. Thank you. I'm Coach Lowe, and I have two assistants I want you to meet: Felix and Adrian."

Just then, the YMS jump suited ninjas came running from each side of seated spectators and leaped on to a minitrampoline positioned on the floor below. Their rebound from the trampolines launched them high into the air toward Coach Lowe, where they executed a perfect front flip and a tuck and roll before springing to their feet just inches away from Lowe.

The surprise performance brought the kids to their feet, cheering and clapping.

"Felix and Adrian will now help demonstrate some of the activities we're going to be doing along with your classroom instruction."

"Does anybody play soccer?"

"Yes!" screamed several kids in the audience.

"How about you, Isaac Foreman?"

The big screen behind the stage changed to a live video of a freckle-faced, red-headed kid in the audience, sitting between his parents. He mouthed the words "Wow," as he pointed to his larger-than-life image that everyone was now watching.

Just then a Quadcopter Drone buzzed overhead carrying a soccer ball. Stopping directly over the Foremans in row two, it made a whirring sound as it hovered. When Isaac Foreman looked up in shock, the ball dropped into his arms. It was all displayed on the giant screen behind the stage. The audience loved it, clapping and laughing.

The attention went back to the Coach at the microphone, "Isaac, now's your chance to score a goal. I want you to kick that ball into the net by Felix."

Carrying the ball in his right arm and leading with his left, Isaac immediately pushed his way to the isle on Felix's side of the stage. Placing the ball on the turf, he backed up and measured the angle and distance. The determination on Isaac's face was on full display on the big screen.

Without hesitation, he lunged toward the ball planting his left foot and kicking it with his right directly into the net just five yards away. The crowd erupted with cheers. Isaac jumped up and down, hands extending overhead and a broad smile on his face.

"Good job, Isaac!" shouted Coach Lowe. "Now, does anybody know how to throw a football?"

The big screen video displayed the audience. Screams from the kids, "I do! Me, me, pick me!"

"How about you, Allan Talbert?"

The live image of Allan Talbert materialized on the big screen. Flashing a big smile, the towering kid of only nine years old had dark curly hair and a maroon sweatshirt with "USC" on the chest.

Randall looked over at Eve, raised his eyebrows, and flashed a perplexed smile.

Another drone appeared, this time carrying a junior-sized football. Buzzing the audience and generating maximum enthusiasm, it then hovered directly over Allan Talbert, who was now standing and waiting. The ball dropped, and he caught it perfectly.

"Move out to the isle, Allan, and fire that ball to Adrian!" yelled Coach Lowe.

Allan knew exactly what to do and threw a textbook forward pass to Adrian. The crowd was ecstatic. Allan gave an appreciative fist pump and returned to his seat next to a proud mom and dad.

Coach Lowe brought the audience's attention back to the stage by saying, "Now, are there any drone pilots in the audience?"

Again, the expected refrain, "I am. Pick me, me, me!"

"How about you, Melissa Farnsworth?"

Melissa sprang to her feet, looking for a hovering drone. Felix came running toward her carrying a remote-control unit with twin joy sticks. The live feed to the big screen projected the image of Melissa smiling and looking for the drone to appear. She was no stranger to Quadcopter Drones and immediately fastened the device around her waist while looking upward for the drone it controlled.

"Melissa, I want you to land the drone on the top of the Yucca Mountain School sign over to our right."

A drone appeared overhead. With a few anxious adjustments, she broke the code and assumed control. The drone buzzed right, then left, and finally flew directly toward the sign that Coach Lowe indicated. Landing it exactly on the sign, she smiled and removed the strap supporting the control panel. Felix congratulated the expert pilot and took the controls. The mesmerized audience broke out in cheers. Melissa waved to her fans and to the big screen, then took her seat next to the congratulatory strangers next to her parents.

"Thank you, Melissa. Great job. Kids, look on the big screen behind me. Here are some of the other activities we will be doing," the coach urged. "We're going to have a lot of fun here at YMS."

The screen flashed images and captions of swimming, basketball, field hockey, gymnastics and archery. Squeals of joy and applause erupted from the captivated audience.

"Now for you big kids, yes I'm talking to you parents, we have activities too."

The big screen changed, and a new list appeared: swimming, golf, pilates, yoga, zumba, volleyball, pickleball, bridge, book club, weightlifting and ping pong, bocci ball, basketball, music and arts and movie discussions.

"There will be no boring, idle moments in Yucca Mountain." The seated residents applauded.

The big screen refreshed with the YMS logo. Coach Lowe summoned two staff members to the stage: Angela Murphy and Marion Duncan. Standing on each sides of Lowe, and wearing burgundy YMS blazers, they were introduced as the staff faculty at Yucca Mountain Academy. The audience politely applauded.

"Now, I would like all of the fourth graders to stand up," directed Coach Lowe.

Prodded by their parents, about twenty kids cautiously stood, including Allan Talbert and Melissa Farnsworth. Each student instinctively examined the other standing students. "Look around," said the coach. "These are your new Yucca Mountain classmates. And your teacher is Ms. Murphy," he said extending his hand toward Angela. "Okay, you can take your seats.

"And, will all of the third graders please stand.

Having learned the routine from the fourth graders, thirty-two youngsters, ages eight and nine, rose from their seats and peered at the others standing. "These are your new third-grade classmates and right here is Ms. Duncan, your new teacher.

"And finally, all second graders, please stand up. You third graders can sit down."

More prodding was required by the parents, but eventually a couple dozen bewildered kids were on their feet, looking around. "Now, everybody point to one of your new classmates and wave."

"Now, wave to me, your new teacher."

More animated than either of their older schoolmates, the second graders energetically waved to a smiling Coach Lowe.

"Now, it is eleven o'clock, time for our first Yucca Mountain Bar B'Q lunch. Parents, take your kids to the far end of the plaza where the grills are fired up and the picnic tables are waiting. At 1 o'clock we will reconvene right here while your children will report to their classrooms."

CHAPTER XII
THE DETAILED BRIEFING

RETURNING FROM THE MIDDAY BBQ, THE ADULT RESIDENTS FOUND A smaller grouping of chairs in front of the stage. They engaged in small talk while reading as they waited for the orientation to continue.

When the Merediths took two seats in the third row, they were distracted by a couple in the row behind them. The lady's head was buried in her hands on her lap. Rubbing her back and neck, her husband was obviously attempting to console his distraught wife. Two staff members were kneeling directly in front of her, one holding her hand. Occasionally looking up toward the stage, then at the gathering audience taking their seats, the man returned his attention to his wife. Her wailing was somewhat muffled by her hands and was partially obscured by the upbeat music playing from the big speakers.

A lady seated close by leaned toward Randall saying, "They won't let them out!" Her stage whisper did little to reduce Eve's already nervous mindset.

All seats were full when the bright and sunny sanctuary ceiling gradually dimmed as if evening dusk had settled over the stage and audience. The big screen came to life with the familiar YMS logo, music, and the authoritative voice:

Welcome back to the second part of the Yucca Mountain Sanctuary orientation.

Frank Lowe was now in his classroom and Adrian and Felix were on the stage. Adrian took the mike and cleared his throat as the residents on him.

"Well, did you enjoy the BBQ?"

A muffled chorus responded affirmatively.

"Your students are now safely across campus in their classrooms with their new teachers," he proclaimed through a smile. "They're going to have a fun-filled afternoon." Pausing, to breathe, he continued, "This period will be a little more serious as we cover some of the administration and logistics of our facility."

Eve peered over her shoulder to check on the distressed couple, who were now sitting upright but did not seem to be totally recovered.

"But before all that, I'd like to introduce the visionary and founder of the Sanctuary. The man who salvaged an abandoned, fourteen-billion-dollar storage facility and turned it into the world's most complete and secure bunker complex…the prophetic creator of our shelter, our home, and our village community: Dr. Heinze Globitz."

Just then a powerful stage light focused on the dimly lighted balcony above the big screen. A cherub-faced, elderly gentleman with flowing white hair, wearing a white percale shirt and white corduroy pants appeared in the spotlight, smiling as he descended the stairs.

"Care for a little drama?" whispered Randall to his wide-eyed wife.

The audience exploded with applause. Wild enthusiastic whistles and cheers came from the back rows and gradually spread to the patrons in front. The Merediths glanced at each other before grudgingly joining the enthusiasm.

The spotlight followed the man moving slowly down the stairs to the stage. An invisible wind wafted his hair and caused his tailored shirt to shimmer, adding to the moment's regality. Dr. Globitz seemed to glow as if gazing at his loyal subjects. Reading from a prepared script, he began:

"Ladies and gentlemen, I am honored and privileged to stand before you today on this historic occasion—the salvation of civilization."

More applause from the back.

"I congratulate you on your foresight and decision to join an association committed to weathering the storm of global calamity. We are the lucky ones. We will survive!"

Applause. Whistles and cheers from the back rows—the staff.

"We may all sacrifice a little comfort today so that our children will live to see a better tomorrow. They will eventually understand and thank us for our insight. The future of mankind lies, not with our current standing, but where the torch gets carried by our progeny.

"As you know, I have direct access to the White House. When I summoned you, the world was headed for a catastrophic disaster. President Cranston has personally conveyed new information to me. I am happy to report that the magnitude of this disaster has been re-assessed by the authorities and is now regarded as survivable."

Applause. The air blowing toward Globitz did little to prevent his perspiring. He wiped his brow and continued.

"It could have been a nuclear attack by North Korea, China, or Russia; or perhaps a total collapse of the power grid, a viral epidemic, a civil war, or any of a dozen other scenarios. And you would be safe here at Yucca Mountain. The danger we face today, however, is not man-made. It originated from space and, at first glance, it looks to be worse than any of the above."

Eve reached for her husband's assuring hand.

"In fact, it is a massive asteroid on a path to collide with planet Earth. Efforts to disrupt the path of this asteroid, called *Onesimus*, have partially succeeded...*partially*. Reduced by only ten percent, it is now projected to impact somewhere near Lavrentyia, Russia, in four days.

"The impact of this asteroid will be severe and earth-altering. Fires, flooding, earthquakes, volcanic eruptions, and global cooling are expected. This situation could last for months, even a year or two. But we are safe here in Yucca Mountain.

"During the coming darkest moments, we must keep our focus on surviving. When it may seem as though you can no longer hang on, never give up. For that is the time and the place that the tide will turn. Believe me."

Mild applause.

"We will endure this together, in the safest shelter on the planet. We planned for the possibility of an event like this, we installed the necessary infrastructure and facilities, and now we will ride out the storm like Noah did, five thousand years ago. We in this very sanctuary are the next generation of Earth's inhabitants."

A thunderous applause erupted from the rear seats, but the response from the fifty couples was somewhat lukewarm.

"Now, I'd like to answer any questions you may have regarding your time here in Yucca Mountain. Yes, the gentleman in the front row."

"Dr. Globitz, how long do you expect we will have to stay here?"

"That's a difficult question to answer, sir. Until it is safe above ground, is my best response. One or two months? Maybe a year."

Globitz earnestly continued, "When you first entered the mountain, you may have seen the thick glass globe mounted into the mountain's rock surface above the heavy steel gate?"

No response from the new residents.

"Mounted inside that globe is a group of instruments that measure air quality, temperature, radio activity, UV values, wind velocity, electromagnetic radiation, even video—an electronic periscope of sorts. The Yucca Mountain Command Center upstairs," pointing toward the loft behind him, "monitors these instruments outside, as well as the systems that operate within the sanctuary. When these monitors indicate that the outside environment is habitable, we will unlock the sealed exterior doors and open the gate to exit."

"How much food do we have stored?" asked another resident.

"Rest assured, our storage lockers have enough rations to sustain everybody here for up to twenty years."

One of the mothers asked, "Are there medical capabilities here if we need them?"

"Yes, we'll cover that in his briefing next."

"Can we communicate with others outside Yucca Mountain?" asked one man.

"Your residence is currently receiving cable TV and has WIFI internet connection. We will continue with that as long as it is working. And you have already seen our internal, closed circuit TV capabilities—remember this morning's announcement of this meeting this morning?

"I am sure there will be many questions as we settle in, but Adrian and Felix have a briefing that will cover many of your concerns for now. Thank you for your attention and again, welcome to Yucca Mountain."

"Thank you, Dr. Globitz. I direct your attention to the big screen," Adrian said, assuming control of the microphone.

All eyes focused on the outline of topics displayed behind the announcer. Heinz Globitz returned up the stairs, while Adrian continued the orientation with a Power Point presentation showing an outline on the big screen.

YMS ORIENTATION

- Staff Introduction
- Sanctuary Configuration
- Health Considerations
- Services Available
- Safety Precautions
- Rules & Regulations
- Governance
- Participatory Roles
- Grievances

"You can follow along in your information packets or take notes and jot down questions you may have concerning any of these topics. Our staff is here to help and provide details," Adrian.

"In addition, we have provided 'Yucca Pads' in your residences that contain this and other information electronically."

CHAPTER XIII
THE SECRET'S OUT, OR IS IT?

RUMORS AND CONSPIRACY THEORIES ON SOCIAL MEDIA, PODCASTS, AND YouTube videos mushroomed from the usual suspects. Late-night talk show hosts clambered onboard, inviting "alternative scientists" (weirdos) to comment on plausible scenarios. Their ratings soared. An atmosphere of wild speculation and doomsday obsession entertained enthusiasts in all forms of social discourse. A documentary report was in the making by one of the most insufferable film makers in Hollywood. The news reports were all labeled fake partly because of the government's aggressive media campaign to dispel them.

Disgraced, former presidential candidate Alfonso A. Gordon took the opportunity to bash the president. Attempting to rally a new support base with a series of "the-sky-is-falling while the White House fiddles" speaking engagements, the former senator's message found superficial traction. A circus atmosphere ensued, and the poor chap was ridiculed and summarily dismissed by most of the establishment press.

Predictably, Burning Man worshipers assembled in the Nevada Desert to "witness and participate" in the asteroid event. The Druids turned out at Stonehenge. Christian prayer vigils were organized at public gatherings and churches. Survivalists were migrating to their bunkers and government militaries were placed on alert. Water, canned food, blankets, and batteries became scarce items on stores shelves.

The dripping faucet of asteroid conspiracy leaks just wouldn't go away. Gossip and rumors morphed into public beliefs. Protests by emotionally charged college students sparked more protests which seemed to spread like the plague. Seattle, Portland, and San Francisco were first and worst cities for protesters. Paris was running a close second to Tokyo on the international scene. Outbreaks of demonstrations in China, Australia, even Chile were reported on the evening news.

Governments involved in the coverup had their hands full trying to put out the fires, especially when challenged by other heads of state who were not in the loop. Alliances that once bound world leaders devolved into diplomatic skirmishes. Long-time loyalties were challenged as suspicion permeated the diplomatic scene. The questionable stratagem of keeping secret the danger so as to prevent mass chaos and panic required those in the know to deny everything. It was an ugly burden to bear.

The White House press secretary was designated the official scapegoat to lie to the press corps. His razor-sharp wit was complemented by a Boy Scout persona and convincing manner. But his soothing mantra did little to dispel the uproars. The disinformation and denials intended to contain chaos only added to it. It was a lost cause. The leaks kept appearing. Plausible deniability was overtaken by the obvious. Too many leaks from too many authorities made the narrative problematic. News anchors echoed their "high government sources" of a pending asteroid collision while government credibility all but collapsed.

Some communities, however, were not persuaded by asteroid paranoia; Nome, Alaska among them. Like mid and rural Americans, they were skeptical of most TV news broadcasts emanating from Washington and New York. For them, uninhibited news anchors with their selected talking heads were trumped by the honest-looking White House press secretary or by a local broadcaster—after supplementing his coverage of the local high school football score. To them, the asteroid story was analogous to another Big Foot or Loch Ness monster sighting.

But it was only a matter of time. An unauthorized government leak surfaced, revealing Lavrentyia, Russia, as the point of impact with just fifteen hours to prepare. But broadcasts of the leaked dispatch were sporadic. A midnight news flash on the East Coast couldn't rouse sleeping Americans. Yet, time zone differences would not suppress panic for the rest of the world. *Onesimus* was going to hit and humankind would forever change.

Utter chaos eventually erupted throughout the world. Riots, looting, traffic jams, and the worst of mankind were on full display. Churches rang their bells non-stop, calling their followers to gather in prayer. Store shelves were totally stripped by panicking shoppers and looters. Mobilized National Guard troops were completely overwhelmed by the sheer mass of out-of-control civilians.

In sharp contrast with the chaos of the outside world, pleasant background music permeated Yucca Mountain Sanctuary. The home channel TV featured greetings, instructions, and personal messages from Dr. Globitz. Other channels ambivalently broadcast movies and cartoons on demand. Outside news was relegated to one or two channels. iPad and cell phones had no cell towers, limiting their internet communications.

The Merediths held hands to say grace then nervously consumed their garlic shrimp pasta dinner. It was their third night in Yucca Mountain, and the most tense.

"Whose turn is it to clear the table?" asked Randall.

"My turn and I get to choose the game." stated Rex.

The family ritual of reward for work performed was immediately picked up in their new quarters at Yucca Mountain as part of the plan to keep things in balance.

"Okay, Rex. What'll it be, Progressive or Pass?" Dad asked, referring to their family's invented parlor games. One involved linking up imaginary details from one member into your own details for one continuous story. The other, reading a segment from a chosen book (device, actually) until one falters, and must pass the book.

"Pass the Book!"

"I want Progressive Story Telling," argued Samantha.

"Pass the Book it is, Sam. Go get your pajamas on while Rex clears the table."

With dishes cleared and both kids in their PJ's, the Meredith family gathered in the family room to read aloud from Johann Wyss' *Swiss Family Robinson*. Rex had the first opportunity to pick up where they had left off from last night and read until he stumbled with a word in the text and had to pass the book. Eve continued where Rex left off, passing the book to Samantha upon her misstep (deliberate or otherwise). Finally, Dad got to read. Tonight's reading was perfect; it lasted forty-five minutes, was entertaining, and a distraction from the looming event above ground.

"Alright, bedtime."

"Aw, Dad. One more round," Rex protested.

"Off to bed, kids," Mom confirmed.

Without further protest, they each hugged their parents then scampered off to their bedrooms. The twins knew something was brewing but didn't inquire. Randall followed them down the hallway and entered Samantha's room. Sitting on the edge of her bed, he stroked her hair tenderly.

"Are we going to be here for a long time, Daddy?"

"Only until it's safe to go home, honey. Sweet dreams." With a kiss on the top of her head, he turned off the light and backed out through the door.

From the other bedroom, a lonely voice, "Dad, are you coming?"

"What's up, big guy?" Randall sat on the bed and comforted his inquisitive son.

From under the covers, the worried six-year-old responded, "Stevie Jacobs told me that there's going to be a big explosion tomorrow, but we'll all be safe. Is that right, Dad?"

"That's why we're here, Rex. This is the safest place to be. Now, get some sleep," he said as he stood.

"But what if the explosion happens right here?"

"Do you remember the long ride in the golf cart with Ms. Murphy?"

"Do I ever. We kept going down and down, 'til we got here."

"Exactly, Rex. We're more than a thousand feet under a mountain. No explosion can reach us down here. Close your eyes and get some sleep."

"But…"

"No buts, Rex. Go to sleep," he firmly said.

"Dad, are you and Mom gonna be with us when the explosion comes?"

"We'll all be right here, Son. Now go to sleep."

"Will we hear the explosion from here?"

"I doubt it, Son. It will probably be a long way from here. Are you sleeping?" He walked down the hallway when he heard another voice.

"Daddy, can you come in here?" Samantha appealed from the other bedroom.

"Sam, aren't you asleep yet?"

"What explosion were you and Rex talking about?"

"Samantha, there's nothing to worry about. Rex and I were talking about an explosion that might happen a long way from here, but we're all going be safe," he whispered through the doorway.

"Randall, tell the kids to go to sleep."

"Daddy, you didn't kiss me."

"Oh yes I did, but here's another one," his soothing voice muffled as he pecked Samantha's cheek. Then Randall joined Eve in the master bedroom.

From her side of the bed, Eve looked up from reading her Bible and whispered, "It's happening tomorrow, isn't it?"

"I'm afraid so, Eve. This time tomorrow night it will all be behind us," Randall responded with feigned confidence.

"We're safe, right?"

"Absolutely. Don't even think otherwise."

"Will the kids be in class when it happens?"

"I doubt it. They plan to send them home so that we can all be together during the predicted critical time frame."

Moonlight trickled onto the hallway floor and faint sounds of crickets emanated from the virtual reality windows as Randall's warm arm wrapped around Eve's shoulder. The apprehensive couple snuggled into their familiar spooning position, trying to blot out the reason for leaving their Santa Barbara home.

The rest of the Yucca Mountain Sanctuary residents were all similarly tucked in. Meanwhile, a half million miles out in space, the remnants of a rock named *Onesimus* was in a 35,000-mph descent toward earth.

CHAPTER XIV
ANTICIPATION AND IMPACT

THE FOURTH DAY OF SCHOOL PROMISED TO BE FUN-PACKED ONE, ACCORDING to Coach Lowe. The twins were eager to attend class. Having gulped down Cheerios, toast, and juice, they were oblivious to the galactic calendar and the rendezvous with *Onesimis*. Lingering over their sendoff was Mom's issue, not the kids.' Randall sipped coffee at the kitchen counter, choosing not to add to his wife's emotionalism seeing the kids out the door. Their unescorted walk to Yucca Mountain Academy was now a rite of passage for the proud third graders.

"Mom was sure smoochy today," noted Samantha during the walk down the residential corridor to the town square.

"Yeah, she's been like that since we got here, but today was really bad," Rex replied as matter of fact. Shifting to more important matters, "Wonder what Coach has for us today?" he resumed. The two blithely joined the other kids crossing the village green and entered the classrooms.

Predictably, nervous anticipation was an understatement for the Yucca Mountain adults. Outside, pandemonium gripped everyone else. Unsubstantiated projections: zero-two-forty-seven, GMT, the time of asteroid impact (8:47 PM local). All calendars had the day and time marked.

While school was in session, the adults in the Sanctuary were invited to a briefing in the Village Square. Emergency procedures were explained and rehearsed. It was a dreadful syllabus. Intermixed with the horrifying possibilities was a reassuring sales pitch proclaiming the many advantages of their Yucca Mountain investment. Riding out the storm "top side" or in some lesser form of bunker would be tragic, the staffers proclaimed. No matter what disaster materialized, this was the safest place to be; a good decision by the fortunate, intelligent patrons.

The reinforced concrete survival chamber of the apartment within each residence had survival gas masks, decontamination items, water, food, flashlights, and emergency medical supplies. It also contained a version of old WWII Navy hammocks that could be put up or taken down as the need arose. The chamber's function was strictly for emergency use and the family's survival. It would be the first-place rescue teams would search, if required. This last point was reiterated.

The briefings also included demonstrations of CPR, defibrillator use, CBR (chemical, biological, and radiological) hoods and breathing masks and emergency rescue procedures delicately mixed with humor by the Yucca Mountain staff. It was a well-rehearsed and tasteful orientation, but a grim reminder of the reason for being where they were. The adult residents were reminded of the time of the expected impact and told to gather all family members near their respective resident survival areas to wait for the siren.

Briefings concluded when the children were let out of school. Their anxious parents were waiting to greet them and walk them back to their quarters.

"Hi Mom, hi Dad. Coach had us play Action Charades."

"What's Action Charades, Sam?"

"It's when Zoey pretended to brush her hair, and we guessed what she was doing and had to write it down."

"Yeah, and Raymond pretended he was playing golf with his dad, and I guessed it right away!" exclaimed Rex proudly.

The short walk with the twins confirmed it had been a fine day at school. Advised by staff, parents were reminded to maintain a positive, cheerful demeanor for their kids. It was a tall order. For the Merediths, the rest of the day would be homework, dinner, and Pass the Book, extended indefinitely, without explanation.

Moving the game and chairs into a new corner near the survival chamber door didn't seem to alarm Rex or Sam. It appeared as just another closet door, irrelevant to where they played their favorite past time. The twins were also A-OK with the longer game session, unaware of the day, let alone the hour of impact. Both were sheepishly indisposed to concede that it was a school night.

H HOUR

The digital clocks from the various electronic devices in their apartment indicated the dreadful hour had arrived. Eve and Randall mentally braced for the alarm. Their eyes met with anticipation. Eve squeezed her husband's hand. Their ambivalent daughter enthusiastically embraced her turn at Pass the Book.

Nothing happened.

The digital clock kept ticking while Samantha continued reading. When she muffed one of the words, Rex immediately pounced in his Tattletale voice, "Pass the Book, Samantha!"

By 9:30, the most welcomed "non-event" in recorded history was being nervously celebrated by everyone under Yucca Mountain. Randall lost track of who's turn it was to read. Still squeezing her husband's hand, Eve stared at the front door, lost in thought. Rex's reading of *Swiss Family Robinson* fell on deaf ears. The magic hour had passed; no alarm was sounded.

The twins were fighting heavy eyelids and struggling with their reading. Dad finally called it, "Time for bed, guys." Without protest, Rex inserted the marker and handed the book to his mother. Dad followed the twins as they wobbled off to their bedrooms. There was a faint sound of people yelling and cheering outside the Merediths' residence.

"What's that, Dad?"

"Nothing, Rex. Just some happy people down the corridor."

Morning came.

A sigh of relief wormed its way among the inhabitants of Yucca Mountain as the children were summoned to school. There were no panic-stricken crazies or irrational residents running about. Calm and order prevailed. Emergency procedures had not been required. The predicted asteroid disaster had not materialized, and Yucca Mountain was starting to feel like a bizarre guest home.

Now what?

Was it possible to simply settle in—and wait? Residents were encouraged to remain vigilant but go about their daytime activities. If possible, try to not worry about the asteroid event. It may have been less of an incident than forewarned. Maybe not at all. Globitz and his staff would provide the "all clear" when the situation became known. "In the meantime, consider Yucca Mountain a vacation getaway," they said.

Vacation? "Is that a joke?" questioned most of the residents. Business and work was obviously "off the calendar" for the accomplished inhabitants; nobody really brought their office work with them. But vacation? Enjoy some recreation? In a bunker complex?

Resigned but cautious, the inhabitants took collective a deep breath. "While we're here, let's make the best of it," Randall petitioned to his family. "I think I'll try out that High Definition Golf Simulator. Always wanted to play Pebble Beach."

Visibly annoyed, Eve feigned a smile and nodded. "Maybe I'll join the bridge group."

One day passed.

The virtual golf game was wearing thin. Gossip among the frustrated bridge players was running rampant. Murmurs of an asteroid hoax spread. Was it possible this was some kind of scam? At a very hefty price? Paid in solid gold bricks, no less?

After dinner, the Merediths left the twins at home and joined their neighbors in the commons to discuss the situation. Virtual twilight activated the streetlamps surrounding the village green. A circle of chairs accommodated the impromptu gathering. Taking turns to speak, each participant stared uncomfortably, voicing concerns about the possibility of having been duped. No one had answers.

Twenty minutes into the bitch session, a slight shiver in the earth directed attention to the few rattling empty chairs among the group. Then it stopped. Talking resumed as some residents dismissed the shivering as air turbulence when the ventilation system kicked on, or possibly from noisy refrigerators in the storage alcove down the corridor. California residents among the group knew otherwise. Their eyes met; corresponding in concern.

Then, more shivering. Heavier. And, prolonged. Again, it stopped. The residents' conversation went silent; replaced by eye contact—voiceless horror. The beginning of the nightmare was immediately confirmed by the sound of an earsplitting siren.

The group sprang from their seats. Terror contorted every face. Pulse rates skyrocketed. A deep rumbling vibrated the floor beneath their feet, triggering screams. The growl from within the one-thousand feet deep belly of the beast was more than a tremor. The deafening siren sounded its woop-woop warning signal reverberating throughout the Sanctuary tunnels. Terrifying shrieks erupted from the panicked residents. They scattered from their impromptu meeting like central park pigeons escaping an unleashed dog.

"Come on, Eve!" Randall grabbed his wife's hand and raced back to their residence and their kids.

The pathway under their feet heaved and swayed like a carnival fun house. Eve stumbled but hung on to her husband, avoiding a face plant into the concrete floor. Their pulse rates skyrocketed from the horrifying rumblings punctuated by the screeching alarm. Randall glimpsed upward toward the tromp'el loi ceiling; its sunsetting illumination was flickering. So were the streetlamps lining town square.

The rumbling intensified and a swaying broke into a pitching and rocking motion. The recently vacated folding chairs clattered as they fell like dominos. Women screamed, igniting a series of shrieking and wailing. Children's squeals echoed up and down the residential corridor. Men cried as they yelled. No one concealed fear.

Obeying their father's instructions not to leave the front porch, the screaming and crying twins anxiously waited. Mom and dad wasted no time grabbing the kids and bursting through the front door. The lighting dwindled from the swinging chandelier in the dining area. Bouncing off the family room walls, the Merediths plunged through the access door to the security chamber. Eve and the kids were crying while Randall hugged all three in a futile attempt to establish calm inside the safe confines of the security chamber.

"Our Father who art in heaven," began Eve, as the four sat on the floor cushions, embracing each other. "Hallowed be thy name."

The lights flickered then went out. The chamber was totally black.

Screams echoed throughout the darkened Sanctuary. Like a jetliner in thunderstorm, Yucca Mountain rocked and lurched while the helpless and blind passengers cried and screamed in darkness.

Several octaves lower than the human shrieks bellowed the deep rumbling of Earth communicating with Hell. Mom and Dad clung to the kids and to each other. The fear of death in a black cave constricted his breathing like a python with its prey. The screaming of the other family members continued.

Randall's voice crackled, then merged with Eve's, "Thy kingdom come, thy will be done, on earth as it is in heaven." Then the twins joined, "Give us this day, our daily bread…" A mixture of primal yells, screams, cries, and prayer emitted from the four as they trembled in the confines of their uncomforting safe place.

The interior structure seemed to torque as the ground shook. Creaking noises from the reinforcement beams of the facility challenged confidence in the Yucca Mountain engineering. Like the rest of the inhabitants, the Merediths were now at the mercy of the Sanctuary for their survival. Would it hold? Would they survive?

The rumbling and shaking suddenly stopped. Rattled nerves persisted in the total darkness. The twins maintained their death grip on Mom's arms. Randall fumbled and found the stowed flashlight. The modest illumination only slightly eased the tension. Thirty minutes passed. Whimpering languished in the dimly lit chamber while Mom and Dad held their breath.

Then the gut-churning sound of earth moving and shaking started again. The human shrieks resumed. The four family members huddled and prayed for the next hour. It felt like days. Dad's watch indicated an irrelevant 3 am, but sleep was hopeless. A waking nightmare was happening, and nothing would suppress it.

Then it stopped. A welcomed calm allowed a deep breath among the sanctuary residents. Screaming and crying had silenced; replaced by muted whimpering. Was it over? Everyone waited. Five minutes. Then ten. All quiet. One hour passed.

Suddenly the lights flickered, then went on. Cheering echoed throughout Yucca Mountain. The Sanctuary had held. They had survived. Their prayers were answered.

CHAPTER XV
THE AFTERMATH

FOUR MONTHS LATER.

THE ERRATIC HEAVING AND SHAKING CONTINUED, THE RESULT OF A grumpy, unsettled Earth having absorbed a vicious punch by *Onesimus*. The meteoric collision had caused tectonic plate shifting and surface faulting that propagated a swarm of earthquakes and volcanic eruptions within the Ring of Fire.

These quakes and eruptions heaved and shook along both the eastern and western shore of the Pacific, north to south and stretched inland all the way to Nevada's Amargosa Valley and beyond. Like bricks in a shifting rock pile, masses of earth moved and resettled, spewing gases, rocks, and molten lava. Coastlines changed, mountains and valleys formed, and a new topography was born.

Yucca Mountain, situated in the Amargosa Desert fault system near the south end of the Mono-Inyo chain of volcanic craters that included Mammoth Mountain, was due east of the Death Valley. During the Mesozoic Era, extensive tectonic activity had resulted in a period of volcanism and faulting in that area. Relatively dormant for the next 30 to 60 million years, the area now became reactivated by movement from a swarm of spreading seismic activity.

The reinforced tunnel system under Yucca Mountain swayed and trembled for months. Nearby volcanos erupted, leaving a large accumulation of magma that formed a curious-shaped bowl directly around the sanctuary entrance. But the one-thousand-foot-deep bunker held.

No one had predicted nor understood the length of stay that would be necessary. Residents were growing weary of the in-and-out occupation of their survival chambers whenever the warning siren wailed, and the mountain shook. The concession, however, and a grateful one at that, was that each day, they woke up—alive. There was no assurance that anyone had survived "top side."

All during this uncertain period of earth rumblings, residents were confined to their apartments and internal survival chamber. A daily venture outside their residence was a necessary risk taken by family heads for a resupply of food from the central commissary. Off and on rumblings made the trek extremely frightening. Holed up in residence #9, the family was always apprehensive whenever Randall ventured out for provisions and were grateful upon his return.

"How's the family holding up, Peters?" Randall said to his neighbor during one of their mutual ventures to the central commissary.

"Nervous, jittery but still intact, Randall. How about yours?"

"The survival chamber ritual is really getting tiresome but we're managing."

"Sleeping in those old, Navy hammocks is a bitch, isn't it?" Peters quipped.

"Sleeping? Who's sleeping?"

Their walk together was a hurried ten minutes with little time for pleasantries. The commissary packages were marked and ready for pickup, so Peters and Meredith made a quick turnaround.

"Grab and go," quipped Peters, attempting to add some humor to the trepidatious situation.

"Walking drive-through convenience, alright."

Suddenly, a rumbling quake turned violent, knocking Peters to one knee, spilling the groceries from the bags in his arms. Randall was able to maintain his balance and helped his shaken neighbor gather the rolling canned goods from the sanctuary floor. Both picked up their pace heading back to their homes. Then a yell was heard from the far end of the corridor.

"The reservoir gate!"

Lights blacked out. Background music went silenced. Dreadful seconds passed. Then the whir of backup generators was noticed, and electricity returned. Simultaneously, the piercing alarm sounded. Then the loudspeaker, "Return to your quarters! Return to your quarters! This is not a drill!"

"God, what is this!" Peters exclaimed at the sight of a gush of water flooding down the corridor.

The quake had caused a breach in the water reservoir which flooded the main corridor. Momentary panic swept over Randall and his neighbor as they splashed through the knee-deep water back to their families. Death by drowning, flashed through their minds. The water level was just below the porch and entrance heights and allowed both men to get in to their respective apartments without delay.

Brave maintenance crews fought through the onrushing water to find the problem. One worker waded through the rushing water and pump controls to shut off the source, while another scrambled the Caterpillar dozer into action and pushed mounds of backfill against the weakened segment of the gate. The whine of activated sump pumps confirmed that Globitz' design engineers seemed to have thought of everything. The leak stopped, the water drained, and the sump pumps did their part.

The next day a new sound generated from huge fans that dried the concrete floor and helped to restore calm—relative calm.

Two weeks passed without another incident. The shaking and heaving had seemingly run its course. And yet, the "all clear" notification had not been sounded. Updates from outside Yucca Mountain as promised by Globitz were conspicuously absent. Without confirmation or some kind of safety clearance, everyone inside the Sanctuary remained on alert.

It had already been established that all external communication links were down. The sealed Observation Chamber, with its framed glass copula, could have provided a view of the status outside, but it remained airtight and closed during the eruptions and shaking; too dangerous to enter. The rest of the five-mile-long tunnel complex had other vulnerable areas that had to be inspected. It could take several days to evaluate the residents were told. Finally, Globitz ordered his maintenance staff to inspect the critical areas of the sanctuary and provide a damage assessment.

During one of his rare ventures outside his residence and the Command Center, Dr. Globitz was approached by a disturbed resident with a strange request: "Is it possible to adjust the alarm setting from the repetitive shriek to, say, a subtler type of ring? It's frightening enough, but a softer sound would reduce fear and anxiety."

Bemused by such a request, the reclusive mogul responded, "I'll see what I can do."

Eventually, at a status briefing in the Sanctuary Command Center, the head of Facilities and Maintenance reported, "We have some very bad news, Dr. Globitz."

"And, what would that be, Rafael?"

"Well, sir, everything held pretty well during the eruptions.

Even the Observation Chamber. The air-tight door seal and copula are intact."

"That's good news, not bad!"

The veteran engineer and facilities maintenance guru continued. "One of the five trapezoidal windows is cracked but not leaking. The problem is that rocks and debris have piled up against the copula so that only a small part of a window has any view outside."

"We had two copulas made but only installed one. Right?"

"Right, sir. The other copula is in the back tunnel with our maintenance parts and supplies."

"Can you remove one of the trapezoidal windows and weld it right over the cracked one on the inside of the Observation Chamber?"

"Yes, but that's not the problem."

"What is it, Rafael?! What's the problem?" a frustrated Globitz demanded.

"The problem is what I could see, outside of the one small window. Water. All I could see was water. I believe we're underwater!"

The next day, rumblings among the residents were mounting due to the lack of information by Globitz and his staff. So Globitz decided to call a community meeting to pacify the inhabitants and explain what had happened outside the bunker. There was little good news and some VERY bad news.

Globitz and his wife slowly descended the staircase from their residence to face the concerned citizens of Yucca Mountain Sanctuary. Enough folding chairs were placed in front of the stage to accommodate all the residents and staff members. The cherub-faced seventy-year-old Globitz had aged significantly since their last meeting just four weeks earlier. His flowing white hair was perfectly coifed, but the lines on his brow had multiplied and deepened. The bags under his eyes were double-layered and pale gray. His shapely young wife stood politely behind her worried husband.

The forced smile and greetings were the only bright spot of the news he would deliver: "We have survived the worst disaster of mankind. The world as we knew it, outside Yucca Mountain, has forever changed. The human toll is unknown, but we have survived."

Gasps and murmurs swept through the audience. Faint cries and shrieks broke out. Randall grasped his wife's hand and squeezed. It was the only act of comfort he could muster.

"What does that mean, Daddy?" Samantha inquired, looking for some positive reassurance.

"It means we may be here for a while longer, Sam." Her father's voice cracked as he looked away so she would not see the tears welling in his eyes.

Globitz continued:

"All of our monitoring equipment outside the Sanctuary has been destroyed by rocks and debris. The view from our Observation Chamber has been obscured. Once we have any communication links to the outside, we will send that information to the video panels in your residences. You all will have access to the Command Center's latest status when we have information to report.

"The view from the Observation Chamber, the portholes, the outside cameras and the periscope will all be made available as soon as we can. But for now, everything is dark. It is obvious that entrance to our sanctuary is buried and/or underwater. Our visual capabilities and all communication with the outside world have ceased. I wish I had better news, but all I can say is—we survived."

Coach Lowe emerged from the stage behind a faltering Globitz. He dutifully took the microphone relieving Globitz, who retreated with his wife back up the stairs.

"Ladies and gentlemen, it's been a very difficult few months for all of us," he conveyed in a positive, authoritative manner. "We recommend that you and your families return to your quarters and focus on the positives—we have survived. We will prevail, and we will emerge from this experience when the time is right."

"In the meantime," he resumed, "Yucca Mountain will continue to operate as planned. Our staff is here to serve and, barring a few inconveniences for repairs, we are open for business."

Too dispirited to hear answers to questions they dare not ask, the residents accepted dismissal. One by one, they rose from their seating and straggled back to their residence.

The ceiling lights showed bright, fluffy clouds and friendly sunshine and the background music was upbeat. But the feelings of uncertainty of each family heading back to their quarters would test each person's character to the maximum.

CHAPTER XVI
COMFORTABLY NUMB

FIVE MONTHS AFTER IMPACT.

"That was a nice shot, Max,"

"Thanks, Randall. Now if I can put it on the green and two-putt for par, I'll be set."

Max Schwab moved off the tee, bagged his driver, and stepped on to one of the two synchronized treadmills. It was Randall's turn to drive the ball into the screen and watch the virtual golf ball sail down the life-like fairway. Fifty yards short of Max's ball but still on the short grass was considered a success for the novice golfer.

"Yes!"

Meredith slid the driver into the golf bag next to the treadmill on his side of the tee box and hopped on to its conveyor belt. The mechanical whine of the treadmills had an ironic similarity to the sound of his golf cart back in North Carolina, Max thought. He was a tall, lanky man from Woodcliff Lake, New Jersey, by way of Duke University, thanks to a full-ride golf scholarship, and then Harvard. He made his millions at Lehman Brothers on Wall Street before moving to Cary, North Carolina. It didn't hurt that he married a sole-surviving tobacco heiress he met in college.

"Nice not sleeping in the chamber for a while, eh, Randy?"

"Yeah, I thought the temblors would never end," his golf partner confirmed.

"My grandmother used to talk about the sirens and the fallout shelters in London during World War II. Wonder how she would fare, down here."

An imaginary hike down the fairway allowed them to rendezvous with their respective golf balls. Walking, talking, and golfing while the scenic fairways unfurled in front of them in high definition was a four-hour escape from the reality of being entombed a thousand feet underground. Staying active with exercise, if chasing a dimpled ball is considered exercise, was good for the body, soul, and mind.

"I'd use your 3 wood for the next shot, Randy."

"Thanks, coach."

The whine of treadmills stopped as Randall dismounted, and Max observed. Placing the ball from the retrieval bin onto the turf a foot away from the embedded rubber tee, the humble golfer followed the pro's advice and took another swing. Whack! Zipping past Max's nose by two feet, the ball shanked into the containment netting to his right.

"That was some slice, Randy. Hit another."

"Sorry, Max. Just can't seem to keep my head down."

"Relax, swing easy. It'll come."

"You know, Max, this is such a frustrating game," Randall said, placing another ball on the turf. This time, he eased up, swung easy, and delivered the ball just short of the green. It was a good recovery.

"The virtual walk idea was probably what Globitz had in mind to occupy our time in this dungeon. Our kids have school, the wives have bridge, and we have golf. Brilliant!"

"I've also been swimming in the lap pool." Randall said. "You should try it. The water's warm, and rather soothing before bedtime. And my wife is totally into the spinning class."

"Julie is too! It's too much like work for me. Besides golf, I prefer the spa," Max responded. "Whatever works, right? How are the Leibovitz's doing?"

"Not good. The whole family is on Prozac, I heard. They're having a hard time adjusting to living like moles."

"I sometimes wonder if our water is being spiked with some kind of sedative. More of us should be going nuts down here."

"Like my dad would say, 'Don't think, Marine. Just keep walking.'"

Whack. Schwab's second shot slammed into the screen. The red trail of his virtual ball projected a beautiful arc over the fairway, biting in to the cybernetic green. A slight thump, courtesy of the programmed sound effects, triggered grins from both golfers.

For Max and Randall, it was a beautiful day at Torrey Pines Golf Course in San Diego and a four-hour make-believe escape from being sequestered and entombed. There were many outlets for the Sanctuary residents to engage in, but golf was Max and Randall's.

Back to reality. Yucca Mountain's bunker complex was floundering like a buttoned-up submarine at one hundred fathoms. Even if the air-tight entrance was operable, its porthole still revealed they were underwater.

From the top of Yucca Mountain's crest, three mini-hangers bored into solid rock, harbored the Yaneec Tornado drones and their HD Hazzelblad cameras. One deployed spontaneously with the first eruption and had never been heard from since. Inundation of the Amargosa Valley could not be confirmed by the other drones, implying they were also dysfunctional.

Near the tunnel entrance, another problem arose. Boulders and rocks heaved against the blast-proof reconnaissance robot door prevented its opening and the robot's deployment. All electronic surveillance outside the sanctuary was now kaput. A human safety exploration beyond the tunnel entrance was out of the question.

"The cables, wires, fibers, and splitters checked out, sir," reported Stew Hawkins, a former Navy electronics technician. "Everything's okay from the Command Center right up to the panel box at the tunnel entrance. The problem we have is outside the walls of the sanctuary."

"So, none of our sensors or cameras can transmit?" asked Globitz.

"Correct, sir. They're either destroyed or their links to us are broken," responded the apologetic worker.

Computer screens and camera monitors all sat silent around the Command Center near Globitz' office. Despite the perfectly controlled temperature and humidity throughout the Sanctuary, nervous sweat saturated the visionary's brow and under arms. His experts had exhausted all strategies to revive the environmental instruments and communication links to the outside.

Even the radio and TV signals from the government's Emergency Broadcast System were silent. The feverish attempt to connect to something, anything, that would indicate survivability above ground was futile. Nothing worked. And, for another one of the few times in his adult life, Globitz had no control of the matter. His eyes darted from one staff member to another in search of alternative solutions.

It was obvious they were stranded. Drilling an escape tunnel to the surface was an impossible option, considering the equipment necessary and the depth of the sanctuary. Blasting open the tunnel entrance was the one event reserved only after the "all clear" atmospheric conditions could be assured. The occupants, both staff and patrons, became resigned to settling in for a while. There were no other options.

From the depths of despair at the Command Center to anguish and exhaustion across the commons and in the Services and Support side of the complex, nothing seemed to be operating as planned. Overworked and understaffed, physician, Dr. Jammicit and Nurse Higgins tended to a throng of residents and employees for hypertension, depression, insomnia, anxiety, and panic attacks. Minor scrapes, bruises, diarrhea, and fevers took second place to the incessant requirement for mental therapy. The pallets of prescription sedatives that filled the cavernous medications locker were dwindling at an alarming rate.

The unused dental chair in Jammicit's clinic was symbolic of the medically unprepared team—no dentist on staff. Last minute cold feet dissuaded Dr.Kenneth Martino to jump ship before the gate was closed. An unappreciative medical doctor would pull teethe if required but drew the line on filling cavities.

Dr. Audrey, Jammicit's wife and a practicing clinical psychologist, was pressed into action, providing triage and counseling for her husband's patients. Considered an authority in mental health issues, the dark-eyed beauty had authored a book on mental health and self-hypnosis. Combatting a preventable situation called "learned helplessness," was her specialty. Her warm and understanding manner helped assuage and often mitigate the emotional effects of underground confinement. Talk therapy was preferred to medicating whenever possible.

It appeared the Jammicits were a perfect hire by Globitz. They were young, workaholic professionals of complementary expertise. As newlyweds and idealists, they could totally immerse themselves into their work without the demands or constraints of children. They envisioned that the experience working at the Sanctuary would enrich their lives immeasurably. But for now, they both were up to their eyeballs with frantic patients.

Between work, sirens, and bunker slumber, they tried to enjoy candlelit dinners in their apartment. Conversation inevitably turned to patient assessment:

"Frank Jamison is about to blow, Jim. I'm passing him to you for some heavy meds."

"I'm already treating him for high blood pressure. How is he in your group therapy sessions?"

"God, he's an emotional time bomb, and affecting a couple borderline participants. We've got to get him out of there; he's a cancer."

"I'll call him in tomorrow."

The two doctors confirmed Mr. Jamison's fate with a smile and continued with their romantic dinner date in their cozy confines. The issue was a page turn of a paperback novel. Not even a frantic patient could interfere with their marital bliss.

During his early-morning walk, Roy Bartholomew discovered some black scribbling on one of the storefront doors: "Globitz fiddles while the rest of us fidget." He notified Toby, the morning maintenance guy, who immediately removed the graffiti. Roy thought to himself, *What good would a message like this do? Maybe it would help demoralize the adults, but the kids, probably not.* Unfortunately, this theme was subconsciously carried by many dispirited residents and staff.

Heinz Globitz was often seen driving his golf cart throughout the Sanctuary with Rafael Ochoa, his facilities engineer, to check on the equipment and services. But it was rare for him to ever stop for a visit in the clinic. Frank and the two doctors were seated in the snug waiting area when he walked in.

"Good morning, doctors. Frank." Globitz's smiling and cordial demeanor were welcomed by the respectful staff members, as he sat down.

"Thanks for meeting with us, Dr. Globitz. My husband and I thought that you and Mr. Lowe might help us reduce some of the medical issues we have been dealing with here in the clinic."

"Yes, of course. How can we help?"

"The issue is depression. Several of the residents are slipping into a depressive state that may be minimized by some non-medical intervention. We thought that you and Frank could assist," said Dr. Audrey.

"By all means. What exactly do you need?"

The other doctor spoke up, "Audrey and I have noticed that the staff members have fewer recreational outlets on their side of the tunnel, yet their incidence of medical needs is miniscule compared to the patrons. Meaningful work dominates their day and they have less leisure time on their hands to feel depressed. We feel that is the critical difference."

"Yes," Audrey said. "We feel that the abundance of leisure time has an adverse effect on morale, and ultimately, mental health. If the residents were inspired to contribute, in some way, to the function of the Sanctuary, that it may reduce boredom, which often leads to mental health issues. The residents here are talented, educated and accomplished, yet there is little outlet for them to apply their abilities other than recreational activities."

Frank picked up on the two doctor's inspiration. "We could encourage them to contribute in some form, not only as schoolteachers, physical trainers, and lecturers but in the actual operations of the Sanctuary. Helping the maintenance staff, the food prep teams, the supply warehouse, the weekly newsletter or running the closed-circuit TV broadcasts, could all become meaningful "jobs" so to speak."

Globitz nodded in agreement. Frank and the doctors made a good case. Virtual golf, swimming, pickleball, weightlifting and exercise could only go so far to meet physical needs, and mentally stimulating activities like the book club, art classes and bridge were nice, but the residents needed another outlet to keep them busy. Meaning full work was needed during the day to complement their evening time with their families.

The parties agreed and Frank was tasked to put a program together that would involve the residents in working alongside of the staff. Occupying the daytime hours and preventing boredom for all inhabitants became a priority.

And life went on in Yucca Mountain.

CHAPTER XVII
THE ROUTINE

YEAR NUMBER TWO

REX AND OCTAVIO WERE IN ANOTHER SCUFFLE NEAR THE BACK OF THE classroom which required intervention by Ms. Duncan, the third-grade teacher. The two eight-year-olds had developed a highly competitive relationship since first meeting in Yucca Mountain. Both athletic and smart, they came from opposite corridors of the Sanctuary. Octavio was the adopted son (and nephew) of the staff facilities engineer, Rafael Ochoa. The fracas this time was prompted by the smirk from Rex to Octavio over the grades received on their math tests: Octavio's 96% versus Rex's 97%.

Their twenty other classmates were mostly harmonious and civil but had grown accustomed to the two boy's rivalry. It was a brief encounter immediately snuffed out by an authoritative look by the petite Ms. Duncan. Her artful handling of such situations confirmed her reputation as a tough but talented educator, despite her youthful appearance. Her hiring by Globitz was another stroke of genius.

At lunch time, when the students sat at the tables in the common area for their peanut butter and jelly sandwiches, Rex and Octavio were at their usual, sitting next to each other, laughing and joking. The morning's din had passed like flies in a windstorm, exactly as their teacher knew it would.

A wealth of teaching talent held by the adult residents resulted in classes being offered to their kids that likely exceeded the quality of curriculum they might have found outside the sanctuary. Everything was designed to render as "near normal" as possible a school experience for the students from both sides of the tracks. Modern desks, computers, digital white boards, science lab equipment, and a digital reference library provided a variety of resources for cultivating the "next generation"—the Yucca Mountain progeny.

Extracurricular activities for the students included sports (soccer, archery, swimming, gymnastics, etc.), drama, debate, chess, and choir. "Outdoor" activities were necessarily downsized under the constraints of the subterranean facilities. It can be said that youth adapt more easily than their parents, and this was the case with the students at YM Academy. It was a school as conventional as it could possibly be, albeit underground.

Three alcoves down from the Academy classrooms, adults occupied their recreational time in the Community Center playing duplicate bridge, attending lectures, reviewing books, and participating in other social or cultural-oriented activities. A projection TV hung from the ceiling aimed at the white screen on one of the walls. Three easels with paintings in various stages of completion were located near the single pedestal desk with a laptop computer. The dry-erase board on another wall served as a community bulletin board and displayed the coming week's activities. This week it featured Monday—Book Review (*Anna Karenina*), Wednesday— Lecture (Dr. Jammicit: Vitamin D requirements), Saturday—Lecture

(Chef Diaz: Wise Company tasty desserts), and Sunday—Church Service.

The two after school soccer teams composed of third, fourth and fifth grade players were determined by names fairly extracted from a ranking list. The two teams alternated practice times between the tree-lined village green, laid out as a miniature soccer field and the basketball court near the other end of the commons. Rex's team, the Rhinos, were coached by Ms. Angela Murphy, the fourth-grade teacher. Although Rex was smaller than some of his teammates, his reputation as a fast, aggressive player earned him a starting position on the team as a striker.

The other soccer team was coached by Activities Director/ Teacher, Frank Lowe, whose reputation as an All-American college soccer player invited "coach envy" concerns from the parents of team Rhino. The Polar Bears' prized goalie was none other than Rex's best friend and nemesis, Octavio. Samantha proudly played forward and was one of three girls on the team. Both teams were taught soccer basics, team play and sportsmanship. Both coaches strove to instill the concept of "team" versus "individual" mindsets which would payoff later in the students' lives. With only two teams in the league, a lot of practice scrimmages preceded the big game for season bragging rights.

The men of Yucca Mountain gravitated to several available activities; Randall to virtual golf, swimming and weightlifting. NBA Hall of Famer Toby Styles attracted a dedicated group to the basketball court for a daily ritual of three-on-three. The archery range and bowling alley became novel venues for adults as well as some of the kids. Everyone found at least one activity to hold their interest and to combat boredom.

Globitz cleverly anticipated that coping with prolonged underground survival would require multiple hobby outlets for adults as well as kids, and for patrons as well as staff. His detailed planning for the activities within Yucca Mountain may have been adequate for long stays with a foreseeable exit. Would it hold, however, for an indefinite length of time and an uncertain exodus?

At some point, resident ingenuity became necessary to overcome tedium. Randall stepped forward to call a meeting with all interested parties. The Community Center became a long-overdue town hall forum for the topic of new activities to avoid endless boredom.

Adult residents poured into the Community Center. Kids were requested to stay at home. With all the folding chairs filled and residents still arriving, the meeting became a squeezed-in, standing room only situation.

"Thank you all for coming. Can you hear me in the back?" Randall asked.

A shuffling and mumbling among the standing attendees prompted someone to voice, "Can you speak louder, please."

"Yes, I'll try." Smiling and digging deeper into his chest, the earnest resident continued. "A few of us thought it would be nice to come up with some alternative recreational activities to occupy our time while we're here in Yucca Mountain."

"How much longer are we going to have to be here in this hell hole?" was gruffly offered from someone in the standing audience. A smattering of like-minded residents, nodded and turned toward Randall for response.

Blindsided by the tenor of his detractors, he paused. Then frowning and looking in the direction of the complainer, he nodded, and restated the purpose of the meeting, "We're here to talk about things we can control, not the things we can't. Our topic is Alternative Activities."

Fortified by the surrounding cluster of murmurs, the brazen spokesman shouted, "Alternative activities be damned! We need to know when we can get out of here!"

Shouts of "Yeah, yeah!" were echoed by his group of supporters, spreading quickly among the seated residents. A pall of vengeance engulfed the potentially volatile audience. Pent-up anger reverberated within the confines of the packed room, turning many residents into adversaries. Their irritation was now a matured boil that needed lancing.

All eyes turned on Randall as if he were personally responsible for the conditions that kept the Yucca Mountain survivors confined; that he should have done something to alleviate their predicament. Their misery was no longer placated by Globitz' plans and activities.

Randall swallowed, gathering his composure. *Leading an organization of computer geeks was child's play compared to this,* he thought. His chest noticeably swelled as his lungs filled to speak, when a tall angular man in the fourth row stood up, pre-empting his response.

"That's enough! That's enough of the horse crap!"

The residents around him became quiet, shushing the noisy patrons seated nearby. The murmuring diminished slightly, when someone else yelled, "Quiet, let the man speak!"

Just then, a white board eraser came flying over the heads of the angry audience, flung by an out of control man next to the wall. It was headed directly toward the man's face. There was a muffled thump, as he instinctively caught it mid-flight with his enormous right hand. Lowering his arm to his side, the dispassionate speaker held it for future emphasis. The audience gasped. A cold quiet immediately fell over the entire gathering.

"Now that I've got your attention, I have something to say."

His six-foot, five-inch sinewy frame supported a handsome, honest-looking face, weathered by sun and wind. His baritone voice and imposing figure commanded their attention, as he studied their looks and bearing.

"For those who don't know me, my name is Henry Henson. And I'm as sick of this place as you are. Unlike most of you, I didn't live in a multi-million-dollar mansion, run a billion-dollar company, or inherit a fortune from my family. I'm not used to chauffeurs, servants, or maids. A lucky, hundred-dollar Power Ball investment got me here. My wife and two daughters lived on a family farm in Langford, South Dakota. And we miss it every day, just like you miss your homes."

Using the eraser and his extended arm as a pointer toward his audience, he continued. "But holler'in at Mr. Meredith here ain't going to get us home any sooner. In fact, if we were in our homes today, we'd probably be crispy critters, buried in molten lava. Or at the bottom of a new ocean, fish food for whatever whales or crabs survived.

"So, let's get real. Meredith had a good idea with good intentions. He's not the bad guy here." Henson then took his seat. His wife added her proud support, linking her arm with his.

Silence lasted ten seconds, broken when a small number of listeners started clapping. Then others chimed in, until most of the room came to their senses and showed approval of Henson's assessment.

When the applause subsided, Randall cleared his throat to reconcile the situation. "Those of you who want to stick around and talk about some ideas for new activities and entertainment, please stay."

The grumbling and shuffling of feet toward the door by some of the participants clearly indicated who was not on board. The ones choosing to stay angry slowly filed out, leaving about thirty-five in their seats to work through the agenda. The lines had been drawn; the rebels versus the realists. A confrontation in the future was inevitable.

CHAPTER XVIII

THE HOAX

ONE YEAR LATER

"R ANDY, WAKE UP! S OMEONE'S BANGING ON THE DOOR."

Blurry-eyed and still half asleep, he responded, "It's eleven-thirty, who in hell..."

Randall fumbled for the nightstand light and clambered to his feet. Fastening the top few buttons of his pajamas, he straggled down the hallway to the door. His movement caused the front room lights to turn on, prompting him to shade his eyes with his right hand.

"Who's there?"

"It's Nathan, Randall. Nathan Jones."

Opening the door, Randall complained, "It's awfully late, Nate. This better be important."

Nervous and shaking, Jones entered. After Randall's nod toward the dining table, the guest humbly explained, "We've got a problem down here. You're the only guy I'm comfortable talking to about it."

Seating himself in the dining chair opposite his distressed neighbor, Randall asked, "What's going on, Nate?"

A concerned voice muttered from the bedroom, "What's happening out there, Randy?"

"Nothing, Dear. Just talkn' to Nate Jones about something. Go back to sleep."

With the anxious look of a worked-up college boy, the young multi-millionaire said, "Randy, Jack Abram and Neil Acosta are coordinating a rebellion against Globitz and Yucca Mountain. They want outta here, and they mean to force the issue."

"Interesting. Disappointing, actually."

"They've convinced themselves and a few others that this is all a hoax," Jones stressed.

"A hoax?"

"Yes, a giant money-grabbing scam made to look like a natural disaster."

"Preposterous! This place was shaking like a funhouse on steroids for months. How do they explain that?"

"Bombs. That's why we're feeling it down here. They were blasting the whole mountain with heavy artillery for several months."

"It's awfully late for all this talk, Nate."

The wild-eyed visitor continued. "Globitz's wife, Krishka, is Russian, you know. Abrams thinks she's the SVR Russian spy the Feds were looking for before we were sealed in."

"And?" the exasperated host yawned.

"Well, Acosta claims that she was directed to hook up with Globitz down here to arrange their escape."

"Where does the hoax part come in?"

"Remember when Russia lost billions in a currency scam? That was Globitz! He was sent to White Swan Prison Colony for life."

"So, here he is. With us," the tired skeptic proclaimed.

"They released him early to carry out this hoax. He paid Russia back with the gold we gave him."

"You're losing me, Nate. Let's talk about it tomorrow."

"No! They swore me secrecy, Randall."

"How does all this effect Yucca Mountain?"

"Abrams and Acosta believe the gold bullion we paid to get in here went directly to Moscow. Globitz made a deal to repay them to get out of prison. His Yucca Mountain Sanctuary brainchild is the vehicle. As long as this bunker is sealed up, nobody knows or misses us. Or will ever see us again."

"Nate, this is way too complicated for me to digest tonight. Figure out a better time to talk to me and I'll listen. But not tonight."

He rose from the dining table and awaited Jones to follow him to the front door. Like a disciplined puppy, the visitor obeyed.

"Good night, Nate."

Walking back to his bedroom, the would-be counselor tried to dismiss the last hour from his memory. Cautiously slipping under the covers and rolling into his curled sleeping position with his wife, Randall finally closed his eyes. Eve waited for the sheets to settle, then sprang into interrogation mode.

"What was that about, Randy?"

"Not tonight, dear. Nathan's hair brained ideas are not worth losing any sleep over."

The two kissed, then rolled over into their respective slumber spots. Within minutes the harmony of peaceful snoring favored the night.

2 A.M.

Randall's bladder urged him to quietly stumble out of bed, into the bathroom. The familiar ritual was a "pain in the ass," as he had explained to his urologist in Santa Barbara. Returning to sleep was now up for grabs. Nathan Jones' visit had not helped matters.

2:30 A.M.

Rolling to one side then the other to find the perfect position was not working. Counting backward, deep breathing, pleasant thoughts, and cuddling Eve failed as well. "Damn it. Go to sleep." he quietly uttered. *Think happy thoughts, You're better than this. Close your eyes and go to sleep!* he silently demanded. Nothing worked.

He soon gave up the idea of sleep. He rolled onto his back and began to revisit the ludicrous scenario Jones had laid out. Thinking to himself, the erstwhile computer genius imagined what Mr. Alexander, his eight-grade science teacher, would require. He began to organize the steps in his head. Step 1. Hoax or No Hoax? Step 2. Nathan's data dump. Step 3. Hypothesis: the cause-and-effect relationship of data. Step 4. Test by changing the variables. Step 5. Analysis. Step 6. Conclusion.

This is too complicated for such a ridiculous allegation, he thought. *Cut to the chase.*

Could this whole sanctuary thing possibly be a hoax? he wondered.

True: We all bought into the global disaster picture. True: The Yucca Mountain Sanctuary appears to be well constructed and extensively provisioned. True: We all paid in gold. True: Globitz and his Russian wife are bunkered in with us. True: We can't see or communicate with the outside. According to Nate, Acosta and Abram would risk everyone's safety to break out of the Sanctuary."

Possible: Globitz was a Russian prisoner. Possible: Globitz cut a deal with the Russians. Possible: Our gold got shipped to Russia. Possible: We're bunkered in and nobody knows, or we're locked in down here and forgotten. Possible: Globitz' wife is a Russian spy. Possible: Globitz and his wife could secretly escape, leaving us to die.

Doubtful: Globitz and the Russians concocted this whole plan. Doubtful: The asteroid was a coverup. Doubtful: The earthquakes

SURVIVAL BENEATH YUCCA MOUNTAIN

were actually planted explosions. Doubtful: The conditions outside of Yucca Mountain are currently calm and habitable.

On into the wee hours of the morning, the chattering monkeys in his head conducted a debate.

"How could Globitz pull off a hoax this big?"

"There's a lot of money involved, and with the Russians…"

"But it took great effort to put this facility together."

"Planning, patience, and effort all made it more believable…"

"But the approaching asteroid is indisputable, isn't it?"

"Yes, according to Globitz…"

"But what did the government and the news say?"

"The government said that it successfully diverted the asteroid…"

"But would the government mislead us on something this catastrophic?"

"No, the government never lies."

"That's not very reassuring."

"Perhaps they wanted to avoid panic and riots over something they could not control."

"Globitz wouldn't lie to us, would he?"

"No, he's an honest man…"

"But Acosta and Abram say he's a convicted international felon."

"He's reformed. His convictions in England, Hungary, and Russia are behind him, now."

"That's not very reassuring."

"What about Acosta and Abram?"

"Both are self-made billionaires. Acosta in narcotics and Abram in arbitrage trading."

"What proof do they have that this is a hoax?"

"Abram knows Globitz' history, was skeptical, but bought in to the Sanctuary anyway. Later, Acosta convinced him to connect the dots of doubt."

"How do they explain away the situation outside Yucca Mountain?"

"They say we're sealed off from reality; that our vision and communication with the outside have been intentionally veiled."

"That's impossible!"

"Is it, really?"

"What do Acosta and Abram plan to do?"

"Nate didn't say, just that they want out of here."

"Who else believes Acosta and Abram?"

"Nate didn't say."

"How would they do it?"

"Nate didn't say, only that they intend to rebel and break out."

"If they do, and are wrong, are the rest of us at risk?"

"Yes!"

"Conclusion: It's a bad situation down here, but a hoax—Dubious. Now try and go to sleep!"

4:30 A.M.

With that encouraging thought, the chattering monkeys were able to finally roll over and fall asleep.

6:30

"Daddy, wake up! We're out of toothpaste."

CHAPTER XIX
THE REBELLION VIRUS

THE PRESENCE OF OSCAR WASHINGTON AND MIKE GEHRING AT THE entrance of the Community Center may have been an indicator. The two overly friendly security guards greeted each resident as they passed through the door. Globitz's eyes and ears were the impetus for positioning his two "prime beef" greeters to dissuade any thoughts of rebellion through smiles, if not rippled muscle.

Affectionately called "Sergeant O" and "Sergeant M" by the kids, who celebrated their police force's preference for big-tired mini-bikes to cruise around the Sanctuary corridors and their bright yellow tank top uniforms, were the law and order guys. Recruited by Globitz for a year or longer assignment, they were assured to hook up with a plush security job with one of the fifty or so multi-millionaires they were babysitting once their Yucca Mountain gig concluded.

"There's a couple of empty chairs here," said Randall to the standing onlookers, pointing toward the second row of a packed Community Center.

The follow-up meeting from the one that had sparked the disturbance three weeks earlier was about to begin. Randall, the unofficially anointed leader, stood in front of the apprehensive patrons of the Sanctuary. The shuffling and hushed chatter by the seated residents yielded to quiet. All eyes turned to Meredith.

"Evening," he offered with a confident smile.

"We had some very worthwhile suggestions at our last meeting regarding recreational activities. Many of them are well underway. But a few issues came up that required investigating. Amanda Guilhaus, Fred Spackman, and I met with Dr. Globitz and his staff."

The interruptions started. An angry voice yelled, "Who appointed you three to meet with Globitz?"

Masterfully staring down the indignant questioner, Randall responded. "The three of us stepped forward when nobody else expressed an interest."

Then taking a long pause to let his words soak in, he continued, "So tonight, we want to brief you all on what we learned. Amanda, do you want to use this mike?"

"Thank you, Randy," she said as she stepped forward.

Gender respect may have temporarily prevailed. And, the tension that filled room diminished somewhat with Mrs. Guilhaus' upbeat voice and pleasant demeaner.

"One of the issues that came up was the alarm blast. Thank goodness, we've not heard it for a few months now. But Dr. Globitz advised that it cannot be changed. We'll just have to live with it."

"Those of you concerned about the food we are eating, take note. A team of certified nutritionists has endorsed our menus for the Grotto and the two fast food carry-outs. The food available at the commissary has also been approved. All the nutritional needs for prolonged underground habitation are available to us here."

"Spirits and alcohol. Two bottles of wine per household will continue to be made available each month. There is no hard liquor or beer available, or in the storage warehouse. Champaign will still be offered if we are here for another New Year's Eve."

A groan from a man in the front row was followed by his rhetorical comment, "We're all adults here, you know." Chuckles from the seated residents behind him helped to lower the anxiety level.

Amanda continued. "The hours of the clinic dispensary have been extended per our request. Appointments are from 8am to 11am; walk in's from 1 pm. to 3 pm. Emergencies; anytime.

"Several of you had questions about the lighted window panels in your residences. Those virtual windows are equipped with special sensors and Vitamin D lighting to simulate sunrise in the morning and sunset in the evening. Turning them off is not recommended. It could alter your biorhythms and result in a drop in Vitamin D levels. It could also induce depression or a general feeling of sadness."

A wisecrack from the back seats sparked some laughter, "Our biorhythms oppose fake sunlight!"

Randall smiled. "Thank you, Amanda. Do any of you have questions for her?"

He paused to scan his audience. No questions.

"Moving right along, Fred and I will address your concerns about what is happening outside Yucca Mountain. Fred, do you want to start off?"

Fred Spackman, the tall, skinny, intellectual introvert, reluctantly took the stage to try to describe the environmental conditions outside the Sanctuary. His detailed narrative of the impact of the four-mile wide asteroid, striking the Earth at 30,000 miles per hour, was as perfunctory as if he were forecasting rain.

The chain reaction of earthquakes and volcanic eruptions, he explained, was spawned from the asteroid's cataclysmic impact. His delivery was so deadpan, that he could have been describing conditions on Mars, not on Earth.

"Whoa, hold on there, Spackman," a raspy voice rang out. Randall identified Jack Abram.

Any thoughts of serenity were immediately dismissed by the tone of the challenger.

"What's your source for that information?" Abram continued. "It sounds like the sales presentation we all got back in Las Vegas."

The sarcastic confrontation immediately elevated hostility levels in the Community Center. The few residents surrounding the antagonist nodded in agreement. Sergeant O cautiously walked along the left side of the room toward the front. Despite his imposing presence, all eyes were focused on Abram, the verbal combatant, and on Fred, his target.

"Thanks, Fred. I'll pick up from here," Randall intervened. "Yucca Mountain, it appears, is a stable mass amidst a very unstable arc of once-dormant volcanoes. All around us, earth masses have moved and reconfigured the landscape.

"What we learned from visiting Observation Chamber was very interesting—but discouraging," he confirmed, pausing to recapture the group's attention. "What Fred described was actually predicted by governmental sources. Because of Dr. Globitz' connections, we were lucky enough to be forewarned. And we survived, thanks to this bunker. There is no certainty that we would have survived outside Yucca Mountain."

"How do you know all that stuff took place?"

"They took us up into the Observation Chamber near the Sanctuary entrance. We couldn't see much because rocks and earth had covered the thick glass windows. One of the smaller windows, however, allowed us a peak outside. All we could see was water. It appears that Yucca Mountain is underwater!"

The audience gasped. Mrs. Jorgenson started whimpering then broke out into wailing. Mark, her husband, attempted to comfort her but ended up taking her home. Others attempted to hide their crying but were too distraught to pretend otherwise. The reality was like a Mike Tyson blow to their collective gut.

Randall's report was more credible than any previous secondhand accounts by staff; after all, he was one of them, not one of the employees. And everyone was now looking at him for his reaction to the situation. One tremor in his voice, one whimper, one forlorn grimace would have launched a chain reaction of panic. They would follow his lead and his emotional response. And he knew the responsibility of keeping his composure.

"So, until the water recedes," he sternly posed, "we will be held captive, *but safe* in our bunker."

From one of the listeners rising from his seat, came the vocalized reaction on everyone else's lips, "What does 'until the water recedes' mean?"

Drawing a long breath while diplomatically composing himself, Randall responded, "It means that the water level outside our entrance has to drop before we can open the gate. We've survived the asteroid, volcanic eruptions, and earthquakes. We wouldn't want to now drown with impatience, would we?"

A queasy silence grasped the entire room.

"This would be a good time for a five-minute recess, before we set up to present the next subject of our meeting here tonight."

The attendees broke out in teary-eyed conversations, yet no one left their seat. They turned to talk to their neighbors, measuring each other's reaction.

"If I can have your attention," Randall appealed after a few minutes. "Please, your attention."

The room came to a gradual quiet as heads and eyes turned frontward. He sensed the group's despair and in a very sober yet confident disposition, he brought the meeting's second period to order:

"During one of Abraham Lincoln's darkest moments, he said this,

'We can complain because rose bushes have thorns or rejoice because thorn bushes have roses.'"

Then looking around the room to ensure full attention, he continued, "Ladies and gentlemen, we have a situation of rose bushes before us. We can complain about the thorns or look for and gather the roses.

"I propose that we consider it a godsend to have survived here in Yucca Mountain. And, while we are here, we can gather the roses and help make this place a little better. Well, maybe a little more enjoyable, is what I meant. We can be of service to ourselves and each other.

"The talent in this room is mindboggling. Wouldn't it be great to contribute some of our skills to the operation so that we all benefit? Making it more enjoyable and valuable would be a worthwhile task. Don't you agree? Putting our expertise to work would eliminate boredom and also improve some of the conditions down here.

"Amanda, Fred and I asked the staff and management how we might help with things in the Sanctuary that would benefit everyone. There are hundreds of daily operational chores that keep this place running. Dr. Globitz and his staff have been doing it all, working day and night, for our benefit; our survival.

"But, how many rounds of golf can I play without guilt? How many laps in the pool, how many games of bridge, how many books can we read while the staff cater to our every need? We're better than that. Every one of us."

Meredith paused, looking directly at each of his neighbors seated before him. Moments passed. Without saying a word, his authoritative challenge of their nobler instincts was laid bare before them. No one breathed. He quickly shifted to a new topic.

"We asked for a list of functions where we might contribute. Amanda has a delineation of those functions and I'll let her talk about them. Amanda."

She stood and distributed lists to the first person in each row. Then, stepping to the microphone, she pointed to a larger version of the same list mounted on the easel.

"Ladies and gentlemen, the handout you are receiving contains a list of potential areas where we residents could augment the Yucca Mountain staff. It's not all inclusive and many of you may have additional areas you know you could help with."

"There are a few functions on the list I'll describe; the rest are self-explanatory. The blank line after each function is for you to fill in your name, if that function is an area of your expertise and you want to volunteer. You can hand it in or see me at the end of our meeting.

"A couple of the functions are for our kids and their school. Our capable teaching staff is in need of a Latin and French teacher. They also could use teacher aid support.

"Our kids also need a piano teacher and a music instructor. They have musical instruments available and could compose a musical ensemble, with proper instruction. Can you imagine a musical concert for our entertainment next spring?

"There are numerous IT requirements for all of the computers we have down here. If you have a background in that area, the staff would be most appreciative of your assistance.

"Anyone with a farming background, or interested, for that matter: The staff could use help with the hydroponic garden way back in Alcove 36.

"Interested in cooking? All three restaurants have openings for a sous-chef. The Grotto could also use a pastry chef.

"The Fitness Center could use a yoga and Pilates instructor.

"Dr. Jammicit and Nurse Higgins need a records clerk and an office manager in the clinic and dispensary.

"Yucca Mountain TV, our own closed-circuit TV network, could use a programming assistant and a local news broadcaster. Weather girl—probably not."

The audience enjoyed Amanda's sense of humor and appeared to be receptive to proposal.

"Those are just some of the positions I wanted to point out. The rest, you can read for yourself on the sheet I handed out. If you have suggestions for others, please write them in at the bottom of page two. I'll collect them as you leave. Thank you."

"Thanks, Amanda," Randall said as he stepped back to the microphone.

He peered into the vacant expressions of his fellow survivors, his friends and neighbors. He realized they were still in denial and disbelief. The enthusiasm balloon for volunteering was losing air, sending the whole idea flying aimlessly to the rafters. Their residence in Yucca Mountain was still considered "temporary." Committing to one of the positions suggested by Amanda was like buying into a longer-term lease agreement than they were comfortable with. They also were too used to being catered to; "to be served" rather then, "to serve."

He had to do something to shake them out of their pathetic self-pity.

"Mr. Ellis, how many rounds of golf did you play last week?"

Surprised to be singled out from the lifeless group, the former securities trader perked up and embarrassingly responded, "About eight."

The entire audience was now watching the exchange, not wanting to also be exposed.

"How many rounds of golf did you play each week when you were working on Wall Street, before Yucca Mountain?

Arnel Ellis, the celebrated author and master of derivatives trading, admitted that before entering the Sanctuary, he played golf only on Sundays and worked eleven-hour days, six days a week.

"So, your contribution to society, to your family, and to your friends since moving into the safety of our presence is a lower handicap?"

The tall, angular golfer was now shrinking in his chair

"Mrs. Tillerman, how many books have you read since coming to Yucca Mountain?"

Edna Tillerman, the former president and CEO of Microsoft, did not like being called out by her old friend and co-worker, but faked a smile as she reported, "one a week, a little over a hundred, I guess."

"How great it would be for you to share what you've read with some of us. A lecture, a book review, a presentation…you'd have an audience lined up outside the door waiting to hear your thoughts and inspiration from some of the things you've read."

"Never occurred to me," she admitted.

"And, Lily, when are you going to teach some of our kids how to write songs, play a guitar, and sing? When should we schedule your intimate Yucca Mountain concert?"

The recording artist quickly caught on to what Randall was attempting to do. Flashing her iconic, trademark smile through her bright red lips, she roared back, "I'm ready!" And in her Tennessee twang, she affirmed, "The concert's in three weeks!"

Randall smiled, and some of the audience respectfully applauded. But not everyone.

Meredith neutralized an element of dissention appealing to their sense of dignity and honor. "Surviving depends on all of us supporting each other." Nervous embarrassment was gradually sanitized by nods of acceptance, then under-breadth affirmations echoed, "he's right."

It appeared to be working. Enthusiasm, slow in developing, had a better chance at lasting longer. The residents were obligingly inspired to look beyond themselves and think about the situation. All had something to contribute. All had time on their hands. And, all were in the same situation—surviving for an undetermined time in a safe place. Contributing to community would add purpose and meaning to their lives. It would help them stay active mentally and emotionally and probably avoid insanity.

The meeting adjourned. Busy responding to questions and accepting the completed volunteer sheets, Amanda did not notice Abram and a small group of his followers skirt past her through the door. But the factions were visibly forming.

CHAPTER XX
YOUTHFUL DISCOVERIES

LUNCH TIME AND AGAIN, REX AND OCTAVIO WERE JOSTLING EACH OTHER. Like the toy magnetic matador and bull, they just couldn't avoid their friendly confrontations. They shared their drinks, exchanged sandwiches, and with a timely distraction, snatched the other's cookie.

After school and soccer practice, they'd kick the ball back and forth on their way home before saying ¡Hasta luego! A friendly competition developed for grades, field goals, ten-yard sprints, and practical jokes. Happily mixing it up with the other kids, they'd validate or discredit each other's actions merely through eye contact. Rex, from the patrons' quarters and Octavio, from the support staff community, were after all, just boys. Through their pranks, taunts, and bumps with each other, it became obvious that the contrast in backgrounds and privilege meant little to their friendship.

One Saturday, the boys embarked on what would become a ritual of secret "exploration hikes" around the Yucca Mountain corridors. Their venture started with a modest stroll while kicking a soccer ball back and forth in new and different places of the Sanctuary complex. The boys encountered a fenced-off area of one of the tunnels with a sign that said, "DANGER, NO ENTRY."

Double swing gates, that were big enough to allow heavy machinery to enter or exit, hinged on galvanized poles supporting the eight-foot chain-link fence stretching across the tunnel entrance. The familiar tunnel lights attached to the walls beyond the fence barrier were clearly turned off. A flatbed utility golf cart sat on the dark side of the fence, connected to an electrical outlet. Peering through the fence into the darkened tunnel provided a creepy, cave-like perspective.

"Come on, Octavio. I'll be goalie, try to kick the ball by me to hit the fence."

Without a word, Octavio stepped back ten paces and placed the soccer ball on the concrete floor. "Here it comes," he said as he unleashed a line drive directly toward the midsection of his friend. His ferocious kick caused Rex to cross his arms to protect himself instead of catching the ball. It deflected off Rex's arms and flew up and over the fence.

"Oh no, *la pelota!*" exclaimed Octavio with both hands holding his head.

The soccer ball flew down a darkened corridor. They heard its reverberating echo as it caromed off the tunnel walls and deep into the emptiness of the inclined concrete pathway.

Realizing what they had just done, the boys looked at each other for a reaction. Rex's furrowed eyebrows and an "o" formed lips indicated "not good." Octavio's raised eyebrows and air-sucking grimace corroborated. With pledged confidentiality, they both confirmed that a stealth retrieval was necessary. Ball-kicking innocence was now eclipsed by secrecy and guile.

The "DANGER, NO ENTRY" sign was more of a problem than

the unlocked gate. Passing through it posed risks: being discovered and the advertised, unknown danger. The corridor was dark for a reason—it was not to be entered. A deterrent for most, it only seemed to arouse their adrenaline urges. Proceeding into the dark, unknown would whet their appetite for more surreptitious outings. It was the first of many spooky getaways for the two, fourth graders. Side by side, they cautiously wandered down the path of secret obscurity to retrieve their ball.

They only heard, but could not see, their soccer ball bounce and roll down the darkened tunnel before finally coming to rest. As they crept down the eerie passageway, the fading light emanating from fifty yards behind them yielded a faint shadow of a small animal moving across their path.

"Did you see that?" whispered Rex.

"There's a cat down here!" Octavio exclaimed.

"I thought we weren't allowed to bring pets."

"Someone must have snuck 'em in."

"Wonder if he's hungry? I've still got some of my sandwich."

The boys' eyes were adjusting to the dimly lit corridor as they explored the area looking for the assumed cat and for their soccer ball. Rex pulled the plastic bag containing a mashed, half-eaten, peanut butter and jelly sandwich from his front pocket and tore off a corner. Placing it near the tunnel wall where they last saw the animal, he said, "Here, kitty. Here kitty, kitty."

Octavio blurted, "There's our ball, over there!"

Rex and Octavio quietly continued down the corridor to where they saw an outline of a ball. It had come to rest against the support beam at the entrance to the alcove. Shuffling toward the ball, Rex then bent over to pick it up, noting the stenciled lettering on the heavy metal alcove door, "STORAGE, Home Goods, Clothing, and Shoes."

"Wonder why they have clothes and shoes down here?" he said, testing the door handle. "Locked."

"We better get back before they find us," Octavio cautioned.

"Okay."

Walking back up the tunnel toward the light, Rex looked for the sandwich piece he'd placed along the path.

"It's gone, it's gone!" he exclaimed. "The cat ate my sandwich."

"See if he wants more. See if he'll come up to us," encouraged Octavio.

The boys knelt on the concrete floor and Rex tore off a larger portion of his sandwich. Holding a piece and extending his hand, he called out again for the cat.

"He's not used to people," said Octavio. "Put it on the ground and see if he'll come out to eat it."

Rex threw the offering in front of where they were, and the two boys sat down to quietly watch and wait. Whispering to each other, they patiently speculated on the animal's appearance. Six or seven minutes went by. Finally, Rex stood and declared, "I gotta pee."

"Go over there; I'll wait to see if he comes out. Here kitty, kitty."

Returning, Rex sat next to his friend and continued the cat-bait lookout. Minutes later, there was movement from the other side of the tunnel. They waited, shushed each other, and watched. More movement. Wide eyes strained and focused on the dimly lit corridor where the small animal inched, oh so cautiously, forward. Closer, and closer it crept. Then snatching it's dinner, it vanished.

"Did you see that!?"

"Yah, that's no kitty."

"It was a rat! I'm sure it was a rat," Octavio delicately shrieked.

"Shh…. see if we can get him to come back," admonished Rex as he threw the remainder of his sandwich out before them. The two adventurers silently waited for their hungry friend to return, when a thundering motor kicked on for the Sanctuary ventilation system. It was a horrendous racket to the unsuspecting, pet-seeking adventurers, and caused Octavio to trickle a leak in his briefs.

"Let's get outta here!"

They both jumped and ran toward the lighted end of the tunnel, back toward the Sanctuary. They covered the distance in record time. Breathless and sweaty, the two pulled up short of the town square and began walking. It had been an exciting day but, they agreed, one that should remain confidential.

Rex remembered two football players on television doing a touchdown celebration with a handshake routine. A successful venture like the one they'd just had deserved a similar celebration. He introduced his version to a grinning Octavio. A top and bottom fist bump and a finger point would seal their experience and understanding of confidentiality.

Entering the front door of his home, Rex was exhilarated returning the friendly greeting from mom. Randall picked up on the enthusiasm, turned from watching the YM daily news on the panel TV, and asked how the day went.

"Octavio and I had a lot of fun today kicking the soccer ball."

"You guys should be very good at it. Where's your soccer ball?"

His father's innocent question caught Rex entirely off guard. He realized that in their haste to leave the tunnel, they left the soccer ball near the picnic area of their new rodent friend. Not wanting to lie to his father, but also not breaking his pledge to Octavio, the youngster said: "I left it outside, Dad."

Just then, Mom called to the back bedroom area, "Madison, your mother called; it's time to go home, dear."

Samantha escorted her friend down the hallway. Seeing her classmate, Rex in the front room near Mr. Meredith, the pony-tailed youngster smiled and said, "hi." Red-faced and nervous, Rex returned the greeting and then retreated to his bedroom.

"Get cleaned up, kids. We're eating at the Grotto tonight," said Mom.

Like many Saturday nights in a small town, the plaza was filled with families strolling along the (artificial) tree-lined (synthetic turf) park. The reflective lights on the ceiling dimmed, causing the streetlamps to flicker on. Rex and Sam were five paces ahead of their parents and heading toward the restaurant alcove housing the Grotto. By coincidence, Octavio and his family were also enjoying an evening out, ambling in a similar direction.

"Octavio! Where you going?"

Hearing his friend's voice, Octavio broke from his stepparent's company and raced over to see Rex. The two of them astonished both sets of adults and Samantha with their greeting ritual of the fist bump-finger pointing routine.

"Good evening, young man," Randall said to Octavio.

"Hi, Mr. Meredith," he acknowledged, looking directly at Rex's dad.

Rafael Ochoa and his wife, Carmen, reflexively followed Octavio toward the Meredith family. It was a rare but cordial meeting of the adults from opposite sides of the Sanctuary. Randall had had occasion to meet Rafael over maintenance issues, but the wives had never met. They acknowledged that their boys were best friends, but the Ochoas recognized that the Merediths had surrendered considerable wealth to reside in Yucca Mountain, while they were merely the hired help.

"Evening, Rafael, out for a walk tonight?"

"Good evening, Mr. Meredith. Yes, we're going to Pizza Hut."

"Our boys seem to have bonded," Randall said with a smile.

"Yes, they have. They're like two peas in a pod."

"Rafael, I'd like you to meet my wife. This is Eve."

"Evening, ma'am. Nice to meet you. This is my wife, Carmen."

Mrs. Meredith courteously extended to shake the gentleman's hand and to eliminate any perception of societal barrier. Then nodding, she reached and shook his wife's hand.

"And, this is our daughter, Samantha," Randall offered, pointing.

The Ochoas smiled and nodded in the direction of Samantha, who was gathered with her brother and Octavio. Pleasantries were exchanged about their boys' friendship, school, soccer, and evening walking exercise. A genuine warmth was garnered from the occasion as they parted for their respective dinner locations.

The Grotto was almost filled to capacity and thankfully, the Merediths reserved table was ready. Several of the patrons offered their greetings as the family weaved their way to be seated. Eve noted of the irony of enjoying a white table clothed dining experience while in an underground bunker.

Across the plaza, the Ochoas were comfortably seated waiting for their pizza and discussing the unusually pleasant encounter with privilege, like the Merediths. Octavio joined the conversation offering his opinion—that Mrs. Meredith was "really nice" and often helped them with homework after school.

In the Community Center the next day, Silvia Ricco led the Merediths and a handful of other religious patrons in a Christian-oriented service. Mrs. Ricco, the only person who responded to the appeal for volunteers, was a perfect match for the assignment, having majored in Religious Studies at the University of Notre Dame before marrying Salvatore Ricco, the multi-millionaire industrialist. The digital app featured the biblical references as well as the chosen hymns for the high-tech chapel service.

After church and after Sunday dinner, Rex buzzed his buddy on the closed-circuit monitor. Without mentioning where, they agreed to go exploring again. They would meet in the plaza in fifteen minutes. Octavio would bring the sandwich this time ("wink-wink").

Sometimes their explorations prompted a learning experience, sometimes it was just an outing for friendship and exercise. Today, it would be a mission to find and retrieve their soccer ball, and to cultivate a potential pet.

Their outings often provoked question-and-answer periods at the dinner table like: Why did some of the tunnels have a locked gate and No Entry signs? How did they dig tunnels this big? or Where does the water come from? The adventures became an excellent learning experience for the inquisitive boys. The parents were often stumped by their queries. It was also a bonding experience that the boys would share with few others.

In school one day, when Ms. Duncan asked Rex and Octavio to help with Marco Tillerman, they agreed without hesitation. Marco suffered from Autism Spectrum Disorder, ASD. The nine-year-old had the outward appearance of a healthy fourth grader but the social and communication skills of a toddler. It was a challenge the boys would honor as if their life depended upon it. And, in fact, it would.

With Marco in tow, the after school journeys became slower, more inhibited. He was easily distracted and unresponsive to the boys' prodding to catch up. Their patience was often tested, but their empathy for a kid with a disability grew. The Merediths and Ochoas were proud of their boys' commitment.

In the classroom, Marco was often out of sorts. His two advocates understood and were there for him, like the time with Ricky Abram. Ricky had troubles of his own; self-inflicted. Teachers agreed that he was a challenge from day one. Caught in the act of stealing Gloria's notebook, the boy vehemently denied it. Pushing Stevie into the bathroom urinal was an accident, he declared. But pointing and laughing at one of Marco's incidents prompted a response.

Rex got out of his desk chair and grabbed Ricky by the shirt collar. A pushing and shoving dispute erupted with Ricky ending up on the floor. Ms. Duncan intervened. Seated in opposite corners of the room, the boys glared at each other for the rest of the day. Any chance for Ricky joining the "exploration hike" trio was unlikely.

That night over dinner, Rex admitted to his scuffle with Ricky.

"I heard about it," responded Dad. "Do you want to tell me the details?"

"It was really nothing. Ricky was just teasing Marco, but Marco didn't know it."

"'Nice of you to stick up for Marco. But fighting solves nothing, son."

"I know, Dad."

Ball-kicking exploration hikes continued, sometimes with Marco; sometimes without. It was always an eye-opening experience, especially in the forbidden areas of Yucca Mountain. The boys discovered large, air-lock chamber doors; food storage lockers; medical supply chambers; clothing storage alcoves; a wine cellar; and even a spring-fed water reservoir (with filtration pumps). The rat they befriended looked for his lunch each outing. They named him Mickey.

It took many attempts to get Marco comfortable. On some outings he seemed more cooperative than others, so the three explorers made their way a little deeper into a corridor than at other times. After each outing the boys swore their secrecy with their contrived fist-pump ritual while walking home. Marco would struggle with the routine.

For these boys, Yucca Mountain life was never boring. It was an adventure every day—a rose on a thorny bush.

CHAPTER XXI
RESENTMENT, REBELLION, AND RAMPAGE

RESIDENTS WERE UNEASY. THE LOW TIRE ON THE GOLF CART STARTED the rumors. It hadn't been moved in over a month. From the parking space below his residence and the Command Center, Globitz used to begin his daily routine of touring the complex.

Then, at the community meeting, it was Krishka, not Globitz, who descended the staircase to address the assembled group of concerned residents and staff. Wearing a tight-fitting yellow jumpsuit with the YM logo on the left breast pocket, the statuesque redhead confidently walked to the microphone.

"My husband is a little under the weather," she politely said in her noticeable Russian accent. "He has asked me to thank you for your understanding and knows you will appreciate this month's briefing by Mr. Lowe."

"Thank you, Mrs. Globitz. Before we start, I'd like to acknowledge the wonderful response from the volunteers among you. You accepted the challenge and have added greatly to the staff's efforts in making our stay here as good as it could possibly be. Thank you."

Polite applause.

Then sighing as he read from the briefing sheet, the formerly energetic master of ceremonies revealed the painful truth of the situation:

"We are still underwater. It has not receded by any measurable amount. The likelihood of that happening has now been ruled out. What this means is that the air-tight entrance gate that we all came through cannot be opened. We would all drown."

Screams, shrieks, and shouts erupted from the seats immediately in front of the messenger.

"Please! Please. I hear you. I know exactly how you feel. We all feel it. You, me, the staff, Dr. and Mrs. Globitz. We'd all like to leave this place."

An angry voice from the seated audience shouted: "Then how do we get outta here? This was only supposed to be a TEMPORARY REFUGE until the danger passed."

"That's exactly right," Lowe forcefully responded. "But the danger hasn't passed. Our limited assessment is that the earthquakes and volcanoes around us have formed a deep lake, putting our bunker complex a thousand feet under water and ice."

More shrieks and cries.

"We have three activities we're working on to safely return to the surface. One involves drilling an escape tunnel. The other involves an escape capsule—a mini submarine, if you will. The third and probably the most hopeful is the resurrection of our communication systems with the outside, in hopes of being rescued."

"But what will we exit to, if it is still considered too dangerous?" yelled another angry resident.

"Thanks for asking that question, Mr. Deuel. We think the

situation at the Earth's surface is still not safe. World-wide fires produced a massive cloud that covers the planet. So, the sun cannot penetrate to warm it up. Freezing temperatures and resettlement of the Earth's surface may have destroyed any friendly habitat."

Lowe continued, "It's a waiting game, and in the meantime, we're working on our three options."

On Lowe's cue, Rafael Ochoa stepped up to the platform and the mike. "Most of you know Rafael Ochoa, the facilities engineer of our complex. He's going to provide a little more detail to what I have just outlined."

Ochoa provided the perfect exodus for Lowe. His calm, authoritative demeaner added credibility and hope to the dreadful briefing they had just received. Tall and firm statured with a sincere delivery, Rafael's well-chosen words and slight Castilian Spanish accent conveyed superbly.

"We have a very serious situation here with no easy solution," he said, looking directly into the eyes of his audience. "But we have a three-pronged attack that, God willing, may remedy the problem by the time it is safe to exit Yucca Mountain.

"There is an abandoned tunnel auger deep in one of the shafts of this complex that my crew is working to make operational. We've had to manufacture some broken parts and refurbish the auger heads, but we're optimistic that it will eventually work as one of our options."

"The escape capsule that Coach Lowe mentioned was left by the government when it owned Yucca Mountain. It's only a two-man vessel and would have to be reinforced considerably to withstand the water pressure at our depth. Launching it from a porthole without flooding the Sanctuary is the biggest problem for this option. And, of course, the two-man capacity issue...the idea being that the two passengers could exit and get help.

"The third, and probably the most hopeful, involves repairing our outside communication capability. As you know, the Sanctuary survived, but all of our external communication systems, our weather-measuring instruments, our camera drones, and our antennas were all destroyed. We are attempting to remotely connect the mechanical arm located outside the Observation Chamber to help us establish an antenna for our communication setup. Once our antenna is operational, we'll be able to broadcast an SOS signal for help."

At this point Neil Acosta stood up and yelled to all the residents and staff surrounding him. Waving his arms, displaying a furrowed brow, and an angry look, he proclaimed, "We've been sold a bill of goods and abandoned in this hell hole."

Clifton Porter stood and shouted, "And they told us we'll be the safest survivors on earth. Now we're all doomed, left to die, in this expensive tomb."

"Gentlemen, gentlemen," Ochoa tried to interrupt.

"Gentlemen, my ass, Ochoa. Where's your boss? We need answers from Globitz!" belted out Acosta.

It was like the end-zone seats at a Super Bowl upset. Everyone was on their feet, screaming and hollering, thinking they could influence an outcome. Boiling-over frustration had surpassed all reason and self-control. The billionaire elites within Yucca Mountain had seemingly snapped, devolving into overindulged toddlers deprived of ice cream.

Only two security guards stood between the seething residents and the platform holding Rafael Ochoa and the stairwell leading to Globitz' residence. From the front row, Krishka coldly witnessed the childish emotions on display by the weak Американский (Americans).

The residents were not buying Rafael's plan. Any thoughts of pacifying their anger or of convincing them to be patient collapsed. Their state of agitation turned to rage. Ochoa imagined the crowd turning on him. Sensing the threat, Sergeant O and Sergeant B jumped on the platform near Ochoa and drew their weapons of choice: a night stick for O; nun chucks for B. Pondering the idea of beating a mob of billionaire geeks one wave at a time, the two veterans exposed their weapons and assumed a ready-for-action position.

Just then, the ghastly, ear-splitting woop-woop siren reverberated throughout the entire sanctuary. The screaming stopped as the puzzled residents contemplated another earthquake. Before they had time to think, the lights went out. The bunker complex was totally black. Panic froze everyone in place.

Absent the usual ceiling and streetlamp illumination, the central plaza diminished to a dark, hollow cave. Subtle lighting gradually flickered on from the pathway landscape lights leading to the residential corridors, encouraging the dwellers to return to their quarters. The mastermind staff member at the controls of the electrical panel intended to quash a riot. It worked.

The village square vacated in a matter of minutes. Nobody lingered. Hustling back to their quarters, all residents felt more secure there than they did challenging Globitz and his staff—for now.

The stress of two plus years underground was taking its toll. The klieg lights of anxiety exposed each resident's temperament and character flaws. First in the home. Slight irritations mushroomed into domestic clashes, clashes into hostilities, hostilities into violence. Dr. Jammicit and Nurse Higgins became the first ones to perceive a rate of domestic incidence significantly greater than societal norms. Under disguise or late hours, embarrassed victims would request treatment and confidentiality.

Eventually, Sergeant O and Sergeant M, became the reluctant referees called in by neighbors, or sadly, by the kids. Both veterans were not expecting security duties to include domestic arbitration. Despite the necessity of their interventions, their friendly image and popularity was waning. They also understood that, for every incident they responded to, there were two or three others that went unassisted; unreported. Their assessment was alarming. Repressed anger and rage within the homes would be the tributary stream that feeds the flash flood of outrage on the village square.

The youth of Yucca Mountain, however, adapted to living conditions more easily than their parents. They experienced an assortment of activities that kept them busy from breakfast until lights out, while their parents dealt with the pesky thorns on the bushes. And yet it wasn't all rainbows, butterflies, and unicorns.

Parental stress eventually worked its way into the classroom. All three teachers and their volunteer aids admitted to an increase in acts of aggression and manifestation of disrespect, rudeness, and contempt for authority. Not just Neil Acosta's son, but other students were acting up. Keeping a lid on things in the classroom became a major problem for the teachers and their aids.

ELEVEN O'CLOCK PM AT RESIDENCE #17

The sofa and all the chairs were filled, and some people had to sit on the floor of the front room at Neil Acosta's. The late-night meeting was a secretive gathering of subversives and disgruntled residents.

"Two nights ago, we heard Globitz' lackeys tell us our situation is hopeless," Acosta began. "It's hopeless for us, probably, but not for Globitz."

George Herman interrupted, "Why not for Globitz?"

"George, have you seen Globitz lately? I think he's gone. He made his exit, leaving us down here to die."

"He's just sick, Neil. His wife was there at our meeting two nights ago."

"If that's even his wife. She's actually a Russian spy."

"I know, we've talked about that. But she's down here with us too. If Globitz got out of here, what's in it for her?" Herman asked.

Jack Abrams expanded the theory, saying, "The Russians don't care. They have little regard for their people. They assigned her down here to watch Globitz, and Globitz double-crossed her and left."

Acosta's convincing assessment backed up by Abrams swayed many of the twelve attendees. Their mood was gradually shifting into a frenzy. The anger of being duped, of being trapped underground with little prospect for escape, and the issue of the golf cart's inactivity was starting to make sense.

They agreed to a plan: verify Globitz' status, get the code for the entrance gate, open it, and exit. It sounded simple to the rich, successful, and duped patrons attending Acosta's meeting.

In their riled-up state, Abrams suggested they pay a surprise visit to Globitz' residence. They could verify his presence and/or retrieve the code to open the entrance gate. "If several of us did it now, while he's in bed, he'd offer little resistance."

Acosta and five others emphatically agreed. The rest quietly grimaced and acquiesced. It was decided that seven of the twelve would force their way into Globitz' apartment that night while the rest would return home and wait for the signal for the next part of the plan. The mutiny had begun.

Walking across the plaza toward Globitz' residence, the band of rebels saw the virtual moon against the darkened trompe l'oeil ceiling—a curious backdrop for their covert invasion. Only a routine security round by one of the sergeants would alter their course. No worries. Single file, up the staircase the commandos crept. The joint Command Center and main residence doors were locked. Knocking would arouse the inhabitants but would at least provide entrance—if opened.

"Who is it?" asked Krishka from behind the door.

"It's Neil Acosta, ma'am, I'm concerned for your well-being."

The door opened a crack revealing Krishka's cautionary peek, which allowed Acosta and the intruders to force their entry. The pajama-clad Olympian screamed and was pushed to the sofa by two of the seven, who now stood over her. From a sitting position, she launched a perfectly placed groin kick into one of her captors and leaped to her feet. Grabbing the arm of the second assailant and twisting it behind his back, she forced him to the floor writhing in pain. With two of her seven attackers dispatched, she encountered a group tackle by the others, knocking her against the dining room table and under a pile of inexperienced, billionaire combatants.

"Hold her down—I'll check the bedroom for Globitz!" yelled Acosta.

The weight of four men was too much for the angry redhead to overcome. Their encounter with the screaming wildcat was not expected—they held on tightly.

"What do you want?!" she screamed. "What's the meaning of this?"

"Settle down, Krishka, we want to talk to your husband," said one of the men.

"He's not here! His bed has not been slept in," exclaimed Acosta, returning from the bedroom.

Grabbing a handful of red hair and pulling Krishka's head back, Jack Abrams yelled into her ear, "Where's Globitz?!!"

The struggling Russian hissed and spit through her guards' grip, saying, "He's not here, you stupid..."

The absence of her husband confirmed one of their theories—Globitz had escaped. Bolstering Acosta's argument that they'd been double-crossed, it was now more important than ever to obtain the code to the tunnel entrance gate. It was obvious, the danger of opening it was a hoax.

"Where does he keep the code for the entry gate?" asked Abram.

Straining the buttoned front of her pajama top, the heavy-breathing wife of Dr. Globitz shook her head and attempted to answer, "I don't know."

"Let her go," said Acosta. "She's been duped, like the rest of us."

Krishka stood up, adjusted her pajamas, and confronted the men in her living room. One of the men offered her the robe he found on her bed. She explained that she didn't know where "any code" was and that opening the front gate would be unwise. "That would drown everybody down here."

Perplexed by her response, the rebels looked at each other for answers. Was she hiding something? Covering for her husband? Willing to take a fall for him? For Russia?

"How did your husband escape from Yucca Mountain?" asked Abrams.

"He's not really my husband. And I don't know if he did escape, or how," she admitted.

"When was the last time you saw him?" asked Acosta.

"He went for a walk around the complex three weeks ago and I hope he never comes back."

Complete shock registered on the faces of the group. If Krishka hated Globitz, as she implied, and wasn't his wife, then what was she doing here?

"He was my sponsor, my 'sugar daddy' as you Americans like to call it. He helped me get a green card."

Her confession sounded sincere, but could she really be trusted? Left unanswered was the whereabouts of Globitz. And why hadn't she told anyone?

Silent until now, Bill Radford calmly spoke to her and everyone, "We're in a bind, Krishka. Please help us. We have reason to believe that we're locked in down here and your husband, ah—Mr. Globitz, has escaped, leaving us all to die."

Radford paused to let that soak in. Taking the cue from the rest of his conspirators, Radford continued addressing Krishka in hopes of winning her cooperation.

"You see, we think that Yucca Mountain is a giant hoax. That there was no asteroid, no earthquake, no hazardous environment outside the entrance gate. We need the code to open the gate to all get out of here and go back to our homes, and our lives."

Unlike her American captors whom revered life more than honor, Krishka knew she was facing death anyway and now had useful idiots to join her. Reaching for the cigarettes and lighter on the sofa table, she sighed. Exhaling two streams of smoke from her nostrils, the gutsy infiltrator nodded and smirked.

"There is no code to the gate," she said to the amazed gathering. "It can be opened by depressing the red button and throwing the lever on the wall outside of the Observation Chamber, but... I don't think it is safe to do so."

The humble group of rebels took a minute to comprehend what she had just said. Each weighing her sincerity against his own self-doubt, they had accomplished the first objective of the plan—the combination to open the gate. The revelation that Krishka was captive like they were was comforting, despite her opinion of the danger. Globitz' whereabouts was now, immaterial.

One by one, the group stood to exit, providing a look to Krishka that suggested "Sorry about the mishap, Mrs. Lincoln. Enjoy the rest of the play."

CHAPTER XXII
THE GREAT ESCAPE—IT'S ON

OUTSIDE THE COMMISSARY, THEIR GUILT-RIDDEN EYES MET IN PASSING when one resident secretively muttered the words "It's on. Two am."

The other acknowledged without expression, "Got it." The plan was set in motion. Ten times during that day, the same routine would occur throughout Sanctuary Square, each time with a different conspirator. Pledged secrecy was imperative because of the intensely polarized atmosphere.

The message and the acknowledgment confirmed the time the rebel contingent would meet at the base of the tunnel ramp leading up to the prodigious, thirty-ton gate system; the air-tight door that sealed in life from all calamity.

Not everyone was on board. Only twelve residents were convinced that Acosta and Abrams were right, that Yucca Mountain was an elaborate hoax and that a prolonged and eventual death of its inhabitants was certain—unless they escaped. The heretics were disparaged in all social corners of the Sanctuary for their bizarre speculation. Little was known of their precarious plan. Opening the sealed gate offered a chance of escape, or it could flood the entire complex, drowning everyone. That risk for the three hundred-plus inhabitants of Yucca Mountain lay in the hands of these twelve men.

Two in the morning was a time seldom witnessed by residents. The lamp post lights encircling Sanctuary Square were dim, accentuating the crescent moon on the darkened ceiling. The pleasant daytime background music that flooded the air was silent, yielding to nature sounds of a trickling stream, crickets, owls, and frogs—all compliments of a virtual reality ambiance.

One by one, the twelve men left their residences to witness the tranquil sounds of artificial nature. They walked toward the far end of the plaza, where the ambiance ended. It was the base of the tunnel they had passed through almost three years ago. Only the haunting memory of lights spaced every so often along the walls remained. Tonight, the lights and tunnel shaft were dark. And quiet.

"We got everybody?" whispered Acosta.

"Jones isn't here, yet," one of them responded.

"We'll give him a few more minutes, I'm sure he's coming," Acosta continued." While we're waiting, everyone turn off your flashlights and remain quiet. We don't want to set off any alarms or invite those two security goons to the party."

Without checking his watch, an impatient Acosta said, "It's been five minutes. Fuck Jones. Let's go."

Led by Acosta and Abrams, the eleven-man group stealthily moved up the tunnel ramp in two columns. Confidence in their plan was absolute by the mavericks near the front of the columns. For the men toward the rear, the confidence was more in the mavericks up front than it was in the plan.

They all understood the mission: to open up the tunnel exit. And, they agreed that they all would participate. They expected the lever and gate mechanism to be a simple operation but going as a group would be more convincing if confronted by security. And the congratulatory celebration on breathing fresh air would be its own reward.

Only two flashlights at the head of the columns were illuminated, leaving a shadowed path for the men to follow and not straggle. It would take thirty minutes or longer for the men to reach the top of the ramp. During that time of walking silence, each man's thoughts wandered. The "What if we're wrong?" question loomed in all but the two leaders and the dutiful few immediately behind them.

Echoing footsteps and heavy breathing of men marching up the half-mile incline reminded Abrams of his days in the Marine Corps. It was called "movement to contact," and it always caused think-time anxiety, more than the adrenalin hurricane of actual combat. The slog continued.

"What the…" Acosta said, breaking the silence.

"Everybody, hold up," echoed Abrams, flashing his light on the roadblock of earth-moving equipment.

A deep voice of authority rang out from the dark as the two flashlights hunted for its source. It was Sergeant O, standing atop a Caterpillar dozer horizontally parked along with the excavator blocking the tunnel pathway,

"That's far enough, boys, now turn around and go home."

The flashlights surveyed the roadblock revealing tandem parked earth-moving equipment stretching from one wall to the other of the tunnel. There were men standing behind and around the heavy machinery, to discourage any attempt to breach the blockade. The stairwell leading to the Observation Chamber and the controls for the gate was just beyond the barricade. To get to the staircase, Acosta and his men were going to have to somehow push through the weakest points of the obstacle—the men between the dozer and the left wall of the tunnel.

Not since their childhood days had these billionaire rebels engaged in a physical scuffle. It became obvious that a confrontation tonight would be necessary if they were going to follow through with their plan to open the ominous entrance gate. The eleven insurgents had now reluctantly gathered for a frontal faceoff with the Sanctuary defenders.

"I'm outta here," hissed one of the campaigners, moving to the rear of the group.

Flashlights from both sides lit up the ranks of opposition, panning for neighbors or friends vulnerable to dissuasion.

"Jones, you rat! How could you?" screamed Acosta seeing the defector next to the excavator.

Randall Meredith stepped forward, to reason with his disgruntled neighbors.

"Gentlemen, your frustration living down here is shared by everyone. We all want out of here. But this isn't the way to do it," he said.

"How would you know, Meredith? You obviously bought into the bullshit hoax Globitz sold us!" yelled Jake Mansfield from a shadow within the hostile group.

The nervous and fidgeting pack were now awkwardly engaged in an ideological skirmish. Acosta and Abrams hadn't warned them of this. It was only supposed to be a walk up to the controls, a flip of the switch and a celebration. Everyone would benefit. The non-believers would be praising them as heroes for their courage in undertaking the task.

"Yeah, have you seen him lately? He's gone... He snuck out of here, laughing at our ignorance!" hollered another angry voice from the pack.

"Hold on, just hold on. Dr. Globitz is sick, up in his apartment," argued Meredith.

"He's not sick, he's gone, Randall! We checked it out. Even Krishka hasn't seen him," said Acosta.

"That can't be. There's 300 of us down here, somebody knows where he is."

"Randy, his golf cart has had a flat tire for three weeks. It'd be fixed and he'd be driving it around every day if he were still down here with us," said Jack Abrams.

"Not if he's sick in bed," responded one of the men behind the excavator.

"You guys get out of the way!" said an impatient Acosta. "We're opening the gate."

"You don't know what you're doing, Acosta. You're gonna get us all killed!" shouted another one of the men next to the bulldozer.

Shouting ensued from behind the flashlights of both hostile factions piercing the cave. Back and forth, they yelled insults, some beyond comprehension. It was like a gaggle of geese squawking at each other over a kernel of corn. Witnessing the spectacle and scratching his head, Sergeant M thought, *So this is how rich people do battle.* Just then, a rock whizzed from the agitators through the air, grazing Randall's forehead.

"Ah, bastard!" he shouted, as the flashlight beam revealed blood gushing from his brow.

The dubious civility shifted. Seeing the injury, Sergeant O instinctively jumped down from his perch on the dozer and rushed into the crowd, nightstick flailing. The reluctant, flashlight-wielding warriors impulsively struck back, causing a rattling sound on impact of the flashlight against his head and body. Sergeant M and Henry Henson jumped into the fray to defend their cohort. Nun chucks against flashlights favored the sergeant. Henson's fists against multiple flashlights, however, was a gallant misadventure.

By this time, all of the men were drawn into battle. Except for the two sergeants, the only weapons utilized were fists, boots, and flashlights. The two dozen or so brawlers kicked, punched, and battered, then wrestled each other to the corridor's concrete floor. Nobody noticed that Jones fell backward, hitting his head on the bulldozer blade. Beams of light thrashed about the ceiling and walls between thumps and pops of the flashlight's impact. The lights flashing, the yelling and screaming of grown men fighting was like an accidental detonation of a fireworks stand.

With most of the men engaged, Acosta squeezed through the gap between the dozer and the tunnel wall and clambered up the stairs, unnoticed. Reaching the top, he couldn't help detecting the intense cold emanating from the round hatch door of the Observation Chamber next to the exit gate lever and throw switch. Despite the urgency to complete the mission, his curiosity took over. He spun the hatch locking wheel and pulled it open. The rubber grommet seal made a squeaking sound as the heavy, air-tight chamber unsealed. Pointing his flashlight into the freezing cold compartment as he climbed in, he saw the spherical copula with the thick glass windows he had heard about.

Acosta's mind flashed on the briefings he had disparaged regarding the chamber's obscured view caused by shifting rock and earth against its windows. He thought about the warnings of being underwater and of the global cooling estimates resulting from the thick cloud barrier blocking the sun. *Could they have been right?* he asked himself.

Bending as he moved toward the glass-windowed copula, he found himself shivering and his breathing accompanied by puffy clouds of steam. The flashlight's reflecting glare off the glass prompted Acosta to move closer into the inner surface area of the heavy, reinforced concave dome. Pressing the lens of his light against the large, center glass window, he confirmed—there were indeed large rocks against the exterior surface. Trying again to peer through one of the smaller, trapezoidal windows offered the same result: a blocked view. Only one of the seven smaller windows allowed his light to shine through, giving him a look outside the Yucca Mountain complex.

On his knees and bending down, Acosta craned his neck for a more favorable view. Pressing his flashlight firmly against the ice-cold window, he could see through the thick glass. He strained to focus, looking beyond the safety of his position within the Observation Chamber. The distracting noise of men fighting below the stairwell brought him back to the urgency of his mission. His moment of curiosity had expired.

One more minute, he said to himself. He suddenly realized he had to confirm what he saw. Shock and horror froze him for a moment. The stakes were astronomical, and he was the instigator of this mission. Bumping his head in haste to leave the cramped chamber, he scrambled to the stairwell. Trembling in panic over what he had initiated, he screamed to the men below, still engaged in battle.

"Stop! Stop!" he bellowed. "It's a mistake!"

Nobody heard. The screaming, hollering, and fighting continued. He tried again, holding out his arm to shine the flashlight on himself. "Stop! Stop! "We made a mistake!"

One battling duo after another pulled up from their confrontation to look for the source of the impassioned command. Disengaging was difficult for the committed warriors. No one wanted to be the recipient of the last blow when the whistle blew. The word spread, one by one, "Hold up, stop. There's some kind of mistake." Everyone was skeptically cautious but willing to separate.

Acosta scrambled down the stairs to the scene of the mêlée. Climbing on top of the earth moving equipment's cab, he stretched out his flashlight arm, shining the light directly at himself so that everyone could see. And he again, commanded everyone to stop fighting. The whirling flashlights, now motionless, began to converge on the man behind the familiar voice standing atop the excavator.

Neil Acosta was in full view, highlighted by the few, still-working flashlights in the shaky hands of the embattled men. His voice quivered as he steadied himself against the equipment operator's cage.

"We have to stop fighting each other," he pleaded. "We made a mistake." Tears rolling down his cheeks glistened from the beams of light trained on his face. Shaking and openly sobbing, the distraught rebel leader announced, "Globitz was right. It's unsafe to open the gate. We are under water."

The fighters stopped in place. Some were still on their knees writhing in pain, others were standing, clutching their injuries. With adrenalin still raging and the sound of heavy breathing filling the cool air, they listened to Acosta's concession. Ghastly agony and despair skewered every man's core.

Both sides had fought gallantly for a worthy cause; one defending the safety of Yucca Mountain's inhabitants, the other for their escape and freedom. The conspiracy hoax was the catalyst, and now it was exposed.

"I would like everyone here to walk up those steps and see for yourself," Acosta continued through his sobs. "Look through the windows. Understand what we are facing. We're not getting out of here this way."

Tending to their wounds and injuries, the men congregated behind the dozer. One by one they climbed the Observation Chamber stairs to look through the copula windows. Returning with the reality of their situation, some openly sobbed. Others provided a more stoic veneer, but deep down they were quaking. Murmuring among them centered around a version of what they saw—it was cold, it was obscured by rocks, and they were underwater.

When the last man down the stairwell joined the group, they all got to their feet for the walk back to the Sanctuary. Flashlights pointing downward kept their faces obscured, yet all knew friend from foe. Randall Meredith moved to their midst. Pointing his flashlight toward himself, his voice quaked as he spoke: "Hold up a minute, guys. I gotta say something."

The murmuring stopped. A few flashlights pointed toward Meredith's voice.

Slowly pointing his light toward each man in the group, he continued, "What happened here tonight must never happen again. Look at what we did to each other."

His light shown on each of the two dozen men, some with blood still gushing from their noses, some with swollen eyes and cheeks. A couple were cradling an injured arm, shirts were torn and spattered with blood, trousers ripped, and fewer than half had an undamaged flashlight that worked.

"Does anybody need tending to by Dr. Jammicit?"

"I do," said Gordon Ashcroft. "I think my arm is broken."

"I can't see out of my eye," said another.

"I might need some stitches," said another.

Meredith continued, "I'll get him to open the clinic when we get back to the Sanctuary."

"Now, I recommend we put tonight's event behind us. Our families, especially our kids, deserve to know there are better ways to resolve our differences."

The few working flashlights had minimal relevance in the path down the pitch-black tunnel shaft. The men's silence surrendered only to the echo of their footsteps and an occasional sob and sniffle. Their devastated morale played the dirge in their vacuous minds.

It was 4 am when the battered, tired, and weary men reached the base of the ramp, entering a dimmed Sanctuary Square. Just before scattering to return to their residences or to the clinic, Meredith asked, "Where's Nathan Jones?"

CHAPTER XXIV
POSTMORTEM

THREE MONTHS LATER

THE REGULAR SATURDAY MORNING AEROBICS CLASS GATHERED AT THE NORTH end of the Sanctuary Square. Its popularity had waned slightly after the death of Nathan Jones, in consideration for one of its most enthusiastic participants, his wife, Lisa. Today, however, the power amplifier, mixer, and four corner speakers reestablished the lively, energetic atmosphere for the group, which was warmly welcomed throughout the Square. Lisa pensively participated, encouraged by everyone there.

All day on Saturday, the area was filled with activity. With the aerobics platform dismantled, the pilates class took over. Many of the aerobics participants stayed for a double workout. Then it turned into a pickleball court. Lively rounds of two-on-two paddled a wiffle ball over the net for games of eleven points, with stacks of new players watching and waiting their turn.

It was also back to normal for the rest of Yucca Mountain residents, including Randall and Max Schwab's four-hour virtual golf outing. Other resident activities consumed the Saturday, almost eliminating concern and boredom. Almost.

Rex and Octavio were warned not to be gone all day; that the special event required them to be home, cleaned up for dinner, and seated with their family for the concert. Both agreed, especially since Marco would be with them.

With soccer ball under arm, Rex led his buddy and Marco toward the familiar "NO ENTRANCE" tunnel of the Yucca Mountain complex. His guardian hosts had breached the entrance many times, but this would be a first for Marco. Plopping the ball down, he swiftly kicked it toward Octavio; Octavio to Marco. Marco fumbled and the boys sportingly chased it down the lighted corridor. It would be a fun day for two of the boys but foreboding for their autistic-impaired companion.

Nearing the woven-wire fence, Marco was starting to fidget and screech. His inability to speak led to his friends to speculate on his discomfort. The fence? The darkness beyond the fence? The distance from his home? Both Rex and Octavio prided themselves, on their ability to calm Marco. This too they turned into competition. Venturing down the dark tunnel with Marco would be the true test.

"What is it, Marco?" Octavio appealed, as he picked up the ball and walked toward his friend.

Marco no longer looked at the ball nor at his friends. He was rocking back and forth looking through the fence, making a faint squealing noise. With the gentleness of a medical intern, Rex approached his buddy and grasped his hand.

"Hey Marco, don't worry."

A squeal diminished to a squeak as a result of hearing Rex's soothing voice. Their clasped hands held tightly as he continued to talk.

"Do you want to go with us to our secret clubhouse?" Rex asked with a smile.

The squeaking stopped and Marco's grip loosened. His attention was appearing to shift to Octavio, then to Rex, and back to the darkened tunnel. The boys interpreted Marco's behavior as positive. Octavio picked up the soccer ball and walked toward the unlocked gate. Rex pointed his flashlight down their path, and all three gingerly proceeded.

Reaching the area where their friendly rodent sometimes appeared, Rex and Octavio knelt and waited. Marco respectfully cooperated. It was eerily dark except for the parabolic brightness directly in front of the grounded flashlight.

Reaching into his pocket, Rex pulled out his snack bag with a peanut butter and Ritz cracker sandwich. Placing a portion of it on the concrete path, he asked, "How do you call a rat, Tavo?"

"How would I know? Try whistling."

The three intently waited, while Rex whistled and adjusted the cracker sandwich.

Marco began to squeal.

"There he is! Marco spotted him. Let's all be quiet," Octavio whispered, gesturing a shhh with his finger to his lips.

All three boys sat in suspense as they strained to see the dark image of their long-tailed, four-footed friend. The rodent moved in spurts, stopping to ensure safety. Then, then, after snatching the cracker, it disappeared. Marco squealed in delight. The boys laughed and rose to their feet. Grabbing the ball and the flashlight, they turned to continue their journey.

"Come on, Marco. Wanna see our igloo hide-away?"

Without incident, the boys wandered deep into the darkened tunnel, carefully following the oval glimmer moving along their path. Marco nervously held on to Rex's sleeve but remained quiet.

"We should be close by now, Rex, shine the light over there."

Barely within the reach of the beam of light lay the alcove marked OSSUARY. The glass-windowed igloo and the MAINTENANCE alcove were directly across the corridor. Rex intuitively aimed the light in the direction of their intended rendezvous. Marco squealed.

The boys moved in concert with the flash-lighted approach toward their hide-away. Marco seemed mystified by the light reflecting back from the glass windows as Rex aimed his beam toward their objective.

"The opening's on this side, guys," advised Octavio. "Over here."

Rex and Marco watched Octavio climb through the opening and disappear into the strange glass and metal structure. Rex shined the light through one of the glass windows, allowing Octavio to temporarily look around. From inside the dome-shaped copula, he called out, "All clear." Knowing that encouragement was probably necessary, he added, "Come on in, Marco,"

Pointing the flashlight into the aperture, Rex reinforced Octavio's invite, lighting the way for Marco. Both were surprised by his eagerness to wriggle through the opening. Rex followed. Inside, they laughed and bantered about their secret hiding from the rest of Yucca Mountain inhabitants.

Sitting with their backs against opposing walls, legs in a "v," and flashlight on the floor, they passed the soccer ball back and forth. To the boys' delight, Marco squeaked and laughed at the unique experience. If the day had ended there, it would have been perfect. But it didn't.

The tunnel lights suddenly went on. Then, the sound of music approaching.

"Quick, Rex, turn off the flashlight. The workers are coming."

Holding his finger to his lips he said, "If we're quiet and they don't see our light, they'll never know we're here."

Marco's eyes opened wide at the boys' concern, yet he remained silent. The gravity of the situation was somehow understood. The flashlight went dark. Lighting outside the cupola reflected off the glass, obscuring any gaze inside by the men in the golf cart. The boys were safely hidden, for now.

The music got louder as the flatbed golf cart pulled up and parked near the boys' hideaway. Two workers stepped out of the cart and walked directly toward the structure with the boys inside. They stood outside the cupola contemplating something, while the boys were fear-frozen inside. Talking to each other, it became obvious the workers had not spotted the boys, now huddling inside the glass-windowed dome.

"Hay seis ventanas. Sólo necesitamos uno," said one of the men.

"Necesitaremos algunas herramientas para eliminar una de ellas," responded the other.

"Y, el oxi acetilénica antorcha."

The men turned and walked toward the maintenance alcove entrance. Once they had entered and were out of sight, the boys exhaled in relief. Marco was surprisingly unmoved.

"What did they say, Tavo?"

"I dunno? Something about a window. We gotta get outta here before they come back!"

"Quick, Marco! Follow me."

Rex pulled on Marco's hand as he climbed out of the cupola. Marco followed, then Octavio. The music emminating from the golf cart helped to mask the sound of the boys' sprint across to the other side of the tunnel. They entered the darkened Ossuary. Peeking back toward their secret hide-away next to the maintenance alcove, they watched and wondered what the workers were up to.

The men returned to the cupola pulling a wagon filled with tools. Studying their project, they walked completely around it. One retrieved a stepping stool. Placing it next to the structure, he climed up and peered into the hole where the round window was supposed to be.

"Manny, la ventana superior y una de las ventanas laterales faltan!"

"Vamos a decirle al jefe, a que hora volvamos", responded his partner.

The two men busily set about working on one of the side windows. The music played on. Talking as they worked, they were unaware of the three stowaways less than fifty feet across the way, watching them.

"Let's take off before they see us," said Octavio.

"Yeah. Let's go," said Rex. "Hey, where's Marco!?"

"I thought you were watching him," challenged Octavio.

"He was right here, I didn't see him leave."

"Flash your light around this cave; I'll tell you if the workers notice."

Rex turned and pointed his flashlight around the darkened cavern in hopes of seeing their friend. Nothing. Alarmed, he walked deeper into the cave carefully calling out "Marco." No response. Flashing his light down deeper into the shaft, he thought Marco may have climbed behind the machinery they had previously labeled the "hole driller." The curious piece of equipment would attract the attention of almost anyone, including Marco. It had a strange auger system on a boom in front, with protruding black hoses that found their way to what must have been a pump of some sort near the engine, all mounted on two steel tracks.

Rex walked behind the strange-looking "hole driller" calling out for Marco. Kneeling down at the hole driller's front, he directed his light and peered under its belly, between its tracks. No Marco.

Dismissing any thoughts of losing his friend in the forbidden areas of Yucca Mountain, Rex swallowed and continued shining his light around the cave. Except for the hole-drilling machine, a mound of rock near its auger, and a pallet of bags marked "mortar," the entire alcove tunnel appeared empty.

Walking back toward the mouth of the cave, Rex was now flashing his light back and forth along the floor and walls. The numerous tubular holes along the walls cast moving circular shadows as he proceeded. Octavio turned to watch his best friend find his way back to the entrance empty-handed.

"Where's Marco?" he asked.

"I've looked everywhere. I couldn't find him, Tavo."

"He didn't walk out of here or I would have seen him. Flash your light in one of those hollow holes."

Rex walked closer to where the hollow cylendrical holes rows started and flashed his light on the first one, then the second.

"Tavo, two of these holes have been closed up, it looks rocks and cement."

"Forget those two, look into the others," Octavio instructed.

One by one, Rex pointed his flashlight into the tube-shaped holes, alternating from the closest to the floor to the one above. Three feet in diameter and ten feet deep, the hollow chambers would be a perfect place for a game of hide and seek. Rex worked his way up and down shining his light in each hole; deeper and deeper toward the "hole driller." Octavio split his attention between Rex's progress and the men working on the igloo across the corridor.

Frustrated by having reached the end of one side of the cave without success, Rex moved to the other and continued. The number of holes tested his patience, but the responsibility of looking after Marco was a strong motivation.

Rex heard a familiar squeal coming from one of the holes he was about to illuminate. The tension in his neck and shoulders was instantly relieved. Shining the light directly into the suspect hole, he found their hiding friend, mischieviously grinning ear-to-ear.

"I found him!" he yelled softly toward the cave's opening.

"Great, now let's get outta here before it's too late."

The lighted tunnel made for easy running by the three boys. Beyond the sight of the workers at their hideaway, they stopped running and began to walk. As promised, they would make it back to their homes in time to clean up, have dinner, and join their families for the concert. They wasted little time trying to teach Marco their secret fist pump. Octavio left for his side of the Sanctuary. Rex walked Marco back to Residence #27, then headed home. It had been another exciting outing, especially for Marco.

The evening's entertainment by resident country music artist

Lily Ashton was another of a series of her performances intended to elevate spirits. It would be the evening's highlight after the scheduled staff briefing and a talk by Randall Meredith. The first rows of the folding seats in front of the stage would be filled early by the eager residents; the rest by residents and staff immediately after their dinner. It was expected to be a delightful evening.

The four Merediths dutifully sat in the front row seats, while master of ceremonies Coach Lowe set the stage for the evening's program. But first was a brief update on the state of affairs by Randall Meredith.

The assumed leader stepped forward to inspire hope, yet his discussion on the physical and practical constraints of an immediate rescue from the Sanctuary were met without celebration. Explaining the disappearance of Dr. Globitz was more troubling. It was "highly unlikely he found a way out of here, alive," Randall said. Globitz, "had suffered severe depression." It's more probable, Randall explained, that he "retreated to the back catacombs of Yucca Mountain and ended his life."

Globitz' disappearance, the death of Nathan Jones, and the bleak outlook for a possible rescue would have been a difficult climate even for a speaker with the power of Dr. Martin Luther King Jr. to transcend. For a computer geek from Santa Barbara, it was dreadful. Randall's brutal honesty nullified the advertised uplifting evening's entertainment.

In an emotional appeal, he encouraged everyone to dig deep into his soul to find the reason God had spared them from extinction, a purpose for their survival. Then, quoting best-selling author Rick Warren, he said, "The greatest tragedy is not death, but life without purpose. Your purpose becomes the standard you use to evaluate which activities are essential and which aren't."

Then he reiterated, "It is essential that we all survive. Let's make that our purpose."

His words of encouragement required a few seconds to soak

in before mild applause could be heard. Then it spread, eventually erupting into a standing ovation. The difficulties of surviving life underground didn't evaporate but they no longer seemed insurmountable.

"And now, let's sit back and enjoy some music by Lily Ashton," Randall concluded with a smile.

CHAPTER XXV
ISSUES SURFACE

AFTER FOUR YEARS

Yucca Mountain had operated without its founder and leader, Heinz Globitz, who had disappeared and was presumed dead. His wife, Krishka, had seemingly withdrawn from any leadership responsibilities, choosing to defer to others. Day-to-day operations were assumed and routinely conducted by the head Facilities Engineer, Rafael Ochoa, who felt obligated to liaise with Randall Meredith.

Ochoa and his staff were the unheralded superstars of Yucca Mountain, responsible for preserving its operational integrity. On one occasion a perilous situation was avoided thanks to their resourceful response. Removing one of the trapezoidal windows from the unused cupula near the maintenance alcove and welding it over the leaking window frame in the Observation Chamber prevented a catastrophic flood of the Sanctuary. They were instrumental in repairing a breach in the air filtration system which would have asphyxiated every resident. Numerous other occasions required their immediate response; they had always kept everyone safe.

Liaison with residents was managed by Coach, Frank Lowe. His routine briefings provided the assurances needed to maintain reasonable harmony. Issues surfaced once in a while that prudence dictated more than just staff involvement. Randall, Amanda Guilhaus, Fred Spackman, and Jake Mansfield were tacitly delegated. Their involvement wasn't seamless, but over time, became invaluable. Randall emerged as the recognized leader.

No one could have predicted the length of stay in Yucca Mountain. The envisioned bunker complex was meant for all calamities, each requiring different survival protocols and underground durations. The Globitz organization prided itself in having the safest, underground sanctuary able to withstand the most devastating world disasters. But uncertainties remained.

After four years, resident safety concerns were overshadowed by mundane issues like boredom, diet options, dental health, cosmetic provisions, and replacement clothing. Pallets of Vans tennis shoes were on hand to accommodate growing feet of the Yucca Mountain youth.

Surprisingly, colds, the flu, and infections were negligible. Minor cuts and bruises were routine, but depression intervention and counselling were still predominant concerns. All physical and mental health issues were closely monitored by Dr. Jammicit and his wife. Lenient terms for prescribing anti-depressants—Zoloft, Lexapro, Prozac, Paxil, Cymbalta, and Luvox medications had dwindled supplies increasing the roll of therapy sessions, both group and one-on-one with psychotherapist Audrey Jammicit, PhD. Dr. Galina Vasylyuk, a resident volunteer frequently assisted.

Vitamin D supplements were offered for every man, woman and child in the sanctuary. The sunshine vitamin was deemed an important safeguard for the underground inhabitants because it supported healthy bones and bone marrow, and many other health issues normally benefitting from sunshine.

Replenishment of everyday household necessities: packaged non-perishable foods, powdered drinks, soap, toothpaste, shampoo, and over-the-counter medications was well-organized and administered by staff. The hair salon stocked plenty of lipstick, nail polish and hair coloring, but still drew complaints by women demanding different colors or brands. By all accounts, forecasted survival requirements were brilliant.

There's a knock on the door of residence #14.

"Edna, who could that be, it's seven thirty?"

"I have no idea. I'll get it," responded Mrs. Tillerman moving from the kitchen to the front door.

From his living room recliner, Marco's father, Maxwell, heard a brief discussion followed by his wife's friendly invite to their neighbor Galina Vasylyuk.

"Come in, come in, Dr. Vasylyuk."

Setting his iPad on the coffee table, Maxwell smiled, stood, and greeted his neighbor, "Hello, Galina. What brings you out to visit us tonight?"

"Good evening, Maxwell," holding a large white envelope the petite psychiatrist with the heavy accent said, "As I was just telling Edna, I'd like to talk to you about my research project at the Mayo Clinic. It could possibly help your son."

"Please, come in. Sit down."

With her eager audience attentively seated and their pajama-clad son sprinting toward them from the bedroom, the unassuming doctor sat down for a polite discussion. Clutching his iPad like an ice cream bar, Marco reached the front room with the adults, spun around, and disappeared to the back as swiftly as he came. The Tillermans were unmoved by his momentary appearance. Dr. Vasylyuk smiled, accepting their indifference and continued with pleasantries.

The sincere doctor provided an incisive prologue of the research that had been conducted at the Mayo Clinic involving TMS, Transcranial Magnetic Stimulation. The government had endorsed its application for depression before the asteroid strike and the Mayo Clinic had been researching it's efficacy for some of the symptoms of Autism Spectrum Disorder, ASD.

"Max, Edna, I recently discovered that there's a machine in Dr. Jammicit's clinic that could possibly help Marco."

"What kind of machine?"

"Dr. Globitz anticipated that despair could be a major issue among some residents. He wisely acquired a Transcranial Magnetic Stimulator to help treat and minimize depression without prescription drugs or invasive treatments. This is the same equipment we used at Mayo Clinic."

"Depression?" questioned Max. "What's that got to do with Marco?"

During the next hour, Dr. Vasylyuk provided a summary of her fourteen years of research. Repetitive Transcranial Magnetic Stimulation (TMS), she said, used magnetic fields to stimulate nerve cells in the brain. It had successfully produced changes in neuronal activity associated with mood control. The FDA approved the novel, non-invasive method to treat major depressive disorders in 2008. Her research at the Mayo Clinic continued testing its efficacy for the treatment of ASD. She cautioned that ASD has many potential causes and that her research addressed only one.

Galina had been the director of the clinic's TMS research department when she and her husband were hastily summoned and evacuated to Yucca Mountain. Her interrupted research indicated that a magnetic influence on cortical inhibitory neurons appeared to improve movement-related activity in some patients. She explained that they may have found the pathology of autism, the treatment of which may lessen autistic symptoms without compromising the creativity and savant abilities that make autistic people so extraordinary.

Dr. Vasylyuk cautioned the Tillermans against drawing conclusions, however. But they were flabbergasted at the suggestion that Marco's disorder could possibly be treatable. She asked some background questions relative to family history and provided the Tillermans with documents describing her work and a procedural outline. She would be willing to work with Marco with their permission. She said that Dr. Jammicit had been briefed and welcomed her expertise.

Despite his enthusiasm, Max questioned some of the procedures outlined in the treatment plan. The elimination of many of the electronic conveniences in their apartment was the biggest concern. The cordless phone was first on the list. Their iPads was second. Their Yucca Mountain wi-fi linked many of their electronic devices. Disconnecting the wi-fi would be very difficult. Unplugging the microwave was also a problem. Removing the fluorescent and LED lights was doable, providing suitable replacements were available.

"What do the electronic disconnects have to do with this?" Max challenged.

"Eliminating any and all potential detractors, like ambient electronic frequencies, will help us determine the effectiveness of our treatment," she explained.

A line item in the instructions referred to cell phone limitation but was abandoned by the doctor in view of their underground inoperability. Also dismissed as impractical was the lab testing of blood for mercury, lead, or arsenic. Activities she suggested for the measurement of progress included piano playing, golf, Lego blocks, and dominos.

The Tillermans were shocked by the detail offered during Galina's visit. Her sincerity rose to angelic levels and deserved their deepest gratitude. Both Max and Edna agreed to read through the packet of information and get back to her.

THREE DAYS LATER

Marco's TSM therapy with Dr. Vasylyuk in Dr. Jammicit's clinic began at 8:00 a.m.

Krishka, who was assumed to be Globitz' wife, emerged from her apartment after more than two years of self-imposed hibernation. She had become bored with treadmill workouts, lap-pool swimming, e-book reading, and watching movies on demand. Approaching the fourth-grade teacher, Krishka offered to help in the classroom.

Surprised to see Ms. Globitz in school, let alone volunteering, Coach Lowe warmly welcomed the offer.

"What subjects would you like to help with," he asked.

With perfect diction, swathed in Russian-British inflection, she responded, "I don't know. Languages? Geography? History? Civics? What are your needs?"

Lowe gulped, realizing the windfall. Recovering, he humbly asked, "What language could you teach?"

Krishka sighed, replying, "English, French, Japanese, Latin, or Russian. Whichever."

"That would be very nice, Ms. Globitz," Lowe said while hiding his expression of wow! "I'd like to talk to the other teachers so that we may best utilize your skills. Can you come back tomorrow?"

"Of course."

ONE MONTH LATER

Krishka comfortably fit in to her faculty role at Yucca Mountain Academy. The students easily gravitated to their new instructor and the parents were thrilled—most of the parents. Some were a bit suspicious of her. During the course of the next semester's instruction, Latin was the chosen language based on a survey of the parents.

"Eat your carrots and peas, Samantha," Eve implored her daughter.

"They taste awful."

"Be thankful, dehydrated food is better than going hungry," her mother said while clearing the table.

Dinner at the Meredith residence was a time to catch up with the day's events and reinforce family values. Conversation was by parental design, upbeat and educational with a moral-shaping subtlety.

Discussions were free-flowing and informative. Rex described the new semester's activities. Replacing soccer, he had chosen weightlifting and basketball. Eve's objections to weightlifting were tactfully assuaged by her husband as Samantha proudly that announced she chose golf and drone piloting. The other choices included archery, swimming, and drama. Both parents were amazed with the variety of activities available and offered their endorsement.

"Come on, kids. The sooner we finish dinner, the sooner we can continue with *Narnia*," said their father.

A few minutes passed as the twins reluctantly finished their dinner, looking toward the arranged chairs and sofa where Dad had relocated. The evening ritual was still a favorite of the growing Meredith twins, partially because of the attention received from their parents while reading, partially due to in their rivalry in reading skills and, fortunately, partially due to their interest in the stories of the books they read. To the parents, it would be cherished moments of family time during their fleeting years of influence as well as anti-boredom mental stimulation.

All four Merediths had settled into their favorite family room reading space, anticipating the next round of Pass the eBook. It was their fourth book in the seven-book *Narnia* series by C.S. Lewis, *The Lion, the Witch and the Wardrobe*. "Who's turn was it when we left off last night?" asked their father as he picked up the iPad from the coffee table.

"It's my turn! Sam was reading, Chapter 7 last night before we went to bed. Lucy, Peter, Ann, and Susan were eating dinner with the Beavers," recalled Rex. It was another treasured evening for the close-knit family. By nine o'clock, sleepy-eyed reading faltered. It was time for lights out.

School the next day was a-buzz with the excitement of the new activities. The shift from soccer to other events was welcomed by all. Rex was first in his class to announce and hand in his chosen pursuits. Breaking from identical routines with his best friend, Octavio chose archery and swimming. The raised eyebrow of Coach Lowe indicated his surprised approval. Enthusiasm was high among the kids and boredom would not be an issue. The new schedule would begin the following Monday.

Saturday adventures for Rex and Octavio continued. Marco accompanied the boys when not in therapy. Ventures into the forbidden areas of Yucca Mountain satisfied their curiosity/exploring passions. They discovered large air-lock chamber doors, food storage lockers, a medical supply chamber, clothing storage, a spring-fed water reservoir (with filtration pumps), and a surprise—a small shed with evidence of a resident.

CHAPTER XXVI
A NEW RESIDENT

SATURDAY MORNING

WITH THEIR BACKPACKS BULGING WITH FRISBEES, TENNIS BALLS, sandwiches, chips, candy bars, and drinks, Rex and Octavio set out for their regular Saturday discovery hike into the darker segments of Yucca Mountain. Their pace would be quicker without having Marco along. They reached the chain-link fence and the gate beyond which the darkness loomed.

"Look at this, someone left the gate open," Rex declared. "It's never been opened that far before, wonder if one of the workers forgot."

Undaunted, the boys briskly followed their flash-lighted oval in front of them. Proceeding into the pitch-black tunnel provided the necessary adrenalin rush for their young appetites. Their Saturday-morning ritual bestowed bragging rights and rather conspicuous confidence for the ten-year old's. Less than five minutes into their excursion they encountered a petrifying jolt.

"What's that! I heard moans, Tavo," whispered Rex.

"It's coming from over there. Shine the light over there," Octavio responded.

There was a rustling sound and people scrambling to their feet as the flashlights zeroed-in on the source of the noise. Two entangled adults, shading their eyes from the blinding flashlights, looked as startled as their two intruders felt.

"Mrs. Silvester, are you okay?" Rex innocently asked. "And, Mr. Beaufort do you need help?"

"No, boys. We lost something over here and were just trying to find it," the man sheepishly responded as his companion stepped into his shadow.

Moving toward the rattled and disheveled couple, Rex and Octavio offered to help. Shining their flashlights on the ground beneath the couple, they saw a blanket and a pair of shoes.

"There it is, Mr. Beaufort. A blanket and some shoes. Is that what you were looking for?"

"Yes, thank you. Now we can go," he responded, hastily gathering the blanket and hiding his shoes. "What are you boys doing here? This area is supposed to be off-limits."

Octavio was first to respond, after briefly stuttering, "A-a-a-our soccer ball got kicked over the fence and we're trying to find it."

Rex chimed in, "Yeah, have you seen it?"

"No, haven't seen your ball. But if I do, I'll set it by the gate," Mr. Beaufort said as he and Mrs. Silvester shuffled back toward the lighted portion of the Sanctuary.

"Okay, sir. We'll just keep lookin'," said Rex.

The embarrassed couple plodded out of sight and hearing while the boys thought about their next move. Should they continue into the tunnel or would Mr. Beaufort and Mrs. Silvester squeal on them?

"If my dad finds out, I'm in big trouble, Tavo."

"Me too."

"But we did lose a ball here…once," said Rex.

"That was a long time ago, Rex."

"But we didn't actually lie."

Reaching into his backpack, Octavio pulled out a tennis ball. Clutching it in his right hand and winding up like the Yankees center fielder, he launched it into the tunnel darkness, toward no man's land. The ball made diminishingly faint sounds as it caromed off the concrete floor and walls.

With a sheepish grin, he pointed his flashlight down the corridor and said, "Let's go find our ball."

"Yeah, let's find it," Rex agreed.

The adventurers continued on their trek down the corridor. Passing the area where their appreciative rat inhabited, they paused and sprinkled some breadcrumbs. Not waiting for its appearance, they pressed on, deeper and deeper into the tunnel shaft. As they walked, they pondered some of the issues troubling them since arriving at Yucca Mountain: the death of Aaron Jones' dad and Jimmy Solis' mother, the friends they missed from their old school, Christmas time, Rex's mom's hair turning brown, and family vacations. They agreed to be friendlier to both Aaron and Jimmy.

Their flashlight beamed toward the tunnel alcove marked OSSUARY, then directly across the tunnel to the alcove marked MAINTENANCE. "Here's our hideout. Let's eat our lunch here," said Rex.

The boys crawled through the familiar open window and sat down. With one flashlight on the concrete deck, they had enough light to sort through their backpacks and retrieve lunch.

"I know what they did with the other window they took outta here," said Octavio as he chomped into his sandwich.

"What?" asked Rex through his mouth full of chips.

"My uncle said they welded it into place right over a leaky window in the Observation Chamber. Kept the place from flooding."

"We almost got caught that day, remember?"

"Yeah. That was a close call," laughed Octavio. Wonder where the top window went."

Reflecting in a more serious tone, Rex attempted to discuss a deeper topic; one they dare not broach amongst their classmates.

"I heard my dad tell mom that Jimmy's mother killed herself."

"Yikes! How'd she do it? Why!?"

"Some kind of pills. She took a bunch of pills," said Rex.

"¡Chale! Give me a break!"

"What happen to *your* mom, Tavo? You're living with your uncle and aunt, right?"

"My dad took a new job and they had me live with my uncle for a while. When he moved down here, I just came with him," he said. "I miss my mom and my dad; I hope they're safe. 'Feel sorry for Jimmy though—no mom."

"Yeah. 'And Aaron with no dad."

"Let's go." Octavio said, changing the mood and picking up his flashlight. "Let's see what we can find farther in the tunnel."

"I'm ready, let's go."

Saturdays were the best days of the week to explore since daring to enter the restricted area. The boys ventured deeper into the bowels of the tunnel than ever before; cautious but confidence still soaring. They were determined to explore all five miles of tunnels and alcoves of the complex—especially the forbidden areas. While following their flashlight beam, they walked and talked as though they owned the place.

"Tavo, there's a light up ahead."

"Yeah, and it's not the tunnel lights hangin' on the walls. It's something else."

With eyes bulging and tiptoeing steps, they inched toward the glowing light. The tunnel darkness gradually dissipated with each step. Soon, their flashlights were superfluous. The glimmering bluish-green light emanating from a horseshoe-shaped, five-foot high concrete berm provided a magnificent reflection off the ceiling and walls of the otherwise-dark tunnel. And, the connecting alcove/tunnel glowed from the lights and water it contained and extended out of the alcove. Powerful ultraviolet lights beneath the water level were the source that luminated the portion of Yucca Mountain that, until now, had been witnessed only by its workers.

"Wow! It's like a giant glow-in-the-dark swimming pool that goes back into that alcove," exclaimed Rex.

"Yeah. Amazing!"

"What are these motors and pipes for?" asked Rex.

"Pumps. They must be water pumps," Octavio said.

With a mischievous grin, he took off his shoes and socks. Then his shirt.

"What are you doing, Tavo?"

"I'm going skinny dippin'. Come on!"

Rex burst into laughter at the thought of Octavio swimming naked in the glowing water tank. Watching his buddy jump from the berm into the water ignited their symbiotic connection immediately. Rex found himself gleefully stripping down and joining the escapade. With tip toes just inches from the water reservoir's bottom, the boys were secure enough in their swimming ability to frolic without concern.

Suddenly the pool lights flickered and the motor from the nearby pump kicked on. The noise from the pump started with an angry growl then leveled off to a whirr that was loud enough to cause concern. A startled Rex hastily paddled to the edge of the pool and climbed from the water to the top of the berm. From the other side of the reservoir, Octavio swam directly over the large circular water drain in the reservoir floor. The fierce suction from the drain created a whirlpool effect that captured and redirected Octavio's course, preventing him from reaching the edge of the berm.

In an instant, Octavio began to panic. He struggled to break from the overpowering pull of the drain. He was just ten feet from the edge of the berm and safety. Flailing with his tired arms and kicking his feet frantically, he fought the powerful vortex of swirling water. He was losing the battle.

Rex was still naked, standing on the berm watching a tragedy unfold. Octavio's body was circling powerlessly around the perimeter of the spinning water. With each revolution, his eyes and terrified look were helplessly witnessed by his friend. Rex's impulse to jump in to the rescue was shut down by his own survival instinct. Octavio's scream for help was drowned out by the noise of the pumps and by the water flushing over his hapless form.

Just then a piece of wood flew through the air landing on the edge of the swirling water, narrowly missing Octavio's head. It appeared to be a 2X4 about three feet long, attached to a long rope. The makeshift lifeline for the potential drowning victim was apparently flung from the edge of the berm. Octavio seized the lumber and rope with a death grip and continued kicking to escape the sucking vortex.

It didn't matter that the other end of the rope was wrapped around a mysterious person from outside the reservoir berm. It was not his friend Rex. A frightened, exhausted, and very thankful Octavio was awkwardly pulled from certain death by the boy with the rope and by his best buddy. It was a surprise, face-to-face encounter for all three.

Sprawled on the top of the reservoir berm, Octavio's naked body recoiled from coughing and spitting up of water. He gasped for air and reflexively attempted some modesty by covering his crotch. His two lifesavers watched with concern—silently. Minutes passed. It appeared his lungs had expelled enough water to allow breathing, albeit still forced.

"You okay, Tavo?"

Through a strained voice and a concerned look, he nodded and rasped, "Okay."

Both boys, still naked on top of the berm, realized the presence of a skinny Mexican boy next to them. His quick action of throwing a piece of lumber and rope had saved Octavio. A faint smile from Rex was returned while Octavio saw his rescuer and mouthed, *"Gracias."*

"De nada."

Rex acknowledged the boy's presence with a nod and a smile, unable to communicate in Spanish. Turning to help his friend, who was still supine on the concrete berm, Rex noticed blood trickling from Octavio's scraped knees and elbows. Desperate clambering of a young naked body over the rough-hewn concrete berm had its consequences; trivial it seemed, to the alternative he had just faced.

Without warning, the mysterious Mexican boy vanished.

Over the noise of the whirring pumps, Octavio barked, "Who was that?!!"

"I don't know. He's gone!" yelled Rex.

Like a mallet striking a giant gong, a realization confronted the boys. They were not alone!

Scrambling down from the water reservoir berm to claim the two piles of shirts, shorts, and tennis shoes next to their backpacks on the corridor floor, the boys understood they had been discovered. And naked. It would be hard to explain to any adult accompanying the older Mexican kid. Hurriedly donning clothes over their still-wet bodies, the two saw the boy who had just saved Octavio's life reappear from around the water pump structure.

"Mi amigo, para eusted!" shouted the friendly fellow bearing an earth-toned, heavy Mexican blanket. He smiled as he approached the two, holding out his arms to offer the blanket. It was an honorable gesture by the eleven- or twelve-year-old boy, presented with an expression of sincere honesty and compassion.

Octavio nervously muttered something about "not necessary" as he tucked his shirt in his pants. The pumps suddenly stopped and the cave-like atmosphere with the glowing reservoir returned to its eerie calm, allowing the three boys to communicate without yelling.

"*¿Como te llamas?*" asked Octavio. "*¿Qué haces aquí?*" ("What's your name? and What are you doing here?")

Relieved to be face-to-face with a Spanish-speaking youngster who was obviously not a Yucca Mountain authority, the young man grinned and gestured, offering the blanket again. "*Envuélvalo con mi manta, si quieres. Tengo otro en mi casa, y no lo necesito.*" ("Wrap yourself with my blanket, if you want. I have another in my house, and don't need it.")

"What did he say, Tavo?"

"He said he lives here and doesn't need the blanket. "*¿Como te llamas?*" he said looking at the boy.

His response, in Spanish:

("My name is Paco. My father and I live here so we can fix things when they break. We work for Mr. Globitz and his staff. Mostly, we just work on our own.")

With a friendly but quizzical expression, Octavio sat down next to his backpack. Taking the hint from his friend, Rex also sat, and they were soon joined by the slender lifesaver. Rex took out a Hersey's bar from his pack and offered it to Paco. Politely thanking and accepting the candy, Paco opened the conversation with a flurry of Spanish that lasted five minutes. Both hands motioned and his eyebrows raised as he chattered away. Rex was flabbergasted by the rapid-fire of strange-sounding words from Paco.

"What's he saying, Tavo?"

"He said the water pump automatically turns on every three hours and it often wakes him up when he's sleeping. He said it is unsafe to swim whenever the pump is on."

"All that, just to say that?"

"Where is your house, Paco? Where do you sleep?" Octavio asked in his native language, leaning in and looking directly at their new acquaintance.

"*Yo vivo allí,*" Paco said, pointing to a makeshift metal structure with a curious-shaped trapezoidal window on one side panel. It was a workers shed behind the water pump equipment, obviously converted into a shelter. *"Ven, te mostraré"* he said as he stood and motioned.

Reluctantly, Rex and Octavio rose to their feet and followed the older kid around the pumps to the ten-foot by six-foot structure that Paco called his house. The inside resembled the likes of a jail cell that Rex had once seen on television. An upper and lower bunk hung from the metal walls by chains. A small sink held a glass with a toothbrush and a collapsed tube of Pepsodent nestled in the corner. A hot plate with a cast iron frying pan rested on the shallow countertop. Curiously, there was a Casio keyboard next to the folding chair that leaned against the only wall space available. The blanket on the upper bunk was neat and perfectly tucked in over a thin mattress. The lower bunk mattress was exposed.

"Where do you go to the bathroom, Paco?" asked Octavio in Spanish.

Paco pointed outside to a small outhouse with a showerhead attached to the exterior wall.

"Awesome," responded Rex.

The three boys left the tiny dwelling and sat at the picnic table just ten feet from its front door. There were a thousand questions each could have asked the other, but for now it was just names, ages, school grade, and parents. Parents? Paco's story went over the heads of Rex and Octavio. They had no inkling of what ICE was or where it could have sent his mother. Neither did they understand how Paco's father could be working someplace else in the dark tunnels of Yucca Mountain leaving his son to fend for himself.

The magnitude of the situation for this twelve-year-old kid didn't occur to them. They neglected to question the older boy's story of why Paco and his dad lived in obscurity in such humble conditions.

They were in awe of the autonomy and apparent maturity of their host and his compelling request for secrecy, lest their swimming adventure be exposed. A bond was formed, and the spellbound neophytes found themselves enmeshed in the life of their "secret Mexican friend."

There would be time for more discussion later. It was getting late and Rex and Octavio needed to head home. As graciously as a ten-year-old could possibly convey, Octavio thanked his new friend and suggested they meet again the following Saturday. Offering the remnants of lunch from their backpacks to the reluctant recipient, they rose and said goodbye.

Walking back down the increasingly darkened tunnel, the boys' flashlights became necessary to illuminate their path. Their excitement and conversation of discovering a secret swimming pool and a new friend was somewhat diminished by Octavio's near-drowning. Reinforced by a progressive throbbing of his scraped knees and elbows, his clouded thoughts dwindled to a trivial conversation with Rex. The reservoir and Paco were secondary.

Returning to his shelter, Paco's concern about being discovered by Yucca Mountain authorities was interrupted by his growling stomach. It was almost time for dinner time—fried tilapia, rice, and beans. The chocolate bar would be dessert—courtesy of his new friends.

CHAPTER XXVII
CHARACTERS REVEALED

FRIDAY NIGHT

AFTER TUCKING IN THE TWINS FOR THE NIGHT, EVE RETREATED TO THE front room sofa for her nightly escape into the realm of another Nora Roberts novel. Randall, in swim trunks and sweatsuit, headed out for a relaxing swim in the lap pool. These nightly activities were how the Meredith adults tried to cope with the strain of their prolonged underground confinement.

Randall's ten-minute walk through the Sanctuary's moon-lit town square was enjoined by the after-dark arias of crooning nightingales and whip-poor-wills, the hooting of owls, and chirping of crickets and frogs. If the evening's swim or the spas' water jets didn't relax Randall, certainly the walk through the life-like sounds of nature would.

Through foggy swimming goggles, he easily followed his lane in the underwater lights of the pool, mostly unmindful of everything else. Flip-turning with each lap, he became conscious of another swimmer two lanes over, but was not inclined to break his rhythm or routine to investigate. After completing his twenty laps, he pulled and twisted his body into a sitting position on the pool's edge and observed the proficient freestyle swimmer two lanes over.

He walked to the jacuzzi, set the timer for ten minutes, entered the hot water, and began to relax with his eyes closed. After a few minutes he noticed a dripping, shapely figure wearing a black one-piece swimsuit, looking down at him.

"May I join you?" asked a warmly smiling Krishka.

"Yes, of course, Mrs. Globitz. The water's fine."

The former Olympian/alleged Russian agent, and now widow, had retained her youthful, athletic figure; tall, sinewy, small breasted, and striking. Long dark-reddish hair unfurled from her swim cap as she carefully stepped down into the bubbling spa. A closer look revealed a jagged, rose-tinted scar about four inches long with a void of muscle on her inner thigh. Settling in directly in front of one of the jets, she looked at him and asked, "Do you normally swim at this hour, Randall?

He swallowed, then responded, "Yes, I've been doing this for over a year, now. I find it relaxes me. Helps me go to sleep. What brings you out at this hour?"

In her slightly accented voice, she replied, "I've been helping out in the classroom during the day, but it's been interfering with my normal workout routine. So I thought I'd try swimming at night, like you."

Attempting to hide his nervousness while pushing the accumulated water jet air from his swimming trunks, he responded, "I've never really spoken with you, but I'd like to say that I was very sorry when I heard of your husband's disappearance."

"Yes, it's been almost a year now, and they still haven't found him or his body," she said. "It's hard to believe he could just disappear down here, isn't it?"

"Indeed," apologetically sighed Meredith. "If there's anything we can do, you know to ask, right?"

"Thank you, Randall. Yes, everyone's been quite supportive."

The timer expired and the jets stopped to Randall's relief. He smiled and rose to step out of the quieted spa. "I'll reset the timer if you want, Mrs. Globitz."

"Thank you, Randall. Yes, five more minutes please," she said with a winsome a smile.

He retrieved his towel from the bench and reset the timer. As the throaty sound of the jets resumed, she said, "Good evening to you, Randall. Thanks for sharing your thoughts."

Krishka had watched him as he toweled off and admired his healthy physique. Her assumed marriage to Globitz, decreed by her SVR handlers, had been anything but ideal. He was twenty years her senior, fleshy, and with a lowered center of gravity, the white-haired billionaire was noted more for his brains than his brawn. State loyalty or penance for transgressions would define her spousal obligation to Globitz until relieved of duty by higher authority. Tonight, her momentary escape from reality afforded a beguiling smile and sendoff to her new swimming companion.

Randall donned his sweats, flung his towel over his shoulder and ambled through a moon-lit village square, heading home. During his ten-minute stroll, he indulged in a few salacious thoughts. Flushed and surprised by his arousal, Randall quickly whispered to himself, "Get thee behind me, Satan."

SATURDAY MORNING

"Hurry, Mom, I'll be late for Drone Comp," implored Samantha.

"Drone Comp?"

"Drone Competition. It's a game Coach Lowe has on Saturdays for students in his drone class."

"Here's your lunch. Finish your cereal. Then you can go."

To her mother's chagrin, Samantha slurped directly from the bowl, grabbed her lunch bag, and launched through the door shouting, "See you later, Mom!"

Rex was not in such a hurry. He deliberated over his cereal, watching his sister leave. After the door slammed, the quiet time between mother and son became obvious to the intuitive parent.

"What's bothering you, Rex? You're awfully quiet this morning," said his mother.

"Nothin'," he shrugged.

"You've got something on your mind. Let's talk about it."

Reluctantly, Rex placed his spoon down and searched for words. Finally, he asked, "How come Daniel Lockhart's mom died?"

Eve sat down, reached for her son's hand, and explained. "Daniel's mother developed a case of bronchitis. Her condition was considered mild at first, but as a precaution Dr. Jammicit prescribed both medication and bedrest. But it didn't seem to help. Her condition gradually worsened and nothing he could do helped, so she finally died." Her detailed, melodically delivered explanation conformed to the Merediths' parenting style: age-appropriate truthfulness; no baby talk.

"What's bronchitis?"

"It's a bad cough that gets into your lungs. And you can't breathe."

"What's medication?"

"That's just another word for medicine; mostly pills designed to fix the lung problem to try to make it go away."

"Are those the same pills that Jimmy's mom took?" he asked, looking very concerned.

"Heavens no, Rex. Jimmy's mom had a very different problem. Don't confuse the two."

"Just wonderin'." He paused. "They both took pills from Dr. Jammicit, didn't they?"

"Yes, but the illnesses were different, and the pills were also different." She took a deep breath before trying to explain. "Rex, every day is a gift from God. We aren't always in control, but God is. We have to accept that some people die before they get old, even though it can be very painful for their families. Jimmy and Daniel's moms are in a better place now, and you should do all you can to support both of your friends."

"Is ICE kinda like God?"

"I'm not sure I know what you're talking about. What do you mean by 'ICE?'"

"I don't know. I heard that they take people away, and you never see'em again."

"No. It's not the same. I'll let your dad explain ICE some other time. Now, get that worried look off your face and come here and give me a big hug." The two hugged longer than usual, providing some relief for both of them. Then Mom arched her neck back, looking at her little man and asked, "What are your plans for today?"

"I'm meeting Tavo at archery, then we're gonna pick up Marco to play soccer."

LATER THAT MORNING

Randall's personal and precious family time was constantly encroached upon by community obligations, which he tried to fulfill as best he could. He was very conscientious and knew that somebody had to provide leadership. But, whenever possible, he took the time to escape in his personal world of Clive Cussler novels, golf, and swimming.

In the area of community support, he continually tried to rally both the residents and the staff, serving as liaison between them. His efforts were so well-received that he became recognized as the ex officio mayor of the complex. He held regular meetings with staff department heads, and relayed important news to all the other residents, becoming the honest broker of all things necessary to survive.

But this morning it was Saturday, time for a round of golf.

"Nice shot, Randy. Lookin' to set a course record?" said Max Schwab.

"I wish I could play like this on a real golf course."

"You're hitting the ball farther than ever, man. The weight-lifting and swimming must be paying off."

For Eve, Saturday morning found her joining her neighbors for bridge.

"One spade," opened Mrs. Dubois.

"Pass," responded Eve.

"Two hearts," said Mrs. Ellington.

"Pass," said Eve's partner, Jane Kota.

"Three hearts."

"Pass." "Pass." And "Pass."

"You gals are killing us today," complained Jane.

After bridge club, it would be time for lunch, followed by various household chores. The games filled a three-hour gap between breakfast and lunch, after which household chores would be tackled. Then she would prepare dinner, which would be followed by family activities such as Pass the Book, Progressive Story Telling or a movie from the digital library.

During weekdays her routine included being a teacher's aide in Sam and Rex's classrooms with Mr. Lowe and Krishka and giving or listening to lectures at the Women's Support Group. She also participated in zumba, book club, and yoga, so that, unlike many of the wives at Yucca Mountain, her "free time" had almost every minute accounted for. As a result, she was one of the most popular wives of the bunker community.

Rex watched Octavio and three other boys receive instructions on their takedown recurve bows. It was obvious that Octavio had developed a huge interest in archery. The thump of arrows penetrating their targets supplied a rewarding testimony of skill and training. Octavio's target accumulated more arrows in the small rings than the others. When the class was dismissed, their enthusiastic chorus of the Lakota Sioux war cry, *"Hokahey!"* signaled their farewell.

Joining his buddy, Octavio grabbed his backpack, waved goodbye to his teacher, and scampered from the archery range, dribbling the soccer ball back and forth in the direction of Marco's house.

"I got three bullseyes this morning, Rex!" exclaimed Octavio. "The teacher said I was the best archer he's ever coached."

"I signed up for it next semester, then we'll see who's best," retorted Rex. "Let's go, we gotta get Marco."

This would be the first time Marco would get to see the glowing water reservoir and meet Paco. His therapy was progressing, but he was still unable to articulate any sensible thoughts. Rex and Octavio understood his condition on an instinctive level, and they embraced the idea of including him in their recreational time. Marco was unable to express his gratitude, but his extended comfort zone when he was with the boys was plain to see.

Generally, Marco showed zero emotion, neither enthusiasm nor worry. The boys were accustomed to this seeming indifference and always wondered what he was really thinking. Today would turn out to be a significant challenge for Marco's equanimity.

Marco began to squeal as the three approached the lighted reflections on the tunnel ceiling cascading from the reservoir and its glowing water. His response to the unusual radiance prompted the calming voice of Rex, "Isn't this pretty, Marco?" Octavio reflexively grabbed Marco's hand to also provide reassurance.

Hearing the boys voices, Paco called out from behind the metal shack that served as his home. *"Hola, Estoy aquí."*

Hearing the unfamiliar voice from behind the structure, Marco jumped behind Octavio. Rex laughed at Marco's reaction, then provided an assuring hand. "Come on, Marco. Let's go meet Paco."

The boys followed the voice to the picnic table outside the shack where Paco was busy filleting a fish on a plywood cutting board. After exchanging nods and smiles, Rex and Octavio looked at Paco's endeavor in utter amazement. They had never seen a fish being prepared to eat. They silently gasped; Marco squealed. Paco explained he was preparing the evening's dinner—fried tilapia.

Captivated by a knife-wielding, experienced hand and nonchalance of the twelve-year old across from them, Rex and Octavio began to chat with Paco about what he was doing. Their friend systematically separated the bones and skin from the edible protein, dropping the latter in to a water-filled saucepan, occasionally looking up at his visitors. Octavio continued to translate Paco's words for Rex and Marco, and the conversation created a friendly discussion. But Marco's attention had shifted to the keyboard just a few feet away.

Suddenly, Rex, Octavio and Paco heard a commanding refrain of "chopsticks" emanating from the tiny shack.

"What the…"

Paco recognized the sound of his keyboard but had no explanation. He quickly looked at his friends and realized that they also were clueless.

"Where's Marco?" interrupted Octavio.

"He was just here!"

"¡Está tocando mi piano!" laughed Paco.

The three rushed into the tiny structure to witness a gleeful Marco plunking away on Paco's keyboard. It was a delightful moment for Rex and Octavio to realize that Marco had a musical capacity, albeit "chopsticks." Then, Marco began to play a new melody, more complex, and beautiful. His head bobbed and weaved but his expression was without emotion. In total shock, they watched as Marco played a sophisticated version of the theme from *The Lion King*.

Paco nodded and smiled at Marco's keyboard dexterity before realizing that the other boys' were stunned. The beautiful music filling the tiny habitat was an obvious surprise, bringing Rex to tears. A more stoic Octavio shook his head in disbelief, turned to Paco, and said, *"Increíble, no sabía que podía hacer esto."* ("Unbelievable, we didn't know he could do this."). *"Marco tien necesidades especiales."* ("Marco is a special-needs kid.").

When the music stopped, the three spectators clapped and cheered their magnificent pianist and friend. This was an accolade that Marco had never heard before. It was a wonderful moment for all four, but Marco broke the spell as he turned from his stool, stood, and said, "Pee."

"Come with me, Marco. Paco's got a toilet," Rex said as he led their newly discovered maestro to the outhouse.

In Spanish, Octavio and Paco exchanged thoughts about Marco's performance as they moved back outside to the picnic table area. Paco resumed his dinner prep. The rumble and whirr of the adjacent water pumps kicked in, making conversation more difficult. Marco burst out of the outhouse still half-naked, frightened by the noise. Calmed by his friends, he returned there to finish his mission. The boys agreed it was probably time to say *adios*.

Before leaving, Octavio pulled from his backpack a half loaf of bread and a jar of peanut butter and set them on the table. Paco's eyes lit up in delight, and he thanked him profusely.

The glow from the reservoir allowed for easy walking home, initially. Fading gradually, flashlights became necessary. It was a happy hike back down the tunnel as the boys recounted Marco's unforgettable recital. It would be a joy to report Marco's piano expertise to his parents. But that would mean telling them where they were and explaining everything to the adults. Perhaps it would be better left unsaid for now.

The subject changed as they discussed and compared Paco's dinner with what they would be eating tonight. His keyboard was a nice diversion, but their TV at home was better. And, where did he learn to clean that fish? Where did he get that fish!? How could they have not asked? And one troubling issue Paco communicated to Octavio in their mutual language—Paco's father had died two months ago. Rex was stunned to learn the sad news. "A kid with no parents—that's bad," he muttered as they walked on.

The boys decided it would be good to continue to help Paco. They would kind of "adopt him" and see him every Saturday, if possible. They'd bring him food, some clothes, and maybe some new shoes and stuff. The ramifications of the situation didn't occur to them. They naively vowed to secretly harbor his existence—kind of like kids adopting a puppy without their parents knowing.

After delivering Marco to his residence, the two boys performed their secret fist pump and went their separate ways. It had been another eventful Saturday.

CHAPTER XXVIII
INNOCENT SECRETS

MONTHS LATER

FOUR YEARS OF PROLONGED UNDERGROUND LIVING HAD TAKEN ITS TOLL. Boredom and stress increased, while morale plummeted. The will to survive was slowly diminishing among the YM inhabitants. A suicide occurred. Pneumonia and congestive heart failure occurred with increasing frequency. Mrs. Fitzsimons died of complications while delivering her second child. Dental issues became increasingly alarming, as several people were losing teeth.

Randall and a select group of concerned residents devised a comprehensive plan to mitigate these effects. This plan consisted mostly of an increase in the variety of entertainment activities, including games and music and dance.

The First Annual Soap Box Derby races were a huge success, involving kids and their dads making model racers with limited materials from the supply warehouse. Excited boys and girls guided their cars down a portion of the long ramp that went up to the Yucca Mountain entrance. The cheering by the fans at the finish line did wonders for all the contestants and their parents.

An archery competition gave many of the students an opportunity to demonstrate their skills and compete with each other for prizes and adulation from their parents and the spectators. Not surprising, Octavio won first place in his division. Samantha Meredith piloted her drone through a maze of obstacles past all the competition, but it crashed at the finish line, destroying her craft. An evening of karaoke revealed some exceptional talent among the residents not known for their musical skills. Many of the adults enjoyed the ballroom dances they initiated on Saturday nights.

Another Lily Ashton concert filled Village Square with appreciative residents. Her backup singers, consisting of teachers Angela Murphy and Marian Duncan, as well as a couple of their students, bellowed out their accompaniment of the best of Nashville tunes. Long-time forgotten college musicians Jake Farnsworth accompanied Lily on the electronic keyboard and drums. Marco made a "special guest" appearance on the keyboard that won a standing ovation. The whole ensemble captivated an appreciative audience with the help of an amplifier and oversized speakers that rattled the cavernous walls. Capping the whole evening, Lily sang a new composition that brought the audience to its feet as it spoke of pain, perseverance, and an inevitable reward.

It was clear that the diversionary tactics helped everyone, if only for a short while. It was a brief timeout from the drudgery of captivity, and a time to refocus and enjoy their existence.

DINNER TIME, THE MEREDITH RESIDENCE

The video monitor signaled an incoming face chat. The worried face of Rafael flashed on the screen. "Mr. Meredith, I hate to interrupt your dinner, but we've got a problem."

"What is it, Raf?" answered Randall as he walked to the wall monitor.

"The boys have been keeping a secret, and his name is Paco."

"What?!!"

"Octavio slipped up and told me about this tonight at dinner. They've been taking food to a young stowaway at his hideout every Saturday."

Randall turned to look at Rex as he addressed Rafael, "What kind of hideout are you talking about? Who is this Paco?"

"I don't have many details, except that he's a young kid himself. I'm thinking we should take a cart to go find him."

"If you know where to look, let's go."

"Tavo says he lives in a maintenance shed by the reservoir. It's at mile four, deep in the Sanctuary tunnel."

"My God!" Randall said with a piercing look into the guilt-ridden eyes of his son. "I'll be on the front porch waiting for you."

"Be there in six minutes," Rafael said.

Without a word he turned and walked past the three at the dinner table to retrieve his shoes from the bedroom. After a moment of rustling, the only noise in their apartment was the faint flushing of a toilet. Then a determined cadence echoed from the hallway, as Dad emerged from the bedroom and calmly asked, "What do you know about this, Rex?"

Before Rex could answer, they heard the brakes of Rafael's cart squeak as it stopped in front of Unit #9. Randall turned and exited.

"Evening, Mr. Meredith. Ready for a little journey?"

"This should be interesting, Raf," he acknowledged, returning the greeting. "Who's this Paco, kid?"

As the two pulled away in the golf cart, Rafael's neck veins expressed more than his clenched teeth and explanation ever could have. "Octavio confessed: they've been meeting with him for months. He's a twelve-year-old; the son of a former worker."

"Twelve!?"

"If I'm not mistaken, he could be the son of Manuel Camacho, one of the construction workers who built this place five years ago. He and his son must have snuck back into the Sanctuary, before the gate closed."

"A couple of stowaways."

"Well, we don't really know where the señor is. Tavo says he died."

The golf cart squeaked again in front of the familiar gate bearing the sign "DANGER NO ADMITANCE." Rafael dismounted to swing the gate open just wide enough for the cart to enter. Then he threw the lever on the electrical panel mounted on the tunnel wall, lighting the tunnel for as far as they could see. After he climbed back onto the golf cart, they motored toward the reservoir.

"It's hard to believe that a kid could be living down here without the rest of us knowing," Randall said.

Para seguro. ("For sure.") "How did he get by unnoticed for this long; food, facilities, even security? My staff drives back here a couple times a week to check on things, pick up fresh produce, fish. Nothing. Nobody reported anything."

"Don't be too hard on yourself. We don't know yet what the actual situation is."

The golf cart hummed along the concrete pathway as the two men pondered the baffling circumstance.

BACK HOME, TWO A.M.

Trying not to disturb her, Randall quietly slipped under the covers and snuggled with his wife.

"Did you find Paco?" she softly asked.

"No, we didn't. It's late, Eve. Let's try to get some sleep."

"I think I know what happened to Mr. Globitz," she said to her frustrated husband.

"Globitz! What are you talking about? We're worried about a twelve-year-old kid, not Globitz. I'm really tired, let's talk in the morning."

The whirr of air flowing from the ducts became more obvious than ever before as both lay silent, eyes wide open.

THREE A.M.

"What does Globitz have to do with anything?" Randall said, breaching the unspoken gag agreement.

"I'll tell you in the morning, Randall. Now let's try to rest."

The importance of routine sleep was emphasized at every meeting by the Yucca Mountain medical team. Mental and emotional balance starts with sleep habits and impacts physical well-being, crucial in an underground survival situation. Tonight, however, sleep was illusive, as the spouses lay quietly awake, not wanting to disturb the other.

EIGHT A.M.

Breakfast for the twins would have been routine except for Rex trying to avoid talking to his parents. He hurried to down his milk and scamper out the door to go to school, while Samantha finished her breakfast at her normal pace, then also left for class. Eve turned to clear the table. Pouring herself a fresh cup of coffee, she settled into a dining room chair and contemplated the shocking details revealed by the conversation she had last night with Rex and wondering how she would tell Randall.

Her husband entered the kitchen and said, "Morning, Eve. Thanks for allowing me a little extra sleep time. Our excursion last night was a bust."

"Good morning, Randall. Eggs and sausage?"

"And toast, please."

"He started by saying that they had found a tool shed that workers had used during the Sanctuary construction, near the water reservoir. It even had bunkbeds and a hotplate. According to Rafael, a couple of the workers often stayed there during the week but went home on weekends, and there were no signs of anyone using it recently. There were no signs of a kid named Paco or his father, either. The small shelter was quite clean, orderly, and empty.

Eve listened intently, allowing Randall to finish telling his story. He went on to say that they looked high and low around the whole area. They called out for Paco in Spanish and in English. Walking and looking all around, they came up empty-handed. They eventually decided to call it quits.

Sipping his coffee, Randall revealed, "Riding back last night, Rafael admitted that Octavio had been acting a 'little strange' lately." He continued, "Rafael thinks that Octavio misses his real parents, Rafael's brother and his wife. Quite possibly, he could be acting out, imagining things due to the stress of prolonged loneliness."

He said that Rafael seemed almost relieved in their investigative "dry run," and that they both had decided to dismiss the likelihood of the boys' venturing into the back corridors of Yucca Mountain. Roaming that deep into the darkened tunnel would be unfathomable for their little guys. Right?

Randall's naïve bubble burst with Eve's simple question, "Was there a keyboard inside the tool shed?"

Randall coughed, and his coffee sprayed all over his breakfast plate. Stunned by her implied knowledge of that essential detail, he instantly knew he had been wrong. He had wanted to believe that Rex and Octavio had not been there.

"While you were out looking for a boy named Paco last night, Rex and I had a long, heart-to-heart talk. Randy, those boys know a lot more about Yucca Mountain than you think!!"

During the next hour, Eve revealed details that only someone who had actually been in the restricted area would know: the cupola clubhouse, the pet rat, the glowing water reservoir, the tool shed/residence of Paco, the aeroponic and aquaponic gardens and fishponds, and the Ossuary with a glowing circle on the floor—a glowing circle on the floor! She paused to catch her breath and ensure that she still had her husband's attention.

"Do you know about tickling for fish?" she said with a smile.

"What?!! Tickling for fish?"

"Yes, the boys do. They learned it from Paco. They have learned a lot of things, including about survival."

"So, you're saying…"

"Yes, I'm saying Paco is real. He lives in that shed. And, the boys visit him every Saturday."

"I'm speechless!" Randall admitted, shaking his head.

"They also know what happened to Mr. Globitz."

"Oh my God! Please tell me."

"According to Paco, his body was dumped behind the tool shed in the middle of the night. A lady did it. She was dressed in black, but he didn't see her face. She covered the body with scrap lumber and then sped away in a golf cart."

"My God!"

"Paco and his dad retrieved the body and buried it in one of the burial chambers at the back of the Ossuary. Paco's dad said Globitz' neck was broken."

"I've got to tell Rafael!"

"There's more," she said.

"How could there possibly be more?"

Tears began to form in her eyes. "When Paco's father died, the boy had to bury him back there as well. Now he's an orphan."

A hushed murmur came from her husband's lips, "A twelve-year-old on his own back there. No father, nobody looking out for him. Terrible."

Eve grabbed her husband's hand and squeezed it. Through tears and a forced smile, she corrected him, "Your son stepped up. Rex and Octavio did what they could to help Paco. Religiously; every Saturday. And we should be proud of them."

Randall slumped into his chair. His chest pleaded for reserves as he tried to breathe normally. "We've got to do something. We've got to find that boy!"

CHAPTER XXIX
A LEGAL MATTER

MONTHS LATER

HARDLY RECOGNIZABLE IN HIS CLOSELY CROPPED HAIRCUT, NEW JEANS, polo shirt and classic Vans sneakers, Paco nervously fidgeted on the Sanctuary Square park bench next to his new adoptive mom, Carmen Ochoa, Rafael's wife. Excused from school and waiting for the call from the jam-packed Community Center just twenty steps away, he was beginning to understand the gravity of his presence.

The Community Center classroom, now Court Room, was abuzz with muffled speculation by the curious residents. Reluctantly presiding and sitting at the front of the room behind the folding table, sat Stephan H. Hayes, a New York real estate lawyer. Hayes' last criminal trial was as a first-year law student; the case was a mock trial among his fellow classmates. Hayes' white shirt and tie would suffice for a black robe today.

Representing the prosecution and equally qualified as a lawyer was E. J. Hardwick, an M & A (Mergers and Acquisitions) attorney from San Francisco. The team of defense lawyers consisted of Thomas F. Madigan, a tax attorney from Los Angeles and his assistant, Ruth Hopkins, a former legal secretary and wife of billionaire Arthur Hopkins from San Diego. The reluctant participants were all far removed from any experience in criminal law, but they bore the dubious distinction of having attended some form of law school.

Spectators near the back of the room strained to look over the heads of other observers to see the defendant and the legal circus about to unfold. The long dark red hair was easy to identify. Flanked by Madigan and Hopkins at the folding table on the right front, Krishka Globitz appeared confident, if not amused.

Two rows of empty chairs at the far right and front of the classroom awaited to be filled by selected residents; a jury of Krishka's peers, if that is even possible. A single empty chair to the left of the appointed judge, Mr. Hayes, had a sheet of paper with the words "witness" taped to the backrest. Two bailiffs in familiar bright yellow T-shirts added to the spectacle. Minus their bicycle helmets and shorts, Sergeant O stood at parade rest on the front left as did Sergeant M in the back of the room. Dutifully nodding to their new role, the muscular campus cops opted for more formal attire—long pants.

The tension-filled spectacle was hushed as movement on the front row indicated the court was about to come to order. Meredith stood up from his front row seat, turned, and addressed the gallery: "Ladies and gentlemen, the proceedings about to take place are what any civil society does under similar circumstances. Lacking any formal jurisdiction or governmental authority, you have appointed me and a committee to assemble our best-qualified neighbors to determine the guilt or innocence of one of our residents accused of violating a common, acceptable societal rule of law.

"I ask your understanding and patience during these proceedings.

Please refrain from vocalizing your opinions and respect the process as it unfolds." Turning, and facing the front, he continued, "Now Mr. Hayes, please proceed."

A black robe of authority was missing, but the deep voice and furrowed brow of Hayes made it clear, "Court is in Session. Sergeant O, please ask the jury to come in."

Twelve residents, eight women and four men, filed in from the back doorway and proceeded down the center aisle. Once they were seated, Judge Hayes looked directly at the defendant and said, "Mrs. Globitz, you've been accused of murdering your husband. How do you plead?"

Sitting erect in her folding chair, arms comfortably resting on the defense table, and staring through Hayes, she delivered an unemotional response, "I am not guilty!"

"Very well. E.J. will you proceed?"

Hardwick stepped from behind his Prosecutor's folding table; his enormous stature commanded everyone's attention. The one-time, All-Southeast Conference tight end from Vanderbilt dwarfed his rivals huddled behind the Defense table. The buttons on his white shirt were stretched to the max to contain the girth he had added from his college football days. His booming voice left no doubt who would dominate the proceedings.

"Ladies and gentlemen, we have a murderer among us." He paused. "Let that soak in," he continued. "A murderer." Pausing again, he continued saying, "Life is precious for all of us. We want to survive down here; to live for the day we can go back to our homes, beyond this bunker complex. The defendant, Mrs. Globitz, chose to deny that privilege to her husband by taking his life and hiding his body so that we would never know.

"Dr. Globitz, the genius behind our safe survival, will never see the fruits of his success." Hardwick turned, and with a look of total disgust, pointed his thick index finger and massive outstretched arm directly at Krishka and bellowed, "That woman, willfully and deliberately killed her husband by breaking his neck. She then loaded the body in his golf cart in the middle of the night, drove it to the deep depths of the back tunnel, and buried it under some rocks and lumber.

"She maliciously carried out this plot to satisfy her selfish desire to even a score and silence her betrothed over a trivial marital dispute."

Recognizing the bold tactic used by the prosecutor turned to the defense team for an opening statement.

"Your honor, the defense will show that this is all a big mistake. Dr. Globitz' personality changed significantly after the earthquakes and the isolation from all outside contacts. He grew more and more aggressive toward his wife that culminated in the night of our fifteenth month of sanctuary. He attacked Krishka with a knife. She tried to defend herself and he fell hitting his head and died from a broken neck.

"Mrs. Globitz chose not to alarm the residents in Yucca Mountain for fear of their panic, and so buried her husband's body, mourning his loss for several months. In fact, she suffers today from severe depression from the loss of her husband." For a tax attorney, Hayes' uncharacteristic emotional appeal was heartfelt and believable.

"Mr. Hardwick; your evidence please."

Over the course of the next hour, Hardwick paraded a series of witnesses proclaiming the virtues and the contributions of Dr. Globitz. One witness even suggested Globitz was a modern-day Noah for "shepherding us residents" to safety while the rest of the world was annihilated.

Several of the workers also testified, noting the routine visits by Globitz, often accompanied by Rafael or Mr. Meredith. "They drove up in his cart and Mr. Globitz would explain the importance of the work we were performing. Then he'd ask us how we were and thanked us for doing a good job."

Hardwick knew exactly what he was doing, presenting the best image of Globitz. And, the associations he had with Meredith and Rafael, both well respected, would transfer to Globitz—virtue by association.

Mr. Madigan and the defense team declined objection or cross examination.

Finally, it was time for the main witness. Hardwick provided a detailed explanation of the newly discovered boy found hiding in the back tunnel of Yucca Mountain. "Sitting outside this courtroom and waiting to be called is a twelve-year-old boy. He was a stowaway, the son of a hardworking construction man who helped build this facility. He did his best to save his son from certain death outside this bunker. Clearly, not in a financial position for a front-door invitation like we got, they were understandably determined to survive.

"Unfortunately, the father succumbed to severe respiratory failure and died. Can you imagine," he pleaded, "his twelve-year-old son having to bury his father? In the cold, dark, back tunnels of Yucca Mountain?"

Hardwick continued, "His name is Paco. His deceased father, Manuel Camacho, worked in this facility for years. Manuel and his son secretly took up residence in one of the maintenance sheds by the water reservoir. Last year, Manuel died. Paco did what he and his father had done earlier, he buried the deceased's body in one of the chambers of the Ossuary."

Hardwick paused to make sure the jury was listening. Then with emphasis, he said, "That's right, Paco and his dad had previously buried a body in the Ossuary—the body of Heinz Globitz!"

Hardwick went on to explain that the Ossuary had several rows of burial chambers for deceased residents, should that be necessary. "As you know, three of our residents have already been buried there in the first row. But, in the back-row chambers, deeper into the alcove, there are two sealed chambers—those of Manuel Camacho and Dr. Globitz."

"And now we will solicit Paco's testimony. His English is limited, and my questions will have to be translated into Spanish. He will provide the details I have just outlined. Bailiff, will you call for Paco and Mrs. Ochoa, his interpreter?"

Led by Mrs. Ochoa, Paco walked down the center aisle of the crowded courtroom as though he were being led to the gallows. The terrified witness surveyed the spectators, looking for a rescuer. His hand shook atop the bible held by the bailiff, as Mr. Hayes smiled and asked Paco to be truthful. Mrs. Ochoa's assuring nod and softly spoken message prompted a faint "*Sí*." Paco took Mrs. Ochoa's motioned lead as they both sat down.

"Your witness, E.J.," said Hayes.

Hardwick rose from his chair, cleared his throat, and soothingly spoke directly to his star witness. Mrs. Ochoa repeated the questions in Spanish, soliciting Paco's brief and nervous response. She in turn translated and conveyed to the court. Establishing Paco's credibility and the facts of his case, Hardwick's gentle questioning verified the information he had already presented the court: Paco's age, his father's name, and their circumstances living in the back tunnels of Yucca Mountain. Paco's tears became apparent when the questions addressed his mother's seizure by ICE (Immigration and Customs Enforcement).

Hardwick hadn't wanted to upset his witness before the real "meat" of his case. He asked the court for a brief recess. Hayes recognized his issue and responded, "Granted. Actually, let's all take forty-five minutes for lunch. Members of the jury, please do not discuss anything you've heard this morning and return to your seats by 12:45. Thank you."

BACK IN SESSION.

A cup of water was provided Paco and Mrs. Ochoa. The small packet of tissues offered was declined. It was now time to resume; time for Hardwick to establish the case of murder against Mrs. Globitz.

"Paco, we are all very sorry to hear of your father's passing. But it's important for you to tell us about it. Okay?" Hardwick's words were conveyed by Mrs. Ochoa.

"Sí."

Then, the necessary yank of the band aid, "When did your father die and where did you bury his body?"

Hearing the questions in Spanish, Paco gave a horrified look, dropping his head and uncontrollably shaking with grief. Minutes passed before his head raised revealing bubbling mucus under his nose and tears still flowing down his cheeks. The bailiff returned with the tissues. This time accepted.

As if he were on trial himself, Paco took a deep breath, mustered his maturity, and launched an eruption of hand jesters and explanations. Uninterrupted and lasting five minutes, his rapid-fire narrative captivated the courtroom attendees and established an aura of wholesome respect for the young man.

Finally, nodding in understanding, a teary-eyed Mrs. Ochoa compassionately tapped Paco's forearm. Composing herself, she turned to Hardwick and explained.

> "Paco and his father were asleep in their shelter near the water reservoir when they heard the sound of a golf cart approaching. The glow from the reservoir provided enough light for them to see it was a woman, struggling to lift a limp body from the cart and dragging it toward a pile of debris."

> "She hastily covered the body with the surrounding lumber and some strewn rocks then hopped aboard her golf cart and sped back down the dark tunnel."

"Was the woman you saw Mrs. Globitz?" Hardwick interrupted, pointing toward the defense table.

Paco nervously looked at Hardwick then at Mrs. Globitz. *"No sé."* (I don't know.)

> Mrs. Ochoa continued to explain that Paco and his father recognized *"El Jefe, un hombre muy agradable,"* ("The boss, a very nice man.") "Mr. Globitz under the debris. He was not bleeding, but his head was awkwardly positioned. Paco's father said his neck was broken—probably why he died."

Hardwick interrupted again, "Was there blood on his head or face?"

"No, señor," Paco confirmed.

> "Paco and his father used a wheelbarrow to move the body to the Ossuary. They placed it in the lower, back chamber and sealed it with stones and mortar," summarized Mrs. Ochoa.

Mrs. Ochoa openly wept while relaying:

> "When his father died, Paco placed him in the chamber next to Mr. Globitz and sealed it like they had previously."

"Do you remember which chamber is your father's and which is Globitz'?"

> *"Si. iniciales 'HG' talladas en cemento para El Jefe."* ("Yes, we carved initials 'HG' in the cement for the boss," relayed Mrs. Ochoa.)

"There you have it, ladies and gentlemen. The missing body is in one of the burial chambers in the Ossuary. It was innocently placed there by Paco and his father. The only woman who could have killed him was his wife, Krishka, who used his golf cart to transport the body to the back corridors of this sanctuary. And there she left him to rot under a pile of debris." He confidently strode back to his chair.

Judge Hayes cynically looked at the defense table and affirmed, "Your witness, Tom."

Madigan recognized the authenticity of Paco's testimony. He was a blameless interloper and witness to a macabre set of circumstances. He also was mature beyond his years, surviving alone as he had. The defense team was reluctant to challenge him or his story.

"No questions, your honor."

Having heard the defense decline further questions of the prosecution witnesses, Hardwick rose and confidently stated, "The prosecution rests."

An uneasy Tom Madigan paused and looked at his client, then rose from his seat to address the court. He flashed on his daughter's encouraging words at breakfast, "Make us proud, Daddy."

"First we would stipulate the prosecution's claim that the chamber marked 'HG' in the Ossuary contains the body of Dr. Globitz. There is no need to exhume and identify. Second, we even agree that Globitz may have died from a broken neck based on Paco's description and testimony.

"The series of events and witnesses presented by Mr. Hardwick are reasonable and irrefutable, but do not establish a case for murder.

"You must be certain, beyond reasonable doubt, that Mrs. Globitz killed her husband without justification and did so with premeditation. Please keep those two elements in mind as you hear the testimony of defense witnesses.

"We would like to call a series of witnesses. Mr. Ochoa, please come forward."

Carmen Ochoa and Paco departed the court as her husband Rafael rose to fill the vacant witness chair. Sergeant O held the Bible while Mr. Ochoa affirmed the oath and sat down. Madigan's questions were intentionally upbeat, a departure from the depressing atmosphere left by Hardwick. He attested to the years of construction of Yucca Mountain and of Manuel Camacho's employment. Rafael explained how Paco's presence was revealed.

Rafael was asked about the weekly meetings he and the staff had with Dr. Globitz' and his noticeable declining disposition. The meetings stopped about six months ago "because of Dr. Globitz health issues," he said. Rafael was asked to describe the wine storage alcove back in mile four of the back tunnel and special locker for Globitz' own selection of scotches. Madigan summarized Rafael's testimony saying, "Would you agree that Mr. Globitz' temperament seemed to diminish over time?"

"Yes."

"Would you agree that his consumption of scotch may have contributed to his declining temperament?"

"Probably," Rafael reluctantly responded.

"No more questions. Your witness, Hardwick."

Hardwick sarcastically asked, "How do you know Dr. Globitz consumed his Scotch?"

"Because the empty bottles were collected and disposed of with his trash every other day by my staff," Rafael responded. "The empty scotch bottles also stopped (presumably) when his health issues arose."

"No further questions," Hardwick exhaled.

Rafael was dismissed and Dr. Jammicit was called. Confirming Globitz' weight, blood pressure, and general condition, the doctor's assessment: "He was in poor health." The physician said Globitz' was overweight. His reading habit and lack of physical exercise compounded by heavy drinking likely led to his unhealthy lifestyle. He also admitted the victim's depressive state necessitating the medications he had prescribed.

Madigan asked, "Dr. Jammicit, were you concerned about the declining mental state of Dr. Globitz?"

"Yes."

Hardwick had no questions.

Madigan called several workers and Yucca Mountain staff members who seemed to love their boss but sadly, watched his deteriorating health effect his disposition. One worker in the Air Purification department suggested that Globitz, in a fit of anger, threw a dirty air filter at him. It became a situation where "we were all walking on eggshells when he came around," the man said

Hardwick declined to cross examine.

Buoyed by the testimony of his witnesses, Madigan was aware that his case was still iffy. The charge of murder was daunting and required absolute closure. He had addressed the issue with the defendant and they both agreed.

Nodding to his client and assistant, Ruth Hopkins at the defense table, he confidently rose from his seat and announced his final witness: Mrs. Globitz.

CHAPTER XXX
A TRIAL OF MURDER

KRISHKA GLOBITZ ROSE FROM HER CHAIR TO MOVE TOWARD THE WITNESS stand. Wearing a black blazer pant suit, a white silk blouse, a modest pearl necklace and pumps, she could have been mistaken for the attorney, not the accused.

Sergeant O held the Bible while Krishka hesitated, then placed her hand atop it. Judge Hayes administered the oath. As she settled into the witness chair, Krishka calmly looked over the scene, including the judge, attorneys, and spectators.

Defense attorney Madigan stood and asked Krishka to state her name and place of birth.

She glanced at Randall sitting in the front row of spectators and said, "My name is Krishka Globitz. I was born in Odessa, Ukraine."

"Please tell us how you met your husband, and how you ended up in the United States."

Krishka said that she was working in Moscow when she was

introduced to the wealthy, businessman. "It was purely a business arrangement at first. Then, for me it became a way to improve my status and gain entry into the U.S."

"I'm hesitant to pry into your personal life, but the seriousness of the charges against you may require the discussion of some uncomfortable topics. Are you okay with that?"

"Of course."

"Thank you. So," he assertively asked, "how long was your courtship with Dr. Globitz?"

"Three weeks. Then we came to U.S."

"Did you enter as husband and wife?"

"Yes, he had some papers so that the authorities didn't question anything," she explained.

"Where did you live?"

"We had apartment in the Upper East Side, New York. He split his time mostly between Las Vegas and New York over the last several years."

"Was that because he was overseeing the construction of Yucca Mountain?"

"Yes."

"So, you were together in the U.S. for four or five years?"

"That is correct if you include the time we have lived here," she clarified."

"Did your husband treat you well?"

"Yes, until his health declined," she admitted.

"Was there any issue that you recall that may have angered him?"

"The water level. The water outside the Observation Chamber."

"What exactly do you mean?" queried Madigan.

"He was very upset after the big earthquake, when he discovered the water covering the windows in the Observation Chamber. That was also when all of the equipment outside the chamber was destroyed," she said.

"How did he express his anger?"

Pursing her lips in disgust, "He was crying and told me we were underwater."

"Did he have any thoughts about how to deal with the situation?" urged Madigan.

"Not much. He just began drinking a lot."

"What do you mean by 'a lot'?"

"Well," she offered, "after that night, he seemed to drink more and more each day. He became difficult to talk to. Angry. Some days he never got out of bed, except to go to the bathroom or to retrieve another bottle of scotch."

Madigan asked Krishka about the night Globitz died.

She replied, "He had grown despondent and his drinking increased. His medications were not helping. I pleaded with him to compose himself, and to act like a leader. But he turned on me."

"What do you mean, 'turned on you'?"

She continued to describe the fateful night as if she were reporting news from a crime scene. "I became the object of his anger. He acted like it was my fault. So, he finally lashed out and attacked me with a kitchen knife."

"Was Dr. Globitz inebriated when he attacked you?"

"Yes. He stumbled over the coffee table, slashed my leg, and then fell and hit his head on the arm of the sofa. He never got up after that."

Lowering his voice, Madigan quietly asked, "Is that when you realized he was dead?"

"Yes. That's when I freaked out." She added in a humble voice, "I knew that if the workers and all of the residents realized that Dr. Globitz had given up, it would cause a panic, maybe even be catastrophic if they knew that there was no leader or no hope for ever leaving Yucca Mountain."

"So, you decided to bury him?"

"I waited until everyone was asleep. Then I loaded him on his golf cart and drove it to the back tunnel. I needed time to think about what to do!" she explained in a stressed voice. "The next night, I planned to place the body in the Ossuary, but when I got there the body was gone." Sinking in her chair, Krishka seemed resigned.

Madigan decided it was time to summarize the death. "So, Dr. Globitz, in a drunken craze, attacked you with a knife. He stumbled in the struggle, fell, and broke his neck when his head hit the edge of the sofa."

"That is correct," she confirmed. Adding, "Also slashed at me, cutting my leg."

"Yes, of course. And when you realized he was dead, you panicked." He quickly continued. "Then your immediate concern was the impact his death might have on the residents and staff of Yucca Mountain. You were afraid that it might cause a riot or an insurrection."

Krishka straightened up and declared, "Yes, it could have caused a rampage that would endanger all of our lives."

"So, you thought that secretly burying his body was the only way to prevent an uprising."

"In my panicky state of mind, that was my assessment, yes."

The cagy tax attorney seemed to have built a case that Krishka was the victim, not the culprit.

Madigan took a deep breath to gather his final thoughts. He looked at each of the jurors and said, "So, you are now faced with the decision to either convict or exonerate Ms. Globitz. I pray that you will understand the sad circumstances in which she found herself. That she is the victim in this case and panicked at first when trying to do what she thought best for all of us. I know that you will do the right thing and find her NOT GUILTY."

Madigan turned and nodded to Judge Hayes, then took his seat.

"Your witness, Mr. Hardwick."

The prosecutor rose from behind his table, realizing that he had a lot to overcome. He began his cross with a voice that was soothing, almost mellow.

"Mrs. Globitz, when exactly did you get married to Heinz Globitz?"

"Well, we were never 'actually' married," she demurred.

"But you routinely went by the last name, Globitz?"

"Yes, it was just easier that way," she explained. "My real name is Krishka Konstantine Zhukova."

The jury looked baffled, but Hardwick smiled at her confirming what he already knew.

"Did you respect Dr. Globitz?" he asked.

"Yes, of course."

"I mean, did you *like* him?" Hardwick pried.

"I liked him, yes."

"So, you considered yourselves friends?"

"I suppose. That's a term you Americans have bastardized." she grimaced as she responded.

"Were you and Dr. Globitz, intimate?"

Krishka lingered, protruding her lower lip, blowing and looking upward, "Yes, of course, but it waned."

Madigan was visibly nervous with the line of questions, and Meredith watched Krishka squirm at the details of her private details. His late-night swimming associate and spa companion's personal life was being dissected; necessarily but excruciatingly invasive. Their benign, pool-side conversations would be eclipsed by smarmy details of her personal life.

"Krishka, your "maiden" name is quite famous in Russia, isn't it?" asked Hardwick.

"Yes, I suppose."

"You were an Olympic swimming champion, is that correct?"

"Yes."

"But your father was a legendary military commander, right?"

"It was my grandfather."

"Yes, of course. It would have to have been during World War Two," he paused. "Your parents were at one time members of the Soviet Politburo. Correct?"

"Yes."

"And Communist Party members?"

"Objection!" Madigan screamed. "That has no bearing on the case and is prejudicial to Mrs. Globitz."

"SHE'S A RUSSIAN AGENT!" was shouted from the back of the courtroom.

"Bailiff, please escort that person out," directed Judge Hayes.

Sergeant O stepped past several seated residents, walking sideways through the back row of chairs toward the protesting spectator. The hot-headed resident reluctantly cooperated with the bailiff's tug and was dispatched out the door.

"Thank you. Now, the objection is sustained. Jury, please disregard the reference Mr. Hardwick has suggested," intervened Judge Hayes.

Of course, the damage had been done, as the jury could not "unhear" what had been said.

Hardwick continued, "I'm sorry. Would you say that your family has been in a position of privilege in Russia?"

"Objection!" yelled Madigan.

"Where are you going with this, counselor?" frowned Hayes.

"The court needs to understand the real reason that Krishka is in our midst. I'm trying to establish her and Globitz' ultimate objective. It is pertinent to our case."

"Carry on."

"My family has proudly served our country, if that's what you are suggesting," she retorted. While she was responding, Madigan tried to drown out her reply by shouting,

"Objection!"

"Objection, overruled. Proceed, A.J."

Hardwick picked up a paper and handing it to Krishka asked, "Would you read please the headline of this *UK Daily Mail* article, which is from our computerized library?"

"It says, 'Convicted Currency Scammer Secretly Released from Russian Prison'" she reluctantly uttered.

"Objection!" shouted Madigan.

"Overruled," Judge Hayes responded.

In the next hour, Hardwick kept everyone guessing as he presented copies of international news articles from the Yucca Mountain Library data files. Intending to evoke a reaction, he asked Krishka to read them. As she did so, he began to link them together to suggest that Globitz had agreed to "pay off" certain Russian interests with the gold bullion that he had received from his fifty Yucca Mountain investors. He tried to get Krista to acknowledge this angle, but she would not. He suggested that Globitz was a useful pawn for the Russians to replenish their gold reserves. Multiple objections were raised by Madigan, but most were overruled.

Hardwick continued. "Were you aware of Mr. Globitz' legal issues with the Russian government?"

"No, not really. Not at first, anyway."

Hardwick then seemed to shift gears. His next few questions appeared more gracious and sympathetic. A courtroom seduction of sorts was taking place.

"Krishka, what was your job in Moscow when you met Dr. Globitz?"

"I was an interpreter and translator for a large oil company."

"So, you translated business arrangements for your company?" Hardwick asked.

"Yes, agreements, contracts, transactions, and communications. Things like that."

"And, the company you worked for?"

"It was called Rosneft."

"Isn't Rosneft a state-owned company?"

"Yes."

"So, you worked for the government, the Russian government?"

"Indirectly, yes."

"OBJECTION! OBJECTION! OBJECTION!" interrupted Madigan, standing and pounding is hand on the table. "This whole argument is preposterous, prejudicial, and injurious to my client's innocence."

"Sustained," Judge Hayes admonished. "Wherever you were going with this, A.J., it is now over."

Hardwick glared at Hayes and wondered, how he could make his case now. His attempt to establish that Mrs. Globitz, actually Ms. Zhukova, was not who she pretended to be, had failed. He was actually trying to prove that she was a Russian agent, not just a company employee. He was trying to show that she was not only trained in several languages, she was also trained in self-defense, martial arts, and intelligence services. As a former Olympian she was certainly strong enough to overpower her elderly husband. It was obvious to him that Krishka had been assigned to monitor Globitz for the Russians until he was no longer useful and then had been authorized to exterminate him at that point.

Hardwick's zeal had exceeded the court's legal protocol.

Madigan's intervention prevented the court from hearing the prosecutor's full-blown conspiracy theory. In his view, such a theory would not only have been preposterous, but also injurious to his client's innocence. It would have made a sham of the Yucca Mountain court proceedings.

"I move for a MISTRIAL," Madigan put forward.

"Objection!" interrupted Hardwick. "There are no grounds for mistrial."

"Objection sustained. No mistrial," Hayes ruled. "A.J. you may proceed your cross examination under the precautions I have already made."

"Yes sir," Hardwick humbly replied. Then stumbling through his notes and turning to Krishka, he meekly resumed questioning. "Krishka, did you ever visit the Observation Chamber with Dr. Globitz?"

"Yes, on several occasions."

"What did he point out to you on those visits?"

"He showed me everything: The chamber door, the entry lever, its water-tight seal, the cupola windows, and everything inside. What specifically are you referring to?"

"Was he upset that the instruments for measuring outside conditions were inoperable?"

"Yes, very upset."

"And, the view from the cupola windows, did he mention the view?"

"Yes. He was extremely upset that only one of the seven windows provided a look outside. All of the other windows were totally obstructed by rocks and earth. Each time we went back to look, there was water outside the one window with a view. The fact that we were under water made him very distressed."

"Did Dr. Globitz explain the emergency escape plan through the cupola window?" Hardwick was now probing, not knowing how the accused would respond. He acted as though such an escape route was common knowledge.

She paused to assess Hardwick's query. Then, assuming that he might actually know about the escape mechanism, she confirmed, "Yes, and the igniter switch is on the wall, outside the chamber."

"The igniter to set off the explosives around the cupola escape window?"

"Yes." Krishka was now questioning herself. *Have I mistakenly revealed secrets that were really not common knowledge?*

Looking sterner, and recovering from his previous line of questions, Hardwick boldly asked, "Krishka, did you ever question Mr. Globitz about his failure to design a secondary escape route from Yucca Mountain?"

"Not really."

"Were you disappointed to learn there was no backup escape plan?"

"Of course."

"Didn't the two of you ever discuss how to get out of here?"

"Well, yes. I guess we discussed that."

"Did you criticize his poor planning? No Plan B for escape?"

"No. That was not my place!" she screeched in defiance.

"Every couple argues at some time in their relationship. You said you were together for over five years, even intimate. Are you suggesting that you never voiced your concern over being doomed under this mountain because of his poor planning?"

"Maybe. I don't remember."

Hardwick was on to something. His Russian conspiracy theory could be tabled, but a hypercritical, nitpicking spouse could easily provoke her egotistical partner into a deadly confrontation. And, a former Olympic athlete was obviously capable of winning the confrontation—with neck-breaking thoroughness.

"When you argued, did Dr. Globitz ever raise his voice?"

"I guess."

"Then you did argue." Hardwick immediately asked Krishka to show the court the injury she sustained the night Dr. Globitz attacked her with a knife.

Squirming and looking toward her defense team for help, Krishka paused, and asked, "Are you asking me to remove my slacks?"

"Objection, your honor!" shouted Madigan.

Judge Hayes sustained.

"No, I'm not asking that," Hardwick said. "I only wanted you to point to the area on your leg that was slashed by the knife." Krishka hesitantly raised her arm, then circled her left palm directly over her inner thigh.

"Judge Hayes, this is unsatisfactory. Are we just to assume the defendant is telling the truth about her injury?" pleaded Hardwick.

"I'll not have Mrs. Globitz disrobe in this court, counselor, just to prove whether or not she has a scar," insisted Judge Hayes.

"Then I recommend a third party inspect her leg in suitable privacy," Hardwick offered.

"Objection. This is ridiculous!" insisted Madigan.

Through clenched teeth, Hayes directed Hardwick and Madigan to confer in private.

Finally, the counselors returned to their respective tables, and Judge Hayes announced to the court, "We will take a ten-minute recess while Dr. Jammicit and Mrs. Globitz excuse themselves to a more private place to examine the wound."

When the two returned, a hush descended again. Dr. Jammicit was directed to the witness chair and was reminded that he was still under oath. When he confirmed, Judge Hayes looked at Hardwick and said, "Your witness."

"Dr. Jammicit, did you see evidence of an injury on Ms. Zhukov, err, Mrs. Globitz' leg?"

"Yes."

"Please describe the nature of the injury for the court."

"There was scar tissue on the inside of the thigh *and* on the back side of the thigh," Jammicit said.

"So, a knife went all the way through Mrs. Globitz' leg?" Hardwick asked.

"Yes, I would suggest a sharp object entered the inside front of her thigh and extended through the back of her leg. It was a wicked injury, but it looks to have healed quite nicely."

"How long would you estimate an injury like that would take to heal?" Hardwick prodded.

"Objection!" screamed Madigan. "The witness is testifying beyond the scope we agreed to."

"Sustained."

"So, it had sufficient time to heal since Mr. Globitz turned up missing?"

"It is well healed," Jammicit stuttered, knowing that what he didn't say was pivotal.

"No further questions, your honor," Hardwick said begrudgingly.

"The defense has no further questions."

"The witness may step down," said Judge Hayes. "Mrs. Globitz, you may resume your place on the witness stand."

The damage was done. The description of the wound on her leg left doubt in the jury's mind as to the source and the occasion of the injury. Could it have happened in a previous situation? Even by someone other than Globitz? Could it have been an old injury from her former work environment? Hardwick wondered about these possibilities as he continued his cross examination.

Krishka was slowly being dragged into a murky scenario, the potentiality for murder. It was difficult for Madigan to intervene. The questions were reasonable, without badgering, and were offered in a very mannerly way. Hardwick knew he was making points and continued to probe, finally getting Krishka to acknowledge that she had verbally aggravated Globitz to a breaking point on the night he died. However, the shrewd defendant yielded just enough information to appear cooperative without confessing to delivering the fatal blow. She was smarter than that, and Hardwick knew it.

The jury retreated for deliberations while the whispering spectators remained in place.

One hour passed after the jury was dismissed to deliberate. A shroud of restlessness engulfed the courtroom occupants. Murmurs amplified to a more vocal grumbling, grumbling to loud talking, even open laughter. All silenced when the juror's door opened.

Sergeant M entered carrying a note addressed to Judge Hayes. Everyone quietly watched as Hayes scribbled a response and watched the sergeant return to the deliberation classroom.

Moments later the door opened, and the jury delivered its verdict: Excusable Homicide; Not Guilty of Murder.

Among gasps, Hayes declared "case closed." Krishka displayed a smile of measured restraint, thanking her attorney, and briefly waving to the jury. The courtroom emptied.

Hargrove, Hayes, and Madigan retreated to the faculty lounge where they saluted each other's performance over shots of scotch.

CHAPTER XXXI
A MEMORABLE FIELD TRIP

KRISHKA EMERGED FROM THE TRIAL ORDEAL AS SORT OF A "FOLK HERO," with Globitz as the actual culprit. It was HIS lavish scheme to buy his way out of a Russian prison with American gold. Krishka was merely the assigned watch dog. She really did no harm to the Yucca Mountain residents and was caught in the middle, as the jury saw it. When Globitz's plan failed, he triggered his own death by his violent intemperance, and the pitiable Krishka was left holding the bag (body in this case). Her solution, though not fully accomplished, would have spared her fellow residents trauma and avoided a rebellion. It was an honorable undertaking. "NOT GUILTY" was the community's unanimous verdict.

THREE YEARS LATER

"You're joking. Right?" pleaded Samantha, gulping the last bit of milk from her cereal bowl.

"No, *whale poop*! That's what Isaac's dad said we'd find," insisted Rex.

"Enough of the potty mouth," said their mother. "Finish your breakfast or you'll be late for school. The lunches for your field trip are here on the counter. Don't forget them."

The twins raced out the front door, both yelling, "Thanks, Mom." They continued discussing today's field trip.

"Mr. Lowe said we'll get to look out the window of the Observation Chamber and Isaac's dad said that whale poop is all we'll see. That's what he said," Rex insisted.

"Yeah," Samantha said. "But we're gonna see the whole back tunnel—all five miles of it. I can't wait to see the fishery!"

"Wonder if they'll let us tickle for fish?" Rex posed.

Rafael, Coach Lowe, and a classmate's father, Mr. Willingham, stood outside the classroom next to four golf carts and their tag-along passenger trailers receiving final instructions from Randall Meredith. In a few minutes the carts would be filled with Mr. Lowe's class of boisterous students.

The classroom door burst open and twenty-four ninth graders spilled out to clamber aboard the trailers. "Sit by me," seemed to be the most popular phrase amongst the enthusiastic teenagers. Paco and Marco had evolved into best buddies and, sat next to each other in the motorcade, behind their other best buddies, Rex and Marco.

When they were all aboard, and the caravan made its way to the beginning of the ramp that had brought them all to the Sanctuary seven years ago. A chatter of anticipation was spirited by the roller-coaster effect of the convoy slowly making its way up the steep ramp toward the Observation Chamber. The glowing and fading tunnel lighting, with fixtures spaced every 100 feet, added to the carnival-ride sensation. It was going to be a wonderful day out of the classroom.

When they finally arrived at the end of the tunnel, Mr. Lowe stood at the top of the Observation Chamber stairs. From their golf carts, the students waited patiently. All eyes looked up at Mr. Lowe; they had been thoroughly briefed on the rules and their teacher's expectations of compliance. Still sitting behind the driver's wheel of the last cart, Mr. Willingham was impressed.

"Okay, from the first cart, two at a time. The rest, wait your turn and stay in your golf carts until I call." The first two students scrambled to the stairs, as Mr. Lowe warned them, "Slow down; hang on to the railing. Be careful."

A few minutes passed; then the students who were coming back down the stair warned their nervous classmates of their impressions, saying, "Oh my god!" Awaiting their turn seemed a lifetime for the rest of the impatient youth. Rafael was positioned inside the tiny capsule to brief each pair of kids on all of the gadgets, buttons, and monitors within the chamber. He answered as many questions as their three-minute visit allowed. One observant student asked why one of the windows had a second window welded over it. Another asked why the flashlight held against the partially obstructed window showed only dark water outside.

Rafael calmly explained that the cupola was exactly like the one used by the astronauts in the International Space Station. He explained that a window from an extra cupola had been welded over the leaky window as a safety precaution and was a "lifesaving suggestion by one of the workers." "Ooh," was the students' response.

Amber Trissler and her best friend Britney Sabado were finally called. Amber, considered the smartest kid in the class, was also the quietest, and the one most timid about entering the capsule. Rafael did his best to calm the pair, pointing out all the controls, the buttons, switches, and the monitors. He tactfully explained their inoperable condition and held the flashlight against the only window with any sort of view. Amber was trembling after seeing only "dark water" beyond the glass. Her trembling deteriorated to squeals, then shrieks of horror.

Mr. Lowe crawled partially into the Observation Chamber to

console his favorite student. As he gently guided her out of the tight-fitting compartment, he hoped the cooler air circulating below would soothe her fears. It helped some, but she still clutched Mr. Lowe's arm all the way down to the carts.

Some of the kids wondered if Amber had bumped her head when leaving the capsule. Their perception of what was really bothering her was luckily vague. Each naïvely offered sympathy and encouragement. Britney and Mr. Lowe kept quiet about the probable cause of Amber's hysteria.

When all had visited the cupola and were seated in the carts once again, the caravan made its way back down the ramp. Randall and Mr. Trissler were waiting at the base of the ramp when the golf carts arrived. They helped Amber and Britney exit their cart, since the adults had decided these two girls should forgo the rest of the field trip.

Rex didn't even notice his dad during the brief stop of the caravan and was oblivious to Amber's suffering. He and Octavio were joking with the boys sitting behind them, "We didn't see any whale poop. Did you guys?"

The procession of the golf carts continued through Sanctuary Square around the bend and down the corridor to the woven wire gate marked "DANGER NO ENTRY." Rafael dismounted from his cart, slid open the gate, and flipped the lights on in the tunnel beyond the gate. "We didn't need those sissy lights," Rex said privately to Tavo and Paco. "Yeah," they responded. Sitting next to Paco, Marco squealed in agreement, but the rest of the passengers couldn't figure out what they were whispering about.

Down the tunnel they sped. For all but a few, it was a first-time adventure. Occasional yelps from the students echoing off the walls added to the field trip merriment. The intermittent lighting provided the same "spooky" effect it had in the ramp tunnel. "We just passed our pet rat area. Wonder how he's doing?" Octavio said.

Like a high school hayride, the spirited caravan proceeded all the way to the end of the tunnel before U-turning and stopping. Through the speakers, Mr. Lowe explained they had reached the point where a closed-off exit gate sat behind a large mass of rock and earth. A Caterpillar dozer and scoop loader left over from the initial tunnel excavations sat nearby.

From the last cart, one of the students asked, "Is the gate behind these rocks underwater too?" When their teacher answered affirmatively, the feisty class began booing as though it were an umpire's bad call at home plate. Then, oblivious to the seriousness of Lowe's answer, they broke out in giggling. With a jolt, the carts and their merry passengers were off again, moving back in the direction from which they had come.

Mr. Lowe continued to narrate during the return trip, pointing out the alcoves of food storage, supply warehouse, medical supplies, clothing and shoe storage, and maintenance equipment. Stopping at the alcove labeled "Aeroponic and Aquaponic Gardens," Mr. Lowe explained how Yucca Mountain food supplies were augmented by the products grown in the ecologically efficient gardens.

Rex reminded his teacher that a school of fish was also maintained in the water under the plants. "If you want, Paco and I will show you how to tickle for fish." Laughter from his classmates and a quizzical look from Lowe prompted him to say, "Back on the carts, class. We're running short of time."

The students noticed a slight bluish glowing effect on the ceiling and walls as they approached the water reservoir. When the carts stopped, the students piled out to gather around the outside the berm to hear Mr. Lowe explain the water aquafer and purification system. In the middle of his discussion, he stopped.

"Where did Paco and Marco go?"

"They went to the outhouse, behind the tool shed, Mr. Lowe," answered Rex.

The rest of the group was puzzled. Not everyone knew what an outhouse was. Mr. Lowe continued his discussion. When it was time to get back into the carts, Rafael walked over to the shed to discover

Paco and Marco combing through some of the belongings Paco had left behind when he moved into the Ochoa residents. "Come on boys, we gotta load up."

The next stop on the tour was the area where there were two alcoves on opposite sides of the main tunnel. "Look over there, class," Lowe said pointing toward the alcove with the MAINTENANCE sign. "Let's go look at that glass igloo."

The students quickly gathered around the cupola. Four of the boys were quite familiar with the glass-windowed dome. Marco climbed inside.

"This cupola is the twin of the one you were inside earlier this morning in the Observation Chamber. Rafael is going to tell you a little about it."

Rafael stepped forward where all could see. Placing one hand on the structure, he read from a laminated card,

> "This titanium-reinforced glass structure was built in Italy by a European Space Agency contractor. It is nearly ten feet in diameter and five feet tall. It has six side windows and a top window, all of which have multiple layers of high-strength bulletproof glass."

Then adding his own words, "This is identical to the structure mounted on the International Space Station. It was designed so that two astronauts could maneuver inside and operate the controls for the robot arms outside the station."

Pointing to the empty window frame, Lance Richmond asked, "What happened to that window?"

"We removed it and welded it over one of the leaky windows in the Observation Chamber."

"Oh, that's right."

Olivia raised her hand and asked, "What about the round window on top? It's missing too."

Smiling to acknowledge the observant student, Rafael replied, "The construction workers who built this tunnel erected a concrete monument outside, on the very top of Yucca Mountain. They installed the round glass window and its frame from here into the monument for decoration."

"Gucci!" she exclaimed.

Paco's chest swelled as he beamed. *"Mi papá fue uno de los trabajadores."* ("My father was one of the workers.")

Rafael reinforced his words, "That's right. Paco's dad was an important member of the staff who built this place."

The class broke out in appreciative applause. Paco smiled, glowing with pride.

Lowe cut in, "Okay guys, let's move over to the Ossuary. We're running short of time." The class crossed to the other side of the main tunnel.

"Rafael Ochoa will tell us about this alcove."

Rafael waited for them to settle down. He said, "All of the alcoves we saw today, and even the ones where we have our apartments, were originally supposed to look like this one. The rows of round holes you see," as he pointed, "were drilled into the walls as storage compartments. The one in the ceiling was a pressure-relief shaft." He paused as the kids jockeyed for position.

"The power companies and the government spent over twelve billion dollars to dig this tunnel and these alcoves for storing all of the nation's nuclear waste. Fortunately for us, President Barrack Obama and Senator Harry Reid shut the project down. That's how it became available for our use as a Sanctuary."

One of the students raised his hand and asked, "Why did they shut the project down?"

Rafael responded, "Because they had a better plan."

Another curious student blurted out, "What was their better plan?"

"I don't know; they didn't tell us. Now, your teacher is going to explain what an Ossuary is."

"An Ossuary is like an underground cemetery where we bury our dead."

Rafael cringed, hearing the words out of Mr. Lowe's mouth. They should have warned him. "Let's pay our respects to Jimmy Jones' dad and Jessica Lockhart's mother." They all knew Jimmy and Jessica from a previous class.

Showing some reluctance to follow, the group awaited Mr. Lowe's move toward one of the sealed-up holes. Paco broke from the cluster and went deeper inside the dimly lit cave. The class cautiously followed their teacher.

He somberly murmured, "Notice the hollow chambers drilled into the walls of this alcove? That's where we bury our departed loved ones." The seriousness of his lowered voice triggered a reverential hush from the students. "These three here on the left are where Jimmy's dad, Mrs. McClintock, and Jessica Lockhart's mother are buried. And, farther back in this alcove are where Paco's dad and Dr. Globitz are buried."

Seeing the outline of Paco, deep in a back part of the alcove, kneeling with bowed head in front of one of the tombs, Lowe grimaced. Silently cursing himself, and in a hushed tone, he motioned to the class to quietly exit.

Whispers from the obedient students shuffling back to the golf carts asked, "What's going on?" One-by-one the students learned of Paco's situation. Some of his classmates were more informed than others; all became sincerely respectful as the caravan quietly waited for Paco's return.

Rex and Octavio gradually found their seat in the cart and remained uncharacteristically silent. The rest of the students respectfully sat and waited. Mr. Lowe nodded in appreciation to the class.

After a few minutes had passed, Paco quietly emerged from the Ossuary and assumed his seat among the group. His moments of remembrance were unconditionally accepted. The boy sitting behind him patted his shoulder without saying a word. It was now time to go, and the caravan jerked and began to roll.

"Wait!" shouted Paco. Surprised, all heads turned to look. "Where's Marco!? He's supposed to be sitting here."

The procession halted. "'Anybody seen Marco?" asked Mr. Lowe. Silence.

The teacher panicked. Still unsettled by his insensitivity to Paco and now by the possible loss of a student, he was stammering. "Where's Marco?"

Blank looks from his kids; he asked again, "Has anyone seen Marco? Where did we last see him?"

"He was sitting with Paco right behind me when we stopped," said Octavio. "He must have gone into the cave," he said pointing to the Ossuary.

"I can find him," said Rex. "Come on, Tavo, we've been through this before."

Wrinkles across Mr. Lowe's forehead expressed both exasperation and hope as he nodded permission to the volunteers. The two entered the Ossuary while Rafael stood by the entrance. Mr. Lowe and the rest of the class waited in the golf carts. Walking toward the back of the tunnel, Rex looked at the empty burial chambers on the right; Octavio did the same on the left. Both called out, "Marco, Marco!" Paco watched and waited next to Rafael.

Lighting in the Ossuary was not ideal, but it was considerably better than the flashlight search for Marco the boys had previously conducted. They peered inside each chamber as they walked. Calling out Marco's name with no response, they became increasingly concerned. Deeper and deeper they went, apprehension growing. They reached the Caterpillar "hole driller" in the back of the Ossuary tunnel—no Marco.

"Marco!" they yelled. Their voices echoing inside the cavernous burial den seemed to amplify to the outside. Waiting by the caravan near the entrance to the Ossuary, Mr. Lowe sensed the alarm in their calls. Returning to the Sanctuary without Marco would be a gut punch for Lowe. He was responsible, regardless of the three other adult chaperones. How could he lose one of his students? Or explain it to Marco's parents?

Paco considered himself Marco's best friend. He turned toward Mr. Lowe, "I think I know where he's hiding." With a sense of confidence, he entered the alcove. With Rafael and Mr. Lowe's approval, Rex and Octavio followed their friend.

"Marco, Marco!" he called in the hollow cavern.

The students were abuzz, waiting in their golf carts. Mr. Lowe and Rafael paced back and forth outside the entrance. Minutes passed. The echoes continued, fading slightly as the boys went deeper into the alcove.

Rex and Octavio watched Paco climb up on the "hole driller." Reaching and pulling himself into the tight-fitting shaft in the ceiling, he had obviously done this before. It took only seconds for his legs and feet to disappear into the chamber. The boys quizzically looked at each other. And waited.

Faint sounds of "Marco," trickled from the opening, muffled by Paco's body as he crawled deeper and deeper into the tight shaft.

"Tavo, what if they get stuck? And don't come back?"

"Shut up! They've both climbed up there before. At least I think they have." The uncertainty in Octavio's voice was unsettling for both. They waited.

"Boys, what's happening in there?" an impatient Rafael shouted.

"Paco's climbing after him, sir. Don't worry," reported Rex.

ONE HOUR LATER

Cheers erupted as all four boys emerged from the Ossuary tunnel. Paco and Marco were noticeably tired and covered with dirt. Marco's knees were bleeding and exposed through his worn pants. His elbows were scraped, and his lips appeared blue. Unmindful of this pain, Marco was smiling and babbling an unrecognizable sequence, "ite,ite,ite." The celebrating adults and kids treasured their ASD friend and ignored his limited vocabulary.

Without fanfare Rex, Octavio, and Paco led Marco to the golf carts. They all took their respective seats, and the caravan headed home. Rafael exhaled in relief. The fast-moving air from the speeding motorcade sent a slight chill through Mr. Lowe's sweat-saturated shirt. When the group finally got back, they were about two hours overdue. It was truly a memorable field trip for all the participants, both adults and kids.

CHAPTER XXXII
A MYSTERIOUS DISCOVERY

SIX MONTHS LATER

THE MEREDITHS' AFTER-DINNER RITUAL CONTINUED, THIS TIME including a Friday night sleepover guest, Octavio. They voted to play Progressive. Samantha raised her hands and clenched her fists in delight, especially at the prospect of incorporating Octavio into the game. Both parents chuckled at the twins' enthusiasm.

The story game lasted well after normal bedtime, but since it was the start of the weekend, the parents allowed it. Finally, Dad called out, "Time to hit the sack, folks." The boys went to go "camping" in the survival chamber, while Samantha went to her normal bedroom.

The boys continued to laugh, giggle, and make weird noises well past midnight, but the closed-up survival chamber mercifully contained the interspersed creepy sounds and laughter while the rest of the household slumbered. It was a giggle fest for the two teenagers. The topics of conversation included the normal subjects: girls and sports, along with more girls and sports. With the flashlight they verified whose underarm and pubic hair exceeded the other's. Saturday morning found the boys still asleep at ten thirty.

Four doors down the residence corridor, Marco's parents had invited Paco to drop by for Marco's birthday party breakfast. They kept the party low-key because of Marco's difficulties with overstimulation. The single candle on his cupcake remained lit despite everyone's encouragement for him to blow it out.

Paco was sensitive to the needs of Marco, and they both enjoyed their shared time at the electronic keyboard that Paco had given to Marco. Marco was still undergoing transcranial magnetic stimulation (TMS) therapy as prescribed by Dr. Vasylyuk, and their shared musical interests complemented the therapy as well as just being fun. Later that morning, Rex and Octavio joined Paco and Marco for their regular Saturday exploration.

Saturdays found Samantha participating in a martial arts class with six other young women. She had become the star student at Adrian Ho's *dojo* and first to earn the prestigious green belt. Her mastery of martial arts ended up being a big surprise for Rex and Octavio when she broke up their last fist fight and dispatched both ruffians before they knew what happened. Picking themselves up from the ground, they humbly promised not to fight again, now aware that Sam was not a pushover anymore.

With Eve and the kids all busy with Saturday activities, Randall was home alone and able to prepare for his weekly podcast to the residents of Yucca Mountain. The notes passed to him from Rafael and the staff gave him the information he had requested about the levels of foodstuffs, clothing and medical supplies, the status of maintenance and repair, and several other concerns. He also included the regrettable status of the view of the water level at the Observation Chamber: unchanged. Other routine announcements included highlights of the week just past and the schedule of upcoming events.

He usually concluded his remarks with a motivational quote, a Bible verse, and a short prayer.

But everyone embraced his religious penchant. The residents seemed to fall into two camps: believers and skeptics. However, the skeptics were not offended because his presentation was considered to be honest, reliable, and informative. No other resident, in fact, seemed to have the ability to marshal consensus like he did. But he stayed humble, and all the residents appreciated it. When there were difficulties along the way, Randall invariably rose to the occasion.

It had been three years since Rex, Octavio, and Paco were forbidden to venture into Yucca Mountain's restricted tunnels. However, time had a way of eroding such constraints. Thus, the three boys decided to ignore the ban on this day because they all wanted to go skinny-dipping. With Marco innocently in tow, they slid through the gate and snuck along the forbidden tunnel, using the flashlight only when necessary.

They left crumbs for their pet rat but didn't wait to see if she came out to eat them. They pressed on and stopped to visit their old six-window hideout. With his affinity for tight places, Marco immediately crawled inside and then squealed with joy. Paco, Rex, and Octavio tried to follow, but they had grown a lot in three years, and finally decided it was too uncomfortable to even try getting in. They did take a brief look at the Ossuary alcove but decided to head directly toward the pool instead. Eventually, they saw the familiar blueish glow as they approached. They glanced at Paco's old "house" nearby, and Paco reminisced sadly, but briefly, about living there with his father.

Rex and Octavio were excitedly stripping down for their jump into the water.

"Come on, Paco, the water's waiting!" shouted Rex.

Paco quit thinking about his dad and grabbed Marco's hand to join the others. He sternly reminded them of the whirlpool effect when the pump activated, and that they only had about twenty minutes to swim. He was able to convince Marco to sit on the berm and watch before jumping in himself.

The boys splashed and frolicked like toddlers in a bounce house. They engaged in primeval water fights, wrestling and dunking as they each tried to dominate the other. But it all came to a screeching halt when Paco looked up and said, "Alto! Alto! Marco's gone."

They madly stroked their way back to the edge of the pool and climbed out. All three felt personally responsible for Marco, and hurriedly began the search for him.

"Marco! Marco!" they yelled while zipping up their jeans.

Paco was dressed first and raced to his former home. Rex climbed atop the berm and looked around to ensure that Marco was not in the water. Octavio ran around the berm's outer side to look for their buddy. It was a momentary lapse in judgment that could have ended tragically, when Paco suddenly called out, "He's over here, in *el baño*."

After that, they regrouped for the hike back to the sanctuary. They enjoyed recounting their swim and the fun they had there, and soon began to approach the location of the maintenance and Ossuary alcoves. Once the glow from the water reservoir faded, Octavio's flashlight became necessary to light their way. Laughter and joking continued but in hushed tones the closer they got.

The clubhouse cupola next to the maintenance area received a courtesy scan from their flashlight, but they were not tempted to enter. They turned to continue down the tunnel, when suddenly Rex exclaimed, "Look, there's a light in there!"

A bright light in the form of a crescent appeared about half-way into the Ossuary alcove. It was a strange circumstance for the otherwise pitch-dark tunnel. The boys stopped to observe.

"It's moving!" whispered Octavio.

"Let's get otta here!" answered Paco.

"No, wait. It's getting bigger. Look at it."

"ite!" Marco squealed.

"The lights are all turned off, so maybe this is one that is blinking or broken," Rex reasoned.

"It's getting bigger!" whispered Paco.

"Come on, let's go look," said Rex. "There's got to be a reason."

Hesitantly, the boys followed Rex and inched their way into the otherwise pitch-black Ossuary. As they got closer, the boys confirmed the appearance of an oval-shaped spot emanating from the Ossuary floor.

"It's still moving," exclaimed Paco.

Pointing at the image, a gleeful Marco cried, "ite! ite!"

"Yeah, and now it's getting smaller, and it looks like a sliver of a moon."

In less than three minutes, the bright spot on the Ossuary floor was gone. Its last appearance seemed to be a dim, crescent-shaped flicker, then nothing. The alcove became totally dark. Octavio fumbled and turned on his flashlight. Pointing it at the floor, then the walls and then the ceiling, he searched for the source of the vanishing light. Back toward the walls, his light exposed the creepy chamber holes that awaited Yucca Mountain's next occupants. Next, he moved the beam toward the grave chambers where the bodies of Globitz and Paco's father rested. But the source of the light on the floor was nowhere to be seen.

Hoping Paco didn't follow the flashlight beam, Octavio then turned and illuminated the area near the three sealed chambers close to the Ossuary entrance. Whether Paco wanted to or not, none of the boys were inclined to linger any longer in what they had labeled the Chamber of Death.

"This place is spooky. Let's get outta here," Octavio said.

Nobody objected. The boys tiptoed out of the Ossuary. Paco grabbed Marco's hand and they all turned to see if the strange and weird light had returned. Then they used the flashlight to continue their journey home.

"Do ya think we should tell my dad or Rafael what we saw?" asked Rex.

"We'll be in trouble if we do," responded Octavio. "They'll just ask what we were doing back here."

"I don't wanna tell 'em," replied Paco.

"We don't have to tell 'em we went swimming," argued Rex.

"Doesn't matter," said Paco. "We aren't supposed to be here."

"Yeah, we'll only get in trouble," echoed Octavio.

They continued their walk toward the main area of the Sanctuary. Except for the sound of their feet hitting the stone passageway, a peculiar quiet pervaded the space while they thought about the strange light they had seen. How could they explain it? Who could they tell? Who would believe it?

The silence was broken when Octavio asked, "We all saw the light on the floor, right?"

Paco immediately agreed, "*Si*, we saw it."

Rex picked up on Octavio's question, saying, "Maybe it was one of those mirages."

Mispronouncing the word, Paco asked, "What's a mirages?"

"It's one of those imaginary visions people get when they've been prevented from seeing a lot of stuff."

"You mean like being stuck down here, underground?" said Octavio.

"Yeah. Like that."

"It's no mirages. I saw it," Paco disputed.

"Then, where'd it go, Paco?" Rex challenged.

"*No sé*," Paco said, extending his arms out with his palms turned upward.

Silence again surrounded the boys for several minutes as they continued along the tunnel. Even Marco sensed a need to be quiet. Eventually, the gate was within sight and Sanctuary lighting beyond it eliminated the need for the flashlight. Once through the gate, they stopped to figure out what to tell the adults.

Rex took the lead. "Okay, we've all gotta be together on this. We didn't see anything, right?"

"Right," Octavio immediately responded.

"I dunno," said Paco. "What if..."

Octavio cut in, "No what if's, Paco. We didn't see anything!"

"*Si, Si.* Okay. Okay."

"ite!" squeaked Marco.

"No, Marco," Rex said while holding his finger to his lips. Octavio added, "Shhhh."

"Okay, let's seal it and sign off," Rex decreed.

Marco gleefully demonstrated his ability to participate in the boys' secret fist bump, and they turned to go home. Each held a secret, and one day each will have wished he had not.

Samantha's nightlight went dark after her dad's comforting peck on the cheek. His next stop was Rex's room, where he hoped to impart another life lesson to his son. Tonight, it was a Biblical reference from the Book of John: "Then you will know the truth, and the truth will set you free." His inspirational talks were always reassuring, but tonight it seemed to make Rex very uncomfortable as he tried to get to sleep while remembering the Ossuary experience.

Meanwhile, Eve settled comfortably onto the living room sofa as she started yet another digital Nora Roberts novel. Randall made his way toward the door for his nightly swim.

"Keep the light on, Eve. It should be a short one tonight."

"Okay, dear. Don't drown."

Even after years of bunker confinement, Randall still marveled at the life-like atmosphere of his walkthrough Sanctuary Square. The virtual stars and moon on the ceiling, the sounds of frogs, crickets, and owls, and the twilight shadows all made for a pleasant walk to the pool. *Globitz was really a genius,* he thought. *Too bad he's not here to witness all this, and to receive our appreciation, at least from most of us.*

As he adjusted his goggles, he noted the proficient swimmer in lane three and another in lane two. He launched into a front crawl stroke in lane number one for his planned twenty laps. Swimming had a magnificent therapeutic quality for him amid the burdens of Yucca Mountain. Something about the semi-weightlessness, aerobics, and mind-cleansing solitude provided him with a kind of spiritual balance and enlightenment. The rest of Yucca Mountain recognized and admired his serenity but were reluctant to make the effort to acquire it themselves.

Climbing from the pool, he moved toward the heated spa. The powerful pressure of the jets kneaded his tired muscles and helped him to relax.

In five minutes, he would be ready to float home and collapse in bed.

A few feet away, one of his spa companions suddenly sat up and spoke.

"Good evening, Randall."

"Hello, Krishka."

CHAPTER XXXIII
PURSUIT OF AN EXIT

THE USUAL CROWD OF TEACHERS AND STAFF ENJOYING THEIR FRIDAY-night dinner and conversation in the designated "noisy" corner of the Grotto included elder newcomer, Krishka Globitz. Recently exonerated from her husband's murder, she emerged never the worse for wear, accepted more by this group than by some of the skeptical patrons.

No longer holed up in the "Globitz penthouse" as it was dubbed, she increasingly stepped out to engage in the social events, especially those involving the teachers. Ms. Globitz was a highly respected Latin instructor by her students, but also as a team player capable to instruct in algebra, literature classics, and history. Her "folk hero" status for beating the rap was gradually surpassed by her prominence as Yucca Mountain's First Lady "emeritus,"

After-school lesson planning with Frank Lowe was depicted as "team teaching" prep work, whose frequency and duration surpassed the actual classroom event. A true friendship evolved under the accepting noses of the other teachers, and oblivious students. Dinners at the Grotto were becoming a common occurrence for the two.

They shared classroom experiences, like the day Mr. Lowe overheard Rex and Octavio quietly reveal that they saw a glowing spot on the floor in the "Chamber of Death," as they called the Ossuary. Krishka's comment? "Boys and their imaginations." Frank was less dismissive and more intrigued by their sincerity. Both boys were good students, reasonable, and not known to exaggerate. When Paco chimed in to corroborate their story, their classmates' eyes lit up. As unlikely as it seemed, it sounded genuine. Yielding to Krishka's assessment, however, Lowe joined her and laughed at the absurdity.

What began as shared thoughts on classroom episodes evolved to more personal feelings, experiences, and yearnings. Lowe was fascinated with the background mysteries of his attractive Russian associate, and Krishka was drawn to her likeable and trustworthy confidante. Limited to the confines of Yucca Mountain, they gravitated toward each other. Both shared a knack for competitive swimming—one recognized on the world stage, the other a seldom mentioned, college competitor. Both felt betrayed by Globitz. And both wished they could escape.

Rumors of a relationship accelerated after Mr. Lowe was seen descending the stairs of the Globitz residence. To the naïve science teacher, rumors didn't seem to matter. Shared dinners and rendezvous were warranted by fate and Yucca Mountain comradeship. Krishka revealed her experiences growing up in the shadows of a famous military hero and party leader. Frank admitted to the pressures of being the first member of an Irish immigrant family to attend college. It seemed like soul-bearing episodes on an *It's Just Lunch* mate-seeking date.

They talked about their families, their hometowns, the schools they attended, their joys and disappointments, and about the prospects of ever seeing daylight again. They shared their concerns about the five students who, for various reasons, lost a parent while living in the Sanctuary. Frank was fascinated by the extensive book collection the Globitz' maintained in their residence. Krishka admired Frank's dedication to his students. Their mutual admiration was blossoming.

One night, Frank asked Krishka about the peculiar cardboard tubes sticking out of the umbrella stand next to the desk in her residence. "Blueprints," she responded. "Blueprints to Yucca Mountain."

"Mind if I look at them?"

"If you like," she replied.

Lowe was fascinated with the architectural detail outlined in the layers of CAD (computer-aided design) paper he spread out on the desk. Page by page, he poured over design specifications of the engineering marvel that provided the blessing of safety yet the curse of inescapability. *How could the genius who built this bunker not provide for an escape?* he thought. Krishka gave him permission to take the drawings home.

Later that night, back in his own apartment, Lowe's imagination was unleashed as he examined the prints. *There must have been an exit mechanism in Globitz' design, someplace,* he thought. *Globitz was too meticulous in all the other details of this complex to forget something as important as a secondary exit.*

Into the wee hours of the night, he mulled over page after page of the blueprints. He examined the Observation Chamber details, thinking about its disastrous underwater situation. He scrutinized the drawings of the thirty-ton, air-tight gate at the tunnel entrance. It was underwater too. *There had to be some other method of exiting at a higher point in this mountain. But why doesn't Krishka know about it? She had to know.*

Frank went to bed with his imagination churning about Globitz; the genius behind the cherub-faced mask. *He didn't intend to die down here,* he reasoned. *There had to be some escape. Where was the escape exit? Why didn't he use it?*

Lowe's mind tumbled deeper. Any chance for sleep was lost that night. *What role did Krishka have in Globitz' strategy? Why didn't she know about an exit?* At her trial, he remembered that it had been revealed that the couple were together as a matter of convenience. Convenience?!

His suspicions turned to Krishka. *How could she accompany Globitz into Yucca Mountain for 'convenience' if she didn't have some plan for exiting?* Frank's own insecurities played out, as he thought, *Was she a Russian agent as some have suggested?*

Before dozing off, he tried to dismiss the wild notion of a Globitz-Krishka conspiracy. Everything was too coincidental, too nebulous, to implicate them in a dishonorable scheme. He would, however, keep an open mind to possibilities and continue to probe for a hidden escape route from Yucca Mountain.

The next day he contacted Randall about the blueprints he was studying. He requested a technical visit to the Observation Chamber to satisfy his quest for clues to an exit. Randall was doubtful but obliging and suggested that Rafael join them.

The three met after Frank's science class and climbed aboard Rafael's golf cart. During the drive up the ramp, Frank explained that the Observation Chamber could contain a clue to how Globitz might have designed an alternate escape exit.

Only two people at a time could enter the chamber because of its tight quarters. Randall deferred. Frank and Rafael spent more than an hour examining every significant square inch, conferring as they progressed. They cursed the water that pressed against the glass-enclosed capsule preventing an easy escape. The cursed the instruments, tools, and cameras that were rendered useless because of the damage they incurred just outside the chamber. They cursed the rocks and debris that had piled up against most of the observation windows. It seemed like a futile hunt; they were grasping at straws.

Then, Frank noticed two small wires leading to the O-ring around the large circular glass window. Tracing the wire channel raceway from the window, around the glass framing, through the wall near the chamber's entrance, he said, "Bingo!"

"What is it?" asked Rafael.

Frank had uncovered what the blueprints lacked—an escape hatch. The wires were the give-away. They led through the wall to a locked cover plate and throw switch next to the entry hatch. With his fingernail, he dug out a sliver of a white, puttylike substance of the O-ring that was packed inside the window's casing. Holding it in his palm, he showed it to Rafael. As he envisioned, this was the critical ingredient to blast open the window. It had to be C-4.

"This window is rigged with explosives: military-grade plastic explosive, C-4."

Rafael looked shocked. He was supposed to know every component of the Yucca Mountain facility. This was not in his wheelhouse.

Frank continued, "That locked switch outside this chamber is connected to an electrical detonator that would set off the C-4, blowing this window out, and creating an emergency exit."

Randall peered into the chamber from the hatch to see what they were talking about. He registered his amazement, as well.

"Great. How does that help us? We're still underwater," Rafael said sarcastically.

"It won't help us in here. But it's a clue for another possible escape hatch."

"Hmm. There's no other windows down here like this one. And, we're still underwater," declared Rafael. "Like I said, how does this discovery help us?"

The three hopped aboard the cart and headed back down to Sanctuary Square. During the twenty-minute ride, Frank was rather upbeat about their findings, explaining that he now had more to work with than before. "If Globitz was willing to secretly close up the observation capsule, blow open the window and then escape, leaving the rest of us behind, he would also have kept secret an alternative plan.

"I'll continue studying the blueprints. I have a feeling we'll find another exit—a more viable alternative," he said.

"You sure that white stuff is plastic explosive?" asked a skeptical Rafael.

"I'll burn it tonight to see if it is."

"What!" exclaimed Randall.

"Don't worry. If its C-4, it'll just burn like a solid fuel, cooking tablet."

The three agreed that their adventure today should be closely held so as not to create false optimism and disappointment among residents. Rafael delivered his passengers to their quarters and they parted.

Meanwhile, life below Yucca Mountain trudged on. Randall developed a heart-warming bond with his son through their Sunday-afternoon sessions on the virtual golf course. Rex absorbed his dad's expert instruction and technique and became quite good at the game, occasionally, even beating his father. Among his classmates, Rex was considered "top golfer."

Eve and Samantha entered the Sunday-afternoon pickleball league, competing against other students and their moms. They played on the Sanctuary Square pickleball courts erected on the soccer field Astroturf, which worked surprisingly well. Week after week, the female Merediths were very competitive, owing their reputation to Eve's gritty pickleball instincts. Samantha was inspired and proud of her mom and keen to carrying the mantle.

Once a month they joined Samantha's Girl Scout troop on bicycle ventures—rides that were deep into the restricted areas of

Yucca Mountain. Unlike her brother's slogs, however, the girls had permission and the tunnel lights were turned on for safety.

Between soccer, basketball, and swimming, Octavio and Paco spent their recreational time at the archery range, becoming expert with bows and arrows. Since Paco's foster parents were also Octavio's, they proudly declared stepbrother status, which was readily endorsed by the Ochoas and the boy's classmates. Paco's love of music and his loyalty to Marco continued. They were best buddies despite the verbal communication gap between them. Everyone in Yucca Mountain, especially Marco's parents, admired Paco for his commitment to his friend.

The lack of fresh air and sunlight had taken its toll. Premature aging seemed to be a communal scourge. Thinning and graying hair, wrinkles, and dental issues were most loathsome. Weight gain by some and weight loss by others were all attributed to BBS: bunker blahs syndrome.

The Ossuary chambers now contained the remains of sixteen bodies. Four of the deaths were determined to be suicide. Randall's weekly video updates and "pep talks" could only do so much to stave off depression among the residents. Many had resigned to the fact they might never leave Yucca Mountain. Others buried the thought and hoped for a breakthrough. Still others deferred to their Higher Power and lived each day, one at a time. Frank Lowe occupied a spot on the second category: hoping for a breakthrough. He was determined that a solution lay somewhere in the drawings. Every spare minute for the next few months, found him studying them and consulting with Rafael.

There were two separate sets of plans for this alcove; one old and faded, the other newer and more clear. Lowe's focus eventually turned to the Ossuary. The older plans dated 1997 depicted fifty drilled chambers, three feet in diameter and sixteen feet deep, neatly aligned on each side of the Ossuary alcove. They were labeled "cask storage cavities," which were initially intended to stow containers of spent nuclear fuel; Yucca Mountain's original design. As part of Globitz' survival bunker, they conveniently became burial chambers.

The older plans also indicated that there was one oddball chamber angularly drilled into the ceiling toward the deep end of the alcove. It was labeled "heat/pressure relief chamber." It was also two feet in diameter, but its depth was unclear. Indicated by two broken lines in the plans, the relief chamber extended onto another blueprint sheet. How deep and where it concluded were omitted. The other sheet would be necessary to clarify.

There was no other sheet.

Stymied by the blueprints, Lowe turned his investigation toward Krishka. He and Krishka shared the same classroom. They ate together—at the Grotto and occasionally, in Krishka's apartment. They enjoyed late-night swims together—often at the same time as Randall. They attended community events together: picnics, movie nights, and school soccer games. And, they occasionally slept together. Frank, however, was determined to find out if Krishka, knowingly or unknowingly, held the key necessary to break the Yucca Mountain "escape" code.

The two shared thoughts and ideas over a sampling of the scotch, left by Globitz in his liquor cabinet. One night after a casual dinner, Frank learned about the Russian poem that was framed and hung on her living room wall. He learned of her loyalty to the motherland. And, in a deeper, comforting moment, asked, "What are your plans, once we are rescued? Will you return to Russia?"

"Rescued? That's a nice thought," she paused, swirling her scotch and shaking out her hair so as to clear her mind. "If we were rescued tomorrow, I'd like to return to Russia, to continue my work."

Neither had discussed what Russia, or the world for that matter, would look like outside Yucca Mountain. Krishka was clearly detached from the possibility of an Armageddon-type scenario. In her mind, Russia would survive, unaffected by what ravaged the United States. Her life underground was merely a temporary setback.

"Interesting," he told her. "Do you think your home and your job are still intact?"

"Of course," she said matter-of-factly.

Surprised by Krishka's candor, Frank interpreted her response as a clue. This would require further probing, on another night.

CHAPTER XXXIV
THE GOOD, BAD, AND UGLY

THE GOOD

Rex had assumed a leadership role following in the footsteps of his father. He was an honor student and class president. He and Octavio were popular and respected and co-captains of the soccer team. Octavio was the better archer, Rex the better golfer. Both had become somewhat interested in girls.

With the announcement of Friday's after-school disco, both boys had anguished about embarrassing themselves on the dance floor. Samantha volunteered to help. Dance lessons at the Merediths provided the necessary nerve-easing therapy. Fast and slow dance and hip-hop were the lessons offered by Sam. Her selected music, from the unlimited memory on her hard drive, became the backdrop for her "dance workshops."

The tight quarters in Rex's room hindered the hip hop and fast dance lessons but afforded the necessary privacy the boys insisted on. They took turns dancing with Sam with hilarious critiquing by the idled dancer. Their tomfoolery prompted Samantha to send the noisy critic to the living room to wait to be called. Ten-minute routines were all the boys' attention span could handle. Rex had become obsessed with the dance steps, Octavio with the dance instructor—to the point of embarrassing arousal during a slow dance.

The days leading up to the big event had caused nervous jitters for the boys. The dance workshops were supposed to inspire confidence, instead they only made them more aware of their inadequacies. Worried about how they would look on the dance floor was only part of it. There was vulnerable risk having to ask for a dance. "What if she says 'no?' If she says 'yes,' I now have to dance," they whined. "Everyone will be watching."

When Friday's after-school event began, it was a fast dance that neither Rex nor Octavio would risk initiating. Their vanity and insecurity had hindered their asking a girl to dance. They had been out-maneuvered, watching their carefree classmates boogie. The three minutes of the first dance seemed like an hour for the humbled boys. When a confidence-shattering second song immediately struck up, their intended dance partners, Madison and Samantha, continued laughing and dancing with others. The floor was filled by their classmates and they were on the sidelines, watching. Forced smiles and dull jokes couldn't hide their embarrassment.

"Look at that! Paco is out there with Silvia," lamented Octavio.

"Wow! Where'd he learn to dance like that?"

"Next dance, I'm cuttin' in," announced Octavio.

"Me too."

Rex and Octavio were relieved to see the floor clear after the second song. Both watched their preferred dance partners return to the sidelines. On cue, Rex and Octavio walked toward the girls like men on a mission, as the music began. It was a slow dance and the boys were prepared. The remainder of the dances found both vigilantly attentive to their preferred partners while their friend Paco made the rounds with the rest of the girls.

Some of the class members planned to meet for pizza after the school dance, where Rex and Octavio had reserved a cozy table for four. With their confidence somewhat restored, they risked inviting the girls to dinner. Waiting for their pizza while talking between sips of soda was awkward at first, but the ice was broken with a few jokes and reflections on the music and gyrations they had attempted. The raucous gaiety and laughter from the group claiming the neighboring table caught everyone's attention. It was Paco, entertaining three of his dance partners. Rex looked at Octavio with an expression that said, "How does he do it?"

THE BAD

Three residents had called a confidential meeting with Randall. Sylvia Ricco (the volunteer chaplain), Amanda Gelhaus, and Dr. Vasylyuk wanted to discuss a serious medical issue. Sylvia had become the respected spiritual leader for the residents. Gelhaus and Vasylyuk were often called upon to assist in the Sanctuary clinic.

They met privately at the Merediths, since Eve had voluntarily joined the twins at school. Were it not for the gravity of the subject, the seated group around the table could have been mistaken for a bridge foursome.

"Coffee, anyone?" Randall offered.

"No thanks," by all three guests.

"Now, what's this about?"

Dr. Vasylyuk opened the discussion. "Randall, we're concerned. Dr. Jammicit and his staff are not facilitating the needs of the residents any longer. You're the only one we could talk to about this, in hopes of some intervention."

"Interesting, Galina. What seems to be the doctor's problem?" Randall asked.

Sylvia nervously interjected, "there's been entirely too many deaths among our otherwise healthy residents. I've conducted many more funerals than should have been required, even considering our predicament in Yucca Mountain."

"I'm not familiar with actuarial statistics, or how they might apply to our circumstances down here. Are you?" Randall asked, downplaying the assertion.

Amanda added, "There once were some 300 people in this Sanctuary, all under age forty-five. Except for Dr. Globitz, of course." She paused. "In eight years, we've lost thirty-one people. Twenty-three were women. Mothers!" she exclaimed.

Meredith was actually well aware of the casualty numbers. He had personally visited and prayed with too many suffering families. But he intentionally moderated his visitor's assertions in an effort to avoid panic.

"Randall, we think many of the deaths were preventable," Dr. Vasylyuk clarified.

"Whoa," he paused. "Are you suggesting that Dr. Jammicit is to blame?" He said scrutinized each of the accusers.

"Yes," all three said in unison.

"What could our clinic and Dr. Jammicit have done differently?" asked Randall.

"We're not sure. But ever since his wife died, Dr. Jammicit has gone downhill. We've had several complaints," said Sylvia.

"What do you propose I do?"

Moments passed.

Galina spoke up, "There's no way of knowing what the life expectancy is in a bunker. It's a first time for all of us to be subjected to living underground this long. But the incidence of mortality seem high. We should try to do something."

No others had offered a solution. Their silence was deafening and indicated the complexity of the problem. Jammicit was the only medical doctor they had. He was obviously overworked, stressed, and floundering. They had attempted to provide relief for him with volunteers, but the health issues and fatalities had still mounted.

"I'll talk to him, to see what can be done," Meredith offered.

"Thanks, Randall. You're the person that people listen to. Maybe Dr. Jammicit will improve and come to his senses."

He realized that Dr. Jammicit had become more and more distant from his fellow residents. Frequent outbursts and irritating conduct had rendered him ostracized from the rest of the occupants. His arguments with patients often required intervention by Nurse Higgins. Both Sanctuary cops had responded to incidents at the clinic. Was it possible that Globitz' superb draft choice had bombed? That brilliant graduate of George Washington University and the Perelman School of Medicine at the University of Pennsylvania had been reduced to the "medical maniac" of Yucca Mountain?

Not mentioned during their meeting were the reports that Jammicit's clinic had become unsanitary, his living quarters unkept, and his body odor pronounced. Medical records, instruments, supplies, and medications had been neglected. Prolonged underground living, lack of sunlight exposure, and plummeting morale were more than a single doctor could remedy. His inability to deal with their diminished immunity, infections, and isolation had taken its toll. And, like many of the inhabitants, Dr. Jammicit was not impervious himself to those conditions.

Randall had agonized over his promised investigation. He understood everyone's concern, and yet his family was healthy and unaffected by the doctor's situation. He realized that for the good of the community, he had to evaluate, confront, and, if necessary, intervene.

A pre-emptive call from Sergeant O had summoned Randall to the clinic hours before he had even planned. Once there, he found Jammicit being treated by Nurse Higgins. According to the Sergeant, his broken nose, black eye, and cracked ribs were the result of a confrontation with Neil Acosta. Acosta's wife was not happy with the treatment she received for her allergies, so her husband paid a visit. A little motivational warning was administered, to make sure his wife and others didn't end up like some of the doctor's patients--in an Ossuary chamber. Acosta was the canary in the coalmine.

Holding a saturated towel and an ice bag to his face, Jammicit was able to see that Randall had arrived. Through the blood still flowing from his nose and lips, Jammicit hoarsely said, "Acosta did it. That drug kingpin did it."

"Okay, Nelson, we'll take care of it. Now let's tend to your injuries."

Meredith waited for Higgins to finish her treatment before hearing her assessment. It was obvious there had been some kind of struggle in the office. Sergeant O was attempting to tidy up the chairs and the papers strewn on the floor and upright the table lamp on Jammicit's desk.

"He's done this before, Randall. Not to the doctor, but his wife. We've had to intervene several times," said Sergeant O.

"When we're done here, we'll have to pay him a visit," said Randall. "In the meantime, Nurse Higgins, is there anything we can do?"

"No. The doctor's nose has to be set. I can do that. His ribs and eye will heal naturally. We should notify the residents that the clinic will be closed for a few days."

"Okay. I'll see to that." Looking at Sergeant O, Randall grimaced and said, "Ready to go confront Acosta?"

THE UGLY

With the clinic closed, Dr. Jammicit was able to reduce the swelling his face. His black eye and the tape over his nose would become a conversation topic when his patients returned. Sergeant O and Randall chose to keep secret their warning to Acosta, but a holding chamber (jail cell) would be readied for any future incidents.

Jammicit begrudgingly returned to his duties but his anger would not subside. On Saturday afternoon, he snapped. Several residents witnessed the doctor storm through Sanctuary Square. He clambered aboard one of the golf carts parked near the commissary and spun it around, toward the entrance ramp. The astonished bystanders had to scramble out of his way to avoid being run over. He paused to make sure they had received the full exposure of his animosity.

"You're going to die!" he yelled. "We're all going to die!"

Then he sped toward the ramp and disappeared into the dark tunnel.

Rafael was driving Octavio and Rex home from the archery range when he saw Jammicit racing the golf cart up into the tunnel. Without hesitating, he turned and pursued the doctor. The commissary manager's shout prompted Randall and his golf partner, Arnell Ellis, to commandeer a nearby golf cart to follow Rafael. While making their rounds, the security team also had witnessed the disturbance and peddled their bikes after the three golf carts.

Jammicit's cart had tripped the alarm sensor, setting off the ear-shattering siren and flashing tunnel lights. Undeterred, he continued racing up the tunnel ramp toward the entrance. Rafael and the boys, Randall and Arnell, and the two security guards all followed. He itched his cart at the base of the stairs leading up to the Observation Chamber. Shouting indecipherably and crying, he bounded up the steps. It became obvious that Dr. Jammicit had decided to take matters into his own hands and breach the escape access, ending the suffering—for everyone.

With the parking-break not engaged, Jammicit's vehicle started to beep and slowly roll backward down the ramp. Rafael swerved and missed the wayward cart, but it plowed into Randall's, causing a temporary delay. Sergeant O caught up and helped disentangle the vehicles and they resumed their pursuit.

Jammicit reached the top of the stairs and the entrance to the

Observation Chamber. He clumsily turned the door wheel, opening the water-tight hatch adjacent the locked cover plate to access the switch for the explosive-charged copula window.

Opening the chamber hatch without the proper sequence had set off another alarm. The upper end of the tunnel ramp had become like a macabre feature in a horror movie, filled with competing siren shrieks and blinking lights.

Rafael's cart was first to stop near the stairwell below. Randall and the bicycle-riding security team were immediately behind. They all scrambled to watch the crazed Jammicit flounder with the mechanisms of the emergency escape hatch. They were frozen in disbelief. If he succeeded with his efforts, the cupula window would blow open, flooding the entire sanctuary. Everyone would drown.

"Don't do it!" yelled Rafael.

Negotiating with this madman would be tricky, more consequential than talking someone down from a window ledge. They had to avoid inciting his emotional state. They had to appeal to his core values, his sense of morals, and his obligation to his community—his fellow residents and neighbors. Randall stepped forward.

"Dr. Jammicit, we understand your anguish. Please stop to reason with us."

Jammicit paused and looked down to the group at the base of the stairs and without a response, turned and opened the hatch.

"Dr. Jammicit," Randall desperately appealed, "whatever your objection, we can address it."

Pulling a screwdriver from his pocket, he turned and snarled through phlegm and tears, "You can't fix anything, we're all doomed." His hands were shaking as he fumbled with his tool and turned his attention to the chamber entrance.

"What do you mean, Doctor? We're all still alive and well. We're not doomed."

"We're all gonna die down here. Everybody knows that," he said, forcing the screwdriver head under the security plate.

Rafael made a move toward the steps, but Randall pulled him back. He whispered, "Nobody move, it may set him off."

"Dr. Jammicit, I understand your concern, but really, we're going to make it. We're going to all walk out of here."

The security cover to the explosive detonation switch popped open from the force of Jammicit's screwdriver, as the men below gasped. Even with the flashing lights, they could see that the switch was totally exposed, available for activation. Whimpering, and delirious, the doctor looked down at his intended victims and between the screeching alarms, announced his decision.

"I am going to end this insanity. I already have for some. I killed their wives," he said sobbing uncontrollably. "If my wife couldn't live, why should their wives? I killed them. I let them die."

Resting on the throw switch, his hands shook. "I saved them from having to live indefinitely in this hell hole."

Again, Randall yelled to the doctor to stop. "Think about what you are doing! Flipping that switch will flood the entire Sanctuary, killing every one of us."

"I let them die, I don't care," he muttered. His hand continued to rest on the switch.

Randall pleaded with him to stop. There was a nobler calling that taking other people's lives, he said yelling up the stairway.

Suddenly, a muffled thump sounded from the top of the stairs. The doctor was knocked against the tunnel wall. The flashing light briefly revealed the doctor's hands clutching his chest around the feathered end of an arrow. When the lights flashed again, the group saw him staggering near the stairwell railing. A loud, thud was heard near the feet of the spectators below. The flashing lights exposed Jammicit face down on the tunnel floor with the bloody head of an arrow protruding from his back.

The witnesses were shocked. Sergeant O was the first to summarize, sighing, "now we have *no* doctor."

CHAPTER XXXV
THE CLUE TO EXIT PLAN B

EIGHT PM, THE MEREDITH RESIDENCE

"I'm stepping out for a while, Eve. I'm meeting Frank Lowe."

"What's that about, Randall? Rex's algebra grade?"

"No, not at all. We're just meeting on some facilities-related matters," he replied.

Waiting on one of the park benches lining Sanctuary Square was a rather nervous Frank Lowe. The moon and star lights were on, the crickets and frogs were chirping, and the pleasant evening atmosphere created by lights and sound effects inside the cavernous tunnel complex provided an ironic backdrop for the unpleasant news Frank was about to convey.

"She's dirty, Randall."

"What do you mean, Frank?"

"She and Globitz were planning to break out. They had gold

stashed and had a plan to escape with it, leaving us here to flounder. If we weren't underwater, they'd be gone."

"How did you learn this? Are you certain?"

"It's a long story. Let's just say we got very friendly. In an inebriated state last night, she spilled the beans."

"God!" Randall sighed.

Both men sat silent, looking at the moon and stars on the Sanctuary ceiling. Minutes passed. The streetlamps offered just enough illumination to reveal their distraught expressions.

"She offered to include me in on the plan, if I ever find the other exit."

More silence.

"Does she know of an alternate escape access?"

"Globitz kept her in the dark on that. 'Kinda his insurance plan," Frank confessed.

"Insurance!? Insurance from what?"

"They hated each other. Krishka was tasked by the Russians to find out if Globitz held back some of the gold they got from Yucca Mountain residents. Globitz was afraid to show her an alternate exit fearing she would rat on him," Frank revealed.

"Gold? Did he keep gold down here?"

"Yeah, that's the good news, I suppose."

"You mean Krishka knew where gold was held and Globitz knew where the alternate escape hatch was? 'Sort of a Mexican standoff?"

"One way to put it."

"Did she confirm that there was definitely another exit?" Randall asked.

"No. In fact, she's not sure Globitz did. They both were counting on escaping through the Observation Chamber window with the gold they stashed. When that option collapsed, they were screwed."

"So, she killed him."

"She intended to do that, anyway. She's an SVR agent, a Russian spy. Once she recovered the gold, Globitz was expendable."

"And our sympathetic jury bought her story."

"Yep."

The two men again sat silent and allowed these revelations to soak in.

Randall shook his head in dismay and asked, "Any progress on the blueprints?"

"Not really. I've spent two months trying to decipher Globitz' plan. He didn't leave a clue."

"So, we've got gold, but no way to get out of here."

Shaking his head in disgust, Frank said, "Not exactly. We don't know where the gold is, nor do we know of an alternate exit."

"Suddenly I've got a severe headache," Randall confessed. "We're almost better off not knowing anything about Krishka, Globitz, or the Russians." He paused. "Staying alive and positive down here until we find an escape would have been a lot easier." He paused, then asked, "Does anybody else know about this?"

"Just you and me."

"I think Rafael needs to hear about this. I'll talk to him in the morning. In the meantime, I want you to continue your friendship, or whatever it is, with Krishka. But, watch yourself—she's obviously dangerous."

Frank nodded. The two men parted and walked back to their homes.

ONE MONTH LATER

Angela Murphy interrupted Mr. Lowe's math class and handed him a note. He grimaced and asked Ms. Murphy if she could take over for a while. Waiting outside the classroom, Rafael and Randall sat in the golf cart.

"Hop aboard, Frank. We're going for a ride," said Randall.

The three sped off in the direction of the restricted area of the tunnel. The cart came to a stop and Rafael hopped off to open the gate and turn on the tunnel lights. Continuing on, they proceeded to the back areas of Yucca Mountain. Approaching the widened area where the maintenance alcove opposed the Ossuary, they slowed and then stopped.

"It's in here, guys," said Rafael as he turned on the Ossuary lights.

Eagerly walking toward the deep end of the alcove, next to the hole-drilling machinery, Rafael motioned for them to follow. Past the sealed chambers with the remains of the thirty-one deceased residents and near the two isolated ones containing the remains of Paco's dad and Mr. Globitz, Rafael turned and smiled. His two associates caught up and looked mystified.

"What is it, Rafael? Why the face?" asked Randall.

"Look at this, it's a locked cover plate to an electrical switch," he said, pointing to his discovery on the Ossuary wall. "The wires from here lead to that two-foot tunnel opening in the ceiling above that piece of equipment."

"Holy shit! This could be it," shrieked Frank. "This shaft could lead to an escape hatch, wired with C-4 like the Observation Chamber window."

In restrained gratitude, Randall mouthed the words. "Wow."

"We need to send somebody up that shaft to see where it ends," said Rafael.

"It'll be a tight fit for one of us. And I'm claustrophobic," apologized Frank.

"Not only that, we don't know for sure where it ends, or what it leads to," Rafael said.

"Can we shine a light up the hole and see anything?" asked Randall.

"I tried already. It's too deep for the light to penetrate."

"This has to be the heat/pressure relief chamber I saw in one of the drawings," Frank said. "The blueprints didn't show where it goes."

Rafael reasoned, "If it was originally bored to relieve heat or pressure and it now has an explosive opening hatch activated by this switch, it's got to reach outside this bunker. Possibly, outside Yucca Mountain."

The three men swallowed and looked at each other. It had been over fifteen years since they had seen sunlight, breathed fresh air, or heard a neighbor's dog bark. This discovery could possibly answer their prayers. Was it the alternate escape shaft Globitz didn't reveal?

"The boys have been up that shaft," Rafael said. "Marco liked to hide up there. Paco had to always climb after him."

"That was a few years ago, Rafael," said Randall.

"I know, and they were a lot smaller then, too. I doubt anyone could turn around in there, if they decided to come back."

"Did they say how far they climbed up into it?" asked Frank.

"No."

Frank flashed on a memory. "You know, the boys used to joke about this Ossuary floor glowing in the dark." He paused, then moved a few steps sideways, pointing directly up the shaft. "If the angle of the sun aligns in a straight line with this shaft, for one brief minute or two, on a certain day of the year, it would cast a bright oval on the floor where we're standing." Pausing, he continued, "The boys may have actually seen it happened."

Randall looked to ensure he had the two men's attention and said, "If that's true, there would have to be an opening at the top of this shaft."

"Your right, Randall. But remember, we're totally sealed up. This whole bunker complex is completely airtight. It's like a giant submarine. The pressurized ventilation system only works if we're buttoned up," cautioned Rafael.

Frank warned, "We're more than a thousand feet below the desert floor, and that shaft reaches beyond that and even higher up Yucca Mountain. It could be well over a quarter-mile long."

The three men went silent, looking at the switch plate, the shaft, and the Ossuary surroundings. A good five minutes passed without a sound. The dejected threesome turned toward the alcove entrance.

"Let's think about all this before taking any drastic measures," Frank said walking back to the golf cart.

Except for the humming of the cart's tires on the concrete floor, it was a quiet ride back to Sanctuary Square.

TWO DAYS LATER

Rafael and Randall were having morning coffee in a secluded corner of the Grotto.

"We've got some old miner's oxygen masks and tanks in the maintenance shed," Rafael said.

"Nice. There's two hundred seventy-one of us alive down here, Rafael. How many do you have?"

"Seven."

"I talked to Rex. He said the shaft angled upward pretty steep."

"Did Rex climb in it very far?"

"He admitted that Marco did, first. Eventually, all four had climbed in it at one time or another. But they didn't climb too deep."

Rafael took a deep breath, "Paco volunteered to crawl up and explore."

"Too dangerous, Rafael. We need an adult to do it."

"Randall, you forget, our boys are nineteen now," Rafael said with a smile.

"God, have we been down here that long?" Randall said in disbelief. "Let's get our boys together and examine the possibilities."

SATURDAY MORNING IN FRANK'S CLASSROOM

With the critical page of the Ossuary blueprint spread out over Lowe's desk, the six men (welcoming Rex, Octavio, and Paco as such) studied the drawing details as though they were planning the Normandy Invasion. Frank pointed to the lines labeled "heat/ pressure relief shaft," to insure everyone was oriented.

"According to the drawing, the shaft angle is about thirty-four degrees," said Lowe.

"How long is it, Frank?" asked Rafael.

"The boys and I used our trig tables to calculate. If the tunnel is only 1,000 feet in height, the shaft length would still be over 3,000 feet (more than a half a mile)."

"That's a long crawl for somebody," sighed Randall.

"Unfortunately, if the shaft extends higher up Yucca Mountain than the desert floor, the shaft would actually be longer. The blueprint page revealing where the shaft exits the mountain is missing," said Frank.

Rex quickly responded, "If it went only to the level of the Yucca Mountain entry or the Observation Chamber, it'd still be underwater."

"Correct," said Frank.

"But if we saw sunlight on the floor in the 'Chamber of Death,' it means it was *above* water level," said an optimistic Octavio.

Rafael beamed at his stepson's contribution. Frank and Randall were equally impressed. Octavio welcomed their concurrence but professed little pleasure in sharing his analysis. His buddies silently cheered Octavio's input despite its woeful truth.

Rafael said, "We'd have to get up there to check it out."

"Someone would be climbing up there, blind. It could be a hell of a lot longer than 3,000 feet," a concerned Randall conveyed.

"I'll do it," said Paco.

"You're fearless, Paco. Ever experienced claustrophobia?" warned Randall.

"I crawled up that shaft several times. Claustrophobia never affected me."

"Easy, son. You were younger and smaller," warned Rafael.

"Somebody's got to do it. I'm as capable as any."

The meeting lasted for two long hours. They discussed the concerns about climbing up the shaft. It was long and tight-fitting, not wide enough for a grown man to turn around and return. Randall raised up the issue of oxygen. Anyone crawling that distance in a confined shaft could conceivably use up all the oxygen.

One of the teenagers related how the shaft surface had previously worn out the knees of his jeans. Knee pads would be an important item for the crawler. Lighting would also be important. The tunnel shaft appeared dark when most of them observed it. A flashlight, if not too cumbersome, would be necessary.

The mere length of the shaft was daunting. It could take a couple hours or more to reach the top. And longer, crawling backwards, coming down.

It would require the stamina and agility of a young man.

"A risky reconnaissance just to see where the shaft ends," concluded Randall.

"If we could verify that there's a glass hatch of some sort, rigged with plastic explosives like the cupola in the Observation Chamber, we could possibly blow it and exit this dungeon," appealed Frank.

"We'd have to verify that it's not underwater. That an exit from here would be sensible," reasoned Rafael.

"What's the shelf life of C-4 explosives, Frank? If it's wired to detonate, will it still explode?" queried Randall.

"It's pretty stable. That should not be an issue. The detonator and wires should be fine, also, as long as they're not severed."

"And if it doesn't blow, we could always use a hammer," said Paco.

"If it's glass like that in the cupola, hammering wouldn't work, son," explained Rafael.

Paco suddenly realized his critical role in their underground internment. His inaction undoubtedly prolonged their confinement. He cleared his throat and nervously confessed something he probably should have mentioned years ago. "I think the missing glass window from the spare cupola is the one my dad mounted up there."

All eyes transfixed on the teary-eyed eighteen-year-old.

"Before he died, he told me something about mounting the glass on top of a *mucho especiales la caracteristica*. ("very important feature"). I didn't really think about it until now."

Randall swallowed when seeing the tears trickle down Paco's face. With his calm and compassionate authority, he addressed the courageous young man so that all could witness. "Paco, you were very, very young, dealing with a lot of issues. It's quite understandable that your father's words were forgotten."

Rafael quickly stepped around the blueprint-covered desk and hugged his trembling adopted son. Everyone felt Paco's grief. The meeting's importance was tacitly suspended for the moment. Randall moved to one of the desks in the classroom and sat down. Frank, Rex, and Octavio followed. They stared at the floor, lost in thought. Any possibility of thinking "if only" in light of Paco's circumstances was summarily dismissed.

"That might explain the light on the Ossuary floor we once saw. The sun was shining through the glass, right down that shaft hole onto the floor," said Rex.

"Highly unusual," said Frank. "It could only have 'exactly' lined up once a year or so, because the Earth rotates out of sync with its revolution around the sun."[3]

The emotional moments eventually concluded. The group circled their desks and resumed their discussion. Rex was tasked to take the notes as Randall directed the group to focus on the heat/pressure relief shaft and develop the Plan B Exit. The escape from Yucca Mountain Sanctuary had begun.

---

[3] **Anthem Veteran's Memorial, Anthem, AZ.** Once a Year at 11:11 am the sun shines through holes in five marble pillars creating an intense solar spotlight into the monument's deep shadow, highlighting a vivid mosaic of The Great Seal of the United States.

CHAPTER XXXVI
RECONNASSIANCE MISSION

DEEP END OF THE OSSUARY

IT WAS A SLEEPLESS NIGHT FOR RANDALL AND RAFAEL, WHO WERE BOTH worried about the day's big event. Paco, the leanest and most agile of the secretive group, had been chosen for reconnoitering the shaft. He had eagerly volunteered, was unaffected by tight spaces, and had experience crawling up the shaft to retrieve his friend, Marco years before.

He was ready to go, all suited up: shorts, T-shirt, tennis shoes, knee pads, leather gloves, head-mounted LED flashlight, and cell phone camera. A couple of energy bars were tucked into his hip pocket for good measure. No problem. Then they strapped the harness on him. Suddenly it became more serious. The weight of the emergency respirator canister, walkie-talkie, water bottle, and three-strand monofilament tether rope provided the gut-punch of reality. This could be dangerous.

"Do you remember how to open the canister and use the respirator, Paco? Or should we practice one more time?" asked Rafael.

"No, I got it. Do I have to wear it?"

"Absolutely."

"What about this plastic rope you tied onto me?" he challenged.

"You just have to be careful that it doesn't get fouled up, especially when you're coming back down. We'll be spooling it as you descend to check on your progress, but we don't want to exert too much downward force and cause you to fall. The rope will also tell us how high you are climbing and how fast."

What Rafael didn't say was that the 3/8-inch rescue rope would also serve as a tow line to pull him back down the shaft if he became incapacitated. They had estimated that the crawl up the shaft would take about four hours but returning would require a little longer because Paco would be crawling backward. A head bump, panic, or exhaustion could require intervention from below. A rescue rope was determined the most practical.

Randall and Frank ensured the waist-high stack of coiled rope was positioned and snag free. Octavio and Rex watched as Rafael gave Paco a hug and some private words of encouragement. Paco turned, smiled at the group, and climbed up the tunnel boring machine next to the heat/pressure relief chamber entrance. A hop from the equipment chassis and he was inside the tunnel and on his way. In seconds, the sight of the soles of his tennis shoes disappeared and the monofilament rescue rope from the coiled mound below was unspooling, providing the only evidence of his progress.

The group below positioned themselves into folding chairs in a circle near the rope on the alcove floor. Rafael shared hot coffee from his thermos. They chatted occasionally and tried to remain upbeat and positive. It was a tall order. Deep down their stomachs were knotted by the uncertainty of Paco's mission. He was tasked to verify the presence of an exit and to take photos. If the shaft terminated with the cupola window, as anticipated, he needed to determine if a C-4 explosive charge was placed around it, and that the detonator wires were also in place.

Paco was instructed to peer through the glass window, if it existed, to determine what the conditions were outside Yucca Mountain, and take photos there, too. And, lastly, he was to return down the shaft safely and report his findings. This mission would determine if critical factors existed that offered the possibility of escape. The enormity of his findings could not be greater.

As the men talked, they watched the pile of rope uncoil and inch its way up the tunnel shaft. Paco was making progress. Octavio decided to communicate with him by yelling up the shaft.

"Paco, you alright?"

"Yeah, I'm fine," came the answer.

An hour went by and the coiled rope continued to uncoil, snaking its way into the shaft. Paco had obviously not stopped to rest. Octavio used the two-way radio to call up again. The answer was positive and assured the group of his progress. Octavio smiled and gave a thumbs up. They all tried to remain positive, helplessly buried in their thoughts. Randall's mind drifted back to his grandmother's anticipation of the report of her wounded son on his return from Vietnam.

The rope continued to unspool.

Waiting bred an unspoken tension across the group. Rex wondered about the likelihood of finding the glass-windowed escape hatch "exactly like the one in the Observation Chamber." This opened a discussion about the explosive charge placed around (hopefully) both windows. Frank picked up on the thought and described the detonation process, the low-voltage wires, the blasting cap, and the locked switch on the Ossuary wall.

"I'm positive it's just like the one in the Observation Chamber," he assured.

Rafael suggested, "If we blow the hatch tonight, we'll have to temporarily close the bottom of the shaft opening with plywood to ensure the integrity of the circulation system down here. Not a big deal, but it would be necessary to prevent overburdening the fans sending air up the opened tunnel shaft."

Frank then cautioned, "Setting off the C-4 might harm the integrity of the shaft walls."

Randall responded, "That's a possibility. We'll have to wait and see."

"Another reconnaissance mission," Rafael moaned.

"Afraid so. We'd have to do that again anyway, to see what's outside."

"Paco, everything alright?" spoke Octavio into his handset.

A brief static sound erupted from the device in Octavio's hand then, "Yeah, everything's okay." More static and squelch, then silence.

"You gettin' tired?"

"I'm good. Right now, I'm taking a short break," squawked the speaker.

They noticed that the line had stopped unspooling. After a short while, it started up again.

"Paco, can you see any light from a window?" asked Frank via the walkie-talkie.

The squawk from the device broke and a breathy voice responded, "No light yet. And the tunnel is pretty much not changing as I go up. But this rope is getting harder and harder to pull."

"Take a rest, Paco. Stop and catch your breath," said Frank.

Randall looked at the coiled rope remaining on the Ossuary floor. It had diminished to only a few coils. "My God, we're almost out of rope! How deep could that shaft be?"

"No wonder he's getting tired. It's been over two hours."

"I don't like this," agonized Rafael.

Moments later: "Any light from a window, Paco?"

No answer. Then the last few feet of rope vanished.

"Paco, can you see the end of the shaft, yet?" Frank yelled into the handset.

Moments painfully passed. Static followed by a squelch from the speaker offered some relief. A faint voice from the other end whispered, "I found two wires, but I can't see out the window. It's totally dark."

"He made it!" yelled Rex.

"Paco, it's very important! Hold your head lamp to the glass, what do you see?" barked Frank.

Thirty seconds seemed like an hour to the five waiting in the Ossuary. They stared at the handset in Frank's grasp.

Squawk, static. No voice. Squawk again and Paco's breathy voice echoed, "It's dark, real dark, but I think I see a moon."

"Yes!" said Randall.

"Yay!" erupted the anxious group, as they congratulated each other. Their hugging and cheering lasted only a few minutes, and then the receiver sounded. They all stopped to look to Frank, still clutching the handset.

"I can't breathe," came the faint voice from the speaker.

"Paco, Paco! Open the canister, quickly. Put on the face mask. Now!" yelled Frank.

No answer.

"Paco, did you hear me? Put on the oxygen mask."

He weakly responded, "Okay."

Minutes passed. Despite the earlier good news, all concerns were now focused on his well-being. He was over 3,000 feet up the tight-fitting shaft and his last statement was very alarming.

"Paco, can you hear me?" bellowed Frank.

No answer.

"Paco!"

Nothing. Everybody looked up. The air thickened to a suffocating mass. The possibility of losing Paco sickened the group. Randall intervened before panic took over.

"Pull him out. We need to help him down the shaft."

Rex and Octavio immediately raced for the coiled rope on

the Ossuary floor. It was gone. It had been dragged up the hole, unnoticed. Pulling Paco out by the rope was now impossible.

Alarmed, Rex leaped on to the hole-drilling machine toward the shaft's opening to look for the end of the rope. Nothing.

"He's pulled the rope up into the shaft. I don't see the end."

"We've got to pull him down!" cried Rafael.

"Paco, Paco! Can you hear me?" shouted Frank into the handset.

"I'm going. I'm going after him!" shouted Rex.

"Wait. Let's think about this for a second," cautioned Randall.

"We have no time to waste! He could die," yelled Frank.

Rex didn't wait for permission. Standing on the drilling equipment, he pulled himself up into the shaft. In seconds, he disappeared into the hole to help his buddy. Octavio stood on the equipment looking up into the hole, watching the bottom of his best friend's shoes disappear up into the darkened shaft.

"Tell him to only crawl as far as the end of the rope, Octavio," said Frank. "Then pull it toward us."

Octavio relayed the message, and from the shaft Rex acknowledged while he continued to climb. Randall, Frank, and Rafael stood next to the hole-drilling machine, looking up toward Octavio and the shaft opening. Grunts and a slight scraping noise from the tunnel indicated that Rex was making progress.

"See the rope yet?" Octavio anxiously yelled up to Rex.

"Not yet."

It was getting too dark for Rex to see, but he was undaunted. He would feel the rope when he crawled far enough. His haste in entering the shaft did not provide for knee pads, flashlight, or his own oxygen canister. It also did not include a tether rope for his own rescue.

Rex crawled for ten more minutes, while Octavio kept talking to him. Louder and louder from Octavio and softer and more distant from Rex, their running conversation provided some assurance of progress.

Meanwhile, Frank kept trying to reconnect over the handset.

"Paco, Paco! Push the talk button if you hear me."

Nothing.

"Paco, you have to put your oxygen mask on. Do you hear me?!"

Suddenly, from inside the tunnel, "Got it! I've got the rope." A welcomed notice faintly heard but relayed by Octavio, "He's got the rope!"

"Can he pull it?" anxiously barked Randall.

"Pull the rope, Rex!" yelled Octavio up into the shaft.

Rex tugged on the rope. It flexed and recoiled some, indicating resistance. He wrapped three loops around his right hand and braced himself with his left, pulling the rope toward his body. Crawling backward, he repeated the maneuver, making a foot of progress.

"Are you getting anywhere? How are you doing, Rex?" yelled Octavio.

Pulling and gasping, he answered, "It's coming, slowly."

Rex was now only ten yards from Octavio at the opening of the shaft. They continued talking through Rex's strenuous efforts to pull and crawl. It was dreadfully slow. The others were watching helplessly as Octavio encouraged his friend in the rescue attempt of Paco. The handset now lay on one of the folding chairs.

Rex pulled and crawled, inching his way toward the shaft's opening. He paused to catch his breath with just five yards to go. Octavio could now talk to him in a normal voice, but Rex's response was raspy and winded. He rested to catch his breath.

"Come down, Rex. I can take over," Octavio directed.

"I'm good," he said as he started moving again.

Pulling and crawling, all he could think about was a helpless Paco attached to the other end of the rope. The pain of the monofilament line cutting into his palm had not registered. He finally reached the shaft opening. With the help of Octavio, Rex found his footing on the piece of equipment that Octavio stood on. His shirt was saturated with sweat; his elbows and hand were bleeding and his bloody knees shown through his torn jeans. But the nylon rope that dangled from the shaft opening was now available for the others to pull.

They took turns pulling on the rope not knowing what condition they would find Paco in when he appeared. The surface of the shaft he was being dragged down would not be kind to his knees or elbows; a price to pay in order save the young man's life. Their effort would take more than two hours. The rescue rope, once neatly coiled, was now hastily strewn on the Ossuary floor as it was wrested from the shaft. Each tug from the men below would move Paco closer to them. The race against time and oxygen was judged to trump the bruises and scrapes Paco would suffer.

Another hour passed. The fatigue factor of only one man pulling demanded the change to two at a time. The accumulation of rope on the floor had become a mound of dirty white entanglement.

"Rex, take the cart and go get Nurse Higgins. Hurry!" commanded Randall.

Fatigue during the second hour prompted shorter intervals of pulling and resting by the two-man teams. Octavio scrambled atop the machinery as they felt Paco nearing the shaft opening. The life at the other end of the rope was limp, uncooperative, and totally dependent on the men's efforts.

"I see him!" Octavio shouted. "He's only got about fifty more feet to go! Just a few more pulls."

Paco's legs were bent and had been forced up toward his body, cannon-ball style, due to the towing from his waist-level harness. The tips of his tennis shoes had been worn through, exposing bloody feet. His legs were first pulled from the shaft by Octavio, who then wrapped his arms around the center of his mass. Ignoring the blood dripping from the shaft opening, Octavio lifted Paco's body and lowered his wounded buddy down to the outstretched arms of his stepfather, Rafael.

Paco was laid motionless onto the blanket next to Nurse Higgins. With Rafael's help, she removed the blood-soaked harness and rescue rope that was intertwined with his legs. The blanket quickly turned red from the muddy liquid oozing from Paco's legs, torso, and arms. The canister holding the mask and chlorate oxygen candle was still attached to the harness, unopened.

Nurse Higgins knelt down to assess Paco's condition. Without deploying her stethoscope, she checked his blood-soaked wrists for a pulse. She quickly moved her fingers to the side of his neck. Frantically, she leaned over to listen for breathing. Then she immediately positioned his head back, opened his mouth, and blew air into his lungs. She blew again, causing his chest to heave. As she raised quickly to inhale and press on his inflated chest, strands of saliva extended from her mouth to his. She continued blowing and gasping. Then placing her hands in the center of his blood-drenched torso, she vigorously pumped with all her weight. The others watched in shock and despair.

Nurse Higgins maintained her attempt at resuscitation for twenty minutes, alternating between mouth-to-mouth and CPR, exhausting herself in the process. Every few minutes she checked Paco's pulse and his own response to breathing. Nothing. But she was unwilling to admit the truth. Her tears were now mixed with the drool washing down his face as she desperately continued, refusing to let his young life pass.

But Paco had indeed passed.

With his hands grasping the top of his head, a distraught Octavio wailed. "NO-O-O-O!" Rex dropped to his knees and clasped his hands to plead with God. Tears flowed down Rafael cheeks as he hugged Octavio and grimaced. Randall stepped forward to console Higgins. He knelt beside the despairing nurse, who was still hunched over her patient, and said, "It's okay, Clara. We tried."

CHAPTER XXXVII
OSSUARY QUANDARY

IN MEMORIUM

ORGANIZERS HAD GROSSLY UNDERESTIMATED THE TURNOUT FOR PACO'S memorial service. Over half of the attendees ended up sitting on the Astroturf behind those in the folding chairs. As she had over twenty-nine times before, Sylvia Ricco led a traditional funeral service, this time for Paco. Most people were still in shock. Her sermon was insightful and poignant, that Paco radiated an unbound magnetism despite a life marked by tragedy. She was followed by Paco's friend, Rex Meredith.

Rex's parents watched as their son rose to speak. His eyes were moist but his jawline firm, revealing an amazing likeness to his father. He delayed a minute while he looked over the audience. They looked back with curiosity and friendliness. An abject quiet blanketed the mourners watching their nascent leader.

"Paco was my friend. He was everybody's friend. And today, he's enjoying a perfect friendship with God." After briefly clearing his throat, he continued with an emotional eulogy, honoring his pal.

"Octavio and I took a forbidden swim one day in the reservoir. Luckily, Paco appeared from nowhere and saved Octavio from drowning. Paco and his father lived as stowaways in the back tunnels, without the services we enjoyed. When his dad died, Paco was only eleven years old, and he had to bury him in the Ossuary. Imagine that, eleven years old!

"Paco cheerfully adapted to our social and cultural norms that were so different from his own. At our first school dance, he outperformed all of us guys to the delight of all the girls. Paco embraced Marco's friendship and shared a mutual enjoyment of music. And, finally, he bravely sacrificed his life in an attempt to find a safe passage for all of us."

Several of Rex's classmates were shaking, many with sobs. Some of the parents openly wept. Paco was the first of Yucca Mountain's younger generation to die. Whether their compassion was for his incomprehensible earlier life, the life they witnessed, or for his heroic final act, it was uniformly felt and expressed. Rex had summarized with great feeling Paco's short but meaningful presence among them. In closing, he asked God's favor on Paco's soul, that he would be able to dance with the angels like he had danced here on Earth.

Rex returned to his seat while Lily Ashton and her band took the stage. A comforting squeeze on Rex's shoulder was conferred by Mr. Smallwood from the row behind.

Lily began, "Paco was such a dear friend to all of us, so my students and I wrote a song to honor him. Julia will join me on guitar, Rhonda on the violin, Marco the keyboard, and Tommy the drums. You may recognize the melody as we sing to the tune 'The Boxer' by Simon and Garfunkel."

When I entered Yucca Mountain
I was no more than a boy
With my papa and his tool kit
And he taught me independence and integrity
But then he died
Leaving me, seeking out an existence
Where nobody would go
Living in a place that only he would know
Mm-mm-mm-mm-mm-mm
Mm-mm-mm-mm-mm
Then I became an orphan
Who'd been blessed in many ways
By friendships and by families
Who saw me as a son and as a brother
Not unlike them
But an equal
I am thankful, for the kindness they've shown
And now I am gone
And now I am gone
Lie-la-lie
Lie-la-lie-lie-lie-lie-lie
Lie-la-lie
Lie-la-lie-lie-lie-lie-lie, lie-lie-lie-lie-lie
Lie-la-lie
Lie-la-lie-lie-lie-lie-lie
Lie-la-lie
Lie-la-lie-lie-lie-lie-lie, lie-lie-lie-lie-lie

The voices of Lily, Julia, and the band concluded with a final strum of the guitars and produced a chilling effect among the attendees. It was a beautiful memorial for a worthy young man who would not be forgotten. Later, Paco was laid to rest in the Ossuary chamber next to his father and Heinz Globitz.

PLANNING RESUMES

After a two-day interval, the remaining five planners resumed their quest for an escape route. By now, the community had been apprised of the potential for getting out of the bunker and were receiving daily updates from Randall's blog. Paco's investigation had revealed enough information for the group to continue in the direction they had initiated: the heat/pressure relief chamber in the deep end of the Ossuary.

The group presumed that the two wires he found protruding from the heavy glass cupola casing led to a detonator for the C-4. This would blast open a viable exit hatch when detonated. The group assumed that the wires to the locked cover and switch in the Ossuary were the same that led to the top of the shaft, similar to what they had seen in the Observation Chamber. The few pictures Paco had taken appeared to confirm this theory.

Activating the detonator would be easy. However, there were many preparatory steps to be taken before they "flipped the switch." They considered the back-blast effect down the shaft into the Ossuary. They talked about the possibility of damage to the shaft, debris that could block its passage, and even cause its collapse. If the shaft became opened to the atmosphere outside the bunker, it could depressurize the Sanctuary, interfering with the ventilation system and the heating cooling.

Once the escape hatch was blown open, someone would have to ensure the shaft was passable, and that the exit at the top was large enough to actually use. The environment and terrain outside would have to be inspected for weather conditions, and for the prospects for food, shelter, and contact with the outside world. Preparation for the mission beyond the exit would need to be thought through carefully, and long-range planning needed to be included.

Randall warned the group that too much haste could spell disaster. "We need to be cautious," he stressed. "Meticulous planning with cool heads must govern our actions. We've been down here almost fifteen years, and a little more time of comprehensive planning won't hurt in the long run."

"I suggest we all take our notes home to study the situation and reconvene in the morning," offered Rafael.

"Good idea," echoed Frank.

Later that night after the women had retired, Rex and Randall had a deep discussion of the situation. Rex was the anxious young idealist, ready for liftoff. His father was more pragmatic and detail-oriented, a strategist whose wisdom was essential. Rex took note.

Sometimes their proposed action items were more obvious than others. This private meeting had suddenly made Rex more appreciative of his father's gray hairs and wrinkles. He thought to himself, *How long has it been since I really looked that closely at Dad, or thanked him for his support and the example he has provided?* His mind momentarily wandered from the details under discussion, toward, "How will this all end?" and, "When is a father's love returned?"

The next morning.

"Coffee, anyone?" said Samantha to the five sitting around the Meredith dining table.

Octavio winked and requested water; while the rest all said, "Coffee, please."

Rex said, "Dad and I have pooled our thoughts and we're a little concerned about informing everybody about the details of our plans until we've actually inspected the hatch and the shaft after it's been blown open. We still want to give daily briefings about our results but prefer to go lightly with the plans."

"Do you mean blow it first, then tell the residents?" asked Frank.

Octavio responded, "Yes, it could cause unnecessary panic if a particular part of our plans fails. It could invite too much second-guessing."

The group thoroughly discussed plans necessary for exploding then inspecting the blown shaft. Detonation was set for Tuesday morning, 0900 hours. Assuming the shaft appeared passable, Rex would enter the shaft on Wednesday. Upon his return and assuming his report was positive, a more detailed plan would be developed, and the residents would be apprised of the details, along with a discussion of possible follow-on plans. They had three days to calm their nerves and mentally prepare.

TUESDAY MORNING

All systems were ready.

"Fire in the hole! Fire in the hole!" yelled Octavio.

Startled, Rex turned and asked, "What does that mean, Tavo?"

"I don't know, I just read about it someplace."

From a safe distance, they braced themselves and watched as Rafael flipped the switch. They looked skyward and held their breath as two nerve-racking seconds passed.

KA-BOOM!

A cloud of dust and debris shot out of the shaft, and instantly covered the drilling machine below. The concussion shocked the eardrums of the five men, causing a reflexive movement of their hands to cover their ears, while an involuntary diaphragm contraction forced an expiration of air from their lungs. It was over in five seconds, but the memory of it would never be forgotten. An immediate swoosh of air rushed up the shaft, causing a draft within the Ossuary.

Without prompting, Rafael and Octavio lifted the plywood to cover the shaft's hole, while Frank and Rex wedged the lumber braces into place. After this, the Sanctuary ventilation system returned to normal. A sigh of relief was expressed by all five.

"The gust of wind going up the shaft is a good sign," said Frank.

"Yes, it means there's an opening up there," concurred Randall.

"And, we're not seeing any water flooding down, either," said Octavio.

The reconnaissance mission would take place the next morning after the dust settled. Rex was somewhat nervous, while getting mentally prepared for the long, arduous climb. Any possibility for experiencing claustrophobia would be moderated by a Xanax pill. It would be a long night for the courageous young man. It would be even longer for his apprehensive parents.

Rex's reconnaissance mission went off without a hitch. He explained the details of his findings to the planning group, and they all decided they would share the results at a community meeting later that night.

WEDNESDAY NIGHT

By special request, the security team was positioned on both sides of the door to the Community Center, indicating the seriousness of the meeting. Their charming smiles and bulging biceps had a calming effect at important gatherings, where otherwise rowdiness was likely to ensue. The standing-room-only crowd had heard rumors of an exit plan and waited patiently for their leaders to make it public. The usual skeptics and hecklers were among the gathering, waiting for their opportunity as well.

Randall Meredith took the microphone and the crowd settled in more quietly than usual.

"Ladies and gentlemen, thank you for coming. We have some very important news to share."

"The Pope is paying us a visit," cracked Neil Acosta from the back of the room.

The residents turned and laughed at the mindless antagonist. It was an inconsiderate yet handy icebreaker, and a smiling Randall made points by just ignoring it. After the tittering subsided, he talked in a quiet voice that immediately drew their attention.

"We've got some news about the ventilation shaft that we found about ten days ago. As most of you know, our friend Paco died only last week during the first attempt to climb up this shaft. However, his effort was not in vain. That shaft leads to the exit out of Yucca Mountain. This morning, a second attempt to climb up the shaft was made by my son, Rex, who succeeded not only in reaching the top, but who also exited onto the ground just outside the shaft exit and had a look around!"

Loud gasps and rumbles shook the room. Wailing and sobbing erupted. Complete pandemonium replaced the prior calm of moments earlier. Paco's sacrifice was forgotten as they all jumped up and began hugging and praising the Lord, congratulating each other as if they had discovered the New World. The excitement lasted for ten minutes before Randall could restore order.

"Quiet, please. Quiet!" he shouted, looking somewhat excited himself. "Please take your seats. There's more to this than you've just heard."

The residents were disinclined to end their celebration, lest there be "a catch" or bad news following the wonderful opener. Another five minutes passed before the excitement gradually subsided. Randall motioned for everyone to sit.

"Thank you. Please listen, there is more to tell." He turned and looked to his left, "Frank will explain some of the other details, and what we think our options are." Randall motioned Frank Lowe to the microphone.

Frank pointed to a poster board he had placed on an easel in front, and said, "Can everyone see this? Ladies and gentlemen, the circle shown here is twenty-four inches in diameter, the same as the diameter of the shaft we have found. That's barely wide enough to crawl through. It is about three thousand feet long, with an angle from the vertical of thirty-four degrees." He paused to allow the murmurs to settle.

"It took Paco a little over two hours to crawl all the way to the top of that shaft. He confirmed what we expected; that the top of the shaft was wired with explosives. You may have heard the loud boom three days ago when it was detonated, opening up the shaft to the outside.

"Since that time, Rex made one round trip, but it took longer than it took Paco because he was trying to be more careful to keep safe."

"It can now be told that Paco died from a lack of oxygen and probable exhaustion in the narrow confines of the air-tight shaft. He died crawling back down from that shaft. God rest his soul." Dozens of the audience members nodded; some crossed themselves.

"The glass dome that sealed the top of the shaft was the same as the circular glass window that you may have seen in the center of the cupola of the Observation Chamber. Both had been installed with an explosive charge that when detonated, would provide an exit from Yucca Mountain." He paused to allow the murmurs to subside.

"As you know, the Observation Chamber has been under water all this time and would have flooded the entire Sanctuary had we blasted it open. In fact, Rex has now confirmed that a deep lake now fills up the entire valley east of Yucca Mountain, presumably because of the severe forces of nature that accompanied the asteroid impact that we felt not long after we arrived here.

"The good news is that the level of the lake is lower than the new exit we found at the top of the ventilation shaft. Rex is here to tell us all about what he saw when he looked around earlier today. Rex?"

Smiles and nodding accompanied jubilant small talk among the audience.

"Thank you, Mr. Lowe. As you can imagine, crawling that distance in such a narrow shaft was very difficult. It was hard on my knees. It was hard on my hands. It was even hard on my elbows, ankles, and noggin. It was also quite exhausting." Murmurs and comments rippled through the audience.

"But the worst thing was the narrow confines and feelings of claustrophobia that almost paralyzed me."

"Nevertheless, I did it. I survived, and I crawled outside through the exit."

"WHAT DID YOU SEE OUTSIDE?!" was yelled from one of the impatient residents.

"That's what I'm about to tell you." He paused, then said, "The desert and mountainous topography that was probably there fifteen years ago has really changed. It certainly is not what you might probably expect. Yucca Mountain is still north-south ridgeline, dominated by rocks and dirt with very little shrubbery. To the east there are distant hills with trees and foliage, but there's lake that fills up the valley in the near distance. We're guessing that the lake developed because of volcanic activity that formed dams at the normal passages connecting the valley to the rest of Nevada."

"I spent an hour and thirty minutes exploring. I climbed to the top of this mountain and looked in every direction. To the west, the terrain looked mostly normal, though when I came here as a boy, I was only six, so I don't remember any details, and besides our arrival at Yucca Mountain was from the east. It's springtime, and there was warm sunlight accompanied by streaks of white clouds high in the sky. It was a magnificent view."

But I saw no sign of civilization. No roads. No buildings. No airplanes. No indications of human activity."

Just then a man's sandal came flying toward Rex. "Son of a bitch!" spewed from the overwrought resident. Sergeant O was quick to intervene, grabbing the disgruntled fellow by the arm and marching him out the door. Mild cheers and applause from the others diffused the menacing situation.

Rex grimaced, then calmly continued. "I gathered a bunch of rocks and made a large 'HELP' sign near the shaft exit. It was great to breathe fresh air, to see the sun and the clouds, and to feel the wind. But as I returned back down the shaft into the Ossuary, I realized that leaving the safety of our sanctuary may have its problems. It will not be easy."

"Thank you, Rex," Randall said moving back to the mike and observing the tension returning to the audience. "With everything you've now heard, we've put together some discussion points that we'd like your feedback on." Octavio placed a large poster on the easel with an outline of their plan. "Frank will explain."

With an expression of deep concern, Lowe pointed at the outline, which read:

EXIT CONSIDERATIONS

- Seek Help vs Totally Vacate
- Passage through the Shaft
- Carry-along Provisions
- Best Qualified
- Number of Participants
- Volunteers

"Before leaving this meeting tonight, I think we all need to agree on a plan with these considerations. If there are other issues you want to address, we'll take them up as necessary."

Throughout the course of the evening weighty discussions ensued, moderated by Frank and Randall. The few regular cynics and jokesters were silenced by their serious-minded neighbors. Everyone had a chance to question and comment. Reasonable and sincere sentiments gradually prevailed as the audience, which included residents and staff, came to realize the new problems associated with their new "freedom."

A general consensus was formed. It would be more prudent to send a small group of physically fit volunteers outside the Sanctuary to seek help rather than to evacuate everyone from the existing safety of the facilities. Each volunteer would need to carry provisions to survive as long as possible. If foraging was not viable, and water and shelter were inadequate, they would have to return for a revised plan.

Volunteers would have to be healthy, physically fit, and mentally stable in order to endure the anticipated hardship. The problem of just getting up the shaft would eliminate many. Seven to ten volunteers was thought to be a reasonable number for the expedition. Its mission would be to find help for the safe evacuation of the remaining survivors within Yucca Mountain.

Everyone was invited to volunteer and to meet with Randall, Frank, and Rafael after the meeting. Seven to ten of the best applicants would be selected. They would depart in one week.

"Do we have any volunteers?" asked Randall.

A painful minute passed before a single hand went up.

"Jammie, is that you?" asked Frank.

"Yes sir," answered the young man.

Then another hand went up, and another. Within a few minutes, a half dozen volunteers from the audience identified themselves; all were the youthful offspring of the original patrons and staff. Among them, and to her parents' chagrin, was Samantha Meredith.

CHAPTER XXXVIII
THE EXODUS BEGINS

E-DAY MINUS FIVE

Swimming laps in the evening had always given Randall time for solitude and thought. His sleeping habits of late, elevated their importance. Tonight, he reflected mainly on the plans that were coming to fruition for the volunteers to leave the bunker and strike out for help. Only five more days! The fact that one of these would be his own daughter, however, gave him chills. At first, he didn't realize it, but then it felt like his whole body was reacting to the dread. Each lap became more laborious. He began to flounder after only eleven laps; suddenly he couldn't believe he might not make it to the edge of the pool.

Frank and Krishka arrived just in time to notice that Randall was struggling. Throwing his robe to the deck, Frank leaped into the water to save his friend. He dragged him toward the shallow end of the pool. Krishka was waiting with a towel, and the two of them lifted and rolled the limp body to the concrete apron.

He had not taken in water or shown signs of drowning, but something was obviously wrong. Krishka checked for a pulse: it was very weak and sporadic. She quickly suggested they get him to the clinic.

When they got him there, Meredith acted like he was confused by the bright overhead lights and by the attention that Nurse Higgins was paying him. At her instruction, he slowly sat up to swallow an aspirin crushed and mixed with water.

"Raise your arms, Mr. Meredith," Higgins commanded. "Can you smile and say your name?" Randall was slow to respond but eventually complied. "Can you stick out your tongue?"

Randall's lips moved but his tongue wouldn't cooperate. By that time, Eve, Rex, and Sam had arrived and were watching with great concern. Eve moved to hug him. Tears formed in her eyes as she affirmed her love and whispered, "Are you okay?"

"It looks like a stroke," declared Nurse Higgins. "Probably a mild one. We have dabigatran and aspirin available. But he'll need therapy, Mrs. Meredith, to recover properly. Lots of therapy."

E-DAY MINUS FOUR

Frank and Rafael were seated next to Randall, who was recuperating in his bed.

"Randall, we've got eight volunteers willing to go," said Rafael.

He nodded and blinked, acknowledging their news. His arm raised and he flashed a thumbs-up but was unable to speak. The men spent the next few minutes sharing words of encouragement, offering help if he needed anything, and suggesting he relax and focus on his recovery.

E-DAY MINUS THREE

Frank, Rafael, Rex, and Octavio were discussing plans for the volunteers once they were stationed topside.

Frank said, "I've been looking at the maps, and it looks like the last part of our route coming here from the Amargosa Valley turnoff is totally underwater, so we've got to think of another way to find civilization."

Rafael said, "What about Beatty? That's pretty close."

Frank replied, "You can't get to Beatty as the crow flies, what with mountains and cauldrons. But it looks like there were some reasonable truck trails that led to it, down the west side of Yucca Mountain, at least prior to earthquakes. I figure it would be about twenty-two miles of rough hiking."

Octavio said, "If we start the hike at noon, we could be there on our second day."

Rex contributed, "I think that's a good plan. Beatty, and then determine where from there. Hopefully they'll be able to help."

Frank said, "Let's pray that they survived the quakes and can help."

Later that evening, Krishka and Frank were enjoying their regular post-swimming nightcap. Sitting on her sofa, she asked, "Have you ever been to Peru?"

With a quizzical look, he responded, "No. Why?"

She responded, "Arequipa is supposed to be one of the most beautiful cities in the world. Arequipa, Peru."

"I never really thought about Peru. I guess they speak Spanish, right?"

"*Sí señor*," Krishka giggled. Her eyebrows furrowed serious and her voice lowered, "When we finally get out of this place, I'd like to go there."

"Great, I'll know where to find you."

Changing the subject, she asked, "Are you ready for your expedition?"

"Almost. I still have to pick up some of the survival gear from Rafael: hunting knife, first aid pack, mylar blanket, and light sticks."

"Wow. He's really got you guys outfitted."

"Yeah. He's even going to inspect each of us before we launch. Rafael's like a demanding army sergeant."

"You'll be the oldest one with those eight kids. Are you sure you can handle it?"

"They're no longer kids, Krishka. And, I'm only fifteen years older than they are. I think I'm in pretty good shape."

"Well, we're all counting on you to find help and to rescue us down here."

Randall was able to sit up in bed and move his arms and legs, but his speech was still slow and slurred. Eve had researched therapy practices from the Sanctuary's massive database library and consulting with the nurse. Breathing and tongue-thrust exercises in front of a mirror, various speech sounds, short sentences, and object naming were all part of the rehab process. Randall was cooperative and understood the routine, but his understanding of everything else was uncertain. His hearing was fine, but a pad and pencil were needed in place of speech.

Samantha sat on the edge of his bed, smiled, and asked, "How're ya feelin', Daddy?"

His eyes and half smile showed welcome for her attention. He motioned for the pad and pencil on the nightstand.

He scribbled a note, asking, "Are you ready for your journey?"

Pleased that he still remembered her volunteering, she nodded. Then she asked, "But I'm concerned about you and Mom. Do you really think I should go?"

Randall abruptly drew a line across the tablet, and boldly scribbled: "YES!"

Rex walked into the bedroom and joined the conversation. "Don't you worry about us, Sam. We discussed all this last night. Dad, Mom, and I will be just fine, waiting for you to return with help."

"That's right," was scribbled on the pad. "You go."

Octavio and Eve walked in to join the discussion. The moisture in her eyes predicted an emotional event looming. She sat on the other side of the bed, holding Randall's hand. Rex looked guardedly at Sam, also knowing what was about to unfold.

"Daddy, Octavio and I want to get married."

They all looked at Randall. His eyes closed for a second as if to gather his thoughts. Then they opened and looked at Sam, then at the others, lastly at Octavio. Before he could respond, Samantha raised her left hand to show him the ring.

"It belonged to Tavo's father. Isn't it beautiful?"

Absent a jewelry outlet in Yucca Mountain, Octavio had turned to his prized possession, a ring given to him by his intuitive father and held in safe keeping for fifteen years by his adoptive uncle. The ring was thought to be an heirloom, though its provenance was a bit sketchy. Instead of diamonds, it featured an oval black onyx in a robust gold setting.

Randall stared at the ring. Tears welled up in his eyes. He looked at Sam, then Octavio, then nodded and attempted to mouth, "yes." Sam thrust forward into her father's arms. They hugged and through flowing tears, she whispered, "I love you Daddy."

They all shared a group hug on the bed. Rex smiled, turned to Tavo, and shook his hand. "Welcome to the family, brother."

Randall grasped Samantha's hand for a closer look. She adjusted the ring so that it was right-side up on her slender finger. He gently pulled her hand to examine the ring more closely, which surprised Samantha. Everyone was a little surprised by his interest. He reached for his pencil and pad. The four quietly watched as he scratched out a question: "INSCRIPTION INSIDE?"

Samantha removed the ring, looked and said, "Yes."

Drawing another horizontal line on his pad, he scribbled another question: "1/5 SEMPER FI?"[4]

Puzzled, Samantha looked inside the ring, then at Octavio, and back to her father. "Yes. How would you know that, Daddy?"

Randall coughed and tried to smile. Looking at Octavio, then turning to his pad he wrote, "IS YOUR REAL FATHER'S NAME ALEJANDRO?"

Puzzled, Octavio mumbled, "Yes."

"Alejandro Ochoa was our butler!" a surprised Eve exclaimed.

Randall scratched on his pad: "GAVE TO ALEJANDRO FOR YOU." He motioned for Octavio to come closer.

The young man sat on the edge of the bed and watched Mr. Meredith frantically scratch out another message on his pad.

"SMALL WORLD, OCTAVIO. COULDN'T HAVE PLANNED ANY BETTER. CONGRATULATIONS."

E-DAY MINUS TWO

The closed-circuit TV interrupted Rafael, who was having breakfast with Octavio. It was Frank Lowe, who looked very worried. He said, "Rafael, did you remove my survival gear from the front room of my apartment?"

"Ah, no."

"It's gone, Raf! Somebody's taken it," exclaimed Frank Lowe.

"What would anybody possibly do with it? There's gotta be some explanation. Tavo, do you know anything about this?"

---

[4] 1/5 Semper Fi is the abbreviation for the storied 1st Battalion, 5th Marines of the 1st Marine Division based in Camp Pendleton, CA. Semper Fi is the moto of the US Marine Corps. The ring was sentimental memorabilia from Randall's father's estate. If you are still reading Footnotes of this novel, I'm impressed.

Between spoon fulls of cereal, Octavio looked at his uncle and at Frank on the video monitor, and said, "No."

"I don't know, but I have a funny feeling about this," Frank warned.

Later that day one of Rafael's workers notified him, *"Tragedia en reservorio de agua!"* ("There's been a tragedy in the reservoir!"). The two men hopped onto a golf cart and raced to mile four of the restricted back corridor. Approaching the glowing section of the tunnel complex, they rolled to a stop next to another golf cart. The men climbed up to the reservoir berm and looked down into the green water. The figure of a woman drifted face down at the bottom of the pool.

Rafael immediately jumped in. It took seconds before he dove under to retrieve the body. He came back up carrying a woman in a black swimsuit with a heavy satchel around her neck.

Krishka.

They strapped her body in the back seat of the cart, and the two men slowly drove back to the Sanctuary Clinic. With the death of Dr. Jammicit, Nurse Higgins had become the acting physician, dentist, pharmacist, and regrettably, mortician. Rafael had removed the heavy satchel that had obviously caused the former Olympic swimmer to drown. *Or it could have been the untimely activation of the filtration pumps,* he thought. Her neatly folded clothes in the golf cart were retrieved for Nurse Higgins to clothe her for later.

Curiously, the golf cart near the pool had also contained a box of survival gear.

Rafael phoned Frank, and said, "I found your gear. Come over to the clinic right away."

Waiting outside the clinic, Rafael dreaded telling Frank about Krishka. It was well known that he and Krishka were more than just friends and fellow teachers. How he would react was a mystery, and Rafael would try to be as sympathetic as he could.

It didn't matter.

When Frank entered the clinic and saw the body in a bathing suit, he was beside himself. Wrapping his arms around the cold, wet corpse, he sobbed uncontrollably. Rafael and Nurse Higgins excused themselves from the scene until he could compose himself. Several minutes passed.

Frank eventually joined Rafael on the clinic steps, where they sat and gazed toward Sanctuary Square. The programmed ceiling lighting had just faded to dusk. Except for the virtual frogs and crickets, it was quiet. Rafael started to speak but was immediately interrupted when Frank blurted out, "It all makes perfect sense, now!"

"What do you mean, Frank?"

"The letter. The letter she wrote to the Russians."

"I'm not sure I understand. What letter?"

"It's right here," he said, reaching into his pocket. "She gave it to me last night, to mail to the Embassy, the Russian Embassy. I told her that the postal service may not even be working. She laughed and said, 'Just get it to them.' She insisted."

"Frank, I'm not following you. Sorry."

"All of our talks, all our plans about escape. To her, it was all theater; entertainment. But she was so convincing about being curious, so dramatic, and yet, she was just fooling me. I am so gullible."

"Don't beat yourself up, Frank. She's met her just reward."

Frank was steaming, oblivious to his empathetic friend. Tears still flowed down his cheeks and lips as he continued. "She used me for her personal indulgence, whenever she decided. And I fell for it."

"It couldn't have been all bad," Rafael said under his breath.

"I opened the letter, Rafael. I used my software to translate. Go ahead and read it. Read it. Read it out loud. I still can't believe it."

Rafael pulled his penlight from is pocket. Taking the paper from Frank, he began reading:

"Товарищ комиссарЯ предоставляю это письменное коммюнике, в случае моей смерти ДО извлечения…

Comrade Commissar:

I am providing this written communiqué, in the event of my death BEFORE extraction.

I have faithfully carried out my assignment as directed. Mr. Globitz was an easy target but time in this underground bunker facility has been difficult. The earthquakes destroyed all communication channels. It was not possible to apprise you of the situation.

The current status of the three objectives is as follows:

- Gold. The gold he failed to ship is all accounted for and stored underwater, in the reservoir deep in the alcove at mile four. (I have secured three bars for my redeployment attempt.)
- Uranium. The powdered Uranium Oxide (U308) is locked in a safe in a hazardous storage chamber in the Yucca Mountain Ossuary at mile marker number two. The combination to the safe is inscribed on the inside cover of Comrade Tolstoy's War and Peace on Globitz' bookshelf.
- Mega data files, security codes and taped political messages are in hollow spaces on numerous books on the shelves in Globitz' office.

Mr. Globitz is dead. His personality changed significantly after the earthquakes and our isolation. He began to blame me, and began to be aggressive toward me. As you authorized, I had to terminate him, though sooner than I planned.

I have kept secret our objectives from the Americans.

If this letter survives and I do not, please convey my love to my son and restore my nameplate to Moscow's Wall of Honor.

Your Faithful Servant...Krishka Zhukova

"Holy shit. She really was a Russian agent!" exclaimed Rafael.

"Even after all these years, she's still one of them. And she would have climbed up the shaft ahead of the rest of us, using my gear," Frank whimpered.

"With three bars of gold," Rafael added.

CHAPTER XXXIX
THE EXODUS

E-DAY MINUS ONE

FRANK STOOD AT THE FRONT OF HIS CLASSROOM ADMIRING THE COURAGEOUS young adults seated before him. Provided with ample opportunities during the previous days, none had withdrawn from the mission. Their briefing would be an eye-opener and a warning of things to come.

He cleared his throat, smiled and began, "Welcome to our pre-embarkation meeting. The bravery you've revealed in volunteering is a great tribute to your character. I am proud to be a part of this team and look forward to our voyaging together. There are some administrative and logistics details and some technical information for our journey. So, let's get into it.

"You've all been provided a backpack and various supplies to carry with you." Handing out a list he said, "here are the necessary items we'll need."

BACKPACK SURVIVAL GEAR

- First Aid packet
- Flashlight and spare batteries
- Duct Tape
- MRE's (Meals Ready to Eat)
- 10' parachute cord
- Mylar blanket
- Fishing hooks and line
- K-Bar survival knife
- Dry Fleece hoody
- Light Sticks
- Sunscreen
- Bug repellant
- Stainless Steel water bottle
- Aquatabs (water purification tabs)
- Magnesium Fire Starter
- Pad and pencil

"Tonight, when you organize your pack, make sure you've included everything on this list. Tomorrow morning at 0700, we will meet outside this classroom for a final inspection. Then we'll load up in the golf carts and ride to the Ossuary. Any questions?"

The group sat silent.

"I'll see you in the morning. Good luck. Now, here's Rex."

Rex walked to the front of the class, turned and with an authority never before witnessed, addressed his former classmates.

"They called you courageous VOLUNTEERS." He smiled, shaking his head. "I wouldn't call you that." A puzzled look gripped his audience. "You didn't really volunteer. You were CHOSEN.

"You actually had no choice in the matter. You were specifically picked for this mission. And, if God himself had asked me whom to choose, it would have been you. Each one of you. So, you didn't really volunteer; you simply responded to a Higher Calling. The calling is sometimes higher for some than for others. This one, the one you answered, is the highest you'll ever experience—to help save your family and friends."

"That is your mission.

"There are three phases of this mission: survive, find help, and rescue those left behind.

"You have to survive your climb up that shaft and survive the trek down the mountain to civilization, if there STILL IS a civilization. That will not be easy. In fact, the first few hours of your journey, the crawl up the shaft, will be a nightmare. Once you start, you cannot turn back. The shaft is too small to turn around, let alone cross over someone to get back down.

"You'll be spaced at fifteen-minute intervals, so as not to bunch up. If you need oxygen, put on your mask. Avoid panic and claustrophobia at all cost. If you think you may need a Xanax, take it before you enter the shaft, not after. Breathe easy. Save your flashlight batteries, crawl in the dark. Except for Mr. Lowe, there will be someone right behind you in the shaft—so you must keep moving up. Your backpack should be dragged behind you about five feet with your parachute rope. Rafael will get you set up and started in your climb.

"Questions?"

Eyes wide open, the volunteers were quiet.

"My recon last week confirmed what the topographic maps indicated: that the best route down Yucca Mountain is south and west. North and east have been flooded and is now a deep lake. Keep the sun on your face and right-side walking down the mountain. Every time you stop to rest or set up camp, mark your spot with an SOS pile of rocks. Maybe someone will fly over and notice. There was a small town, Beatty, not far away. Hopefully somebody there survived the asteroid impact and earthquakes over the past fifteen years and can offer help."

Rafael intervened, "About the rescue. The coordinates of the shaft's exit are written on the board, behind me (36°56'25" N 116°27'30" W). Write it down and store it in your backpack. If or when you find help, they'll need to know where to look for us."

Rex resumed, "There's going to be a time when you are tired and discouraged, when you start thinking about your own misery and pain. It may well be when you are a third of the way up that dark and narrow shaft, or on day eight of your hike to find civilization, or after you've finished your last MRE. And you want to lie down and give up. Don't surrender to those feelings! *You are better than that.* Turn your thoughts to the mission you were chosen for. It's not about you anymore; it's about your parents, your family, your friends—the people you left behind here in Yucca Mountain.

"Now, can we count on you to complete this mission?" he paused. "I wanna hear, 'Hell yes!'"

Deep in thought, and attentive to Rex's coaching, they responded, "Hell yes!"

"That was weak. I want to hear it, like you mean it."

"HELL YES!" they roared awakening from their trance.

Smiling with a fist pump, Rex said, "That's better. I'll see you in the morning."

The team of eight bounded out of their chairs and enthusiastically left the classroom.

Rafael and Frank stayed behind with Rex. Like the young volunteers, both were electrified by Rex's passionate motivation. They moved to shake his hand and pat his back.

"That was a great speech, Rex," gushed Rafael.

"It was awesome!" exclaimed Frank. "Thank you."

"Thanks," chuckled Rex. "Tomorrow's a big day."

"Yes, it is," replied Frank. "Rex, please sit down, I need to talk to you."

"Okay. What is it, Mr. Lowe?"

"Rex, it's become obvious that you are now one of the leaders down here. Not just of your former classmates, but of the rest of us as well. You've picked up the mantle that your father carried so well. And, you've grown into your skin, admirably."

"Thanks, Mr. Lowe. That's a nice compliment."

"Please, call me Frank."

"Yes sir."

Rex, you look a little concerned. What are you thinking?"

"I guess I'm a little shocked that only eight people volunteered. Besides you, of course."

"Don't be shocked, Rex. There are plenty of reasons. Except for your classmates, most of the residents here are older than you by decades. The physical demands of crawling up that tunnel or hiking down this mountain would be too difficult for them. Claustrophobia in that shaft is enough to scare most away. Also, premature aging and illnesses have hit our residents hard.

"Then, like you many of your friends have to take care of their aging parents instead of leaving them to fend for themselves. And, unfortunately, many parents have chosen to die in the little comfort they now have rather than some new unknown future.

"But, there's one other item you should be aware of, it's called "learned helplessness." It's a behavior that doctors have used to describe the people who feel everything is beyond their control. They tend to feel that continuously repeated bad circumstances, like living underground with no possibility for leaving, makes them powerless. They have learned to accept the negative and even when shown an alternative, they have chosen to stay in their funk. It's a sickness, a mental sickness, Rex. And, many of the residents down here have it. They've learned to be helpless."

"I never thought about it like that."

They both paused, looking away into thin air. Then Frank spoke again.

"I'd like to talk to you about something else, Rex: I'd like you to take my place as the Activities Director. That means coordinating all the activities that happen in the Sanctuary. It means working with Rafael and the staff, meeting with the school and the teachers and speaking to the residents about important issues, like your father and I did. I've noticed that you and your mom are already preparing the weekly blog that Randall used to do."

The humbled and flattered young leader gulped, then responded, "Of course. I'd be honored."

0700 E-DAY

Resembling a military inspector, Frank had the eight volunteers perfectly aligned, with their backpacks positioned at their feet. He was standing at attention in front of his "troops" when Rafael drove up to inspect.

Rafael said, "Pretty impressive formation, Frank. Are they ready?"

"Yes, sir," he responded with a smile.

Frank then helped Rafael go through each backpack ensuring all of the necessary items from the list were included. A few were missing fishing line and hooks and extra flashlight batteries which Rafael provided from a box in his golf cart. Overall, the inspection went without a hitch.

Rafael then distributed some extra rolls of duct tape.

"Tear off two six-inch pieces and tape one across each knee of your pants. Now tear off two more and make an X with the tape on your knees. This will help prevent injuring your knees during your climb. Now, tear off two more pieces of tape and wrap them around your palms. This will protect your hands as you crawl."

All complied. Samantha tore an extra piece to secure her engagement ring.

When carts were moved into position, Frank directed everyone to "load up." The gut-check factor kicked in. Everyone suddenly realized the seriousness of the situation. For the participants, this was General Eisenhower's "land the landing force" command for a Normandy Invasion. No turning back.

Led by Rafael, the parade of carts slowly followed in single file. The column snaked through Sanctuary Square toward the once-forbidden tunnel entrance. At the entrance, he flipped on the tunnel lights, and was surprised by the thunderous cheering of the residents lining both sides of the tunnel. The gauntlet of some 200 whistling and applauding residents included Randall in his wheelchair pushed by his wife and demonstrated their appreciation for the brave volunteers. Many of the supporters fell in behind the column of carts and followed on foot toward the Ossuary. Organized the night before by the new "Activities Director," it would be a royal send off with a lasting impression.

The carts parked outside the entrance of what the boys once called the "Chamber of Death." It was now a lighted alcove, the starting point for their exit. It was ironic that the Ossuary had sealed-up holes in the walls that represented *death*, and a shaft hole in the ceiling that represented *life* beyond Yucca Mountain; an ending and a beginning in the same cave. The hole-drilling rig had been moved and a staircase built directly under the entrance to the shaft. The platform atop the stairs would afford an easy entrance into the shaft.

With silver x's on their knees and carrying their backpacks in their taped-up hands, the nine explorers eerily walked toward the staircase launching pad like astronauts toward a spacecraft. Their faith in Rex's promise of light beyond the dark hole in the ceiling was all they had to go on. It was a spine-tingling prospect, yet no one backed down.

They assembled around Rafael at the base of the stairs, where they received his final instructions. He noticed that Octavio had wandered away from the group and was about to call him back, when Rex signaled with one finger to his lips. Octavio was kneeling in front of one of the markers on the Ossuary wall. His head was bowed, and his duct-taped hand was pressed against the mortared-up chamber holding the remains of Paco, his friend and stepbrother. Everyone respectfully waited for Octavio to return.

Rafael waited, then reached into the box on the passenger seat of his cart. Pulling out a small wrapped package, he smiled and said, "This is a little farewell gift, compliments of the Russian government. I am putting one of these into the side pocket of each of your backpacks. It's a piece of a brick of gold we sawed in thirds, worth about $70,000 each, fifteen years ago. It may come in handy on your journey."

"Wow," was the common response.

He encouraged a last-minute visit to the porta potty behind them, and reminded them to also refresh their water bottles. "Remember to keep moving up the shaft. There will be others behind you, and you don't want to bunch up in that tiny space. Talk to each other while crawling; it will help pass the time and also establish your separation." Then he climbed up the stairs to the platform where the whirr of ventilated air could be heard. As planned, it flowed up the shaft and provided insurance of oxygen for the climbers.

The bench below the platform provided a place where the volunteers could sit while waiting their turn to enter the shaft. Nervous conversation of inane topics occupied their time. Every fifteen minutes, another one would be summoned. It had the somber feeling of a nine-man gallows hanging, one man at a time.

With the signal from Rafael, Octavio was first to go. Rex was at the base of the stairs to wish his best friend farewell. They smiled and did their secret fist bump before shaking hands. A bear hug followed as they whispered in each other's ear.

"Don't worry, Rex. We'll be back to get you outta here." Octavio then turned and scampered up the stairs to the platform.

"Make sure your pack is secured to the cord around your waste, son. I'll lift it up once you start moving," said Rafael. "Update your progress on the walkie-talkie." Then the two hugged, shared a few final personal thoughts, before he climbed up into the shaft. In a matter of minutes, Octavio and his backpack had disappeared into darkness. Rafael marked the time: 0803.

Samantha was next and anxious to follow her fiancé. She smiled and hugged her brother at the base of the steps. Her good-byes with Rex and the family the night before had been emotional enough, this should have been easy. Rex struggled with it, however, and remembered that he had never actually told Sam that he loved her. She beat him to it and he warmly returned the same. Their eyes welled up as she turned and raced up the steps.

Rafael tried to maintain his composure and upbeat demeanor, but his emotions got the best of him. With a cracking voice and teary eyes, all he could say was, "Take care of yourself, Sam." Then she bound up into the shaft and Rafael lifted her pack to follow. It was 0815.

Six more times Rafael would assist the young volunteers up into the black hole. Six more times he would offer words of encouragement, and each time a piece of his heart seemed to ascend up the shaft with them. His confidence in their safety was now a moot point; it was their mission that was of overriding concern. They had to succeed.

Horror struck. Thirty minutes into the climb, Octavio's pulse rate skyrocketed. His chest tightened and his breathing was shallow; he was hyperventilating. The tunnel walls were closing in, and he could not yet see light at the shaft's opening. Claustrophobia had immobilized the lead tunnel climber. His trembling body had slowed and eventually stopped crawling, unable to proceed.

Suddenly he heard a curse from behind. Samantha had crawled up and bumped into his backpack. She yelled, "CRAWL FASTER, DAMN IT! You're holding up the rest of us."

Her shout seemed to jar his mental state. Stuttering, he apologized and resumed crawling, not wanting to reveal his weakness. With Samantha pressing from behind, he was determined to persevere, onward and upward.

There were three volunteers still sitting on the bench, waiting for Rafael's call, when the supportive residents who had walked down the tunnel began to shuffle into the Ossuary. Anxious to show their appreciation if not to witness the event, the crowd grew to near capacity in the alcove. Several approached the waiting volunteers to shake their hands and pat them on the back. Then they applauded and shouted encouragement as the next volunteer ascended the ramp and disappeared up the shaft.

Frank Lowe was last to shake hands with Rex before climbing up the stairs for Rafael's sendoff. Still numbed by Krishka's betrayal, his capacity for emotions, even toward his former students had burned out. His brief and perfunctory conversation with Rafael suggested a nervousness toward his pending role. When he turned to witness the cheering from the group that had now packed into the Ossuary, his confidence in the mission was buoyed. He assured Rafael that the team would do all it could to return with help.

Rafael initiated a radio check with Octavio at the head of the column and with Frank standing next to him. "Loud and clear," was the response. Frank shook Rafael's hand and Yucca Mountain's last hope for rescue disappeared up into the black hole. The time was 1034.

Converging echoes of conversations spilled out from the shaft as the brave explorers talked and trudged upward. One female voice faintly rose above the chatter with a song, and suddenly all other voices silenced.

> *You raise me up, so I can stand on mountains*
> *You raise me up, to walk on stormy seas*
> *I am strong, when I am on your shoulders*
> *You raise me up... To more than I can be*

The haunting melody from the soulful songstress had silenced everybody and engulfed the tunnel like fresh air. When she had finished, only the sounds of scraping knees and dragging backpacks could be heard. Then a voice rang out, "Sing it again, Amanda!" "Yes, sing it again!" echoed another.

With spirits lifted, the nine volunteers continued their unrelenting trudge.

Suddenly Octavio screamed down to the others, "I see light. I see light from outside the tunnel!"

"Yay!" rang out from the voices below. The news and happiness spread from one person to the next, and the next, until Frank Lowe finally heard it. The announcement energized the crawlers and raised their spirits.

Forty minutes passed; they all craved for another reassuring message from the head of the group. They labored onward and upward. Octavio was nearing the opening of the shaft, but too tired and winded to convey his excitement.

Finally, his outstretched hand grasped the metal rim of the cupula opening still affixed in concrete around the drilled-out rock of the mountain's summit.

"Yes!" he breathlessly exclaimed.

Pulling himself up so that both arms rested on the outer lip of the opening, he paused in silent prayer. A refreshing mountain wind danced across his face. Then, a waft of a pungent fragrance from a nearby sage brush shocked his olfactory sensors which had been dulled by fifteen years of breathing HEPA-filtered bunker odors. A moonscape of boulders and jagged rock greeted Octavio as he wriggled out of the shaft's aperture. In sharp contrast to the natural setting and lodged between a rock mound and a bush just twenty feet away, was the metal-rimmed cupola window. It had obviously frisbee'd there after being blasted from its mounting days earlier.

Octavio pulled the lanyard and his backpack from the shaft and hollered down to Samantha. "I'm out, I'm out!" A newly formed mountain behind him that dwarfed Yucca Mountain went unnoticed over his concern for the team still in the shaft below. He was out of the bunker. They were next, and nothing could eclipse the excitement.

Samantha grunted and returned his good news, "Great, I'm right behind you."

Octavio activated his walkie-talkie to transmit his announcement to Frank and Rafael, then he yelled down the shaft again to encourage the other climbers. Starting with Samantha, each relayed the message to the person below and added a personal word of encouragement. Rafael relayed the news to the gathered residents and a cheer went up throughout the crowd.

One by one, the volunteers emerged from the shaft. Some cried. Some kissed the earth. It was a joyous celebration every fifteen minutes, when the next person climbing out would shout down to the ones following. As the group outside grew in numbers, they crowded around the opening to send down more encouragement.

One or two gazed at the surrounding mountain tops and the desert below, assessing the route to Beatty. No one remembered the topography as it once had been. Mother Nature's adjustments and rearrangement of the landscape triggered by an asteroid was the last thing on their mind.

When the top of Frank's head surfaced, two of the team members grabbed his arms to assist their senior member out of the shaft. He arose smiling, setting off a euphoric celebration. They hugged and danced in congratulatory oblivion. With outstretched arms, they slowly twirled to simply breathe and relish the moment. Then, gathering around the shaft's mouth they chorused a message to Rafael and the residents below: "WE MADE IT!"

It took seconds for the news to reach the jam-packed gathering below, eliciting a spectacular roar that seemed to compress and funnel up the shaft bursting out of the top like a geyser. Their cheers filled the heavens and electrified the volunteers.

The fresh mountain air, the afternoon sunshine, the wind and freedom from the bunker were all that mattered for the moment. Ecstasy! Fifteen years underground had culminated in escape for these nine members of the Yucca Mountain Sanctuary.

Frank directed the group to help lift the glass cupola dome back over the aperture to protect the shaft from the weather. Before they slid it in place, he removed the batteries and duct-taped them, and the two walkie-talkies, to the underside of the glass. Then, the teary-eyed elder asked the group to gather around for a few words.

"We made it!" Cheers erupted. Smiling in their triumphant celebration, he motioned calm. Several minutes passed before quiet was restored. "The first part of our mission has been accomplished. I'm really proud of you all. This day will never be forgotten."

More cheers.

"Now, we've got about three hours of daylight left. Gather your gear and backpacks and let's launch in ten minutes. We've got about a two-day hike to get to Beatty. Any questions?"

Frank's dictates evaporated into thin air, unheard. The celebrating continued. They hugged and danced and cheered unconstrained, as if they had won the lottery. On a slightly overcast day, fifteen years after entering purgatory, they had emerged victorious. Nothing would hamper their excitement. They had finally escaped Yucca Mountain.

Deep in the bunker below, the celebrants had turned their attention to the walk back to Sanctuary Square. They inched their way out of the Ossuary alcove like cheering fans exiting a packed stadium after a Super Bowl victory. The main tunnel provided more walking space and breathing room that better accommodated their cheerful conversations for the four-mile hike back to their residences. Their celebrating could be heard up and down the corridors, on into the wee hours of morning.

Rex adjusted his father's wheelchair to the left of the usual broadcasting position and sat down in the chair to Randall's immediate right. The camera light flashed "on" and the two began another broadcast of their daily video blog.

"Good morning, ladies and gentlemen. My father and I want to update you on current events in the Sanctuary. Yesterday was fabulous, but first we'll address some administrative matters." Rex fumbled for his notes while Meredith smiled and offered to help.

- "The air filtration system has been repaired and the musty odor some of you detected should now be gone.
- "The Grotto's menu has been revised as per your requests and now includes spicy blackened tilapia. Also, they remind us that reservations help them provide the best service.
- "Our school has a need for two teachers: French and math. See me if you have abilities in those subjects.
- "And, don't forget tonight's concert on the Sanctuary lawn. Lily and her band have a special performance dedicated to our nine brave heroes and their rescue mission. It starts at 8 pm,

"Now, on the subject we're all excited about: It's just a matter of time. Help will be on the way! It will take our team of volunteers at least two days to reach Beatty. There, they should find help. A rescue team will require drilling equipment and mining operation specialists. That may take a while longer. If the folks at Beatty can't help, our team will contact Amargosa Valley or Pahrump. Be patient, help is on the way."

For most, the morning's announcements were well received. Fifteen years in an underground Sanctuary had obviously humbled the privileged class of residents and tempered expectations. Yet, *this* morning-after hangover, like a ticker-tape parade cleanup, would not deter their blissful optimism and euphoria. A few grumpy skeptics, however, would dismiss the team of volunteers like the corpses occupying the chambers in the Ossuary. For them, the prospect for an exit from Yucca Mountain was dubious. "It was a moon landing all right, but what's in it for me," was their troubling mindset. "A new beginning? Pshaw."

EPILOGUE

THERE WERE 296 RESIDENTS (PATRONS AND STAFF) ACCOUNTED FOR entering Yucca Mountain. Nine residents (eight-young adults and one staff member) escaped through a long, narrow shaft with a promise to seek help. After the volunteers' exit, 258 residents remained underground. During the fifteen years and three months in the Sanctuary, the following figures were realized:

11 Suicides
21 Natural deaths
9 Accidental deaths
1 Murder
13 Births
3 Marriages
8 Divorces

Fourteen residents had converted to Christianity, 23 enjoyed significant weight loss (42 suffered significant weight gain), and 31 students had completed two years of college credits. The women claiming natural blond hair begrudgingly watched it turn brown and gray. Dental issues noticeably plagued most adults, a factor of Vitamin D deficiency and no dental staff.

The volunteer's exodus clearly marked a change in some residents' attitude and hope. A rescue from the "hell hole" was a possibility.

9 781480 889422